AENEAS IN THE UNDERWORLD

AND OTHER ESSAYS

AENEAS IN THE UNDERWORLD

AND OTHER ESSAYS

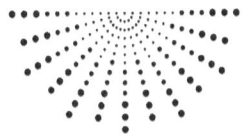

STEPHEN BARBER

APOCRYPHILE
PRESS

Apocryphile Press
PO Box 255
Hannacroix, NY 12087
www.apocryphilepress.com

Copyright © 2025 by Stephen L. Barber
Printed in the United States of America
ISBN 978-1-965646-25-0 | paper
ISBN 978-1-965646-26-7 | ePub

Please join our mailing list at www.apocryphilepress.com/free. We'll keep you up-to- date on all our new releases, and we'll also send you a FREE BOOK. Visit us today!

For Alison
without whom, not

CONTENTS

PREFACE

I have been a student of English literature for most of my life, but in mid-life I brushed up my Latin and began to study Latin literature seriously. I joined a class, hosted by Oxford University, in which we read the texts and discussed them. We also had the opportunity to write essays and most of the pieces here started as essays written for this class. Later, I posted some of them online, and, such has been their reception, that I decided to put them into more permanent form in print. They have been found useful by students and teachers, and I hope would also have something to offer more advanced scholars.

In these essays I have asked myself, and tried to answer, the questions that ordinary readers and students may have when reading the classics of Latin literature and which critics and scholars often seem mysteriously to overlook. They are arranged, not in the order of my writing them, but in what seemed the most attractive structure for reading them. I begin with a group of essays on Virgil.

There are two essays on *Aeneid* II. The first deals with the sequence of events by which the fall of Troy became inevitable. In the course of this, I consider Priam's passivity and poor judgement and the way Aeneas as narrator handles the events he recounts at some distance, although he was present for at least some of them. I also consider some of the other treatments of this episode from the mythological tradition, including some which Virgil rejected or only touched on. The second essay on this book shows Aeneas at his lowest point, wholly dependent on outside guidance. Here he is at the very beginning of the process by which he has to learn to become an effective leader on a new model, since that of Homeric warrior is denied him.

The essay on *Aeneid* IV considers Dido's claim that she and Aeneas were married, against the denial of this by Virgil as narrator, and comes down on her side after considering the evidence within the book. Aeneas comes out very badly from this episode, and this, at least, I believe to have been Virgil's intention.

The essay on Aeneas in the underworld asks what he learned from this adventure and how he learned it. I see this as a version of the mythological motif of the underworld journey and argue that the contradictions and inconsistencies in this book are deliberate and support a coherent view of the meaning of Aeneas's experience. The book is not a scenic tour of the underworld for its own sake but a vision deliberately constructed for the benefit of Aeneas, who is experiencing it.

I then go back to the *Eclogues*. That on Arcadia in the *Eclogues* argues for the unity of the collection in the setting of Arcadia, an ideal landscape, in contrast to some recent views which deny it. I then take up the celebrated use of the fourth Eclogue as a prophecy of Christ and explore the case for reviving this interpretation, which turns out to be stronger than one might expect.

I then turn to Catullus and consider one of the strangest of Latin poems: his poem on Attis, and ask what was the motivation of the central character and what was the point of the poem for Catullus. This is a long and complex essay but I hope will be rewarding to those looking for a coherent interpretation of this poem.

Next, I move to Horace and consider three of the Odes. Ode 1.37 *Nunc est bibendum* and 2.5 *Nondum subacta ferre iugum ualet* first drew my attention for negative reasons: the first seemed unpleasantly jingoistic and the second prurient. However, in working through them I came to a different view of each. The third Ode I consider, 3.3 *Iustum et tenacem propositi uirum* takes a central theme of the *Aeneid*, Juno's opposition to the Trojans, a personification of everything that has gone wrong for them. Horace treats this in one short poem and shows her change of mind expressed in one key word.

'Ovid's happy afternoon' considers *Amores* 1.5 as that rare thing, a love poem, which is actually about lovers meeting and making love. I contrast Ovid's handling of this with poems by Catullus and Propertius. The essay on Ovid's treatment of Circe tries to separate this from Homer's account and show that it has had its own influence.

Dr Johnson's 'The Vanity of Human Wishes' is a free imitation of Juvenal's tenth satire and has a reputation of its own independent of that. I consider both where Johnson follows Juvenal and where he doesn't, to bring out the characteristic qualities of each.

The *Satyricon* of Petronius is a kind of parody of the Greek romances, with the disreputable same sex couple of Encolpius and Giton replacing the devoted opposite sex lovers of the Greek stories. However, there is more to it than that, and I argue that there is more to the attachment of the two than may at first appear.

The tale of Cupid and Psyche is the longest and most celebrated of the inset tales in the *Metamorphoses*, better known as *The Golden Ass*, of Apuleius. I had to abandon my original intention to write about allegorical interpretations of this tale, since there are several of these, all of some length, and to consider them would require a book rather than an essay. Instead, I have concentrated on Apuleius' handling of the psychology particularly of the divine characters in the story.

In writing these essays I have used the techniques of literary criticism, which I learned through the study of English literature, and applied them to the classics. Three schools of criticism of English literature in particular have influenced me. The first is the traditional humanist approach which I associate with C. S. Lewis, Graham Hough and Frank Kermode. This aimed to situate the work under discussion in its historical and literary context and to enter in the minds of its intended first audience. Then came the New Criticism, pioneered by T. S Eliot and I. A. Richards and taken up by many others, including William Empson and Cleanth Brooks. This uses close analysis of the text, together with relevant comparisons, but often without a historical context, with a view to arriving at a contemporary understanding and a value judgement of the work. Then there was the myth criticism of

Maud Bodkin, Joseph Campbell and Northrop Frye, which stressed the affinity of literary works with analogues in myth and ritual which, it is argued, gives literary works their power. All these approaches have been given theoretical underpinnings, and I have found them variously useful in reading my texts.

I also acknowledge debts to classicists who have concentrated on criticism, and four names stand out for me. These are Brooks Otis, Kenneth Quinn, Gordon Williams and Michael Putnam. The occasional references I make to their work do not exhaust my debts. I am also grateful to Dr Alison Samuels, my mentor at Oxford, who saw most of these papers in an earlier form, but who is not responsible for my errors. And of course, I value scholarly work on texts and interpretation and make frequent reference to it. I have given full references to all such works. As I do a great deal of close reading, the reader will find it helpful to have copies of the original texts in front of them. However, to reduce the notes, the texts and commentaries I have used are cited simply by editor's name; details are in a list at the end. Other older texts are given without note, but in a form which can be located in any edition. There is some repetition in the two essays on *Aeneid* II, as I wanted these essays to be able to be read independently. Some interesting side-issues are explored in the Appendices. All Latin is translated.

Stephen Barber
May 2025

1

COULD THE FALL OF TROY
HAVE BEEN PREVENTED?

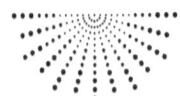

*V*irgil's command of suspense is such that, however often you read *Aeneid* II, each time you find yourself hoping against hope that this time it will be different: that the Trojans will heed some of the many warning signs, dispose of the Greeks in the horse and save their city. It doesn't happen, of course. So the issue is to consider these warning signs and also to reflect on why it was that the Trojans did not respond to them. Virgil's skill is to make it clear to the reader both that the signs are there and why it was that they were not heeded.

There are three preliminary issues. Firstly, Virgil was working here with traditional themes and legends, some of which were unalterable. The givens included the wooden horse, the involvement of Sinon and Laocoön and the return of the Greeks, but the details varied and gave Virgil scope to arrange them to his own satisfaction. Homer was some help, but the action of the *Iliad* ends well before the fall of Troy, though there are some references in the *Odyssey*. We cannot now get a full understanding of Virgil's use of sources, since some of the most important ones are wholly or mostly lost: these include parts of the Epic Cycle, particularly the *Sack of Ilion* by Arctinus, and at least two plays by Sophocles (*Laocoön* and *Sinon*). However, there are versions of the story later than Virgil which are thought to preserve earlier traditions.[1]

And there are some traditional motifs which Virgil sometimes hints at even if he deliberately did not use them and which I shall touch on.[2]

Secondly, the whole of this book, as well as the next, purports to be Aeneas' tale to Dido, told in retrospect and with later knowledge occasionally slipped in. This will sometimes be relevant. Apparently, this is the first time that the fall of Troy had been told from a Trojan point of view. Aeneas can expect a sympathetic hearing since Dido, like him, is an exile from her native country and already knows something of the Trojan war from the temple murals at Carthage which Aeneas has seen in Book I. However, Aeneas himself does not appear in his account of the wooden horse at all; it is only when the doom is already upon the Trojans that he tells her what he did. I shall return to the issue of his absence from his own account.

Thirdly, although the actual Trojan war was supposed to have taken place a good thousand years earlier than Virgil and the details had become absorbed in legends, nevertheless sieges and the sacking of cities were an only too recent memory and fear, because of the Roman civil war. Virgil is too canny to make this point explicitly, but it is a very clear implication of this book that the fall of Troy is the kind of thing that has happened and could happen again. You can think what you like about Augustus, but the fact that he put an end to the civil war comes up in Virgil's first acknowledged poem, *Eclogue* I, and is touched on or implied intermittently and gratefully throughout the *Aeneid*.

With these in mind, let us turn to the actual events as set out by Virgil. He charts the path to destruction in five stages, which I shall consider in turn:

I. The discovery of the horse.
II. Laocoön's warning.
III. Sinon.
IV. Laocoön's death.
V. The horse brought into the city.

I then want to consider more briefly:

VI. Greek duplicity and Trojan trust.
VII. The role of Priam.
VIII. The role of Aeneas.
IX. The role of the gods.

Aeneas starts by telling Dido immediately that the horse was a trap, why and how:

> fracti bello fatisque repulsi
> ductores Danaum tot iam labentibus annis
> instar montis equum divina Palladis arte
> aedificant, sectaque intexunt abiete costas;
> uotum pro reditu simulant; ea fama uagatur.
> huc delecta uirum sortiti corpora furtim
> includunt caeco lateri penitusque cauernas
> ingentis uterumque armato milite complent. (13-20)[3]

The leaders of the Greeks, broken by the war and driven back by the fates and with so many years now slipping by, build a horse the size[4] of a mountain with the divine art of Pallas (Athene, Minerva)[5] and weave its ribs with planks of silver fir; they pretend it is an offering for their (safe) return; that rumour spread. In this they enclose securely within its blind side picked bodies of men and deep within filled the huge caverns of the belly with armed soldiery.

This is almost entirely retrospective knowledge. But how does Aeneas learn that the horse was built *divina Palladis arte*, with the divine art of Pallas, and that *uotum pro reditu simulant; ea fama uagatur*, they pretend it is an offering for their return; that rumour spread? Virgil chose not to use the tradition that it bore an inscription saying explicitly that it was a thank offering to Minerva from the Greeks for their safe return home.[6] Aeneas must have deduced it from what Sinon says later:

> hanc pro Palladio moniti, pro numine laeso
> effigiem statuere, nefas quae triste piaret. (183-4)

They have set up this image (in atonement) for the Palladium, having been warned, for the injured deity, to atone for the dreadful sacrilege.

Sinon is, of course, completely unreliable, but this is the only basis for what Aeneas says, and it may be partly true. As for how the rumour arose, this is unexplained, as the Greeks were no longer around to start it off. Perhaps we are to assume that it was a speculation of the Trojans, given the presence of the horse and the apparent absence of the Greeks. Although in the war Minerva was on the Greek side, the Palladium, named after her title of Pallas, represented her in her customary role as guardian of the city, and in removing it the Greeks had removed her protection from the city.[7] It also had a symbolic meaning I shall come to.

Aeneas goes on to recount the actual discovery as it seemed at the time:

pars stupet innuptae donum exitiale Mineruae
et molem mirantur equi; primusque Thymoetes
duci intra muros hortatur et arce locari,
siue dolo seu iam Troiae sic fata ferebant.
at Capys, et quorum melior sententia menti,
aut pelago Danaum insidias suspectaque dona
praecipitare iubent subiectisque urere flammis,
aut terebrare cauas uteri et temptare latebras.
scinditur incertum studia in contraria uulgus. (31-9)

Some were amazed at the fatal gift of chaste Minerva and marvelled at the bulk of the horse; Thymoetes was the first to suggest that it should be pulled inside the walls and placed in the citadel, whether by treachery or because the fate of Troy was already tending that way. But Capys, and the opinion of those better in their advice, bid us either to throw the suspicious gift of the Greeks into the sea as it was a trap or to burn it with flames from underneath or to bore through the hollow of the belly and test its hiding places. The wavering crowd was split into opposing views.

Notice how the fact that the horse was *innuptae donum exitiale*

Mineruae, the fatal gift of chaste Minerva, is slipped into the narrative, although in Aeneas's account this is again retrospective knowledge. So is also the apparently casually dropped phrase *sive dolo seu iam Troiae sic fata ferebant*, whether by treachery or because the fate of Troy was already tending that way. This latter will prove important in the narrative. In fact, the whole passage is close to Homer,[8] except that there the Trojans take the horse to the citadel first and then argue about what to do with it. Virgil has added the names of Thymoetes[9] and Capys as leaders of the two (in Homer three) factions. Neither, however, commands enough authority to resolve the dispute; the situation called for leadership. There is, however, no mention of Priam at this point.

So the issue is left hanging because of the arrival of Laocoön, storming down (*ardens ... decurrit*, 41) from the citadel. In fact, the debate never resumes properly because each opportunity to bring it to a proper conclusion is interrupted: first by Laocoön's arrival, then by Sinon and lastly by Laocoön's death. This is part of Virgil's technique for generating suspense, because we keep wanting the Trojans to discuss the issue properly and they never do.

Anyway, Laocoön has summed up the situation correctly and warns the Trojans, ending with a line that has become proverbial, indeed a *sententia*:

> equo ne credite, Teucri.
> quidquid id est, timeo Danaos et dona ferentis. (48-9)

Do not trust the horse, Trojans. Whatever it is, I fear the Greeks, especially when bringing gifts.

The tremendous force of his conclusion is achieved by avoiding the usual words for *especially*, such as *praecipue*, *praesertim* or *maxime*, and putting all the weight on the little word *et*, strengthened by the fact it is here long by position, just after the fourth foot caesura, and supported by the coincidence of metrical ictus and stress accent which comes naturally at the end of a line.

He follows his spoken, or more probably, shouted warning with a startlingly aggressive act:

sic fatus ualidis ingentem uiribus hastam
in latus inque feri curuam compagibus aluum
contorsit. stetit illa tremens, uteroque recusso
insonuere cauae gemitumque dedere cauernae.
et, si fata deum, si mens non laeua fuisset,
impulerat ferro Argolicas foedare latebras,
Troiaque nunc staret, Priamique arx alta maneres. 50-6

*Having so spoken he hurled a huge lance with great force into the side of
the monster and the arching structure of its belly. It stood quivering and
from its stricken belly the hollow caverns resounded and gave a groan.
And, if the decrees[10] of the gods had been otherwise and the minds of our
people not been misguided he would have forced us to pierce the Greek
hiding place with steel and Troy would now be standing and you, the lofty
citadel of Priam, would remain.*[11]

We had *Troia … fata*, the fate of Troy, in in a passage I have already
quoted; here we have *fata deum*, the decrees of the gods. Virgil is setting
up his characteristic double motivation: human beings are responsible
for their actions but the gods have a plan of their own all along; I shall
return to this. We should also note that my rendering of *mens*, is slightly
expanded as minds of our people: Virgil does not say whose minds were
misguided and, in particular, Aeneas has not explicitly included himself.
In fact, he may not even have been there: he does not introduce himself
into the action until line 268. Heinze thinks he is speaking as an eyewit-
ness; this need not be true and indeed cannot be true as far as seeing
Laocoön coming from the citadel is concerned, or the serpents disappearing into the temple, if all the time he was on the beach.[12]

Virgil had here another tricky issue to deal with. In at least one early
account Aeneas takes the death of Laocoön as an indication that the city
is doomed and at that point decides to leave.[13] A Roman would have
seen this as desertion and cowardice so Virgil needs to keep Aeneas in
the city until the last moment and to make the decision to leave as difficult as possible for him. (It also means he can witness the beginning of
the sack of the city and the death of Priam.) On the other hand, he does

not want to associate Aeneas too closely with the credulousness of the other Trojans. I shall return to this issue.

Laocoön interrupted the debate among the Trojans, and, in turn, he never gets a proper response because at this moment Sinon is produced.[14] When we next hear of Laocoön, he is making a sacrifice, so at some point he removed himself from the rest of the group. Meanwhile, we have Sinon's three long speeches, which are a tissue of lies from beginning to end, but there are several points at which the Trojans should have been more suspicious. These begin with his very first words:

cuncta equidem tibi, rex, fuerit quodcumque, fatebor
uera (77-8)

I shall indeed tell you, king, everything truthfully.

I cannot improve on Austin's comment here: "Did the Trojans not know what 'I will be perfectly frank' so often means?" I must add that the single word *rex*, king, slipped in, is the only definite indication so far that Priam was present at all.[15]

Then there is the way he avoids naming his father (*pauper ... pater*, my father, a poor man, 87, and *exoptatumque parentem*, my longed-for father, 138). For Virgil's readers this would have been suspicious in itself; some of them might also have known, from earlier accounts now lost to us, who Sinon's father actually was[16] and that the suggested enmity with Ulysses was unlikely, to say the least. Virgil never resolves this in the poem. But Sinon has managed to appeal successfully to a Trojan, i.e. proto-Roman, sense of family.[17] I imagine that when Virgil read this book to his first audience, which included Maecenas and Augustus, one of them might have asked at the end: 'By the way, who was Sinon's father?' He would have smiled and said 'They should have asked, shouldn't they? But as it's you, I'll tell you,' and did so.

There are contradictions in his story, which the Trojans never notice. Aeneas tells us that the horse was made of *abies* (silver fir, 15), but Sinon on first mentioning it says it was made *acernis* (with maple wood, 112), possibly a deliberate mistake.[18] He mentions the horse as standing there (*staret equus*, 113) before Calchas has issued his warning to build it as an offering:

> hanc pro Palladio moniti, pro numine laeso
> effigiem statuere, nefas quae triste piaret. (183-4)

> *They have set up this image (in atonement) for the Palladium, having been warned, for the injured deity, to expiate the dreadful sacrilege.*

Furthermore, Eurypalus has supposedly gone to the oracle of Apollo, presumably that at Delphi, and returns to tell the Trojans that a sacrifice is needed for fair winds, with a reference to Agamemnon's sacrifice of Iphigenia at the beginning of the war:

> sanguine placastis uentos et uirgine caesa,
> cum primum Iliacas, Danai, uenistis ad oras;
> sanguine quaerendi reditus animaque litandum
> Argolica. (116-9)

> *You appeased the winds with the blood of a slaughtered virgin, Greeks, when you first came to Trojan shores; returns must be sought by blood and sacrificing of a Greek life.*

This turns out to be Sinon himself. Yet, when he escapes with no sacrifice made, the Greeks sail away without any difficulty:

> eripui, fateor, leto me et uincula rupi,
> limosoque lacu per noctem obscurus in ulua
> delitui dum uela darent, si forte dedissent. (134-6)

> *I snatched, I admit, myself from death and broke my bonds, and lurked all night in a muddy swamp, hidden in the sedge while they set sail, if by chance they were to do so.*

Which indeed they had done, though only as far as Tenedos, with no problems with the wind, as we were told at the beginning of the book:

nos abiisse rati et uento petiisse Mycenas. (25)

We thought they had gone away and were heading for Mycenae with a favourable wind.

The holes in his story are gaping. Yet no one challenges it and Priam himself takes the initiative in releasing him:

his lacrimis uitam damus et miserescimus ultro.
ipse uiro primus manicas atque arta leuari
uincla iubet Priamus dictisque ita fatur amicis. (145-7)

With these tears we give him his life and furthermore take pity on him. Priam himself first orders his manacles and tight fetters to be removed and then spoke to him with friendly words.

The acceptance of Sinon is the crucial decision in the whole business of the horse and it is the only decision Priam is seen to take. Virgil sometimes likes to make his points by implication rather than directly, and this is one of them: a main theme of the *Aeneid* is leadership, and —leaving aside for the moment the machinations of the gods—it is partly the absence of it in Troy that leads to disaster.[19] I shall return to this.

Then Sinon's whole account of the horse as an offering in atonement for the theft of the Palladium is self-contradictory. Sinon reports Calchas as saying:

extemplo temptanda fuga canit aequora Calchas,
nec posse Argolicis exscindi Pergama telis
omina ni repetant Argis numenque reducant
quod pelago et curuis secum auexere carinis. (176-9)

Straightway Calchas prophesied that the sea should be attempted in flight, nor could Pergama be torn up by Greek weapons unless they sought new omens at Argos and bring back the divine power which they have carried off with them overseas in their curved ships.

Not only is the seeking of new omens, which would have been in addition to the one from the oracle of Apollo, not carried out, but if the Palladium had been restored, it would surely have renewed its protection of Troy, thus defeating the Greeks' purpose. Nor would the supposed offering of the horse have been an adequate substitute for the Palladium, as gods are precise about such things. Sinon then reports Calchas giving advice which is quite absurd:

> hanc tamen immensam Calchas attollere molem
> roboribus textis caeloque educere iussit,
> ne recipi portis aut duci in moenia posset,
> neu populum antiqua sub religione tueri.
> nam si uestra manus uiolasset dona Mineruae,
> tum magnum exitium (quod di prius omen in ipsum
> convertant!) Priami imperio Phrygibusque futurum;
> sin manibus uestris uestram ascendisset in urbem,
> ultro Asiam magno Pelopea ad moenia bello
> uenturam, et nostros ea fata manere nepotes. (185-194)

But Calchas ordered us to build the large structure of interlaced planks so that it could not be brought through the gates or brought within the walls or guard the people under the protection of their traditional faith. But if your hand were to violate the gift to Minerva, then a great destruction— may the gods turn that prophecy first on himself—come to Priam's empire and the Trojans, but if it were to climb to the city by your hands, Asia would come further through a great war to the walls of Pelops [Mycenae] and that fate would remain for our offspring.

Calchas's advice to build the horse so large as to make it impossible to bring into the citadel would have meant it could not expiate the sacrilege of stealing the Palladium, even if it were an acceptable substitute, and so help the Greeks with their return journey, which was supposedly the whole point. No sensible deity would agree to be fobbed off with a wooden horse too big to go into the city as adequate compensation for the theft of the Palladium from inside the city.[20] And as Athene had won the contest with Poseidon in offering Athens the olive tree—

symbol of peace—when he offered the horse, it woould hardly have been an appropriate offering to her. But Sinon distracts attention from this by a specious account of the consequences to the Trojans of bringing it in.

This, the climax of Sinon's account, is also the most internally incoherent part of it. But none of the Trojans challenge it: the faction led by Capys says nothing and Laocoön has not stayed for an answer to his warning but is elsewhere making a sacrifice. By this point the Trojans have been completely taken in:

talibus insidiis periurique arte Sinonis
credita res, captique dolis lacrimisque coactis (195-6)

Through such traps and the skill of perjured Sinon his account was believed and we were caught by tricks and forced tears.

In fact, in the course of Sinon's speeches his deceptions increase as he finds he has got away with the previous ones. No one challenges his frankness, asks about his father, takes up his mistake about the wood the horse is made of, when it was built or when a second group of omens were required. Nor, something which they should surely have been concerned about, did they query the rigmarole about the horse as an adequate substitute for the Palladium or how offering it outside the city would appease Minerva and gain favourable winds. The reader is left wondering how the Trojans could have been so taken in.

However, any debate there might have been is again cut short because of Laocoön's second appearance and the horrible death of himself and his sons dealt by the serpents.[21] This is, clearly, a portent, but what is its meaning? The only clue we are given comes at the end of the account:

at gemini lapsu delubra ad summa dracones
effugiunt saeuaeque petunt Tritonidis arcem,
sub pedibusque deae clipeique sub orbe teguntur. (225-7)

But the twin dragons with a gliding movement escape to the lofty citadel of Tritonia[22] (Minerva), and are hidden under the foot of the goddess and under the circle of her shield.

There is a link between Minerva and serpents, as, for example, that made by Virgil himself in his later description of the aegis on the shield of Aeneas:

aegidaque horriferam, turbatae Palladis arma,
certatim squamis serpentum auroque polibant
conexosque anguis VIII. (435-7)

They [the Cyclopes] were eagerly polishing the dread aegis, the weapon of angry Pallas [Minerva], with the golden scales of snakes and interwoven serpents.

Anyway, for the Trojans, this clinches the matter:

tum uero tremefacta nouus per pectora cunctis
insinuat pauor, et scelus expendisse merentem
Laocoönta ferunt, sacrum qui cuspide robur
laeserit et tergo sceleratam intorserit hastam. (228-231)

Then indeed a new fear creeps into the trembling hearts of all of us, and they say that Laocoön has paid the deserved penalty for crime, who (they say)[23] injured the sacred wood[24] with his lance and hurled a cursed spear into its back.

It seemed obvious to the Trojans that Laocoön's death was inflicted by the will of Minerva because of his assault on the horse, confirmed by the serpents making for her temple. However, this would not explain the death of his sons as well. Here Virgil seems to have made a deliberate break with the tradition about Laocoön as it was handed down. According to this, he was a priest of Apollo. In one version, against Apollo's will he had married a wife and had children. Apollo took the opportunity, when Laocoön had been chosen by lot to sacrifice to

Poseidon (Neptune) on the shore,[25] to send the two serpents to kill him and the wrongly-begotten children.[26] In another version, the offence was not the marriage itself but Laocoön's having intercourse with his wife in the precinct of Thymbrian Apollo and before the images of the gods.[27] It rather looks as if Virgil took this story over and repurposed it with Minerva being the affronted deity, confirmed by the serpents making for her temple. We remember that among the temple murals Aeneas saw one of a suppliant and unsuccessful procession *ad templum non aequae Palladis* (to the temple of unjust Pallas, I.479). Her injustice is compounded in this scene by the deaths of the two children as there is no reason in Virgil to suppose that they were wrongly begotten.[28] In the *Aeneid* we have been told precisely nothing about any previous offence Laocoön might have caused either to Apollo or to Minerva and which, rather than his—perfectly accurate—denunciation of the horse, his dreadful death might have expiated.[29] The Trojans in his account know no alternative to the conclusion they draw. They do not misinterpret the snake prodigy, as Brooks Otis suggests,[30] as Virgil offers no other possible interpretation. The effect is to dispel the sense that they are culpably gullible, which has been encouraged by their acceptance of Sinon's story. By this point the Trojans are in a trap with no escape.

The Trojans then bring the horse into the city. However, even then all was not lost. There were three possible opportunities to reconsider, although we never really think they have a chance. First was the process of getting the horse through the walls. Virgil has Aeneas say:

diuidimus muros et moenia pandimus urbis. (234)

We breach the walls and open the buildings of the city.

Austin says at this point: 'After all the fuss made by Sinon to account for the vast size of the Horse, they got it in without real difficulty; even now they might have reflected on the strangeness of this.' But Austin overlooked the fact that the wall was sacred. It had been built by Poseidon (Neptune) and Apollo,[31] but with the help of Aeacus, a mortal, so that, if necessary, the city could be taken.[32] The breach, probably of the upper threshold of the Scaean gate where Laomedon was buried,[33] undid the magical protection of the wall,[34] and it was important that it was made by the Trojans themselves. None of the Trojans remember that the wall was sacred, although it is possible that Virgil might have intended to write more here, as the immediately preceding line is incomplete. Or he might have deliberately decided only to hint at this motif. It is in any case important that, despite the breach, the gates and their supports remained intact, as it was the warriors from the horse who opened them later:

> caeduntur uigiles, portisque patentibus omnis
> accipiunt socios atque agmina conscia iungunt. (266-7)

The sentries are slaughtered and, having opened the gates, they [the Greeks] *greet all their comrades and unite their participating troops.*

And later we read:

> portis alii bipatentibus adsunt. (330)

Some are at the gates, wide-open on both sides.

Then the horse stopped four times on the way:

> quater ipso in limine portae
> substitit atque utero sonitum quater arma dedere;
> instamus tamen immemores caecique furore
> et monstrum infelix sacrata sistimus arce. (242-5)

Four times at the very threshold of the gods it stopped and four times weapons gave out a sound from its belly; yet we press on regardless and blind with passion we put the ill-omened monstrous thing on our sacred citadel.

Jackson Knight's comment here seems definitive: 'To Roman thought a stoppage in a procession or any other ritual was a bad omen, a stoppage at the threshold a worse omen still, and, since all even numbers, four more than two, might have sinister connotations, four stoppages at a threshold must have been a very bad omen indeed.'[35] We expect the Trojans to be anticipatory Romans here. Yet they not only ignore the omen, they do not even appreciate that it is an omen, because they are *caecique furore*, blind with passion. This is a point which Virgil leaves readers to work out for themselves.

Finally, there is the warning by Cassandra, but of course she is not believed because she never is:

tunc etiam fatis aperit Cassandra futuris
ora dei iussu non umquam credita Teucris. (246-7)

Even then Cassandra opened her mouth about the imminent doom, a mouth commanded by a god never to be believed by Trojans.

In fact, she is ignored, the Trojans have lost their last chance and the city is doomed. Homer had said that the city would perish once the wooden horse was inside it.[36] There is no longer any suspense: we await with sickening dread what will happen when the horse releases its burden.

Turning now to my more general themes, we have first the contrast between Greek duplicity and Trojan trustfulness. Heinze points out that their trustfulness is a Roman virtue, Sinon's deviousness a Greek vice.[37] Aeneas dwells on this repeatedly, from the beginning of his account:

uotum pro reditu simulant (17)

They pretend that it is an offering for their (safe) return.

and at the discovery of Sinon:

accipe nunc Danaum insidias et crimine ab uno
disce omnis (65-6)

Hear now about Greek tricks and from a single crime learn about all of them.

During his account the Trojans are—

ignari scelerum tantorum artisque Pelasgae (106)

unfamiliar with such great wickedness and Pelasgian trickery.

And at the end of it:

talibus insidiis periurique arte Sinonis
credita res, captique dolis lacrimisque coactis (195-6)

Through such traps and the skill of perjured Sinon his account was believed and we were caught by tricks and forced tears.

My point is simply is that this is all retrospective knowledge. (Of course, Virgil was happy to exploit a persistent stereotyping by Romans of Greeks here.) Even if Aeneas was suspicious at the time, he said and did nothing about it. Maybe he was as gullible as the rest of the Trojans. Or, as I shall propose, he was possibly not there. Anyway, it is important that Troy was conquered by trickery, not by force of arms.

I have already suggested that a theme of this whole episode is the poor leadership provided by Priam. In fact, this is conspicuous by its absence. He did nothing to deal with the opposing views as to what to do with the horse, or try to ascertain its true nature or purpose before Sinon's arrival, or to respond to Laocoön's warning. The only thing Aeneas says Priam has actually done has been to welcome Sinon, order his manacles to be released and invite him to give his own account of the horse, which he does not question (147-151). It would be trite to say that Troy fell because of lack of leadership but the more you read it the more glaring does its absence seem. I am not overlooking the role of the gods, but the will of the gods does not exempt human beings from responsibility. There are three possible good reasons and one bad one why Aeneas does not otherwise mention Priam, which might all be true and which support one another. The bad reason is that, according to Homer, there was rivalry between the house of Anchises and the house of Priam for kingship, and Priam did not sufficiently recognize Aeneas' prowess.[38] I do not think Virgil uses this idea or that his Aeneas would have distorted by omission Priam's role if he had exercised it more forcefully. I think we can discard this suggestion. Of the good reasons, one is that he is loyal to his king, whose death he has witnessed by the time he comes to tell this story to Dido. The second is that he might not actually have been there when the horse was found and brought into the city, a possibility I shall take up in a moment. But the third is perhaps the most significant: this is, chronologically, the beginning of his story, and he has yet to learn what leadership involves and this is a major theme of the *Aeneid* as a whole. I believe Virgil intended us to reflect on this.

Turning now to Aeneas' own role in this episode, it is notable that he says nothing about himself at all. He has said to Dido:

> quaeque ipse miserrima uidi
> et quorum pars magna fui. (5-6)

I saw these dreadful things myself and was a great part of them.

He tells the story but does not include himself in it. Virgil had a difficult problem here. He cannot dissociate Aeneas from the rest of the Trojan people, since his destiny is to lead the remnant of them to Italy. One reason Virgil has deliberately kept him back is that he is to be introduced at the nadir of his fortunes in the next part of the book. Another is that he does not want to introduce us to him at the beginning of his account as simply another gullible Trojan. I think Virgil wants us to understand that, although Aeneas is caught up in the catastrophe—it is the defining experience of his life—he was not personally responsible for it. So Virgil finesses the issue: Aeneas might have been an eyewitness of the events he describes, as Heinze suggested, but he might instead have heard of them later, from the refugees whom he met up with at Mount Ida. He does not say in so many words that he was there himself, though we are free to conclude, though we do not have to, that he was, by his use of plural verbs. He implicitly seems to include himself in lines 105 (*ardemus scitari*, we are burning to find out), 145 (*uitam damus*, we give [Sinon] his life) and 234 (*diuidimus muros et moenia pandimus urbis*, we breach the walls and open up the buildings of the city). These need not be taken as meaning 'all of us, without exception, and including myself;' in fact, they clearly did not include Laocoön and we can only infer the presence of Priam when Sinon addresses him as *rex* (king, 77), before Priam speaks to him (148-9). He does not dissociate himself from his compatriots either, but he has slightly distanced himself from them throughout this whole episode; the subjunctive in *qui cuspide robur | laeserit* (who (they say) injured the sacred wood, 231) supports this. So does the fact that the description of the opening of the horse and the release of the Greeks, which immediately follows this episode, is something neither Aeneas nor any other Trojan could have witnessed.[39]

I think we should see him at this stage as more or less the Aeneas of Homer in the *Iliad*: he had a privileged position as the son of a goddess, so in the technical as well as the ordinary sense he was a hero, next to Hector among the Trojans as a fighting man.[40] Homer tells us that his destiny is to become king among the Trojans, or rather what remains of them, though this is said by Poseidon and Aeneas would not yet have been aware of it.[41] Of course it is progressively revealed to him in the *Aeneid*, starting later in this book, but in the account of the wooden horse he knows nothing of it. (In his account of the fall of Troy he does not call upon the knowledge of his destiny he later recounts from the ghost of Creusa or in Book I.) And so far, as also arguably in the *Iliad*, he has had no formal or informal leadership role: he is simply a Trojan warrior among others. He briefly takes a leadership role later but it is only really at the very end of the book that he finds himself leading the whole band of Trojan refugees. So Priam failed to offer leadership and Aeneas was not yet in a position when it could have been expected of him. How it came to be so is the subject of the rest of this book. As Brooks Otis rightly says: 'he had to be a hero on the old model before he could be one on the new.'[42]

Finally, we need to consider the role of the gods. In this episode they feature, with one exception, mainly through hints and suggestions rather than anything explicit; it will be very different in the rest of the book. Aeneas begins his account by saying of the Greeks that they were:

fracti bello fatisque repulsi (13)

Broken by the war and driven back by the Fates

Similarly, at the end of this episode, there are the omens on bringing the horse into the city. Virgil does not dwell on these and Aeneas merely refers to the horse as the *monstrum infelix* (ill-omened monstrous thing, 245). Here again we are in the territory of hints and suggestions.

Then there is the association Aeneas makes of the horse with Minerva. It was built *divina Palladis arte* (by the divine art of Pallas, 15) and is *innuptae exitiale Mineruae* (the fatal gift of chaste Minerva, 31). This is retrospective knowledge, and Aeneas' hearers do not yet know how he came to know it. Instead there are more dark hints, but this time going the other way from the reference to the Fates. He says of Laocoön's warning:

et si fata deum, si mens non laeva fuisset,
impulerat ferro Argolicas foedare latebras,
Troiaque nunc staret, Priamique arx alta, maneres. (54-6)

And, if the decrees of the gods had been otherwise and the minds of our people not been misguided he would have forced us to pierce the Greek hiding place with steel and Troy would now be standing and you, the lofty citadel of Priam, would remain.

I earlier considered the force of *mens* in this passage; I now want to consider the passing reference to *fata deum*, the decrees of the gods. It is equivalent to the divine will, that is, the will of Iuppiter or divine providence.[43] The gods have a plan, and part of this is that they want Troy to fall, but why they should want this is left obscure. A kind of clarification comes with the death of Laocoön. The fact that the serpents go to Minerva's temple (225-7, quoted above) is the exception to the obscurity of the other references to the gods; it makes clear the link between the goddess and the horse and that Laocoon's verbal and physical assault on it was abhorrent to her. Virgil has deliberately discarded the version in which there was a previous offence against the gods by Laocoön, so as to justify the Trojans in taking the horse as a gift offering as Sinon suggested. It does not, however, justify them for accepting his rigmarole about the link with the Palladium. The double motivation still operates: they may have rightly discerned the will of the gods but that does not absolve human beings from acting prudently. However, there was no getting round the implacable opposition of Minerva,[44] made clear by the fact that the serpents went to her temple.

However, it is worth considering why Minerva was so opposed to the Trojans. Yes, there is a long-term plan, at least by Iuppiter, which requires Aeneas to leave Troy to become the founder of Rome. But the double motivation continues to apply. Minerva is, among other things, the goddess of reason. The theft of the Palladium signifies the impending irrationality of the Trojans. Her opposition to them coincides with their abandonment of reason in ignoring Laocoön and accepting Sinon's lies. The irrationality and the punishment are linked not as cause and effect but as the same thing, so are simultaneous. In the next part of the book we shall see something of Aeneas' own irrationality.

The poet later says in his own person that Sinon was:

fatisque deum defensus iniquis (257)

protected by the unjust [?] *fates of the gods*

Iniquis is a strong word to use of the gods but it is ambiguous: it can mean *harsh* but also *unjust*. The Loeb version translates it as *malign* and Bailey[45] as *cruel*, thereby leaning to the first alternative. Horsfall refers at this point to *divine injustice*, leaning to the second. Austin suggests that 'this is Virgil's way of saying that Sinon had luck on his side' but this is surely not strong enough. Virgil is practising a piece of subtle equivocation, raising at least the possibility that the gods are unjust. I have already mentioned his doing so in book I. He will do so again in Book

VI, where Aeneas meeting Dido in the underworld is *casu percussus iniquo* (affected by her unjust fate, 475).

Throughout the account of the horse Virgil has had to hold in tension the inevitability of the disaster, which is the will of the gods, and human freewill. He made a skilful selection from the available traditional motifs, discarding some and choosing those which allowed to him to make a convincing narrative without digressions. He keeps the role of the gods to a minimum and in very general terms, apart from the portent of Laocoön's death. He lays out very clearly opportunities for discovering the true nature of the horse, for heeding the warning of Laocoön and for challenging the lies of Sinon. In also showing how and why these opportunities are not taken, he creates that feeling of suspense which dominates the episode and also shows how the disaster became inevitable.

---

1. There are useful summaries of the earlier accounts by Robin Hard, *The Routledge Handbook of Greek Mythology*, London, 2004, 473-6, and Timothy Gantz, *Early Greek Myth: A Guide to Literary and Artistic Sources*, Baltimore, 1993, 646-50, and fuller discussions by Richard Heinze, *Virgil's Epic Technique* trans. Hazel Harvey *et al.*, London, 1993 (1928[2]), 3-14, R. G. Austin's commentary on this book, Oxford, 1964 and especially W. F. Jackson Knight, *Vergil's Troy*, in *Vergil: Epic and Anthropology*, London, 1967 (1932), 75-102. I have used these as pointers to such primary sources and analogues as survive.

2. These include that there was an inscription on the wooden horse dedicating it to Minerva, that Laocoön was a priest of Apollo, that one or more of his family survived the serpents, that the walls of Troy were magically protected, that there was a rivalry between the house of Priam and that of Aeneas, and that Aeneas left the city at the death of Laocoön and before the catastrophe.

3. Quotations are from Book II unless otherwise noted.

4. The bulk must have been more in the height than the width of the horse, as otherwise it could not have got through the gates. See the discussion with estimates of its size and the material findings at the site of Troy, in Julian Ward Jones, 'Sizing up Vergil's horse,' *The Classical Outlook*, Vol. 89, No. 1 (Fall 2011). See below for the discussion of its passage through the gates.

5. Virgil never uses the Greek name Athena but either the Roman Minerva or another title, such as Pallas or Tritonia. See Cyril Bailey, *Religion in Virgil*, Oxford, 1935, 152-7. I shall use Minerva, even in a Greek context.

6. Apollodorus, *Epitome* 14, in *The Library of Greek Mythology* trans. Robin Hard, Oxford, 1997, 156. Other early references are given by Horsfall in his commentary, Leiden 2008, 72.

7. Cities had tutelary deities and one of Minerva's titles was 'saviour of cities' (*Homeric Hymn* XXVIII.3). One of the temple murals Aeneas sees in Book I is of Trojan

women importuning Minerva in this capacity (I.479-82). Part of Roman siege warfare was to remove the gods' protection through an *evocatio*. This is explained by Macrobius (early Vth century A.D.), *Saturnalia*, III.9.1-16. There is an example of an *evocatio* in Livy V.21.2-3 (the destruction of Veii). Ulysses and Diomedes did not resort to an *evocatio* but to a physical removal of the statue. See Walter Burket, *Greek Religion*, Oxford, 1985, 140, Stephen Benko, *The Virgin Goddess: Studies in the Pagan and Christian Roots of Mariology*, Leiden, 2003, 26-7.

8. Homer, *Odyssey* VIII.506-13.

9. There had been a prophecy that on a particular day a boy would be born who would be the ruin of Troy. On that day Priam's and Thymoetes' wives gave birth to Paris and Menippus respectively. Priam had Menippus and his mother killed but spared Paris; Lycophron (attrib.) *Alexandra*, 224, 316-22 and notes by Hornblower *ad. loc.*; Isaac and John Tzetzes, *Scholia on Lycophron* ed. G. C. F. Müller, 3 vv., Leipzig: Vogelii, 1811, I, 535. Thymoetes therefore had a motive for revenge on Priam, hence the suggestion of treachery (*dolo*), though Virgil neither explains this nor assumes it.

10. I take this translation of *fata* from Bailey, *Religion in Virgil*, 225.

11. I accept here the interpretations of Austin; in this passage see his note on *curvam compagibus alvum*.

12. Heinze, *Virgil's Epic Technique*, 13. On his view, Heinze has to concede that Virgil 'does not stay scrupulously within the confines of first-person narrative,' 10.

13. Arctinus, *Iliu Persis* argument §1 apud Proclus, *Chrestomathia*, *Greek Epic Fragments* ed. M. L. West, Harvard, 2003, 144-5. In Quintus Smyrnaeus (II to IV century A. D.), *Posthomerica*, XIII, 332-86. the Greeks allow him to escape from the city; this would have been even less to Virgil's purpose.

14. In Quintus Smyrnaeus, *Posthomerica*, XII, 427, the Trojans were about to obey Laocoön but Athene intervened directly. See note 29 *infra*.

15. Certainly, Aeneas says that the shepherds were dragging Sinon *ad regem* (to or towards the king, 58), but this is not confirmation that Priam was there, though it seems probable.

16. Lycophron (attrib.), *Alexandra*, 344, says that Sinon was cousin to Odysseus (Ulysses). We know the exact relationship only from late sources. In the fifth century poet Tryphiodorus, Sinon volunteers that his father was Aesimus; *Excidium Troiae*, 291. The late Byzantine commentary on the *Alexandra* explains that Aesimus, the father of Sinon, was the brother of Anticleia, the mother of Odysseus; Isaac and John Tzetzes, *Scholia on Lycophron*, I, 547. See also Simon Hornblower (ed.) Lykophron, *Alexandra*, Oxford, 2015, 194.

17. See John P. Lynch, 'Laocoön and Sinon: Virgil, *Aeneid* 2.40-198,' *Greece and Rome*, Vol. 27 No. 2 (Oct. 1980), for an analysis of the different rhetorical devices in the speeches of Laocoön and Sinon. He also appealed to his audience's sense of religion and law, and shed tears.

18. So Austin *ad loc.*. The alternative view, that the horse was made from different kinds of wood (cf. *roboribus*, 186, *pinea*, 258) has been defended by Horsfall, 60: 'the many timbers used for the manufacture of the Horse have long been understood as having more to do with Parnassus than with wood-yard or carpenter's shop.' Servius suggests that the different kinds of wood named each have a magical significance; Servius on line 16. However, Aeneas' hearers and Virgil's readers would surely notice the contradiction and it seems more telling that Sinon should seem ill-informed about the horse.

19. In his opera *Les Troyens*, based on *Aeneid* II and IV, Berlioz added a scene in which Priam explicitly took the fateful decision to admit the horse, against the warning of Cassandra. (Berlioz removed this scene from the orchestral score in anticipation of a performance, but it has been reconstructed from the vocal score by Hugh Macdonald. It is not usually performed but it is included in Dutoit's recording of the opera.)

20. Virgil does not use the motif that Poseidon was in some sense god of horses and also presided over city walls, so that by accepting the horse the Trojans might have believed they would strengthen the magical protection of the city associated with him; Jackson Knight, *Vergil's Troy*, 113-4. In rejecting this, Virgil emphasizes their credulity and discards a possible justification for it. Virgil was aware of horse magic, as in the story of the horses of Rhesus, *Aeneid* I.469-73, or those Anchises saw on first seeing Italy, *Aeneid* III.537-543.

21. The way Virgil introduces this raises an issue: *Hic aliud maius miseris multoque tremendum | obscitur magis atque improvida pectora turbat* (Then a greater thing, far more terrible for us wretched people, comes upon us and disturbs our unwary hearts, 199-200). Nothing terrible (*tremendum*) has happened yet: neither the discovery of the horse nor Sinon could be called that. This passage looks like an unrevised relic of a version in which Virgil used a different sequence of events.

22. A title of Minerva which goes back to Homer. Its origin and meaning were disputed even in the ancient world, Servius on line 171 and Austin's comment. I am attracted by the argument of J. B. Trapp, 'Virgil and the monuments,' *Proceedings of the Virgil Society*, Vol. 18, 1986, that the link with Triton is the most important; he points out that in Virgil the Tritons are powerful beings and servants of Minerva and Neptune.

23. The subjunctive *laeserit* following *qui* makes it clear that this is what the Trojans say and is not vouched for by Aeneas or the poet.

24. *Robur* can mean oak specifically, but that would contradict Aeneas's statement that the horse was made of *abies* (silver fir, 16) and the primary meaning is simply hard wood; I have already noted Sinon's claim that it was made *acernis* (with maple wood, 112) as possibly a deliberate mistake by him. Virgil uses *robore* for it again in 260 and *pinea*, pine, at 258. See note 18 *supra*.

25. According to Servius, Euphorion, the Greek dramatist and son of Aeschylus, said that the Trojans had killed their previous priest of Poseidon for failing to make a sacrifice to prevent the arrival of the Greeks. It would seem that after the apparent departure of the Greeks Laocoön was drafted in as a temporary priest of Poseidon, as Virgil says (201), so that this time an appropriate sacrifice would be offered; Servius on line 201. The altar had been on the shore so during the war was inaccessible to the Trojans and the cult fell into disuse. It would have spoiled the story for Virgil to interrupt it with these explanations. See the discussion by Heinze, *Virgil's Epic Technique*, 12-13.

26. This is known to us from Virgil's contemporary, the mythographer Hyginus, *The Myths of Hyginus* ed. and trans. Mary Grant, Lawrence, 1960, § 135.

27. This is the version of Servius, *loc. cit.*

28. Although in the famous sculpture in the Vatican museum the two sons are youths, in Virgil they are small boys *(parva duorum | corpora natorum* 213-4). In other versions, summarised by Austin, 95, one or both children were killed but Laocoön spared; in the sculpture it looks as if one boy might be escaping. Virgil is apparently the only writer to have all three killed; see Jackson Knight, *Vergil's Troy*, 88-9.

29. Incidentally, although the serpents devoured the two sons, there is no mention of any burial for Laocoön himself or of the need for it; given the importance of proper burial in the ancient world—think of Sophocles' *Antigone* or indeed Book VI of the *Aeneid*—I find this surprising. Presumably Virgil thought this would have been an unnecessary digression. In Quintus Smyrnaeus, *Posthomerica*, XII.479-537, Laocoön survives but is blinded and after the sack he and his wife build a cenotaph for the dead boys. Heinze thought this would have been the original version, *Virgil's Epic Technique*, 40-1.

30. Brooks Otis, *Virgil: A Study in Civilized Poetry*, Oxford, 1964, 248.

31. Homer, *Iliad*, VII.451-3. Virgil mentions Neptune at II.625. (He omits Apollo, as he did with Laocoön; it would have been confusing.) Homer also refers to a weak place in the wall, *Iliad*, VI.434, though this is not one of the gates.

32. Pindar, *Olympian Ode* VIII, 30-6 with scholium quoted *ad loc.*.

33. Servius on lines 13 and 241; I am indebted here to Jackson Knight, *Vergil's Troy*, 120-3. Dares Phrygius (early VI century A. D.) *De excidio* XL, says there was an (apotropaic) emblem of a horse's head outside the gate.

34. It had already been weakened by the negative magic of Achilles' dragging the body of Hector three times round the wall, *Aeneid* I.483-4—in Homer he chases the living Hector, *Iliad*, XXII.165; 'Hector was in some supernatural sense the protector of Troy or the walls of Troy,' Jackson Knight, *Vergil's Troy*, 117; *Iliad*, XXIV.727.

35. Jackson Knight, *Vergil's Troy*, 121. He is relying on Emory B. Lease, 'A further note to Vergil, *Aeneid* II.242f.,' *The Classical Journal*, Vol. 19 No. 7 (April 1924), who gives references substantiating this.

36. Homer, *Odyssey*, VIII.511-3.

37. *Virgil's Epic Technique*, 7.

38. Homer, *Iliad*, XIII.460-1, XX.179-186.

39. Heinze says of this that Virgil 'once again was not confining himself strictly to the stand-point of the first-person narrative; he wanted to give his audience not merely a bare outline of the essential facts, but a vivid picture,' *Virgil's Epic Tech*nique, 15. Cf. footnote 12 *supra*.

40. Homer, *Iliad*, V.466-9,

41. Homer, *Iliad*, XX.306.

42. Brooks Otis, *Virgil: A Study in Civilized Poetry*, 244.

43. See the discussion in Bailey, *Religion in Virgil*, 220-234.

44. Virgil might have taken this motif from the opening speech by Poseidon in Euripides, *Trojan Women*, 1-47, where it is explicit.

45. *Religion in Virgil*, 224.

2

WHAT IS AENEAS' STATE
OF MIND ON LEAVING TROY?

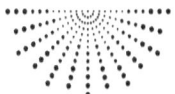

*I*t could so easily have been so different. In a version of the story of Aeneas given by a near-contemporary of Virgil, while the Greeks were taking the lower town Aeneas fled to the citadel, which was fortified, where there were the Trojan holy things, treasure and the best of the army. They repulsed the Greeks and rescued more people from the town than were taken prisoner. Aeneas then sent the women and children on to Mount Ida, escorted by part of the army, while he, with the rest of it, fought off the Greeks. When the Greeks succeeded in breaking through to the citadel he marched away to Mount Ida in good order, taking with him his father, his wife and his children (plural) as well as the best of the treasure. They held this position and then successfully negotiated with the Greeks to surrender the land in return for safe passage. This is the account which the historian Dionysius of Halicarnassus thought most probable.[1] In other accounts, Aeneas left the city before its fall, warned by the death of Laocoön, or was spared by the Greeks.

Virgil chose a totally different approach. At the end of *Aeneid* II, Aeneas is at the nadir of his fortunes. He has lost his role as warrior, seen his city and his home destroyed, seen his king murdered and lost his wife. He has found himself thrust into the position of leader of a group of Trojan refugees, a role for which his previous experience has not prepared him. All he has is his father, who represents wisdom and experience, and his young son, who is his hope for the future. The episodes of this part of the book show him resorting to his role as a warrior, finding it useless, indeed counterproductive, and then being motivated entirely by others, by portents of one kind or another. What I want to explore in this essay is why Virgil chose to represent Aeneas in this way and how he charts Aeneas' withdrawal and future course.

There are three preliminary issues, as I noted in the previous essay. Firstly, as with the first part of the book, Virgil was working here with traditional themes and legends, some of which were unalterable. The givens included Aeneas leaving the city carrying his father and leading his young son, but there were various versions of at what stage in the disaster he did so, whether or not he had his wife with him—and the issue of her name—and whether the Greeks were party to any of this. We cannot now get a full understanding of Virgil's use of sources, since some of the most important ones are wholly or mostly lost: these include parts of the Epic Cycle and at least two plays by Sophocles (*Laocoön* and *Sinon*). However, there are versions of the story later than Virgil which are thought to preserve earlier traditions.[2] And there are some traditional motifs which Virgil sometimes hints at even if he deliberately did not use them and which I shall touch on.

Secondly, the whole of this book, as well as the next, purports to be Aeneas' tale to Dido, told in retrospect and with later knowledge sometimes slipped in. However, Aeneas himself did not appear in his account of the wooden horse at all; I have suggested that Virgil did not want to implicate him too closely in the folly of the Trojans in accepting the horse into the city. In the later part of the book, he gives a first-person narrative of what he saw and did. This is necessary, not only artistically, as his account is indeed thrilling, but also psychologically, in that we need to hear from him how his experiences have shaped him. And as, unlike his creator, he is not a specially reflective or imaginative man, it is from his experience that he learns his destiny.

Thirdly, although the actual Trojan war was supposed to have taken place a good thousand years earlier and the details had become absorbed in legends, nevertheless sieges and the sacking of cities were an only too recent memory and fear, because of the Roman civil war.

There are seven episodes in the fortunes of Aeneas as he recounts them which I intend to consider. These are:

I. Hector and Panthus.
II. Counter-attack by Aeneas.
III. Priam
IV. Helen and Venus[3]
V. Anchises and the oracles.
VI. Creusa.
VII. Departure.

I also need to say something about:

VIII. The use of dream, vision and portent
IX. The narrative context: telling this to Dido
X. The allegorical interpretation of the *Aeneid*.

Aeneas is unaware that the disaster is already upon the city when he dreams about Hector.[4] Hector appears disfigured, as Aeneas would have last seen him. He ignores Aeneas' greeting and immediately counsels flight:

'heu fuge, nate dea, teque his' ait 'eripe flammis.
hostis habet muros; ruit alto a culmine Troia.
sat patriae Priamoque datum: si Pergama dextra
defendi possent, etiam hac defensa fuissent.
sacra suosque tibi commendat Troia penatis;
hos cape fatorum comites, his moenia quaere
magna pererrato statues quae denique ponto.' (289-295)[5]

'Alas, flee, goddess-born, and save yourself from these flames. The enemy holds the walls; Troy is falling from her lofty height. Enough has been done for your native land and for Priam; if Pergama could be saved by combat, then it would have been protected by this hand of mine. Troy

entrusts to you her holy things and her Penates[6]; take them to be companions of your fortune, seek for them the great city walls which you will establish after you have wandered over the ocean.'

This is the kind of dream known as an epiphany dream, as defined by the most recent study of the phenomenon in the ancient world: 'This type of dream consists of the appearance to the dreamer of an authoritative personage who may be divine or represent a god, and this figure conveys instructions or information.'[7] Literary examples go back to Homer,[8] and Biblical examples include Jacob's dream from the Old Testament and the dreams of Joseph, the Magi and Peter from the New. Now Virgil was writing for a Roman audience, and, for a Roman, flight from one's city when under attack would be desertion of the worst kind. The classic exposition of this is the speech of Camillus in Livy when Rome had been largely destroyed by the Gauls. The whole speech takes seven pages in the Oxford text, but I take one sentence as representative:

> Si tota urbe nullum melius ampliusue tectum fieri possit quam casa illa conditoris est nostri, non in casis ritu pastorum agrestiumque habitare est satius inter sacra penatesque nostros quam exsulatum publice ire? (Livy, V.53.8)

> *Even if it were not possible to construct a better or more spacious building in the whole City of Rome than that house of our Founder* [i.e. the hut of Romulus], *would it not be better to live like herdsmen and peasants, among our sacred things, than to go openly into exile?*

Aeneas had to flee to fulfil his destiny as the founder of Rome, but Virgil had to make it clear, both to him and to the reader, that this was not desertion. So he used the device of an epiphany dream. For his authoritative figure he did not choose Aeneas' mother, the goddess Venus, whom he needed to keep in reserve for later, but Hector the fallen champion of Troy. He would also have been aware of the tradition that Hector, whose name means 'he who holds,' was not only physically but also in a magical sense the protector of Troy.[9]

Then Hector warns Aeneas to escape from these flames. This is the first indication that the Greeks have already fired the city. This is another departure from tradition, in which the Greeks first take their plunder and do not fire the city until they depart.[10] Throughout the rest of this book Virgil dwells on the sight of the city in flames, not only because it is dramatic and horrific, but also because it emphasizes that there would be nothing left for Aeneas to preserve or return to.

This dream has the effect of waking Aeneas up. However, he does not engage with Hector's prophecy in his account to Dido, and, in particular, makes nothing of the *moenia ... magna* (the great city walls) which he will found. When he wakes, he sees the city in flames and then:

tum uero manifesta fides, Danaumque patescunt
insidiae. (309-310)

Then indeed the truth is clear and the tricks of the Greeks are evident.

It is important to him that Troy was conquered not by force of arms but by trickery, a point Aeneas emphasized in his account of Sinon (cf. 65-6) and keeps reverting to, and which Dido had already accepted (I.754).[11] And Virgil will go on to emphasize that this was the will of the gods. Heroic fighting would not have helped. Nevertheless, this is exactly what Aeneas immediately and instinctively resolves to do:

arma amens capio; nec sat rationis in armis,
sed glomerare manum bello et concurrere in arcem
cum sociis ardent animi; furor iraque mentem
praecipitat, pulchrumque mori succurrit in armis. (314-7)

Mindlessly I seize my weapons; not that there is any point in weapons, but my spirits burn to assemble a force for fighting and to rush together to the citadel with my companions; madness and anger drove my mind on, and the sweetness of dying in combat sustains me.

In retrospect Aeneas saw that the position was hopeless, but he reacts at the time as a Roman warrior would have been expected to. We remember Horace and his *dulce et decorum est*. This impulse dominates his mind up to the intervention of Venus. However, Aeneas qualifies it in his narrative by using the words *amens* and *furor* (mindlessly or frantically, madness) to characterise his behaviour. What he is displaying here is the heroic impulse, which he reverts to again and again throughout the poem.[12] Horsfall seems to me to be going slightly too far in arguing that 'this is classic tragic irony not irresponsible, delinquent rage.'[13] Furthermore, in his rage he is forgetting his other duties, those to his family, and he does not recall them until forcibly reminded by Venus.

Before he can act on his resolution, Panthus arrives, bearing with him the *sacra* and the *uictosque deos*, the holy things and the conquered gods (320). We do not hear of them again until Aeneas commits them to Anchises in line 717. Exactly what happens to them meanwhile is not clear,[14] but the significance is clear: this is exactly what Aeneas' dream had foretold. However, this has no effect on Aeneas' determination, but he now attributes his motivation to divine forces:

> talibus Othryadae dictis et numine diuum
> in flammas et in arma feror, quo tristis Erinys,
> quo fremitus uocat et sublatus ad aethera clamor. (336-8)

> *By such words of the son of Othrys* [Panthus] *and by the spirit of the gods I am driven amidst flames and weapons to where the grim Fury, to where the roaring, calls and the shouting raised to the heavens.*

In the counterattack which Aeneas leads we see the heroic impulse at full stretch. Two passages are enough to demonstrate this. First, when he rallies his small force:

> 'moriamur et in media arma ruamus.
> una salus uictis nullam sperare salutem.'
> sic animis iuuenum furor additus. inde, lupi ceu
> raptores atra in nebula, quos improba uentris
> exegit caecos rabies catulique relicti
> faucibus exspectant siccis, per tela, per hostis

uadimus haud dubiam in mortem mediaeque tenemus
urbis iter; nox atra caua circumuolat umbra.' (353-360)

*'Let us rush forward and die in the midst of fighting. The only safety for
the defeated is to hope for none.' In this way a recklessness was added to
the spirits of the men. Then, like robber wolves in a black cloud, whom the
nagging fury of the belly has driven out blindly and whose puppies have
been left behind with dry throats, we make our way through weapons and
enemies through certain death and hold the heart of the city; black night
flies around us with enveloping shadow.*

As Otis rightly says, Aeneas here is dominated by *furor.*[15] I pass over
the episode, led by Coroebus, in which they take over Greek weapons
and briefly rescue Cassandra before being caught both by the Greeks
and by friendly fire. Then after they are outnumbered and overcome,
Aeneas exclaims:

'Iliaci cineres et flamma extrema meorum,
testor, in occasu uestro nec tela nec ullas
uitauisse uices Danaum et, si fata fuissent
ut caderem, meruisse manu.' (431-4)

*Ashes of Troy and funeral flames of my people, I invoke you as witness
that in your doom I avoided neither weapons nor any dangers of the
Greeks and, if the fates had been that I should fall, that I would have
earned that by my effort.*

Death in battle was a glorious end for a Homeric warrior and
Aeneas would have welcomed it (316). But his destiny (*fata*) was a
harder one, one which is the subject of the poem as a whole.

Aeneas takes no further part in fighting and witnesses the death of
Priam as an impotent spectator, a scene cunningly set up by Virgil so
that no blame for inactivity can fall on him. I pass over the description
of Neoptolemus, surely quite the nastiest of the Greek heroes, to
consider the effect on Aeneas of witnessing Priam's death:

at me tum primum saeuus circumstetit horror.
obstipui; subiit cari genitoris imago,
ut regem aequaeuum crudeli uulnere vidi
uitam exhalantem, subiit deserta Creusa
et direpta domus et parui casus Iuli. (559-63)

But then a fearful horror first overcame me. I was dismayed; the image of
my dear father came up, as I saw the king of a similar age breathing out
his life with a cruel wound, abandoned Creusa came up and the ravaged
home and the fate of little Iulus.[16]

This is the first time Aeneas has thought of his family and his
concern here is suddenly exclusively for them: there is no recollection of
his dream of Hector, nor of Panthus. It is at this point that, in the Helen
episode, he sees Helen and considers killing her. Even if this episode is
considered spurious, something must have stood in or been intended for
this place to motivate the appearance of his mother, Venus.[17] She
reproaches him for neglecting his family and tells him that she has been
protecting them. But most important, she shows him the gods themselves destroying Troy:

'hic, ubi disiectas moles auulsaque saxis
saxa uides, mixtoque undantem puluere fumum,
Neptunus muros magnoque emota tridenti
fundamenta quatit totamque a sedibus urbem
eruit. hic Iuno Scaeas saeuissima portas
prima tenet sociumque furens a nauibus agmen
ferro accincta uocat...
iam summas arces Tritonia, respice, Pallas
insedit nimbo effulgens et Gorgone saeua.
ipse pater Danais animos uirisque secundas
sufficit, ipse deos in Dardana suscitat arma.' (608-18)

Here, where you see the broken piles and rocks torn from rocks, and smoke
billowing up mixed with dust, Neptune shakes the walls overturned by his
great trident and uproots the entire city from its foundation. Here Juno,

first and fiercest, holds the Scaean gate and, girded with steel, furiously calls her troop from the ships ... Now see, at the top of the citadel, Tritonian Pallas is settled flashing forth with her storm cloud and grim Gorgon.[18] *My father himself stirs up strength to win against the Trojans, and himself arouses the gods against Trojan weapons.*

She immediately follows this theophany with an injunction to flee, the third he has received:

'eripe, nate, fugam finemque impone labori;
nusquam abero et tutum patrio te limine sistam.' 619-20)

Quickly take flight, my son, and put an end to your labour; I shall never be away and shall place you safely on your father's threshold.

Notice that she says nothing about the end of his journey, and, as for putting an end to his labour, that refers only to that of fighting in Troy: he is about to set out on a much more laborious path. Still, he has finally accepted that he must leave.

However, when he gets to Anchises' house, Aeneas finds himself in a dilemma. Anchises also encourages him to flee but says that he himself will stay, endure a heroic death and not be troubled about the lack of proper burial, an issue that is as important in this poem as it is in Sophocles' *Antigone*. He is in the same position that Camillus commended in Livy, and that Aeneas was when he first awoke. But it is unthinkable that Aeneas should abandon Anchises to this fate, particularly after having just witnessed the death of Priam:

'mene efferre pedem, genitor, te posse relicto
sperasti tantumque nefas patrio excidit ore? ...
hoc erat, alma parens, quod me per tela, per ignis
eripis, ut mediis hostem in penetralibus utque
Ascanium patremque meum iuxtaque Creusam
alterum in alterius mactatos sanguine cernam?' (657-9, 664-7)

Did you hope that I would take a step outside, my father, and could leave you left behind and did something so dreadful flow from my father's mouth? ... Was it for this, kind mother, that you rescue me through weapons and fires so that I should see the enemy in the heart of my home and Ascanius and my father and Creusa next to them, slaughtered in each other's blood?

His immediate response to the dilemma is to rush out and fight again but he is dissuaded by Creusa. Then his dilemma is resolved by not one but two portents:

namque manus inter maestorumque ora parentum
ecce leuis summo de uertice uisus Iuli
fundere lumen apex, tactuque innoxia mollis
lambere flamma comas et circum tempora pasci.
nos pauidi trepidare metu crinemque flagrantem
excutere et sanctos restinguere fontibus ignis. (681-6)

For between the hands and faces of his sorrowing parents a light flame was seen from the top of the head of Iulus pouring out light, harmless to the touch, and the flame was licking his hair and playing around his temples. We, shaking with fear, rush to shake out his blazing hair and to extinguish the holy flames with water.

This touching picture of the anxious parents soothing their son is the only moment in the whole poem where we see Aeneas' family acting together.

Anchises recognizes this as a portent and asks for another to confirm it, which is immediately given in the shape of a shooting star. This finally persuades him that he too must leave:

'iam iam nulla mora est; sequor et qua ducitis adsum.
di patrii; seruate domum, seruate nepotem.
uestrum hoc augurium, uestroque in numine Troia est.
cedo equidem nec, nate, tibi comes ire recuso.' (701-4)

Now, now there is no delay: I follow and where you lead, there I am. Gods of my country, protect my house, protect my grandson. This portent is yours, Troy stands in your power. For my part I give way nor, my son, do I refuse to go with you as a companion.

What the divine portent has achieved for Anchises is that, in leaving, he is not deserting his *patria* but confirming his loyalty to a new Troy which is yet to be established: *uestroque in numine Troia est*, Troy stands in your power. It is his change of mind which is decisive, not that of Aeneas. Therefore, as Otis says: 'From now on [Aeneas] looks to Anchises as the father-figure of his new destiny and as the link between his future and his past.'[19] This also maintains consistency with the prophecy of Poseidon in the *Iliad* that Aeneas was to rule the Trojans and his sons after him.[20]

Aeneas is now free to leave and he does so carrying on his back Anchises, who is holding a box with the Penates, and holding his son by his hand, with Creusa following behind.[21] This celebrated scene was one of the givens of the story, with numerous artistic representations;[22] the literary tradition goes back at least to Sophocles.[23] At this point Virgil had to make a decision: in some versions of the tradition, Creusa accompanied him into exile,[24] but he had to remove her. This, I believe, was for two reasons: one was that Aeneas needed to be free to have the relationship with Dido which she could see as a marriage, and then later to marry Lavinia. The other was to emphasize the loneliness of his role. Throughout the *Aeneid* he has no real friends or close advisers apart from his father.

The loss of Creusa is to my mind the dramatic high point of the book, even more so than the death of Priam. There, Aeneas had been an impotent spectator; here, he is active and arguably responsible for her loss. However, although he certainly feels he is, Virgil complicates it. Anchises has warned Aeneas that the Greeks are approaching. Then Aeneas recounts:

> hic mihi nescio quod trepido male numen amicum
> confusam eripuit mentem. namque auia cursu
> dum sequor et nota excedo regione uiarum,

heu misero coniunx fatone erepta Creusa
substitit, errauitne uia seu lapsa resedit,
incertum; nec post oculis est reddita nostris. (735-40)

*At this moment some evil spirit possessed my confused mind in my fear.
For while I follow unmarked paths in my rush and leave the area of
familiar streets, alas my wife Creusa was torn from me by an unkind
fate and stopped or lost the way or sat down in exhaustion, I do not know;
never after was she restored to my eyes.*

Male numen ... misero fatone, evil spirit ... unkind fate: how literally
are we take these? When people use equivalent expressions nowadays it
is usually no more than a figure of speech. But Virgil frequently hints at
dark powers which lie behind the Olympians, drawing on Greek ideas
about μοῖρα, 'the root notion of which seems to be the 'portion,' 'lot,' or
'destiny' of the individual.'[25] How much freewill Aeneas really had and
so how much responsibility he had for the loss of Creusa becomes a
moot point.

Anyway, Aeneas leaves Anchises and Ascanius at the designated
meeting point and frantically plunges back into the burning city,
searching for her and even calling her name aloud. Then:

quaerenti et tectis urbis sine fine ruenti
infelix simulacrum atque ipsius umbra Creusae
uisa mihi ante oculos et nota maior imago. (771-2)

*To my searching and rushing endlessly through the buildings of the city,
the unhappy image and shade of Creusa herself appeared before my eyes
and in appearance larger than normal.*

What exactly has appeared to Aeneas? Is it the ghost of Creusa, as,
for example, Bailey and Austin think?[26] Or do we accept Horsfall's
argument: 'we need only recognize that for [Virgil] Creusa's disappear-
ance from the realm of the living is sufficiently death-like to permit
the attribution to her of an *umbra*, she does not, though, actually *die*,
and on that detail [Virgil] is rather careful.'[27] Horsfall goes on to say

that Virgil does not make a sharp distinction in sense among *simulacrum*, image, *imago*, appearance, and *umbra*, shade, and adds: 'here in particular, where he is so careful to avoid explaining just what has become of [Creusa], a precise terminology would be particularly unwelcome.' This has to be right: she cannot be still alive to return to him; nor is she exactly dead, or Aeneas would meet her in the underworld in Book VI, nor has she been translated to Olympus or Aeneas would surely be told. Where are the shores on which the Great Mother detains her (788)? She seems to be in some kind of intermediate state, to borrow a term from Christian eschatology,[28] and we know no more than that. Ghost is a convenient but imprecise term here. What is clear is that there can be no renewal of their previous relationship.

In considering the effect of Creusa's speech, we should first note that the line which introduces it is somewhat suspect:

tum sic adfari et curas his demere dictis. (775)

Then she spoke and with her words dispelled my anxieties.

This line occurs also in two other places in the *Aeneid* (III.153; VIII.35) and Servius *auctus* notes that many copies omit it here. The issue is not whether it is Virgilian, which it is, but whether it, or all of it, belongs here. Creusa did not dispel Aeneas' anxieties, as is immediately apparent from his reaction to her speech:

haec ubi dicta dedit, lacrimantem et multa uolentem
dicere deseruit, tenuisque recessit in auras. (790-1)

When she had said these words, she left me weeping and wanting to say many things, and disappeared into thin air.

I am therefore attracted by Austin's suggestion that Virgil himself here wrote only *tum sic adfari* and that the rest of the line was interpolated. As there is another incomplete line a few lines later (787) and the passage about trying to embrace her (792-3) also occurs in Book VI.700-

2, and may well be interpolated here (so Horsfall), it seems that the whole passage was still subject to revision.

Creusa's own moving address is a combination of farewell and prophecy:

> quid tantum insano iuuat indulgere dolori,
> o dulcis coniunx? non haec sine numine diuum
> eueniunt; nec te comitem hinc portare Creusam
> fas, aut ille sinit superi regnator Olympi.
> longa tibi exsilia et uastum maris aequor arandum,
> et terram Hesperiam uenies, ubi Lydius arua
> inter opima uirum leni fluit agmine Thybris.
> illic res laetae regnumque et regia coniunx
> parta tibi; lacrimas dilectae pelle Creusae.
> non ego Myrmidonum sedes Dolopumue superbas
> aspiciam aut Grais seruitum matribus ibo,
> Dardanis et diuae Veneris nurus; ...
> sed me magna deum genetrix his detinet oris.
> iamque uale et nati serua communis amorem. (776-789)

What use it is to give way to crazy grief, my sweet husband? Not without the will of the gods have these things happened; it is not permitted that you should take Creusa from here as your companion, nor does the ruler of Olympus above allow it. For you a long exile and a vast expanse of sea must be ploughed, and you will come to a Western land, where the Lydian Tiber flows among fruitful fields. There happy days, a kingdom and a royal wife will be your lot; banish the tears for your beloved Creusa. I shall never look at the proud houses of the Myrmidons and the Dolopians or go to be the slave of Greek women, I a Trojan woman and daughter-in-law of the divine Venus; ... but the mighty mother of the gods [Cybele] keeps me on these shores. And now farewell and show love to our son.

The first thing we notice is that there is no suggestion that Aeneas had abandoned her; on the contrary, in calling him *dulcis coniunx*, sweet husband, and referring to herself as *dilectae ... Creusae*, beloved Creusa, she demonstrates their mutual love. Next there is the prophecy of his future, something Venus had not offered in her appearance to him. The fact that he will make, and will need to make, a dynastic marriage is something she mentions without regret. The fact that he will have to engage in war again is something she does not mention, but I see no significance in this. She stresses the role of the gods in her fate and she reassures him that she will not become a slave, as was the fate of Andromache, Hecuba and other Trojan women, as Virgil's readers would know. She commends their son to him and then vanishes into thin air.

So ends Creusa's role in the *Aeneid*. She is mentioned again only once (IX.297) and then not by Aeneas but by their son, now much older. She is not remembered by Aeneas as his previous love when he encounters Dido, even though she immediately compares seeing him to her feelings for her dead husband Sychaeus (IV.20-29). As for Lavinia, she is little more than a cipher and I do not think that Aeneas has so much as seen her by the end of the poem. C. S. Lewis considered the appearance of Creusa's ghost one of Virgil's most daring successes. He says:

> The sad, ineffectual creature, shouldered aside by destiny, must come to prophesy the wife who will replace her and the fortunes of her husband in which she will have no share. If she were a living woman it would be inexcusable cruelty. But she is not a woman, she is a ghost, the wraith of all that which, whether regretted or unregretted, is throughout the poem drifting away, settling down, into the irrevocable past, not, as in elegiac poets, that we may luxuriate in melancholy reflections on mutability, but because the *fates of Jove* so order it, because, thus and not otherwise, some great thing comes about.[29]

As I mentioned above, Aeneas' attempt to embrace her may well be an interpolation, as Creusa has already departed. As for her prophecy, he never recalls it and it appears to play no part in his motivation.

In the last lines of the book, Aeneas rejoins his father and son and finds a large number of companions, other Trojan refugees. As, presumably, the highest ranking person there, he finds himself to be their leader:

undique conuenere animis opibusque parati
in quascumque uelim pelago deducere terras. (799-800)

*From all sides they come have together with their hearts and their fortunes
ready for me to take them to whatever lands I wish.*

Notice that there is no specific mention of the Western land and the
Tiber. Creusa might as well have remained silent on Aeneas' future.
Still, the death in battle which he was willing to undergo is not his
destiny; instead he has to lead the band of refugees to an uncertain
future, a duty for which his previous experience has not prepared him.

In this book, as elsewhere, Virgil makes a good deal of use of dreams
and portents. We notice that this section begins with Hector's appearance to Aeneas in a dream and ends with Creusa's appearance as a ghost.
In the middle we have the appearance of Venus and the portents of the
flames and the shooting star. Hector's appearance establishes and vali-
dates the need to flee, for the reader as much as for Aeneas, as otherwise
his duty would have been to stay and fight and accept the likelihood of
death in combat. Venus turns his attention from the death of Priam, his
king, to the situation of his own family, which in his *furor* he had
completely overlooked. She also demonstrates that the downfall of Troy
is the will of the gods. However, Aeneas must not leave Troy on his own,
because he cannot abandon his father and his son is the hope of the
future. But Anchises refuses to consider going until he sees the portents
of the flames and the shooting star. It is Anchises' change of mind
which decides the matter. Throughout this book, Aeneas is driven by
factors external to himself, whose authority he accepts and to which he
has to conform. He is right at the beginning of learning to lead.

In considering the narrative context, the fact that the whole of this
book, as of the next, is Aeneas' account to Dido; we need to assess
whether Aeneas is likely to have exaggerated, minimized or distorted his
account to suit his audience. Of course we have no independent check
on this—differing accounts in other authors have no authority here. His
distancing of himself from the episode of the wooden horse I have
discussed elsewhere. His willingness to fight and accept a heroic death in
combat seems perfectly genuine, as does his admission of the *furor*

which possessed him. His inability to decide on an effective course of action emerges unwittingly from his account: it is the dreams and portents and then the change of heart of Anchises which decide him. I do not think that Homer's account of the rivalry between the house of Anchises and that of Priam for kingship[30] plays any part in Virgil or it would have been mentioned somewhere. The finality of his loss of Creusa makes it clear to the listening Dido that he has no current attachment. In general, Aeneas comes across as a straightforward character, who is neither capable nor desirous of the kind of trickery attributed in the earlier part of the book to the Greeks. His account to Dido can be relied on as an accurate account of the events he reports.

Finally, I want to consider briefly the allegorical interpretation of the *Aeneid*. In thinking about the poem as a whole, it is clear that Aeneas is on a journey, one which begins amid the flames of burning Troy and ends with the new settlement in Italy and the promise of future Rome. From this it is but a short step to see this journey as an allegory of human life, and this is precisely what was first done in the late fifth or early sixth century by Fulgentius, in his *Expositio Virgilianae continentiae*. In this work Virgil appears to the writer and says: *'In omnibus nostris opusculis fisici ordinis argumenta induximus, quo per duodena librorum uolumina pleniorem humanae uitae monstrassem statum'* (In all my little works I have represented the order of nature, by which I have shown the whole condition of human life through the twelve scrolls of the books.')[31] He goes on to relate the individual books to stages of life, books I and II referring to childhood.[32] This kind of thinking was taken up in the commentary on the *Aeneid* attributed to the twelfth century poet Bernardus Silvestris. He writes: *'Scribit enim in quantum est philosophus humanae vitae naturam. Modus vero agendi talis est: sub integumento describit quit agat vel quid patiatur humanus spiritus in humano corpore temporaliter positus'* (Insofar as he is a philosopher, he writes concerning the nature of human life, and this is his method of proceeding; under the cover of allegory he describes what the human spirit, placed for a time in the human body, undertakes or undergoes').[33] It was continued in the Renaissance by Cristoforo Landino, who wrote extensively on Virgil, and whose view of Aeneas has been summarized in these words: 'The character created by Virgil was that of a man who gradually purged himself of many great vices, learned the marvellous ways of virtue, and, in spite of obstacles, reached his *summum bonum*, a feat which no man can achieve without wisdom.'[34] And to show that this way of thinking is still, or at least very recently was still, current, here is C. S. Lewis again:

> Our life has bends as well as extensions: moments at which we realize that we have just turned some great corner, and that everything, for better or worse, will always henceforth be different ... All through the poem we are turning that corner. It is this which gives the reader of the *Aeneid* the sense of having lived through so much. No man who has once read it with full perception remains an adolescent.[35]

Virgil opened the way to such interpretations by his decision to let Aeneas recount the beginning of his story and to show him at the nadir of his fortunes. This then leads naturally to the whole of the first half of the *Aeneid*, the so-called Odyssean *Aeneid*, being an account of his education, both as a human being and as a leader. The second half of the poem, the so-called Iliadic *Aeneid*, then shows what he can then do, though there is backsliding right up to the end. In Book II we see how his past as a Homeric warrior is now of no use to him, and is something he must leave behind in setting out for a future of what he has as yet only the vaguest idea.

---

1. Dionysius of Halicarnassus, *Roman Antiquities*, I.46-7. Dionysius says this comes from the *Troika* of Hellanicus (fifth century B. C.), which survives only in fragments.
2. There are useful summaries of the earlier accounts by Robin Hard, *The Routledge Handbook of Greek Mythology*, London, 2004, 473-6, and Timothy Gantz, *Early Greek Myth*, Baltimore, 1993, 646-0, and fuller discussions by Richard Heinze, *Virgil's Epic Technique*, trans. Hazel Harvey *et al.*, London, 1993 (1928[2]), 3-14, R. G. Austin's commentary on this book, Oxford, 1964 and especially W. F. Jackson Knight, *Vergil's Troy*, in *Vergil: Epic and Anthropology*, London, 1967 (1932), 75-102. I have used these as pointers to such primary sources and analogues as survive.
3. I have put an brief note on the authenticity of the Helen episode in Appendix. 1.
4. Virgil deliberately leaves it unclear whether this was a dream or a vision: *in somnis* (270) can mean 'in sleep' or 'in a dream' and *uisus* (271) can mean 'seemed' or 'was seen,' if indeed the Romans desynonymized the word as we do. What Aeneas saw could have been the spirit of Hector, returned from the underworld (where Aeneas

does not meet him in book VI), or a vision sent by the gods or the creation of Aeneas' own dreaming mind. I refer to it as a dream for convenience; Virgil left it ambiguous.

5. Quotations are from Book II unless otherwise noted.

6. The Penates here were the gods of the city, domestic or city gods as opposed to the Olympians, OLD s.v. 2. The distinction was not appreciated by Augustine, *City of God*, I.3. They have a supportive role throughout the *Aeneid*; see Sabine MacCormack, *The Shadows of Poetry: Vergil in the Mind of Augustine*, Berkeley and Los Angeles, 1998, 170-1.

7. William V. Harris, *Dreams and Experience in Classical Antiquity*, Cambridge, Mass., 2009, 4, 26-7, 196-7. There are ten epiphany dreams in the *Aeneid*.

8. See the classic discussion by Dodds, *The Greeks and the Irrational*, Berkeley and Los Angeles, 1951, 104-7.

9. Jackson Knight, *Vergil's Troy*, 115-8, citing, *inter alia*, *Iliad* V.473, VI.403. Knowledge of this tradition appears to have survived at least until the time of Seneca, *Troades* 126-9, 234ff..

10. Aeschylus, *Agamemnon* 334-7, Euripides, *Troades* 1260-4; Heinze, *Virgil's Epic Technique* 17 and note 37 with further references.

11. Odysseus had conceded this, Homer, *Odyssey*, VIII.494.

12. Kenneth Quinn, *Virgil's Aeneid: a Critical Description*, London, 1969[2], devotes his first chapter to a discussion of this.

13. Horsfall *ad loc.*.

14. See Austin and Horsfall (who disagree) on 320.

15. Otis, *Virgil: A Study in Civilized Poetry*, Oxford, 1964, 242.

16. Virgil refers to Aeneas' son by Creusa as both Ascanius and Iulus. Ascanius is an ancient name; it was apparently a tradition among the Iulian clan that they were his descendants and therefore that he was also known as Iulus. Virgil accepts this; cf. Livy, I.3.2.

17. See Appendix 1.

18. This is the rendering of T. E. Page, taking *saeua* as ablative. Horsfall is inclined to agree. Austin takes it as nominative.

19. Otis, *Virgil: a Study in Civilized Poetry*, 246. Austin *ad loc.* agrees.

20. *Iliad*, XX.300-8.

21. She was not necessarily to take the same route: *hanc ex diverso sedem veniemus in unam*, to this place by various ways we shall come together, 716.

22. Timothy Gantz, *Early Greek Myth*, 713-7.

23. Sophocles, *Laocoön*, fr.373.

24. The evidence includes vase paintings and coins as well as literary fragments, see Austin 280-1 and Horsfall, 516-7. Aeneas' wife was originally named Euridica but had become Creusa by the time of Livy (I.3.2) and other near contemporaries of Virgil. Of course, Virgil had already used that name in *Georgics* IV, and indeed there are echoes of that passage here.

25. Cyril Bailey, *Religion in Virgil*, Oxford, 1935, 207 and see the discussion 204-14.

26. Bailey, *op. cit.*, 248-9; Austin, 278-9.

27. Horsfall, 533.

28. The intermediate state is the presumed state of the soul between death and resurrection. See, e.g. Joseph Ratzinger (later Pope Benedict XVI), *Eschatology: Death and Eternal Life*, Washington, 1988, 119ff..

29. C. S. Lewis, *A Preface to 'Paradise Lost,'* Oxford, 1942, 36-7.

30. Homer, *Iliad*, XIII.460-1, XX.179-186.

31. Fulgentius, *Opera*, 86-7.

32. Useful summary in Domenico Comparetti, *Vergil in the Middle Ages*, trans. E . F. M. Benecke, London, 1966 (1908[2]), 109-111.

33. Text and translation from Brian Stock, *Myth and Science in the Twelfth Century: A Study of Bernard Silvester*, Princeton, 1972, 42-3.

34. Landino's commentary as quoted by Don Cameron Allen, *Mysteriously meant: The Rediscovery of Pagan Symbolism and Allegorical Interpretation in the Renaissance*, Baltimore, 1970, 150, and see the whole chapter, 'Undermeanings in Virgil's *Aeneid*.'

35. Lewis, *A Preface to 'Paradise Lost,'* 36-7.

3

WAS DIDO RIGHT TO THINK THAT
SHE AND AENEAS HAD MARRIED?

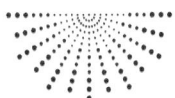

When Dido discovers that Aeneas is preparing to leave Carthage, she reproaches him in their last encounter in a passionate speech including these words:

> per ego has lacrimas dextramque tuam te
> (quando aliud mihi iam miserae nihil ipsa reliqui),
> per conubia nostra, per inceptos hymenaeos,
> si bene quid de te merui, fuit aut tibi quicquam
> dulce meum, miserere domus labentis et istam,
> oro, si quis adhuc precibus locus, exue mentem. (314-9)[1]

By these tears and your right hand (since to my wretched self nothing else is left), by our marriage, by the marriage rites entered into,[2] if I have deserved anything well of you, or if anything of mine has been sweet to you, have pity on a ruined household and, I pray, if there is any place now for prayers, take off that purpose.

This is by no means her only reference to their relationship as a marriage—I shall come to the others—but it is the most explicit, at the crucial point in the tragedy.

Aeneas' reply includes the following denial:

> neque ego hanc abscondere furto
> speraui (ne finge) fugam, nec coniugis umquam
> praetendi taedas aut haec in foedera ueni. (337-9)

*I did not hope to carry out my flight in secret—do not think it—nor did I
ever hold out marriage torches or enter into such a contract.*

The first part of this statement is a lie,[3] but what about the second
part? At first it would appear that he is right, because Virgil as narrator
has stated flatly:

> neque enim specie famaue mouetur
> nec iam furtiuum Dido meditatur amorem:
> coniugium uocat, hoc praetexit nomine culpam. (170-2)

*For Dido is not any longer moved by appearances or reputation and does
not now brood on a secret love: she calls it marriage and with this name
cloaks her fault.*

However, in this essay I argue that the issue is not that simple. As D.
H. Lawrence famously said: 'The artist usually sets out—or used to—to
point a moral or adorn a tale. The tale, however, points the other way, as
a rule. Two blankly opposing morals, the artist's and the tale's. Never
trust the artist. Trust the tale. The proper function of a critic is to save
the tale from the artist who created it.'[4] I shall suggest that Virgil's own
judgement on his own characters and story is belied by the story he actually tells us.

I want to consider this in four stages:

I. Marriage customs, in Troy, Carthage and Virgil's Rome.
II. What actually happens between Aeneas and Dido.
III. Their separation.
IV. The role of the gods.

In representing the relationship between Aeneas and Dido, Virgil had to consider in what social context to set it. Aeneas was a Trojan, Dido a Phoenician, but Virgil's audience were contemporary Romans. Although Virgil had considerable antiquarian interests, he needed to make his story intelligible and accessible to his audience. I consider that he briefly surveyed the issue of marriage customs in Troy, archaic Greece and Carthage before resolving to assimilate his characters to the customs of contemporary Rome.

Aeneas is a Trojan, so we would expect him to be aware of Trojan marriage customs. However, neither we nor Virgil know anything about them. Not a word of Trojan literature—if there was any—has survived, and we cannot even be sure what language they spoke. On the other hand, we have Homer, whom Virgil's first audience would have known either directly or indirectly. On the Trojan side Homer gives us a stable marriage between Priam and Hecuba and a loving one between Hector and Andromache; the relationship between Paris and Helen is seen as irregular.[5] On the Greek side the warriors are away from their homes and wives, if they have them, and they treat women as chattels. Briseis and Chryseis, though one is the widow of a king killed by Achilles and the other the daughter of a priest, are prizes of war whose fate is entirely in the hands of men. Briseis says that Patroclus had assured her that Achilles would marry her but in the *Iliad* she remains only his concubine.[6] In later legend Agamemnon fathers a child on Chryseis before he returns her to her father.[7] In the *Odyssey*, Odysseus has affairs with Circe and Calypso and possibly others, without any exception being taken. None of these relationships are considered marriages.

Virgil could have made Aeneas behave like these Greek warriors. But he doesn't. Aeneas is involved with only three women in the *Aeneid*.[8] The first is his wife, Creusa, who is taken away from him by the gods at the fall of Troy. The second is Dido. And finally there is Lavinia of Latium, to whom Aeneas is due to contract a dynastic marriage at the end of the poem. The relationship with Dido takes up a whole book and shows Aeneas at his worst; it is not a casual or trivial one.

Dido was a Phoenician and ancient Carthage a Phoenican colony. After a long rivalry and then enmity with Rome, it was finally destroyed by Rome in 146 B.C., long before Virgil's time. What do we know about Phoenician marriage customs? Although Virgil may well have known more than us, as some Carthaginian literature survived and was translated into Latin, it has not come down to us. However, nothing we have tells us anything about marriage in Carthage[9] and I rather suspect that Virgil knew no more. He might have known that the principal Carthaginian gods were a couple, Baal Hammon and Tanit or Astarte,[10] possibly comparable to Jupiter and Juno, and that Dido, Elissa in her own language, was accepted as founder, ruler and queen of her city. There were various versions of her story, but one survives, by the historian Pompeius Trogus, of which we have an epitome.[11] As a reigning queen she had status and was also Aeneas's host and so was not remotely comparable to a prize of war. But neither Virgil nor his audience would know or expect a historically precise account of ancient Carthage.

Furthermore, part of Virgil's purpose in this book is clearly to provide a justification or at least an explanation of the enmity between Rome and Carthage by implying that it is the result of the betrayal, as Dido sees it, by Aeneas of her. It is a parallel to the Trojan war being the consequence of the rape of Helen by Paris, and it establishes, if indeed it does not create, the foundation myth for this enmity. Later in the poem Jupiter makes it clear that he does not want the Trojans and the Latins to be in conflict, because the real enemy is going to be Carthage (X.6-15).

Virgil's solution to presenting Carthaginian culture is to Romanise it. He does admittedly use a few Carthaginian names for local colour, such as Dido's own Phoenician name Elissa,[12] Barce, the nurse of Sychaeus, Dido's suitor Iarbas, son of Hammon, and references to the local geography. Nevertheless, he places his Carthage in a Roman religious world. Dido sacrifices to Roman gods, Ceres, Phoebus, Lyaeus and Juno to seek dissolution of her vow not to remarry following the death of Sychaeus (56-63); Iarbas prays to Jupiter who then sends Mercury to summon Aeneas to Troy (205-37); Dido reproaches Aeneas calling on Juno, Jupiter, Apollo and Mercury (371-8) and invokes Erebos, Chaos and Hecate as she prepares to die (509-11). Finally, Juno sends Iris to release her soul from her body (693-705). And of course an unholy alliance of

Juno and Venus oversees the whole affair, a topic to which I shall return.

We may therefore conclude that Virgil assumed Roman marriage customs in presenting the relationship of Aeneas and Dido. So we need to consider what they were when he was writing. Here I rely on authorities, from whom I take the following statements:

> One feature of Roman marriage that seems most surprising to us was the informality with which it could be both made and unmade. A legal marriage (*iustum matrimonium*) was a union between two Roman citizens not otherwise legally disqualified from marriage. Simply to live together by consent as man and wife made a marriage without any formalities, ceremonials before witnesses or signing of registers; and simply to separate constituted legal divorce.[13]

> All that was legally necessary was the giving of consent by the parties and their *patresfamilias*, if any.[14]

> There was nothing to stop a marriage taking place quietly on a country estate ... It was a duty (*officium*) to accept wedding invitations and both the wedding and the group of guests who attended it were also called the *officium*... People of higher social class might be asked.[15]

> Despite the ideal of monogamy for women, Roman practice was mostly against it. Society expected widows and divorcees to marry, unless perhaps they were beyond child-bearing.[16]

The special clothes, torchlight procession by the bride with attendants to the groom's house, the auspices, sacrifice to the gods, the wedding contract and dowry, presents, the joining of hands, witnesses, giving of a ring and so on were all customary elements of at least an upper class wedding but were not obligatory and in actual practice arrangements varied. We may compare contemporary practice, which may range from a royal wedding in Westminster Abbey with a great deal of ceremony and many attendants to a quiet one in a church, register office or licensed venue with a handful of guests or only two witnesses.

Lucan represents Cato and Maria marrying in the last days of the Republic with minimal ceremony:

> pignora nulla domus, nulli colere propinqui:
> iunguntur taciti contentique auspice Bruto. (*Pharsalia*, II.370-1)[17]

No members of the family and no kinsmen assembled: their hands were joined in silence, and they were satisfied with the presence of Brutus as augur.

Let us then set what happens with Aeneas and Dido against these standards. They were not Roman citizens, but they can hardly be blamed for that, as Rome did not yet exist. Were they free to marry? They were both aristocrats and so not constrained by any laws governing slave relationships. Aeneas was effectively a widower. His wife Creusa had been lost from him, and, when her spirit or ghost appeared to him when he searched for her amid the ruins of Troy, she had said:

> terram Hesperiam uenies, ubi Lydius arua
> inter opima uirum leni fluit agmine Thybris.
> illic res laetae regnumque et regia coniunx
> parta tibi. II. (781-4)

You will come to the Hesperian land, where Lydian Tiber flows among with gentle course among the rich fields of the husbandmen. There happy things and a kingdom and a royal wife will be yours.

Some versions of the story had Aeneas leaving Troy with not only his father and son but also with his wife.[18] But Virgil needed her out of the way, both so that Aeneas could get involved with Dido and also so that he could be free to marry Lavinia. Aeneas is therefore both free and predicted to take a new wife. That this should be in Italy and not in Carthage or elsewhere is implied only by the one word *illic*, there. Would it be putting unreasonable weight on that one word to infer that Aeneas could not, for example, find a suitable woman elsewhere and marry her in Italy? No: that is Aeneas's destiny and he should not seek to vary it. He should not get involved with a woman, however royal and with whatever kingdom, otherwise. So there is fault on his side. Should Dido, to whom this narration is addressed, have inferred from the word *illic* that the promised kingdom is not hers and the royal wife not herself? That is a great deal of weight to place on one word, and we are not told that Aeneas at any time elaborated on his destiny to her. It would be unreasonable to conclude from this one speech, and by a ghost too, that Dido should have realised that Aeneas was not free. By using only the word *illic* to indicate that the future marriage would be in Italy, Virgil both incriminates Aeneas and exculpates Dido.

By Roman standards Dido would also be free to remarry, her first husband Sychaeus being dead. However, following his murder, she made a vow not to do so:

> si mihi non animo fixum immotumque sederet
> ne cui me uinclo uellem sociare iugali,
> postquam primus amor deceptam morte fefellit;
> si non pertaesum thalami taedaeque fuisset,
> huic uni forsan potui succumbere culpae.
> Anna (fatebor enim) miseri post fata Sychaei
> coniugis et sparsos fraterna caede penatis
> solus hic inflexit sensus animumque labantem
> impulit. agnosco ueteris uestigia flammae.
> sed mihi uel tellus optem prius ima dehiscat
> uel pater omnipotens adigat me fulmine ad umbras,
> pallentis umbras Erebo noctemque profundam,
> ante, pudor, quam te uiolo aut tua iura resoluo.
> ille meos, primus qui me sibi iunxit, amores
> abstulit; ille habeat secum seruetque sepulcro. (15-29)

If it were not established as unchangeable in my mind that I do not wish to ally myself in the bond of marriage, after my first love deceived my hopes and slipped away in death; if the bridal chamber and torches did not thoroughly weary me, to this one man I could perhaps have yielded to infidelity. Anna (for I shall say it), after the death of my poor husband

Sychaeus and the scattering of our home by my brother's slaughter, only he has changed my feelings and made my resolution slip. I recognize the traces of the ancient flame. But I would pray that the earth should first gape open to its depths for me or that the omnipotent father should drive me to the shades with a thunderbolt, the pale shadows in darkness and deepest night, before, shame, I violate you or relax your laws. He who first joined me to himself has taken away my affections; may he have them with him and guard them in the tomb.

When she becomes enamoured of Aeneas she seeks dispensation from her vow through sacrifices.[19] Virgil does not say whether these were effective or not. He simply says:

heu, uatum ignarae mentes! quid uota furentem,
quid delubra iuuant? (65-6)

Alas, the ignorant minds of seers! What help are prayers, what help are shrines, to one who is crazy with love?

This fine reflection does not tell us whether Dido's sacrifices were effective or not in releasing her from her vow. But there is no reason to suppose that they weren't. However, Virgil insists that her involvement with Aeneas was a fault because of this broken vow. Hence the passage calling it a fault, *culpam*, which I have already quoted. But this is special pleading: Dido need not have made the vow in the first place and anyway had sought dispensation from it by the approved methods. Why should she not think that she had obtained the approval she sought? And her sister Anna was perfectly correct in suggesting that a marriage with Aeneas would both correspond with Dido's feelings and be good for her people:

dis equidem auspicibus reor et Iunone secunda
hunc cursum Iliacas uento tenuisse carinas.
quam tu urbem, soror, hanc cernes, quae surgere regna
coniugio tali! Teucrum comitantibus armis
Punica se quantis attollet gloria rebus! (45-9)

I actually consider that it was by the approval of the gods and the support of Juno herself that the Trojan ships held their course to here on the wind. What a city, sister, you will see here, what a flourishing realm from such a marriage! With the allied weapons of the Trojans, Carthaginian fame will rise to such great heights!

Indeed, Anna is quite right about the role of the gods: Juno with the support of Aeolus diverted Aeneas' ships from their course to Italy and Neptune got them to Libya, as was recounted in book I. And Juno, as we learn shortly after Anna's speech, wants them to get married (124-7).

We come to the issue of *patresfamilias* and here there is a conspicuous gap. Aeneas' father Anchises had just died, as is quietly slipped in at the end of book III. Had Anchises remained alive he would surely have advised Aeneas against any entanglement with Dido. In fact, Virgil presumably deliberately gets him out of the way so that Aeneas makes precisely this mistake, to show, among other things, how dependent he was on his father's counsel and how much he has still to learn. Dido's father has also died and his throne is in the hands of her nearest male relative, her hostile, indeed murderous brother Pygmalion, from whom she has fled.[20] He is obviously neither available nor suitable. There are therefore no *patresfamiliares* on either side available to give or withhold consent.

What about a marriage ceremony? Strictly speaking, there was no need for one; nevertheless Juno's plan, anticipated by Anna, is clear:

diffugient comites et nocte tegentur opaca:
speluncam Dido dux et Troianus eandem
deuenient. adero et, tua si mihi certa uoluntas,
conubio iungam stabili propriamque dicabo.
hic hymenaeus erit. (123-7)[21]

The company will disperse and be covered in thick darkness: Dido and the Trojan leader will come to the same cave. I shall be present, if your [sc. Venus's] *goodwill is certain, I shall declare formal union in true marriage. This will be their wedding.*

Juno's intention is not benevolent, because her long-term aim to block Aeneas from Italy as far as she can. But she is also the goddess of marriage. She, if anyone, should know whether there was a marriage or not. The encounter in the cave follows her plan:

> speluncam Dido dux et Troianus eandem
> deueniunt. prima et Tellus et pronuba Iuno
> dant signum; fulsere ignes et conscius aether
> conubiis summoque ulularunt uertice Nymphae.
> ille dies primus leti primusque malorum
> causa fuit; neque enim specie famaue mouetur
> nec iam furtiuum Dido meditatur amorem:
> coniugium uocat, hoc praetexit nomine culpam. (165-72)

Dido and the Trojan leader come to the same cave. Primeval Earth and Juno fulfilling the role of the married woman who guides the bride to the bedchamber give the sign [for the bridal procession]; *lightning flashed and the sky was witness of their marriage and on the highest peak the nymphs howled. That day was the first in the cause of death; for Dido is not now moved by appearances or reputation and does not now brood on a secret love: she calls it marriage and with this name cloaks her fault.*

I quoted the end of this account above. I can now ask: what fault?[22] That she did not keep her vow not to marry after the death of Sychaeus? But she had sought dispensation from that by the proper route and had no reason to suppose it had not been granted. That she was delaying Aeneas from going to Italy? But that was his responsibility, not hers, and anyway there was nothing in Creusa's prophecy about timing, even if one grants credibility to a ghost. Dido calls their relationship marriage (*conubium* and *coniugium* both mean marriage); so does Juno, the goddess of marriage, and the assisting gods and nymphs. The only fault I can see is that Dido had neglected the building work she had started (86-9) and which anyway Aeneas resumes (260-1). But that is not what Virgil has in mind when he uses the word *culpam* here. Maybe, since he is a subtle writer, he is deliberately provoking us to question him here.

The fault is surely that of Aeneas, not Dido. And while we are about it, when Mercury comes to warn off Aeneas, he says:

> tu nunc Karthaginis altae
> fundamenta locas pulchramque uxorius urbem
> exstruis? (265-7)

Are you now laying the foundations of lofty Carthage and building a beautiful city as a husband?

Mercury may have meant this scornfully—there was nothing about it in Jupiter's charge to him—but he accepts that Aeneas is behaving like a husband.[23] And in Roman terms, cohabitation with consent is enough to constitute marriage. Dido may not have been aware of the gods' approval, but she didn't need it.

Did Aeneas consent to their union? He neither did nor didn't. He went along with it, almost like a Greek warrior taking advantage of an available woman. He could and should have said that he was not free because his destiny obliged him to go to Italy. But he didn't. Admittedly, by the time we get to the quarrel scene, Virgil says:

> at pius Aeneas, quamquam lenire dolentem
> solando cupit et dictis auertere curas,
> multa gemens magnoque animum labefactus amore
> iussa tamen diuum exsequitur classemque reuisit. (393-6)

But loyal Aeneas, although he wanted to soften her in her grief by comforting her and turn aside her cares with his words, groaning heavily and his spirit shaken by his great love, nevertheless followed the orders of the gods and goes back to the fleet.

His loyalty is of course to his destiny, not to Dido, though it takes a moment to appreciate this, but Virgil has not really shown us a man in love, whatever he may say. Only when he sees Dido in the underworld can we really believe that he had loved her, when Virgil says:

demisit lacrimas dulcique adfatus amore est. (VI.455)

He let tears fall and spoke to her with tender love.

The whole episode reflects very badly on him, showing, among other things, how much he depended on guidance from Anchises. But it does not reflect badly on Dido.

What about the absence of human witnesses? Virgil would have remembered the wedding of Peleus and Thetis in Catullus 64, which is attended by both immortals and mortals, though not at the same time. But witnesses, though customary, were not essential for a valid Roman wedding. And do the divine witnesses not count?

Interestingly, Virgil carefully avoids telling us directly about their life together after the encounter in the cave. Instead, he gives us what the rumours are, personifying *Fama*:

haec tum multiplici populos sermone replebat
gaudens, et pariter facta atque infecta canebat:
uenisse Aenean Troiano sanguine cretum,
cui se pulchra uiro dignetur iungere Dido;
nunc hiemem inter se luxu, quam longa, fouere
regnorum immemores turpique cupidine captos. (189-94)

She [Fama], *rejoicing, then filled the people with varied talk, and sang equally of truths and untruths: that Aeneas, born of Trojan blood had come, to whom the lovely Dido deigns to join herself as her husband; now they keep the winter, however long, warm between themselves in comfort, forgetful of their kingdoms and enthralled by vile lust.*

In other words, they are rumoured to be living together; there is no need to characterise this as *turpique cupidine*, vile lust. Indeed, Virgil might have expected his readers to react saying that this was a quite unnecessary slur on them; after all, he does not say this *in propria persona* as narrator. However, Fama does imply that their feeling was mutual; we never learn whether Aeneas was more than a willing partner.

However, the less he was emotionally committed, the worse it reflects on him.

The rumour reaches Iarbas who prays to Jupiter to intervene.[24] Then:

audiit Omnipotens, oculosque ad moenia torsit
regia et oblitos famae melioris amantis. (220-1)

The almighty heard and turned his eyes to the royal walls and on the lovers forgetful of their better reputation.

One might well ask: what was that reputation? Among the Carthaginians, Aeneas was a Trojan prince in exile, who had married their queen, and, by so doing, was fending off Iarbas. And, far from being forgetful, he was also helping to build their city.[25] They hardly cared about Aeneas's destiny to go to Italy, which only those who had been present at his narration and attended carefully would even have been aware of. And their queen had found a suitable second husband. How was that supposed to damage her reputation?

Jupiter sends Mercury to summon Aeneas to Italy. Aeneas prepares in secret to do so; when Dido learns of it she challenges Aeneas, including the words with which I began.

I do not need to consider in detail the pitiful scenes in which Dido comes to realise that she is doomed. But I do need to pick out two points. One is something she says to Anna

non iam coniugium antiquum, quod prodidit, oro 431

I plead not for what once was marriage, by him betrayed.[26]

She could not plead for it had it not taken place, and she had every right to think that it had. Then, when she meditates by herself she raises another possibility:

sola fuga nautas comitabor ouantis? (543)

Shall I alone as an exile accompany the rejoicing sailors?

She goes on, in the same speech, to say:

non licuit thalami expertem sine crimine uitam
degere more ferae, talis nec tangere curas; (550-1)

*I was not allowed to live my life innocently like a wild animal, without
the pain of marriage and without having such cares.*

I need to quote Kenneth Quinn's comment on this, though I
disagree with it:

Dido takes it for granted there had to be marriage and that marriage
took place. The reader has his reservations on both scores: for all her
talk of marriage, what took place was the most abject surrender to
passion. Her words point to a truth none the less, though not the one
Dido intends: they reveal her obsession with marriage; they make us
feel it was her conviction that marriage would put things right which
brought her where she is, even persuaded her marriage was hers when it
was not.[27]

This is powerfully expressed but biased against Dido. It takes two to
tango, as the saying goes, and Aeneas was an equal party. His behaviour
was consistent with accepting a marriage and he did not insist, until
Mercury forced him, that he had to go to Italy straightaway. She was
quite entitled to consider their union a marriage. And in any case, as far
as wild animals are concerned, they are not without marriage, with
numerous species mating for life.

The one possibility which is never raised is that Dido should accompany Aeneas to Italy, go through a public, though strictly speaking
unnecessary, celebration of marriage there, while leaving Anna to govern
Carthage. Of course, they never discussed it; if they had, Aeneas would
have had to say: 'I am afraid I can't do that, as I shall have to marry a

woman in Italy, to consolidate my position there when I have established it.' Virgil contrives never to raise this issue as he needs to show a historical basis for the enmity between Carthage and Rome, so he has to show Aeneas betraying and abandoning Dido without ever being straight with her. He uses this whole episode to show how much Aeneas still has to learn since he is now without the guidance of Anchises.

I come now to the role of the gods. Jupiter sent Mercury to Dido to ensure that she gives the Trojans a warm welcome (I.297-304). Venus enhances Aeneas's looks and sends Cupid to take the form of Ascanius and instil a passion for Aeneas in Dido (I.589-93, 683-8, 715-22). When Juno sees this, she accosts Venus and proposes the plan I have already noted, that Aeneas and Dido should encounter each other in a cave. This leads to Iarbas's petition to Jupiter and Mercury's summons to Aeneas. All this invites the question of how free Dido was to commit herself to Aeneas; was she just a plaything of the gods, or do the gods here represent forces which we would characterise in some other way?

Heinze, in his classic study, suggested that 'Virgil's intention was to use symbols, that is, consciously to change simple psychological processes into instances of divine intervention, counting on the fact that the educated reader these scenes featuring gods would interpret them "allegorically".'[28] Similarly, Brooks Otis says 'the divine machinery ... is brought into play only when it has been called for by the dramatic and emotional situation.'[29] Gordon Williams takes the same approach. For example, he says 'the contemptuous words [Mercury] uses to address Aeneas are clearly also the voice of Aeneas' own conscience, especially the sneer in *uxorius*.' Similarly, in the later appearance of Mercury to Aeneas in a dream, 'what he says follows exactly the line of argument that would naturally occur to a man in Aeneas' situation.'[30] If we follow this line, then Venus's instilling of a passion for Aeneas in Dido simply represents Dido's own motivation and the plot between Venus and Juno represents the pull in Aeneas to resist his destiny of going to Italy and the lure of Dido, while for Dido it represents her wish to make this handsome man and good leader her husband. Williams supports his argument by suggesting that when Virgil employs the traditional mythological trappings of his gods, such as Mercury's magic sandals and caduceus, which Williams calls

Hellenistic rococo, he is deliberately subverting the literal interpretation of such passages.[31]

What then does Virgil intend us to understand by the presence of Juno and other gods at the union of Aeneas and Dido in the cave? Does this represent merely wish-fulfilment by Dido, or by Aeneas, or by both of them? If what Williams would call the Hellenistic rococo trappings of Tellus and the nymphs suggest that we are not meant take this literally, how then are we supposed to take it?

The issue is whether Aeneas and Dido are fully responsible for their actions or whether they are the prey of forces they can neither understand nor control. It then matters little whether we regard those forces as purely internal, psychological processes, or external, the actions of gods. The results are the same. We are all driven, to a greater or lesser extent, by forces of which we are not wholly conscious, and Virgil is showing how disastrous the consequences can be. Aeneas is bereft of the guidance of Anchises, in Freudian terms the superego and in Jungian ones the archetype of the Old Wise Man, while Dido is egged on by Anna, in Freudian terms the Id.

Still, however disastrous the consequences, at least for Dido, there remains their cohabitation—for Fama is surely not wrong about that—and it was enough to constitute a Roman marriage.

I therefore conclude that, for all that Virgil wishes us to see Dido as seriously at fault, while he leaves us to draw our own conclusions about Aeneas, in fact what he has presented us with was indeed a marriage. Admittedly, Aeneas should never have entered into it, and admittedly he betrayed it, but marriage it was and Dido was entitled to consider it so. I end with some lines by Anne Ridler:

> Was not ours a marriage bed?
> Jewelled sword I gave you, purple
> Cloak you wore for me—my passion
> Woke an answering fire in you.
> Winter-long that torch was burning:
> How could you say it was no marriage?
> How could you say you gave no pledge?[32]

1. Quotations are from Book IV unless otherwise noted.
2. Quinn translates this as 'We're as good as married,' 'Virgil's tragic Queen,' in *Latin Explorations*, London 1968, 47.
3. Virgil has made this clear in lines 288-290.
4. D. H. Lawrence, *Studies in Classic American Literature*, London, 1937 (1923), 2.
5. Virgil calls their relationship *inconcessosque hymenaeos*, unlawful marriage, I.651.
6. Homer, *Iliad* 19: 295-9; 24: 675-6
7. Hyginus, *Fabulae* § 121. There are convenient summaries of the legends about both Briseis and Chryseis in Pierre Grimal, *Dictionary of Classical Mythology*, Oxford, 1968.
8. Other versions of his story give him other affairs, with children born from them, Heinze, *Virgil's epic technique*, trans. Harvey *et al.*, London, 1993 (1928²). 95.
9. Glenn E. Markoe, *The Phoenicians*, London, 2005, 107-8, 138-9.
10. *The Phoenicians*, 170-1.
11. Justinus, *Epitome of Pompeius Trogus' Philippic Histories*, 18.4-6. See the discussion of the legends by W. F. Jackson Knight, *Roman Vergil*, Harmondsworth, 1966,126-30.
12. Elissa is a Romanisation of Elath, the feminine of El, God. Justinus says that after her suicide she was worshipped as a goddess and Jackson Knight reports a suggestion that she was originally a Phoenician fertility goddess, *Roman Vergil*, 126.
13. Andrew Wallace-Hadrill, 'Roman marriage,' in Peter Jones and Keith Sidwell (eds.), *The World of Rome*, Cambridge, 1997, 214.
14. Susan Treggiari, *Roman Marriage, Iusti Coniuges from the time of Cicero to the time of Ulpian*, Oxford, 1991, 146.
15. *Ibid.* 162-3.
16. *ibid.* 235.
17. I owe this reference to Jérôme Carcopino, *Daily life in ancient Rome*, trans. E. O. Lorimer, Harmondsworth, 1941, 96.
18. The evidence includes vase paintings and coins as well as literary fragments, see commentaries on *Aeneid* II by Austin 280-1 and Horsfall, 516-7. I consider this in more detail in my article 'Aeneas's frame of mind on leaving Troy.'
19. In Justinus the purpose of the vow is to avoid marriage with Iarbas and this is the reason for her suicide, *loc. cit.*
20. Juno has explained this to Aeneas, *Aeneid* I.340-70.
21. Line 126 is repeated from I.73 and some reject it, though it is in all the MSS and was known to Servius. See Austin *ad. loc.*
22. Quinn, citing Mackail, says '*culpa* means only 'failing' (surrender to passion) and does not imply either criminality or moral obliquity,' 'Virgil's Tragic Queen,' 38n. However, the uses cited by both Lewis and Short and the OLD do not support this.
23. Quinn: 'I don't mean, of course, that Virgil expects us to view the relationship of Dido and Aeneas in strict accordance with Roman laws of marriage. He does, however, expect his readers to interpret the heroic situation realistically, in terms of what might have happened at Rome,' *loc. cit.*
24. Strictly speaking this is what Iarbas is reported to have prayed (*dicitur*, 204). If this is not to be taken as accurate, then it would represent a projection by Aeneas and Dido of their misgivings onto an imagined Iarbas. This is possible but seems strained.

25. Although Dido had been neglecting this (86-9), by the time Mercury came to Aeneas, he was busily engaged in precisely this work (265-7, quoted above).

26. This is the first of Quinn's two alternative translations of this line, taking *antiquum* as 'former' and *oro* as 'ask back.' The other version takes *antiquum* as 'old and honourable' and *oro* as 'plead to get.' He argues 'the ambiguity of Virgil's line well represents Dido's emotional indignation and her failure to distinguish in her own mind between what she had actually lost and what she had only hoped to get,' Quinn, 'Virgil's Tragic Queen,' 50. This is ingenious but I think is a distinction without a difference; Dido was entitled to think that there was marriage.

27. Kenneth Quinn, *Virgil's Aeneid: a critical description*, London, 1968, 337.

28. Heinze, *Virgil's epic technique*, 242.

29. Brooks Otis, *Virgil; a study in civilized poetry*, Oxford, 1964, 67.

30. Gordon Williams, *Technique and Ideas in the Aeneid*, New Haven, 1983, 20ff..

31. *op. cit.* 124-32.

32. Anne Ridler, 'Infelix Dido,' *Collected Poems*, Manchester, 1994, 210.

4

AENEAS IN THE UNDERWORLD

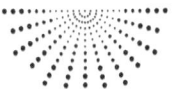

*W*hat does Aeneas learn from his journey to the underworld and how does he learn it? In answering this, the starting point is to note that *Aeneid* VI is an example of the mythological motif or archetypal pattern known as the otherworld journey. This may be presented as direct experience or as a vision or dream. It occurs in literature and also in religion and folklore. Classical literary examples include Book XI of the *Odyssey*, the myth of Er in Plato's *Republic* and the *Somnum Scipionis* from Cicero's *Republic*, all of which influenced Virgil. Non-classical examples include the epic of Gilgamesh, the Biblical books of Ezekiel, Jonah and Revelation and many medieval works including Dante's *Commedia*, in which Dante the author enlists Virgil as a fictional character to be the guide to Dante the pilgrim, the character in the poem. These journeys may include variously a journey through darkness, crossing a threshold often involving water, a spirit guide, encounters with the souls of the dead, a vision of heaven and revelations about the future; as a result of the journey the traveller is strengthened and renewed. In religious practice this process may be symbolically a rebirth or an initiation—which is a symbolic rebirth. Examples include the Eleusinian and Orphic mysteries and the Christian rite of baptism, particularly when carried out, as it was originally, at the conclusion of Holy Week.

The purpose of the journey in Virgil, as in other works, is not simply to offer a tour of the underworld for its own sake, but specifically in order for Aeneas to experience a kind of initiation or rebirth. Virgil arranges his underworld accordingly. I draw here on a comment by T. S. Eliot about the episode with Dido in this book:

> Dido's behaviour appears almost as a projection of Aeneas' own conscience: this, we feel, is the way in which Aeneas' conscience would *expect* Dido to behave to him.[1]

I would take this further and apply it to the whole book: everything and everyone Aeneas encounters is there to form part of his training and development. Everything is arranged so that Aeneas should experience what he needs to, to experience a symbolic rebirth, to prepare him for his future.[2] The success of this is shown by the difference between the Aeneas of the earlier books and that of the later. There is not space to demonstrate this in detail, but in the early books he is constantly unsure of his purpose, and his relation to his father Anchises goes beyond filial piety to a continual emotional dependence. (It is only after his father has died that he gets involved with Dido.) However, in the later books he is consistently steadfast and resolute. Arguably this makes him less interesting as a character, but that is not the point: he has to cease to be the refugee from Troy to become the person who can found Rome. That is his destiny, in modern language his vocation, and his personal feelings have to take second place.

Now Aeneas, unlike his creator, is not an especially reflective or imaginative man, and so he learns best by experience. The purpose of Book VI is to show us the process whereby he becomes able to realize his destiny now that he has finally arrived in Italy. This process gives the answers to the two questions I have put as the topic of this essay. I shall concentrate on some representative moments:

I. Preparation for the descent: the temple gates, the sibyl,
    Misenus and the golden bough.

II. Encounters with Palinurus, Dido, Deiphobus, his father
    Anchises and the sight of Marcellus.
III. Departure through the Gates of Sleep.

Now, as Aeneas took the sibyl as his guide, and Dante the pilgrim
took a fictional Virgil, I shall take Dante the author as my occasional
guide, as he drew a good deal from this book and was as least as good a
Virgilian as modern commentators. Like *Aeneid* VI, the *Commedia* is
not a neutral account of the afterlife but a vision of it, created in each
case by the poet to reflect the needs of the principal character in it,
respectively Aeneas and Dante the pilgrim, though each of these figures
has also a wider symbolic role.

The fact that what Virgil is presenting is a vision of the afterlife will
also help us with the issue of inconsistencies within the book, of which
there are quite a number. Examples include the fact that, despite what
the sibyl says, the re-ascent does not involve recrossing Acheron and is
accomplished without difficulty, that Aeneas does not himself see
Tartarus once, let alone twice, that it is unclear how the judging process
for the souls actually works—how is it decided whether the soul is to go
to Minos, to Rhadamanthus or to Pluto? Virgil does not say[3]—that
there is dawn in the underworld, and that the souls in the Sorrowful
Fields seem to be there for ever, whereas those in the Elysian Fields are
mostly destined for reincarnation. These discrepancies are not trivial
inconsistencies, which can be put down to the unfinished state of the
poem, but flagrant and glaring; they are therefore conscious and deliberate. They make the book more like a dream, an analogy to which I shall
return.

—I—

At the entrance to the temple of Apollo, Aeneas and his companions see the gates with gold relief panels made by Daedalus who
landed there. These show the story of the tribute, the labyrinth,
Pasiphaë and the bull, the Minotaur, and would have shown Icarus
but that *bis patriae cecidere manus* (33, twice the father's hands sank
down). In these panels Daedalus confronts his past as Aeneas is going

to do when he enters the underworld. Particularly significant is the labyrinth:

hic labor ille domus et inextricabilis error (27)[4]

Here is that house of pain and its insoluble mazes.

We had already had a fuller description in the simile of the labyrinth offered in connection with the Troy game at the funeral of Anchises:

ut quondam Creta fertur Labyrinthus in alta
parietibus textum caecis iter ancipitemque
mille uiis habuisse dolum, qua signa sequendi
frangeret indeprensus et inremeabilis error (V.588-592)

As, long ago in lofty Crete, it is said that the labyrinth held a way, wound around with blind walls and a confusing trickery in its thousand paths, by which undiscoverable and irremediable wandering made it impossible to follow the way.

A labyrinth obstructs entry but allows it on the proper terms. It was used in military defences and also, symbolically, in the entrances to sacred buildings.[5] The temple of Apollo, the sibyl's cave and, even more, the underworld, count as sacred places and the labyrinth on the relief panel is an implicit warning of the dangers in these sacred spaces. It can also be taken to symbolize Aeneas' wanderings, both those in the past and those yet to come.[6] It is a central image of the poem.[7] Aeneas has not finished looking at it, and so has not fully appreciated its significance or taken the warning, when he is urged on by the sibyl:

non hoc ista sibi tempus spectacula poscit (37)

Not these sights does the time demand.

And she goes on to explain the necessary sacrifices. Her interruption is not just to move the action on: it is also because Aeneas cannot afford to linger and must proceed forthwith with his spiritual task. This becomes clearer if we note Dante's use of a similar interruption when his fictional Cato scolds Dante the pilgrim who has been listening to a song at the foot of mount Purgatory:

> Che è ciò, spiriti lenti?
> qual negligenza, quale stare è questo?
>   Correte al monte a spogliarvi lo scoglio
>   ch'esser non lascia a voi Dio manifesto. (*Purgatorio* II, 120-1)

What is this, you sluggish spirits? What negligence, what delay is this? Hurry to the mountain to strip off the slough which prevents God from being manifest to you. Trans. Singleton.

The sibyl has two roles, both as the mouthpiece for the god Apollo and as guide to Aeneas in the underworld. In the first role she reveals Aeneas's destiny more clearly than he has previously known:

> o tandem magnis pelagi defuncte periclis
> (sed terrae grauiora manent), in regna Lauini
> Dardanidae uenient (mitte hanc de pectore curam),
> sed non et uenisse uolent. bella, horrida bella,
> et Thybrim multo spumantem sanguine cerno.
> non Simois tibi nec Xanthus nec Dorica castra
> defuerint; alius Latio iam partus Achilles,
> natus et ipse dea; nec Teucris addita Iuno
> usquam aberit, cum tu supplex in rebus egenis
> quas gentis Italum aut quas non oraueris urbes!
> causa mali tanti coniunx iterum hospita Teucris
> externique iterum thalami...
> tu ne cede malis, sed contra audentior ito,
> qua tua te Fortuna sinet. uia prima salutis
> (quod minime reris) Graia pandetur ab urbe. (83-97)

Oh you who have finally survived the great dangers of the sea (but greater dangers await on land), the son of Dardanus will come to the realm of

Lavinia (dismiss this anxiety from your heart); but they will also wish
that they had not come. I see wars, dreadful wars, and the Tiber foaming
with abundant blood. There will not be lacking a Simois, nor a Xanthus
nor a Doric camp; a different Achilles has now been born in Latium and
himself born of a goddess; nor will Juno ever hold back from dogging the
Trojans, while as for you, in your distressed circumstances, as a suppliant,
what tribes of the Italians and what cities will you not beg for help from!
The cause of all this Trojan trouble will again be a foreign bride, again a
foreign marriage ... Do not give in to troubles, but go forward against
them more boldly in the way your destiny permits. Your way to safety will
first lie (which you will hardly believe) through a Greek city.

This then is one of the things Aeneas learns. There are also two
points of detail in this speech of particular interest. Firstly, Apollo
predicts Aeneas's fortunes in Italy almost entirely in terms of the Troy
of the past: the rivers Simois and Xanthus (Numicius and Tiber), the
Doric camp, a different Achilles (Turnus), a Greek city (Pallanteum).
This is consistent with Aeneas as we have known him so far, and with
my general thesis: at this stage he is still looks backwards, to the past.
Apollo has to expound his future in terms he will understand. The
second point is that these problems will again stem from a foreign
marriage. Directly Apollo is comparing Lavinia to Helen, but indirectly
also to Dido. She might also be hinted at the *Veneris monumenta*
nefandae (the record of a monstrous love, 26) in the relief panels.[8] If
Aeneas had stayed with her, he would have cheated his destiny.

Aeneas's reply is expressed boldly. He begins:

> non ulla laborum,
> o uirgo, noua mi facies inopinaue surgit;
> omnia praecepi atque animo mecum ante peregi. (103-5)

Oh lady, no new or unexpected forms of tasks of any kind distress me; I
have anticipated everything and gone over it in my mind already.

Virgil's first audience of Augustus and his circle might well have
been content with this expression of firmness; however, to me it seems

simply bravado. For Aeneas to say that he fears nothing is not courageous but foolhardy, something which he would have known had he been able to read the *Laches* of Plato or appreciated the meaning of the labyrinth on the relief panel. And in fact, for all his show of courage, on entering the underworld he is immediately frightened by the ghosts of the monsters and has to be calmed by the sibyl (290-4). This Aeneas still has a good deal to learn.

To venture into the underworld requires, among other things, that Aeneas should find and pluck the golden bough. The sibyl explains this in these words:

> latet arbore opaca
> aureus et foliis et lento uimine ramus,
> Iunoni infernae dictus sacer; hunc tegit omnis
> lucus et obscuris claudunt conuallibus umbrae.
> sed non ante datur telluris operta subire
> auricomos quam quis decerpserit arbore fetus.
> hoc sibi pulchra suum ferri Proserpina munus
> instituit. primo auulso non deficit alter
> aureus, et simili frondescit uirga metallo.
> ergo alte uestiga oculis et rite repertum
> carpe manu; namque ipse uolens facilisque sequetur,
> si te fata uocant; aliter non uiribus ullis
> uincere nec duro poteris conuellere ferro. (136-148)

A bough, golden in its leaves and pliant stem, hides on a dark tree, said to be sacred to Juno of the underworld [Proserpina]*; an entire wood conceals it and shadows hide it in the dark valleys, but it is not given to descend to the hidden depths of the earth before someone has plucked from the tree its golden-haired harvest. This is what the beautiful Proserpina has prescribed as the offering to be taken to her. When the first is torn away, another golden one is not lacking, and the branch blooms with the same metal. So seek it out in the depths (of the forest) with your eyes and, when it has been found, grasp hold of it*[9] *with due ritual, for it will come away willingly and easily if destiny calls you; otherwise, you will not be able to master it by any force or hard iron* [sword].

She immediately goes on to tell him about the need to bury the body of his friend (*corpus amici*, 149, Misenus, but unnamed at this stage) because:

sic demum lucos Stygis et regna inuia uiuis
aspicies. (154-5)

Only in this way will you see the Stygian groves and realms impassable to the living.

The need to pluck the golden bough is therefore inextricably caught up with the duty to bury Misenus. To make the point explicitly: Aeneas has to demonstrate his *pietas* by burying the dead as one of the requirements for successful admission to the underworld. Burial of the dead is a repeated theme in this book, strengthened by the fact that all those concerned, other than Anchises, have died before their time.

This is reinforced by the fact that he only finds the bough in the course of preparing for the funeral. Even then, Aeneas needs further help, from the doves sent by Venus his mother. His response to them stresses her role both as goddess and as mother:

este duces, o, si qua uia est, cursumque per auras
derigite in lucos ubi pinguem diues opacat
ramus humum. tuque, o, dubiis ne defice rebus,
diua parens. (194-7)

Be my guide, if there be any way, and direct my path through the air to the wood where the rich bough shadows the fruitful ground. And you, my goddess mother, do not fail me in these difficult matters.

Again to spell it out: Aeneas needs divine help to achieve his mission, or to reframe it, he needs his mother's help to find his father. Part of the learning process is to acknowledge the need for help and to accept it joyfully when it is offered. It also involves accepting your parentage.

The actual sight and plucking of the golden bough is a magical passage:

quale solet siluis brumali frigore uiscum
fronde uirere noua, quod non sua seminat arbos,
et croceo fetu teretis circumdare truncos,
talis erat species auri frondentis opaca
ilice, sic leni crepitabat brattea uento.
corripit Aeneas extemplo auidusque refringit
cunctantem, et uatis portat sub tecta Sibyllae. (205-11)

As in the woods in the cold of winter mistletoe is accustomed to turn green with new growth, which does not spring from the trees on which it grows, and to surround the smooth trunks with its yellow[10] fruit, such was the appearance of the golden leafage on the dark oak, and so the gold foil rustled in the gentle breeze. Aeneas seizes it immediately and eagerly breaks off the yielding[11] bough and carries it to the home of the prophetic sibyl.

The golden bough is a complex symbol. The phrase itself comes from the first century Greek poet Meleager, who, in the introduction to his anthology known as the *Garland*, refers to 'the golden bough of Plato, ever divine, all shining with virtue.'[12] In Meleager it is a metaphor for Plato's poetry, not a physical object. It seems that Virgil saw the potential of the phrase as a literal image and then remembered his own account of grafting:[13]

nec longum tempus, et ingens
exiit ad caelum ramis felicibus arbos,
miratastque nouas frondes et non sua poma. (*Georgics* II.80-2)

In a little while a great tree springs up towards the sky with fruitful branches and wonders at its strange leaves and fruit not its own.

He could happily accept the reference to Plato as an anticipation for the informed reader of his use of Plato, particularly the myth of Er. He himself is responsible for the sense of mystery which surrounds the golden bough in this new context,[14] though for English readers this has been enhanced from its use by J. G. Frazer as the title of his enormously influential masterwork. At the simplest level, it is a talisman for safe passage, comparable in this respect to the moly Hermes gives Odysseus[15] and to amulets for travellers, which were popular in the ancient world. But as part of a tree it is reminiscent of the myrtles which the Eleusinian neophytes carried in their procession[16] or of the palm branches and crosses which Christians carry in procession on Palm Sunday. Trees, or branches of them, also have a long tradition in folklore in ceremonies associated with bringing in summer after winter, that is, with rebirth. The Maypole is a survivor of this.[17] Maud Bodkin's summary seems right:

> The bough ... appears as representing the tree-spirit, or, more generally, the power of renewal in vegetation and in other forms of life.[18]

Aeneas will find renewal through confronting his past. This is summed up here[19] in a series of encounters with the spirits of individuals from his past, a technique which turns out to be so powerful that Dante adopted it wholesale for the *Commedia*, which is largely composed of a series of such fruitful encounters with individuals. Aeneas meets them in the reverse order to that in which they met him in life, so he is working backwards, going progressively deeper into his past, a process like that in psychoanalysis and with a similar aim, that of strengthening him by dealing with the implications of his previous experience.

— II —

The first spirit he meets is that of Palinurus. He is among those who are waiting to be ferried across Acheron:

> stabant orantes primi transmittere cursum
> tendebantque manus ripae ulterioris amore. (313-4)

They stood praying to be first to make the crossing and stretched out their hands with longing for the farther shore.

The famous line has been more praised than understood. Why are the souls so keen to cross Acheron? Here again Dante can help us: his equivalent scene is very closely modelled on this. His fictional Virgil explains:

e pronti sono a trapassar lo rio,
　　ché la divina giustizia li sprona,
　　　sì che la tema si volve in disio. (*Inferno* III.124-6)

They are eager to cross the stream, for Divine Justice so spurs them that their fear is changed to desire.

Dorothy Sayers explains this:

God puts nobody in Hell: the damned may wail and weep and curse their parents and the day they were born, blaming everything and everybody but themselves: nevertheless they go, like Judas, "to their own place," because it is the only place where they can bear to be.[20] Hell is the state in which those who choose alienation from God experience the reality of their choice.[21]

Dante's souls crave justice even though they will suffer from it. We remember the inscription over Hell gate:

Giustizia mosse il mio alto fattore;
　　fecemi la divina podestate,
　　　la somma sapienza e 'l primo amore. (*Inferno* III.4-6)

Justice moved my high maker; the divine power made me, the supreme wisdom, and the primal love. (Trans. Singleton.)

Similarly, Virgil's souls crave judgement. However, Palinurus is not allowed to embark because his body has not been buried and Charon may not take him, as the sibyl explains:

> hi, quos uehit unda, sepulti.
> nec ripas datur horrendas et rauca fluenta
> transportare prius quam sedibus ossa quierunt.
> centum errant annos uolitantque haec litora circum;
> tum demum admissi stagna exoptata reuisunt. (326-30)

These, whom the wave carries, have been buried. Nor is it allowed to carry (them) across the frightening banks and the grumbling water before their bones have come to a resting place. They wander for a hundred years and flit about these shores; then and not till then are they allowed back and again visit the longed-for pools.

We can all accept the importance of proper burial, with the *Antigone* of Sophocles as a sufficent reminder, and Aeneas has just demonstrated this in burying Misenus. The judgements in the underworld are inexorable, as the sibyl reminds Palinurus in a weightily spondaic line:

> desine fata deum flecti sperare precando (376)

Cease hoping that the decrees of the gods are to be turned aside by praying.

The fact that the judgements are inexorable does not necessarily mean that they are just. This is where Virgil differs from Dante; no wonder he leaves the actual process of judgement obscure. A person cannot be held to be personally at fault because his body has not been buried.[22] Aeneas' immediate reaction is this:

> constitit Anchisa satus et uestigia pressit
> multa putans sortemque animo miseratus iniquam. (331-2)

The son of Anchises halted and checked his footsteps, considering many things and having pity in his heart on their unjust fate.

This is not the only place where it is either stated or suggested that the judgements in the underworld may not be just. The sentiment may be attributed to Aeneas, to the sibyl or to Virgil as narrator, but it is there. There are other examples. As well as Dido, discussed below, there are the infants, the unjustly condemned (*falso damnati crimine*, 430) and other innocent (*insontes*) sucides, 426-439. Tartarus is called *impia* (unholy) by the sibyl (543) and its threshold accursed (*sceleratum ... limen*, 563). Of course, the last two are examples of transferred epithets but they invite the question as to justice as distinct from judgement in this underworld. We should remember that the underworld is presented as it is for Aeneas's benefit: Virgil does not commit himself as to whether it is really as he presents it, a topic to which we shall return at the end. I therefore pass over the issue that Dante's hell is only for the damned, whereas Virgil's underworld is for all departed souls.

The significance of these passages is that they indicate that Aeneas is learning compassion. This is deliberately understated, but it is an important theme: right at the end of the poem Aeneas would have spared Turnus but that he saw him wearing the belt of Pallas (XII 938-944). Since this is a heroic poem, the plot requires that Turnus should die, but one could argue that the main reason for introducing Pallas was to give a Aeneas a justification for overriding compassion and killing Turnus. But the compassion had to be there to be overriden and Aeneas had to learn it for it to be there.

His capacity for compassion is further tested in the encounter with Dido:

> demisit lacrimas dulcique adfatus amore est:
> 'infelix Dido, uerus mihi nuntius ergo
> uenerat exstinctam ferroque extrema secutam?
> funeris heu tibi causa fui? per sidera iuro,
> per superos et si qua fides tellure sub ima est,
> inuitus, regina, tuo de litore cessi.
> sed me iussa deum, quae nunc has ire per umbras,
> per loca senta situ cogunt noctemque profundam,
> imperiis egere suis; nec credere quiui
> hunc tantum tibi me discessu ferre dolorem.

siste gradum teque aspectu ne subtrahe nostro.
quem fugis? extremum fato quod te adloquor hoc est.'
(455-466)

He let tears fall and spoke to her with tender love: 'Unhappy Dido, was the message that had come to me true then that you were dead and had sought your end with the sword? Alas, was I the cause of your death? I swear by the stars, by the gods above and by whatever trust there may be deep below in the earth, that, queen, I left your shores unwillingly. But the commands of the gods, which even now compel me to go through these shadows, through regions rough with neglect and through deep night, drove me on with their orders. Nor could I believe that I brought such grief to you by leaving. Stay your steps and do not take yourself away from my sight. Whom are you fleeing from? This is the last time that I am fated to speak to you.'

I return to the comment by Eliot with which I began. He continues:

The point, it seems to me, is not that Dido is unforgiving—though it is important that, instead of railing at him, she merely snubs him—perhaps the most telling snub in all poetry: what matters most is, that Aeneas does not forgive himself—and this, significantly, in spite of the fact of which he is well aware, that all that he has done has been in compliance with destiny, or in consequence of the machinations of gods who are themselves, we feel, only instruments of a greater inscrutable power.[23]

He had loved her—it seems clearer here, when it is too late, than anything said about or by him in Book IV—and he had betrayed her. I do not mean that he should have stayed with her; I mean that he should never have got emotionally involved with her in the first place. His duty was to go to Italy. There is now nothing that he can do about it. He has to accept this, though even now he is still partly in denial (*nec credere quiui | hunc tantum tibi me discessu ferre dolorem, Nor could I believe that I brought such grief to you by leaving*). I should add that, though Eliot is surely right about Aeneas, he is partly wrong about Dido. He has overlooked the manner of her departure. She did not stalk off immediately but *tandem corripuit sese* (eventually she wrenched herself away, 472). After all, she had loved him too. But what is even more important is that, by the end of the encounter, Aeneas has stopped justifying himself, thinks not of himself but of her and considers her fate unjust (*casu percussus iniquo*, affected by her unjust fate, 475). He is developing compassion and a sense of justice which is not exactly that which is presented to him. We remember that Dido's place is among the innocent suicides (*insontes*, 435).

What Virgil here expresses by implication, Dante's Virgil expresses explicitly in his discourse on love:

> Lo naturale è sempre sanza errore,
> > ma l'altro puote errar per malo obietto
> > o per troppo o per poco di vigore...
> Quinci comprender puoi ch'esser convene
> > amor sementa in voi d'ogne virtute
> > e d'ogne operazion che merta pene.
> > > (*Purgatorio* XVII.94-6, 103-5)

> *The natural is always without error; but the other* [love of the mind]
> *may err either through an evil object, or through too much or too little*
> *vigour... Hence you can comprehend that love must needs be the seed in*
> *you of every virtue and of every action deserving punishment.*

In the encounter with Deiphobus I want to emphasize his final words and actions in leaving Aeneas:

> 'i decus, i, nostrum; melioribus utere fatis. '
> tantum effatus, et in uerbo uestigia torsit. (546-7)

> *'Go, glory of our people, go; enjoy a better destiny.' Having said as much,*
> *and on that word, he turned on his heel.*

I have translated *decus nostrum* as 'glory of our people;' Deiphobus does not here name the city and it is he who takes the initiative in putting the encounter to an end. Aeneas still needs some helping in letting the memory of Troy go and in accepting the need to pursue his own destiny.

Something similar is also true when he meets the spirit of his father:

ter conatus ibi collo dare bracchia circum;
ter frustra comprensa manus effugit imago,
par leuibus uentis uolucrique simillima somno. (700-2)

Three times he tried to throw his arms round his father's neck; three times, grasped in vain, the ghost escaped his hands, like light breezes and very close to a fleeting dream.[24]

The point is that there can be no renewal of their previous relationship. From this moment Aeneas realizes that he can no longer rely on his father and must find the strength in himself to face the challenges ahead. The past is left behind and Anchises encourages Aeneas by showing him the parade of heroes in the distant future. This is a necessary part of the poem, for its own sake and as a celebration of Augustus, and it is for this reason that metempsychosis is brought in as a piece of essential machinery to achieve it; we notice that this does not seem to apply in the Sorrowful Fields. It is also necessary for the considerable emphasis on the past for Aeneas to be balanced by looking forward and beyond the events of the second half of the poem

The parade of future heroes ends with the appearance of Marcellus, a golden boy who died young. Anchises laments what will be his passing:

nimium uobis Romana propago
uisa potens, superi, propria haec si dona fuissent...
heu, miserande puer, si qua fata aspera rumpas,
tu Marcellus eris. manibus date lilia plenis
purpureos spargam flores animamque nepotis
his saltem accumulem donis, et fungar inani
munere. (870-1, 882-6)

The Roman race would have seemed too powerful to you gods, if these gifts of yours had been lasting... Alas, poor boy, if you could only break your harsh destiny. You are to be Marcellus. Offer lilies with full hands.[25] *Let me scatter bright red flowers and heap the soul of my descendant with these gifts and perform this unavailing duty.*

Marcellus is innocent but will die young. In this he anticipates several of the leading figures of the second half of the poem, such as Nisus and Euryalus, Camilla, and, especially, Pallas. We notice that near the end of this book, as at the beginning, we have a funeral, in this case the imagined funeral of Marcellus, and again of someone who dies before his time. As Otis says: 'The ordeal of empire is based on sacrifice, especially sacrifice of the young.'[26] However, this is a lesson Virgil leaves the reader to draw; the point was well taken by at least one member of his first audience: on hearing this passage, Octavia, Marcellus' mother, is said to have fainted. Aeneas, on the other hand, cannot be allowed to be aware of it. Therefore, we are not told about any reaction he might have had.

— III —

The departure of Aeneas and the sibyl through the ivory gate is one of the most mysterious passages in a book full of mysteries:

sunt geminae Somni portae, quarum altera fertur
cornea, qua ueris facilis datur exitus umbris,
altera candenti perfecta nitens elephanto,
sed falsa ad caelum mittunt insomnia Manes.
his ibi tum natum Anchises unaque Sibyllam
prosequitur dictis portaque emittit eburna,
ille uiam secat ad nauis sociosque reuisit. (893-9)

There are two gates of sleep, of which one is said to be of horn, through which true shades are allowed an easy departure, and the other shining with polished bright ivory, but the spirits send false dreams (through it) to the upper world. With these words Anchises saw out his son there together

with the sibyl and let them out through the ivory gate, and he [Aeneas]
cut a route and went back to his ships and his companions.

This can be taken at several different levels. At its simplest, it was
thought that true dreams appeared only after midnight. One imagines
Virgil offering this explanation to fob off the casual enquirer. At the
next level we notice that Anchises cannot send his still living visitors out
through the gate of horn since they are not *uerae umbrae* (true shades,
taking *umbrae* as referring to them). Thus Austin. But *falsa* need not
mean untrue: it can also mean deceptive or illusory. The contrast is an
unbalanced one between real ghosts and deceptive dreams.[27] Whereas
Dante's otherworld is a vision which is in intention internally consistent
and, I believe, is in execution virtually so, dreams are seldom internally
consistent and literary dreams would be unconvincing were they so.
Aeneas' journey through the underworld was in a way a dream. It is
deceptive in the sense that it may not be a true representation of the
underworld, but rather the one that Aeneas needs. This accounts for the
inconsistencies I noted earlier. It also explains why Aeneas has no recall
of his underworld journey in the rest of the poem. And if it is a dream,
or like a dream, the sibyl as spirit guide and the ghosts he meets, especially that of his father, are at least partly projections of his own
dreaming mind, and so aspects of his own higher self advising his ego:
uolucrique simillima somno, very close to a fleeting dream, 702, could be
applied to the whole of his experience of the underworld. We also
wonder whether there is some kind of indecipherable clue or hint in the
cryptic reference right back to the entry to the underworld and the

ulnus opaca, ingens, quam sedem Somnia uulgo
uana tenere ferunt, foliisque sub omnibus haerent (283-4)

huge shadowy elm, which they say empty Dreams occupy in crowds and
cling under all its leaves.

These are at least some of the meanings latent in this passage and in
this book; they do not, of course, exhaust its mystery.
So we end up with the strange position that the crucial experience

for Aeneas is one that he is not consciously aware of. His journey to the underworld has been the equivalent of an initiation or a rebirth. It has worked as does a successful piece of therapy nowadays: the person functions better than previously but may not remember the process by which this was achieved. He has fulfilled his duties to the dead, acknowledged his mother, separated himself from his father, deepened his understanding of courage, increased his capacity for compassion, reflected on the meaning of justice and been given something to hope for in his future. As a result of all this he has become stronger. And he has done this primarily by a series of encounters with the ghosts of representative figures from his past. As C. S. Lewis once said of Aeneas: 'In a sense he *is* a ghost of Troy until he becomes the father of Rome.'[28] He has, nevertheless, by the end of the book, whether in a journey, or in his imagination, or in a vision, or in a dream, confronted the ghosts of his past and prepared himself for the trials ahead.

---

1. T. S. Eliot, 'What is a classic?' in *On Poetry and Poets*, London, 1957, 62.
2. It is therefore not surprising that this underworld is rather different from that of the Aristaeus epyllion in *Georgics* IV, despite the coincidence of 306-8 with *Georgics* IV.475-7.
3. Gordon Williams, *Tradition and Originality in Roman Poetry*, Oxford, 1968, 395-6 explores this in some detail.
4. Quotations are from Book VI unless otherwise noted.
5. W. F. Jackson Knight, *Cumaean Gates*, in *Vergil: Epic and Anthropology*, London, 1967, 188-201; Mircea Eliade, *Patterns in Comparative Religion*, London, 1958, 381.
6. Brooks Otis, *Virgil: A Study in Civilized Poetry*, Oxford, 1964, 284-5.
7. So Penelope Doob argues, *The Idea of the Labyrinth: from Classical Antiquity through the Middle Ages*, Ithaca, 1990, 30-3, 227-253.
8. Additionally, one cannot exclude a possible incidental reference here to Cleopatra. Virgil avoids direct references to her. In the description of the shield she appears, unnamed, as the *Aegyptia coniunx* (Egyptian wife, VIII.688) for Antony, with the exclamation *nefas* (shame), though this is distanced and could be read as the judgement of Vulcan, Augustus or even Aeneas rather than of Virgil as narrator.
9. *Manu* here can mean 'by hand' but also 'with an effort.' To be consistent with *uolens facilisque* the effort required must not be great, perhaps no more than picking a ripe apple. See also note 11 below.
10. This is not the white North European *viscum album*, but the Mediterranean *loranthus europaeus*, yellow mistletoe. As the golden bough is compared to mistletoe (*talis erat species*), it cannot actually *be* mistletoe.
11. *cunctatem* can also be translated as *resisting*, but this would contradict *ipse uolens facilisque sequetur* (it will come away willingly and easily, 146). Analogues include

Arthur, who pulls the sword out of the stone 'lightly and fiercely,' *Le Morte Darthur*, I. v., Sigmund, who pulls one out from a tree 'as if the sword lay loose for him,' in the *Völsunga-Saga* chapter 3 and Wagner's Siegmund, who does the same in *Die Walküre*, Act I.

12. A. P. IV.1, *Greek Anthology* trans. W. R. Paton, London (Loeb Classical Library), Vol. I, 1916, 114-5. This was pointed out by A. K. Michels in 1945. Austin gives the reference but I take the point from Horsfall's discussion, 153.

13. I take this suggestion not from a Virgil commentary but from an oblique reference in Winthrop Wetherbee, *The Ancient Flame: Dante and the Poets*, Notre Dame, 2008, 36.

14. One might compare the way that the Holy Grail acquires its sense of mystery from the writers who have written of it, not from its probable origin as a dish.

15. *Odyssey* X.287-306.

16. Aristophanes, *Frogs*, 330 and Kerényi, Carl, *Eleusis: Archetypal Symbol of Mother and Daughter*, trans. Ralph Manheim, Princeton, 1967, 64. Jan Bremmer, 'The Golden Bough: Orphic, Eleusinian and Hellenistic Jewish Sources of Virgil's Underworld in *Aeneid* VI', *Kernos* 22, 2009, contends that Aeneas was acting as an Eleusinian initiate.

17. Eliade, *Patterns in Comparative Religion*, 316-9. Additionally, the cult of the Queen of Heaven, which was at one time part of Israelite religion, was associated with a symbolic tree. The menorah represented the tree of life and was made of gold.

18. Maud Bodkin, *Archetypal Patterns in Poetry*, London, 1934, 130.

19. Of course he has already been through some of this in the account of the fall of Troy and his subsequent adventures before reaching Carthage which he recounts to Dido. Otis, *Virgil*, 416, suggests that this replaced an earlier version in which the story is told in the third person by the narrator. This may be so, but his account to Dido is not transformative as are his encounters in Book VI.

20. Dorothy L. Sayers, *Introductory Papers on Dante*, London, 1954, 68. The internal quotation is adapted from Acts 1.25.

21. Sayers, *Letters* Vol, 3, Cambridge, 1998, 276.

22. I appreciate that the theme is traditional: Homer, *Iliad* XXIII.71-4 (Patroclus); *Odyssey* XI.60-78 (Elpenor). The waiting period is derived from Plato, *Republic*, X.615a, where it is a thousand years. Virgil never adopts a topic like this without rethinking its significance in his own context. There is also an apparent contradiction between Palinurus' account here that a god was not responsible for his death and that in V.854-6 where one clearly is, but Palinurus was not aware of this either then or in the underworld.

23. Eliot, *On Poetry and Poets*, 62.

24. This passage is repeated at II.792-4 where Aeneas fleeing Troy encounters the spirit of his wife Creusa. Doubtless in revision Virgil would have modified the wording in one or other place. The motif is taken from Homer, *Odyssey* XI.204-8 though again Virgil transforms its meaning in taking it over. It is taken from here by Dante in the meeting with Casella, *Purgatorio* II.79-81.

25. Dante's use of this line to welcome the arrival of Beatrice and acknowledge the (unstated) departure of his fictional Virgil, *Purgatorio* XXX.21, is one of the most audacious examples of his use of Virgil.

26. Otis, *Virgil*, 303.

27. I take this point from Williams, *Technique and Ideas in the Aeneid*, New Haven, 1983, 48. Nicholas Reed. 'The Gates of Sleep in *Aeneid* VI,' *The Classical Quarterly* Vol. 23, No.; 2 (Nov. 1973), 311-5, argues that Aeneas and the sibyl are false shades and therefore must go through the ivory gate. There is a useful survey of interpretations of this passage by William J. Dominik, 'Reading Vergil's *Aeneid:* The Gates of Sleep (Vi 893-898)', *Maia* New Series, May-August 1996.

28. C. S. Lewis, *A Preface to Paradise Lost*, Oxford, 1942, 37. The whole chapter, 'Virgil and the subject of secondary epic,' is relevant to my argument.

5

ARCADIA AND IDEAL LANDSCAPE IN VIRGIL'S ECLOGUES

To what extent are Arcadia and an ideal landscape really present in the Eclogues? In the middle of the twentieth century this question would have been regarded as settled, thanks primarily to a brilliant essay by Bruno Snell, 'Arcadia: the discovery of a spiritual landscape', which first appeared in 1948. This begins: 'Arcadia was discovered in the year 42 or 41 B.C. ... the land of shepherds and shepherdesses, the land of poetry and love, and its discoverer was Virgil.'[1]

Snell was in fact taking up a suggestion which had been made a few years earlier, in 1936, by the art historian Erwin Panofsky. Panofsky's concern was the use of the Latin motto *Et in Arcadia ego* as the subject of paintings by Guercino, Poussin and others. Before moving to this, his main topic, he sketches in a brief history of the concept of Arcadia in which he says that Virgil idealized the real Arcadia: 'he also added charms which the real Arcady had never possessed: luxuriant vegetation, eternal spring, and inexhaustible leisure for love. In short he transplanted the bucolics of Theocritus to what he decided to call Arcadia ... a bleak and chilly district of Greece came to be transfigured into an imaginary realm of perfect bliss.'[2] In the same year as Snell's essay came a similar statement from Ernst Robert Curtius: 'Pastoral poetry could become a permanent part of the Western tradition only because Virgil took it over from Theocritus and at the same time transformed it. Sicily, long since become a Roman province, was no longer a dreamland. In most of his eclogues Virgil replaces it by romantically faraway Arcadia, which he himself had never visited.'[3] Rosenmeyer, the latest of this group, writing in 1969, is also concerned with the pastoral tradition and says that Virgil 'replaced Theocritus' Sicily and Cos with Arcadia.'[4]

All four works are classic scholarly studies, which have deservedly exercised great influence, and which are still well worth reading. However, we notice that none of the four was primarily a Virgil scholar: Panofsky was an art historian, Snell a Greek scholar—the Arcadia essay is the only one on a Latin topic in his book—as was Rosenmeyer, who was also Snell's translator, and Curtius a medievalist. Incidentally, all four were German. And when Virgilians addressed themselves to the issue they dissented. Putnam has a few dismissive remarks.[5] Alpers ignores the issue.[6] Coleman in his edition notes that Virgil's references to Arcadia are infrequent and that the definitive presentation of Arcadia occurs only in Eclogue 10;[7] Clausen, who also edited the Eclogues said earlier that 'pastoral Arcadia is mainly the invention of Sannazaro and Sir Philip Sidney.'[8] I think he is wrong about Sidney: I shall come back to Sannazaro. Jenkyns surveys supporting and opposing views, comes down against Snell and company and sums up with the words: 'these claims about Virgil's use of Arcadia are simply wrong.'[9] He points to the paucity of actual references to Arcadia in the Eclogues, apart from 10, and declares that the true inventor of the literary Arcadia was Sannazaro.[10]

I want to argue against Jenkyns and defend the older view. I shall argue that all the Eclogues imply a common world and therefore that, since this is Arcadia in Eclogue 10, it is so in all.

But I need to start with Jenkyns' argument about Virgil's actual references to Arcadia in the Eclogues. Apart from Eclogue 10, which is indeed set there, they are indeed few. Let us consider them. So the poet himself thinks he could defeat Pan in singing about the achievements of the wonderful child in Eclogue 4:

Pan etiam, Arcadia mecum si iudice certet,
Pan etiam Arcadia dicat se iudice uictum. (4.58-9)

*Even if Pan were to compete with me with Arcadia as judge, even Pan
would admit himself defeated with Arcadia as judge.*

This is emphatic, as shown by the use of anaphora and the pun on *si*
and *se*: Pan is of course the presiding deity of Arcadia but the poem is
not located there or indeed anywhere; the world (*orbem*, 17, *mundum*,
50) which the wonderful child will come to rule as a man is located in an
indefinite future.

In Eclogue 7 Meliboeus meets Corydon and Thyrsis, described as
Arcades ambo, both Arcadians. Jenkyns argues that his reference means
that the setting cannot be an Arcadia either literal or metaphorical. 'If
some character in a book says "I have just met two Englishmen," we can
be virtually certain that the scene is not laid in England.'[11] He then has
to consider why they are so far from home and has to conclude that 'a
complete answer is not available to us.' This seems clumsily ingenious:
Virgil is a subtle poet but surely here he simply means the equivalent of
'two locals' as opposed to, say, 'two visitors.' Jenkyns also has to deal
with the fact that later in the poem Thyrsis invokes Arcadians in these
words:

pastores, hedera crescentem ornate poetam,
Arcades, inuidia rumpantur ut ilia Codro;
aut, si ultra placitum laudarit, baccare frontem
cingite, ne uati noceat mala lingua futuro. (7.25-9)

*Arcadian shepherds, decorate your increasingly famous poet with ivy, so
that Codrus' sides might burst with envy; or if he should praise me
extremely, wreathe my forehead with foxglove, lest his evil tongue harm
the future bard.*

Admittedly this is part of an amoebaean song contest, one with
alternate rounds of singing, but there seems no reason why Thyris
should not have local shepherds in mind. Jenkyns points out an allusion

to a poem in the Greek Anthology and concludes that here we have an allusion to which we have lost the key. I do not see why we should not take the references in this poem to Arcadians at face value.

We go on to some references to Pan, the presiding deity of the geographical Arcadia. So Corydon in his imagination addresses Alexis:

mecum una in siluis imitabere Pana canendo.
(Pan primum calamos cera coniungere pluris
instituit, Pan curat ouis ouiumque magistros.) (2.32-3)

Together with me in the woods you will imitate Pan in piping. Pan first taught men to join together many reeds with wax; Pan cares for sheep and for the shepherds of the sheep.

But, despite the reference to Pan, Corydon seems to be in Sicily:

mille meas Siculis errant in montibus agnae (2.21)

A thousand lambs of mine roam on the Sicilian hills.

Here Jenkyns appears to be right—unless we could take the argument he himself made about the Arcadians and say that the reference to the Sicilian hills means that we are not or need not be actually in Sicily.

Passing over the mention of Pan in Eclogue 5 for the moment, we come to Eclogue 8, where we have a repeated refrain about Mount Maenalus. This is indeed in Arcadia and associated with Pan, explicitly in these lines:

Maenalus argutumque nemus pinusque loquentis
semper habet, semper pastorum ille audit amores
Panaque, qui primus calamos non passus inertis. (8.22-4)

Maenalus has a grove which is always rustling and pines which are always speaking and he always listens to the loves of shepherds and to Pan, who was the first not to allow the reeds to remain idle.

This is a clear Arcadian reference. And the same is true of the reference in Eclogue 10, which is indeed explicitly set there:

Pan deus Arcadiae uenit, quem uidimus ipsi
sanguineis ebuli bacis minioque rubentem. (10.26-7)

Pan came, the god of Arcadia, whom we ourselves saw, reddening from
the blood-red berries of the dwarf elder and from cinnabar.

So provisionally, it seems that direct references to Arcadia in the Eclogues, apart from Eclogue 10, are few and ambiguous and that both Snell and his companions on the one hand and Jenkyns on the other might have overstated their opposing cases. So I return to my main argument and consider the unity of the poems as a collection. If we are satisfied that they present the same world, the fact that it is only called Arcadia occasionally does not matter.

A few points can be made quickly. We call them the Eclogues, but Virgil's own title seems to have been *Bucolica*, from βουκόλος, a cowherd, which came to be applied to the idylls of Theocritus and so was taken up by Virgil, whose bucolic poems owe a great deal to Theocritus.[12] The alternative title *Eclogae* may derive from the piecemeal publication of the collection, each poem of which was an ἐκλογή or extract from the collection, which was from the first intended as a unified set.

Furthermore there are some marked parallels between the poems: the loss and recovery of a home appear in 1 and 9, the pains and successes of love in 2 and 8; 3 and 7 feature amoebaean dialogues; 4 and 6 both have cosmic scope, one of the future, the other of the past; and 5 and 10 both contain laments.[13]

Then there is Virgil's repeated use of the same names. See the chart in Appendix 2. This list contains some historical figures, such as Pollio, Varus and Gallus, some characters who appear in person, such as Tityrus and Meliboeus, and some who do not, such as Alexis and Alphesiboeus—whose name indeed seems to have been chosen merely to demonstrate Virgil's virtuosity in fitting it into the metre. (It only appears at the end of a line: Ālphĕsĭboēŭs twice, 5.73 and 8.62, and in the genitive ending -boēī twice, 8.1 and 5.) Menalcas is a surrogate for the poet as at the end of Eclogue 5 he claims Eclogues 2 and 3 as his own compositions.

But we must be cautious: the repetition of names does not necessarily mean the repetition of the same characters. In some cases, it seems to, as with Alexis, but in some not necessarily, as with Tityrus. In Eclogue 1 he is a former slave who has managed to retain his right to farm; in Eclogue 6 he seems to be another surrogate for the poet.

Now in arguing that the Eclogues represent a particular world—the idealized Arcadia of Snell—I am not suggesting that they present a consistent or continuous narrative. That was the step which was taken by Sannazaro in the fifteenth century. His *Arcadia*, which is in Italian, unlike his later work which is in Latin, alternates pastoral poems with linking prose narratives. This genre is Menippean satire or *prosimetrum* and it became popular in the medieval period—Boethius' *Consolation of Philosophy* and Dante's *Vita Nuova* are examples—but using it for a continuous narrative which maintains the same characters in a pastoral setting was the distinctive contribution of Sannazaro. This was the origin of the Renaissance use of pastoral, which became enormously popular, and Jenkyns is right to warn us against reading back into Virgil what was in fact a much later convention. But the repeated use of the names does support the view that they come from the same world.

I suggest that an even stronger argument for the unity of the setting comes from Virgil's frequent use of the *locus amoenus*,[14] the pleasant place or ideal landscape. I want to consider some examples in detail. We can start right at the beginning:

Tityre, tu patulae recubans sub tegmine fagi
siluestrem tenui Musam meditaris auena:(1.1-2)

You, Tityrus, lying under the canopy of a spreading beech tree, woo the woodland muse on a slender pipe.

The celebrated opening of the Eclogues immediately presents us with a setting of peace, leisure, a rural setting and a shepherd making music. Meliboeus goes on immediately to contrast this with his own situation, so it is all the more important that the ideal landscape is firmly established first. Virgil does it in two lines. Meliboeus returns to this idyllic setting later:

fortunate senex, hic inter flumina nota
et fontis sacros frigus captabis opacum.
hinc tibi, quae semper, uicino ab limite saepes
Hyblaeis apibus florem depasta salicti
saepe levi somnum suadebit inire susurro;
hinc alta sub rupe canet frondator ad auras:
nec tamen interea raucae, tua cura, palumbes,
nec gemere aëria cessabit turtur ab ulmo. (1.51-8)

Happy old man, here among familiar streams and sacred springs you will find cool shade. On this side, as always, the hedge along your neighbour's border, whose willow thicket blossom has been fed on by Hybla's bees, will often with its gentle buzzing induce you to sleep; on that side, under the lofty rock, the pruner will sing to the heavens; nor yet too will the hoarse wood pigeons, your pets, or the turtle dove cease their cooing from the tops of elm trees.

This more extended passage adds streams, springs, cool shade, bees, various birds and singing. These are all characteristic of the *locus amoenus*. The fact that it is a pruner (*frondator*) who sings suggests that, though work is done, it is done happily. The bees, however, introduce another element: they are from Hybla, which is in Sicily, and their honey was celebrated. Is that where this poem is set? The reference to the land confiscations took us to North Italy. We have to conclude that the poem is set in a parallel world which at times seems like Italy, but here is like Sicily, but in fact is neither.

In Eclogue 3 we have another evocation of landscape:

dicite, quandoquidem in molli consedimus herba.
et nunc omnis ager, nunc omnis parturit arbos,
nunc frondent siluae, nunc formosissimus annus.

incipe, Damoeta; tu deinde sequere, Menalca:
alternis dicetis; amant alterna Camenae. (3.55-9)

Sing on, seeing that we are seated on the soft grass. Now every field, every
tree is budding, now the woods are green, now the year is at its most beau-
tiful. Begin, Damoetas; then you, Menalcas, must follow: you should sing
alternately; the muses like alternate verses.

The season is spring, and the shepherds are going to join in amoebaean verse making, another feature of the *locus amoenus*. The invocation of the Camenae, who were the Roman equivalent of the Greek
Muses, seems to keep us in Italy. Some of the other references in the
poem are Greek, such as Conon the astronomer (40), the other
astronomer, indicated but not named in the same line, who might be
Eudoxus, Orpheus (46), the Muses using Greek terms (84-5), and most
of the named characters; others are Roman: (Jove (60), Pollio (88),
Bavius and Mevius (90). So the world we are in is not exactly Italy and
not exactly Greece either, confirming the impression of a parallel world.

In Eclogue 4 Virgil predicts a new golden age (lines 8-10) and assimi-
lates the *locus amoenus* to this:

at tibi prima, puer, nullo munuscula cultu
errantis hederas passim cum baccare tellus
mixtaque ridenti colocasia fundet acantho,
ipsa tibi blandos fundet cunabula flores.
(4.18-23)[15]

But for you, child, the earth without tilling will pour out its first little
presents, ivy wandering about everywhere with foxglove and the Egyptian
bean blended with smiling acanthus; of itself it will pour out for you a
cradle of smiling flowers.

Similarly a few lines later:

omnis feret omnia tellus.
non rastros patietur humus, non uinea falcem;
robustus quoque iam tauris iuga soluet arator. (4.39-41)

*Every land will bear all things. Earth will not suffer the harrow nor vines
the pruning hook. Then also the sturdy ploughman will loose the yoke
from the oxen.*

The reaction of the natural world to Daphnis in Eclogue 5 is somewhat similar:

ergo alacris siluas et cetera rura uoluptas
Panaque pastoresque tenet Dryadasque puellas,
nec lupus insidias pecori, nec retia ceruis
ulla dolum meditantur: amat bonus otia Daphnis. (5.58-61)

*And so cheerful pleasure absorbs the woods and the rest of the countryside,
along with Pan, the shepherd and the Dryad girls. The wolf does not plan
an ambush for the herd nor nets a snare for the deer: kind Daphnis loves
peace.*

We notice here not only the peaceful wolf but also the presence of
Pan, which could imply an Arcadian setting but this not explicit either
in the Daphnis section or in the frame poem.

I have already mentioned Eclogue 7 because of its reference to
Arcades ambo, but the context of this phrase is another *locus amoenus:*

forte sub arguta consederat ilice Daphnis,
compulerantque greges Corydon et Thyrsis in unum,
Thyrsis ouis, Corydon distentas lacte capellas,
ambo florentes aetatibus, Arcades ambo,
et cantare pares et respondere parati.
huc mihi, dum teneras defendo a frigore myrtos,
uir gregis ipse caper deerrauerat; atque ego Daphnim
adspicio. (7.1-8)

By chance Daphnis had sat down under a rustling holm-oak and Corydon and Thyrsis had driven their flocks together, Thyrsis his sheep and Corydon his nanny goats swollen with milk, both of them in the flower of youth, both Arcadians, equally ready to sing and to reply. To this place, while I sheltered my young myrtles from the frost, my flock's he-goat had wandered and I caught sight of Daphnis.

This is another classic evocation; we notice the harmony between the sheep and the goats, the fact that the latter have milk, that Thyrsis and Corydon are both young—this may not be the Corydon of Eclogue 2—and that the only external threat is from frost and that can be managed.

My next example is the three lines from Eclogue 8 which I have already quoted, since they refer both to Mount Maenalus and to Pan; they also constitute a *locus amoenus*.

In Eclogue 9 Moeris claims to remember the following lines of Menalcas:

'huc ades, o Galatea: quis est nam ludus in undis?
hic uer purpureum, uarios hic flumina circum
fundit humus flores, hic candida populus antro
imminet et lentae texunt umbracula uites:
huc ades; insani feriant sine litora fluctus.' (9.39-43)

Come here, Galatea: for what pleasure there is in waves. Here is a rosy-coloured spring, here the earth pours out varied flowers around the streams, here the white poplar leans over the cave and clinging vines weave shady bowers. Come here; let the wild waves strike the shore without you.

Here we have water, flowers, trees and vines. In the distance there are wild waves but we can leave them alone.

My final example is Gallus sighing for the life in Arcadia which he has rejected:

tristis at ille: 'tamen cantabitis, Arcades' inquit,
'montibus haec uestris; soli cantare periti
Arcades. o mihi tum quam molliter ossa quiescant,
uestra meos olim si fistula dicat amores!
atque utinam ex uobis unus uestrisque fuissem
aut custos gregis aut maturae uinitor uuae!
certe siue mihi Phyllis siue esset Amyntas,
seu quicumque furor (quid tum, si fuscus Amyntas?
et nigrae uiolae sunt et uaccinia nigra),
mecum inter salices lenta sub uite iaceret:
serta mihi Phyllis legeret, cantaret Amyntas.
hic gelidi fontes, hic mollia prata, Lycori;
hic nemus; hic ipso tecum consumerer aeuo. (10.31-43)

But he [Gallus] *said sadly: "Yet you Arcadians will sing of these things in your mountains; Arcadians are experienced only in singing. Oh how softly my bones would then rest if at that time your piper should tell of my love! And oh how I wish I had been one of you, either the guardian of a flock or the vine-dresser of the ripe grape! Surely, whether it were Phyllis or Amyntas or some other person I was crazy about with me—and does it matter if Amyntas is dark? Violets are also black and hyacinths are black —she or he would be lying next to me among the willows under the creeping vine; Phyllis would pick garlands for me, or Amyntas would sing. Here are cool fountains, here are lush meadows, Lycoris, here is woodland; here with you I would be worn away only by time itself.*

This brings together nearly all the features I have mentioned: Arcadians, singing, piping, flocks, grapes, trees, garlands, fountains, meadows, woodland and all dominated by love which in later pastoral is often the primary motive.

I think it will be agreed all these passages show a family resemblance, all evoke a *locus amoenus* and in that way they evoke the same world. This is in fact the most common feature throughout the Eclogues and this, above all, is what serves to bind them together. They do evoke a common world, an idealized landscape and in Eclogue 10 this is called Arcadia. At times it resembles Italy, at times Sicily, at times the geographical Arcadia but at the end of the day it is a country of the mind. So I think Snell and company are vindicated and Jenkyns, to whose argument I may not have done justice, seems to have missed the point.

But we should also notice that these passages are mostly quite short. Part of Virgil's skill is to suggest his ideal landscape but not to weary the reader with extended descriptions. He also constantly contrasts it with other, less attractive settings: the land confiscations in Eclogues 1 and 9 put that issue squarely before us; Eclogue 10 contrasts Arcadia with the harsher places Gallus has chosen to occupy and the other place where Lycoris now is; Eclogue 5 is an elegy for the dead Daphnis. In fact what Virgil conveys is the precariousness of his ideal world, which of course reflects the precariousness of the real world in which he wrote the poems, under the threat of a resumption of the civil war which in fact is what happened. In the same way his shepherds are partly real shepherds with real country tasks, which Virgil understood very well, but they are also surrogate poets and even surrogate politicians from time to time. Here we see the seeds of the later pastoral.

In fact Sannazaro, who was a great Virgilian, did not have to do much to transform the world of the Eclogues into what became Renaissance pastoral. Apart from retaining a continuous cast of characters throughout his *Arcadia*, his other main contribution was to banish or minimize the contrasts with a harsher world which Virgil constantly introduces. This makes for a more consistent but less varied work. Some of his successors took this to extremes, such as Tasso, whose pastoral play *Aminta* is an amazing feat of language since almost nothing happens in it. In contrast, Shakespeare's pastoral plays *As You Like It* and *The Winter's Tale* both introduce strong contrasts to the pastoral settings: a corrupt court and genuine tenant farmers in the former and the jealousy and violence of Leontes in the latter. We learn from these that in literature the idealized landscape is better used in contrast to less ideal settings than simply on its own, but this is a lesson Virgil did not need to learn.

---

1. Bruno Snell, 'Arcadia: the discovery of a spiritual landscape', in *The Discovery of the*

Mind: the Greek Origins of European Thought, New York 1960 (1953), German original 1948; this essay first published 1948, 281.

2. Erwin Panofsky,:'Et in Arcadia Ego: Poussin and the Elegiac tradition' in *Meaning in the Visual Arts*, Harmondsworth 1970 (1955); this essay first published in a slightly different form 1936, 344-5. The two Poussin paintings have since been retitled *The Arcadian Shepherds*.

3. Ernst Robert Curtius, *European Literature and the Latin Middle Ages*, Princeton 1973 (1953), German original 1948, 190.

4. Thomas G. Rosenmeyer, *The Green Cabinet: Theocritus and the European Pastoral Lyric*, Berkeley, 1969, 232.

5. Michael Putnam, *Virgil's Pastoral Art: Studies in the Eclogues*, Princeton 1970, 328.

6. Paul Alpers, *The Singer of the Eclogues: A Study of Virgilian Pastoral*, Berkeley, 1979.

7. Vergil, *Eclogues* ed. Robert Coleman, Cambridge, 1977, 209, 22.

8. Quoted by Richard Jenkyns, *Virgil's Experience: Nature and History, Times, Names and Places*, Oxford 1998, 157. Interestingly, this comment is not repeated in Clausen's edition where he writes more sympathetically about Virgil's choice of Arcadia as a landscape 'remote from experience', Virgil, *Eclogues with an Introduction and Commentary by Wendell Clausen*, Oxford, 1994, 189. The comment about Sidney is true only of the early version, the *Old Arcadia*, not published until the twentieth century; the published version (1590 and reprints) is far more heroic than pastoral.

9. Jenkyns, *Virgil's Experience*, 157. He first advanced this argument in a paper of 1989, 'Virgil and Arcadia', which I have not seen.

10. In this Jenkyns was anticipated by C. S. Lewis, a great Virgilian, whom he does not cite: 'It was Sannazaro, more than anyone else, who ... created one of the great dreams of humanity. To that extent he is a founder', C. S. Lewis, *English Literature in the Sixteenth Century excluding Drama*, Oxford, 1954, 334. Sannazaro's *Arcadia* is available in Jacopo Sannazaro, *Arcadia and Piscatorial Eclogues*, trans. Ralph Nash, Detroit, 1966.

11. Jenkyns, *Virgil's Experience*,162.

12. G. O. Hutchinson, *Hellenistic Poetry*, Oxford, 1988, 144; Coleman, 14-5. The *Vita Vergiliana* of Aelius Donatus refers to the poems as Bucolica, *Vita Donatiana* 19.

13. I have here adapted the schema set out by Brooks Otis,*Virgil: A Study in Civilized Poetry*, Oxford, 1964, 129ff..

14. This term is medieval and was established in modern critical vocabulary by Curtius, 195-200, but, as he points out, the trope goes back to Theocritus and Virgil.

15. Accepting, with Snell, Clausen and Goold, Klouček's transfer of 23 to follow 20 and Campbell's *fundet*.

6

CAN THE CHRISTIAN
INTERPRETATION OF VIRGIL'S
FOURTH ECLOGUE BE REVIVED?

*I*n the year 324 A. D. or thereabouts the emperor Constantine made a speech about the Christian faith, preserved by the historian Eusebius as an appendix to his life of the emperor.[1] In it, he offers as evidence of the truth of Christianity that it was predicted 'plainly and yet at the same time darkly' by the poet Virgil, whom he salutes as 'Maro, wisest of the poets.' He goes on to quote and interpret several passages from the fourth eclogue. The key one is this:

> Ultima Cumaei uenit iam carminis aetas;
> magnus ab integro saeclorum nascitur ordo.
> iam redit et uirgo, redeunt Saturnia regna,
> iam noua progenies caelo demittitur alto.
> tu modo nascenti puero, quo ferrea primum
> desinet ac toto surget gens aurea mundo,
> casta faue Lucina; tuus iam regnat Apollo. (4-10)

> *Now the last age of Cumaean prophecy has come; the great line of the ages is being born anew. Now the Virgin returns, the kingdom of Saturn returns, now a new race descends from heaven above. Only, chaste Lucina, smile benevolently on the newborn boy, at whose coming the iron race will*

cease and a golden one will spring up throughout the whole world; your own Apollo now reigns.

As Constantine expounds it, the Cumaean sibyl is a prophet, the virgin is the virgin Mary and the wonderful child sent from the sky is Jesus. He will be worshipped and will bring a new golden age of peace and plenty. Meanwhile:

occidet et serpens, et fallax herba ueneni
occidet; Assyrium uulgo nascetur amomum. (24-5)

The serpent will also die and the deceitful herb which hides its poison; Syrian spice will spring up everywhere.

The serpent is the one who deceived Adam and Eve, and the spice is the community of Christians. The pagan references, says Constantine, are sops to contemporary Roman understanding. Such is his reading. He was not the first person to see in Virgil's poem a prophecy of Christ; he was merely taking up a line of thinking which had been developed by the Church Fathers Lactantius (VII.24) and Augustine (various places, notably *de civ. Dei* X.28). There are some variations: Lactantius thought the promise related not to the birth of Jesus but to his return; Augustine that the poem foretold the remission of sins, in a passage I shall quote later.[2] But the characteristics of the Christian interpretation are, I suggest, that the Cumaean sibyl is a true prophet, the virgin is the Virgin Mary, the wonderful child is Jesus, that he will bring about a new golden age, that the serpent which tempted Eve will be destroyed and that Virgil through writing this poem was himself also a true prophet, though in some accounts without knowing it. Not all these features are essential.

Constantine's position as emperor assisted the acceptance of the Christian interpretation, which became standard throughout the medieval period. Two examples will suffice. In Canto XXII of the *Purgatorio*, Statius says to Virgil:

Facesti come quei che va di notte,
  che porta il lume dietro e sé non giova,
  ma dopo sé fa le persone dotte,
quando dicesti: 'Secol si rinova;
  torna giustizia e primo tempo umano,
  e progenïe scenda da ciel nova.'
Per te poeta fui, per te cristiano. *(Purgatorio*, XXII.67-73)

You were like one who goes by night and carries the light behind him and
profits not himself, but makes those wise who follow him, when you said,
'The ages are renewed; Justice returns and the first age of man, and a new
progeny descends from heaven.' Through you I was a poet, through you a
Christian. (Trans. Singleton)

Dante is well aware that Virgil's *Virgo* is not the Virgin Mary but Astraea or Justice[3] but accepts the idea of the new golden age, the identification of the *progenies* with Jesus and, with them, the role of the historical Virgil as a prophet who prophesied more wisely than he knew. Indeed, Virgil was commonly enrolled among the prophets, for example at Limoges and Rheims.[4]

My second example is the mosaic of the Cumaean sibyl on the pavement of Siena cathedral. She comes directly from Virgil, and the key passage is shown beside her.[5] I shall return to sibyls shortly.

The Christian interpretation was never without its detractors, such as Jerome, who thought it childish (*puerilia*)[6] but it was broadly accepted throughout the medieval period. After the Reformation it faded from view, without ever being formally refuted or abandoned. However, it continued to be revived occasionally up to the early twentieth century.[7] Now it is treated, for example by Coleman and Clausen in the two current standard editions of the Eclogues, as a historical curiosity, a piece of cultural history rather than a practical option for modern readers. My aim in this paper is to consider whether it can be revived.

However, we need to begin by setting the poem in its original context.[8] Virgil fixes this clearly by saying that it is during the consulship of Pollio (*te consule .../ Pollio*, 11-2), which was in 40 B.C. The occasion was the Pact of Brundisium, which made peace between Antonius—Mark Antony in English—and Octavianus—the future emperor Augustus, but then very much the junior partner. It seemed to people then that civil war had been ended and they could hope for the future. And the peace was cemented by the marriage of Antony to Octavian's sister, Octavia.[9]

With this in mind we can reconstruct the understanding the poem would have been given by its first audience. We begin with the Cumaean sibyl and the new age:

Ultima Cumaei uenit iam carminis aetas;
magnus ab integro saeclorum nascitur ordo. (4-5)

Now the last age of Cumaean prophecy has come; the great line of the ages is being born anew.

Cumae is near Naples and was originally a Greek colony—*Cumaei*, a Graecism, instead of normal Latin *Cumanus* is a tribute to this—and this sibyl is connected with the famous Sybilline books. This particular prophecy is otherwise unknown. Virgil might have invented it together with its oracular tone—notice the rhymes in 'o.' The official collection could be consulted only by order of the senate and so was presumably not available to him. Various collections of Sibylline prophecies were in circulation and some have survived. They are a farrago of material from diverse sources: pagan, Jewish, Christian and others. The extant collection is thought to be a compilation of material of different dates. Some is clearly post-Christian; this, however, may be earlier:[10]

Rejoice, maiden, and be glad, for to you the one who created heaven and earth has given the joy of the age. He will dwell in you. You will have immortal light. Wolves and lambs will eat grass together in the mountains. Leopards will feed together with kids. Roving bears will spend the night with calves. The flesh-eating lion will eat husks at the manger like an ox, and mere infant children will lead them with ropes. For he will make the beasts on earth harmless. Serpents and asps will sleep with

babies and will not harm them, for the hand of God will be upon them.
(*Sybilline Oracles* III.785-95)[11]

This could be an expanded imitation of the famous passage in Isaiah which I shall quote later or it might be independent. It became known to Christians through its quotation by Lactantius, VII.24. This or similar material was presumably in circulation in Virgil's time. Indeed there have been persistent suggestions of a current of influence from Jewish sources to Virgil. He would have known of such things as the Sibylline oracles; he might have known the Septuagint and so Isaiah's prophecy at first hand, and he could have had first hand acquaintance with Jews, particularly if the Pollio who was host to Herod's sons[12] was indeed the Pollio of our poem. There was a Jewish community in Rome from 63 B. C., when Pompey captured Jerusalem and sent Jews as slaves to Rome, and there were strong trade links between Rome and both Alexandria, where the Septuagint was translated, and Jerusalem.[13]

The sibyls were made acceptable to Christians by Lactantius (I.6), who listed them as ten and quoted Sybilline passages, presumably of Jewish origin, affirming one true God. Thereafter they were accepted as prophets, each credited with having predicted one event in Jesus' life and represented in various works of art;[14] as well as the pavement in Siena cathedral which shows the ten of Lactantius, Filippino Lippo included four in his fresco cycle in Santa Maria sopra Minerva in Rome, and Michelangelo five in the Sistine chapel ceiling. So Virgil's implicit ascription of the prophecy to the Cumaean sibyl also told in favour of the Christian interpretation.

The other reference in the line is to the concept of the Great Year, or cosmic cycle, after which the world is remade and repeats its history,[15] an idea Virgil returns to later in the poem:

> alter erit tum Tiphys et altera quae uehat Argo
> delectos heroas; erunt etiam altera bella
> atque iterum ad Troiam magnus mittetur Achilles. (34-6)

Then there will be a second Tiphys and a second Argo to carry chosen heroes; there will be other wars and great Achilles will again be sent to Troy.

However, Virgil is only playing with the idea:[16] he omits the inundation and conflagration at the turn of one cycle to the next and that the cycle would presumably repeat again. What is at hand is a new golden race and this is —at this point of the poem—envisaged as unceasing:

te duce, so qua manent sceleris uestigia nostri,
inrita perpetua soluent formidine terras. (13-4)

Under your leadership, any remaining traces of our sin will become void and release the earth from its continuing dread.

These are the lines which Augustine referred to the remission of sin, though Virgil was surely anticipating the end of the civil war.[17]

The Virgin in the next line, as I have noted, was, both for the first audience and for Dante, Astraea, the virgin patron of Justice, whose departure from the earth marked the transition from the silver to the bronze race and who became the constellation we still know as Virgo. This constellation rises in early October, which is just after the time some think the Pact of Brundisium was made. The story comes from Aratus (96-136) and Virgil assumes rather than expounds it. This leaves the way open for the Christian identification of the Virgin as the Virgin Mary, particularly since in the next few lines we come to the birth of a child. Virgil's original meaning was, however, that Astraea, Justice, had been in exile because of crime, specifically the civil war.[18]

Representations of a goddess—whether a virgin or not—with a child go back well before Christianity, with that of Isis and Horus being one of the best known. Isis had a considerable cult at Rome. In fact it was to be some time before the comparable Christian treatment of the subject emerged.[19]

At this point we have to notice the possibility of assimilating Virgil's account to the celebrated prophecy of Isaiah. Here is a translation of the Septuagint version:

Therefore the Lord himself will give you a sign: look, the virgin shall be with child and bear a son, and shall name him Emmanouel. (Esaias (Isaiah) VII.14 Septuagint; Emmanouel: Hebrew for God is with us)[20]

This might have been known to Virgil. Note that the Greek has 'the virgin', rather than 'a virgin' as in the King James and some other English versions. Who Isaiah had in mind as the child—possibly Hezekiah, son of the wicked king Ahaz to whom the prophecy was addressed—is actually not relevant to our discussion. For us, what matters is the quotation of this passage in Mathew's gospel as a prophecy of Jesus (Matt. 1.23). And at this point there are two large issues which I note only to pass them by. The first is whether the word *virgin* (παρθένος in the Greek) is an accurate rendering of the Hebrew original. The problem here is that the standard Masoretic text of the Hebrew Bible is later than both Virgil and Christianity and it is possible that the Septuagint version of Isaiah was a correct translation of the original which was later altered to contradict the Christian interpretation of it as a prophecy of Christ. The argument over this began at least as early as Justin Martyr's *Dialogue with Trypho* in the second century and is not over yet.[21] The second issue is whether prophecies, such as that of Isaiah or indeed that of Virgil, are correctly understood as predictions of the future. In the ancient world they certainly were; the modern understanding of prophecy is rather different. However, the relation between Isaiah's prophecy and the birth of Jesus is better understood as an example of typology: I shall come to this later.

The birth of the child is associated with a new golden race:

tu modo nascenti puero, quo ferrea primum
desinet ac toto surget gens aurea mundo,
casta faue Lucina: tuus iam regnat Apollo. (8-10)

Only, chaste Lucina, smile benevolently on the newborn boy, at whose coming the iron race will cease and a golden one will spring up throughout the whole world; your own Apollo now reigns.

Virgil here follows Hesiod (*Works and Days* 106-201) quite closely, since he wrote of metallic races, not ages. We might note here another possible Jewish influence or at least an analogue here:[22] in the Biblical book of Daniel, which was probably written in the second century B. C. and is the latest book in the Hebrew Bible, Nebuchadnezzar has a dream of a statue with a gold head, silver chest and arms, bronze middle and thighs, iron legs and feet of iron and clay. Daniel interprets this dream as showing successive kingdoms (Daniel 2.31-45). But the return of the golden race represents a combination of Hesiod with the Stoic Great Year and is apparently new with Virgil.[23]

The growth of the child is recounted in three stages. In his infancy plants cooperate to decorate the boy's cradle, there is fertility and harmony among animals, the serpent perishes and spice becomes readily available:

At tibi prima, puer, nullo munuscula cultu
errantis hederas passim cum baccare tellus
mixtaque ridenti colocasia fundet acantho.
ipsa tibi blandos fundet cunabula flores.
ipsae lacte domum referent distenta capellae
ubera, nec magnos metuent armenta leones.
occidet et serpens et fallax herba ueneni
occidet; Assyrium uulgo nascetur amomum.
(18-25)[24]

But for you, child, the earth without tilling will pour out its first little presents, ivy wandering about everywhere with foxglove and the Egyptian bean blended with smiling acanthus; of itself it will pour out for you a cradle of smiling flowers. Nanny goats will bring home unbidden their udders swollen with milk, and the herds of cattle will not fear great lions. The snake will also die and the deceitful herb which hides its poison; Syrian spice will spring up everywhere.

The plants are among the few pastoral touches in this poem. These ones are more characteristic of the Near East than of Italy, as are the lions—whose range in the Near East at one time reached Greece, though not Italy, and are frequently mentioned in the Old Testament. The spontaneous fertility of the soil comes from Hesiod:

They had all good things: the grain-giving field bore crops of its own accord, much and unstinting, and they themselves, willing, mild-mannered, shared out the fruits of their labours together with many good things, wealthy in sheep, dear to the blessed gods. (Works and Days 116-120)[25]

But the harmony of the animals and the crushing of the snake have closer parallels in the famous passage of Isaiah, with which this of Virgil is often compared; again I quote a direct translation of the Septuagint:

And the wolf shall graze with the lamb, and the leopard shall rest with the kid, and the calf and bull and the lion shall graze together, and a little child shall lead them. And the ox and the bear shall graze together, and their young shall be together, and together shall the lion and the ox eat husks. And the young child shall put its hand over the hole of asps and on the lair of the offspring of asps. (Esaias (Isaiah) 11.6-8)

Virgil is in fact closer to this than to Hesiod, which strengthens the argument that he had access to the Septuagint although he might have drawn on an intermediary text such as the one from the Sbylline oracles quoted earlier.

In the boy's youth the golden race has quietly become the golden age, whose characteristics are intensified as crops ripen towards harvest:

at simul heroum laudes et facta parentis
iam legere et quae sit poteris cognoscere uirtus,
molli paulatim flauescet campus arista
incultisque rubens pendebit sentibus uua
et durae quercus sudabunt roscida mella. (26-30)

But as soon as you can read of the glories of heroes and the heroic actions of your fathers, and can understand what courage is, the field will gradu-

ally glow yellow with waving corn, the reddening grape will hang from wild brambles, and hard oaks will drip dewy honey.

Before moving to signs associated with the boy's maturity Virgil follows Hesiod in inserting a passage on heroes. This is not linked with the golden or any other metallic age, but does suggest the iron age. I quoted it earlier. But he sees the heroes as reflecting *pauca ... priscae uestigia fraudis* ('a few traces of ancient deceit,' 31—it is almost too tempting to translate this as 'traces of original sin' as Augustine seems to have understood it). Since he had stressed that the new age was already beginning (*iam ... iam*, 7-8) this was a wise precaution, as in fact the Pact of Brundisium proved to be merely a truce and the civil war did not finally finish until Actium nine years later. Alternatively we could accept Putnam's suggestion[26] that the life of heroism will be part of the future life of the child since there is a place for heroic achievement in the Roman ideal. We could add that the examples of heroic achievement (Tiphys, helmsman of the Argo, and Achilles) represent respectively a foreign adventure and a foreign war—and by implication clearly not a civil war. However, Virgil does not actually make this suggestion explicitly and, possibly for that reason, it plays no part in the Christian interpretation.

In the child's maturity the fertility of the earth extends so that trading becomes unnecessary, ploughing and pruning become redundant as will—a very curious idea—dyeing.

hinc, ubi iam firmata uirum te fecerit aetas,
cedet et ipse mari uector, nec nautica pinus
mutabit merces; omnis feret omnia tellus.
non rastros patietur humus, non vinea falcem;
robustus quoque iam tauris iuga soluet arator.
nec uarios discet mentiri lana colores,
ipse sed in pratis aries iam suaue rubenti
murice, iam croceo mutabit uellera luto;
sponte sua sandyx pascentis uestiet agnos. (37-45)

After this, when time has given you the strength of manhood, even the merchant will leave the sea and the pine ship will not exchange merchandise; every land will bear all things. Earth will not suffer the harrow nor vines the pruning hook. Then also the sturdy ploughman will loose the yoke from the oxen, nor will wool learn to lie in varied colours, but of his own accord the ram in the fields will change his fleece, now to sweetly blushing purple, now to a saffron-coloured yellow; red will clothe the grazing lambs spontaneously.

The really interesting feature here is the way Virgil represents the new golden age as developing gradually. In Hesiod the golden race enjoys the fertility of the earth and their other comforts all at once: there is no progressive development. There is nothing comparable in the treatment of the golden age by Horace (Epode 16—a poem whose relationship with our eclogue is close but disputed) and by Ovid (*Metamorphoses* I.89-112).

Following this Virgil adds in the fact that the child, who has up to this point been a normal child though a wonderful one, is also in some sense divine. He addresses him as:

cārā dĕ | ūm sŭbŏ | lēs, ‖ māg | nūm Iŏuĭs | īncrē | mēntūm! (49)

dear offshoot of the gods, promise of a Jove to be.

I have scanned the line to show the spondaic fifth foot, and this, together with the alliteration on 'm', gives great weight to the last word. This word Servius considered rather humble, and there is some doubt about its exact meaning here: is it 'a mighty addition to Jupiter', i.e. his offspring, or 'that which will grow into a second Jupiter'? The line is in fact borrowed either from or by the *Ciris* in the *Appendix Vergiliana*:

cara Iouis suboles, magnum Iouis incrementum
(*Ciris* 398)

dear offspring of Jupiter, promise of a Jove to be.

I am among those who think that Virgil was the borrower, and a neat explanation of his doing so comes in the suggestion that the *Ciris* is actually by Cornelius Gallus, whom we know from Eclogues 6 and 10 Virgil both knew and admired.[27] Servius says he borrowed from Gallus in Eclogue 10. However, the attribution is far from certain and Virgil tends to adapt rather than simply borrow lines so the borrowing could be from him rather than by him. Whichever way round it is, his version is surely superior, avoiding the repetition of *Iouis*. In fact the idea that a human child could be the son of a god, or have both a divine and a human father was a common one: Alexander the Great was the son of Philip of Macedon and Olympias but was said also by the oracle of Amun to be also the son of Zeus; Heracles was the son of Zeus in the form of Amphitryon.[28] The term 'son of god' could refer to a divine being or to someone such as a human king, who had been divinely favoured. This usage is common both to classical myth and legend, to the Pharaoh and also to the Old Testament divine court and the Israelite kings. It was also a commonplace that each person's *genius* was divine. Believers are 'children of God' in both the Old and New Testaments; the idea that Jesus was in some sense a son of God is mentioned many times in the New Testament. This language long predates the formal Christian definition of Christ as 'begotten from the Father, only-begotten from the substance of the Father'[29] as agreed at the council of Nicaea in 325 A.D., though Constantine, who actually convened the council, might well have seen this as equivalent to the New Testament usage, as indeed do many Christians both then and now.

The identity of the child is a famous conundrum. Clearly, he has to be a boy. Putting the identification with Jesus on one side for the moment, we should note some of the other candidates.

I.   Given the importance of Pollio in the poem, could it be a son of his? Two are mentioned by Servius. Of Saloninus, we have only the name. The other, Asinius Gallus, apparently claimed to be the child in question. This suggests that the matter was already disputed. The poem says nothing about the child's paternity and his claim has no other merit. Dr Johnson assumed this was the correct identification and commented tartly: 'that the golden age should return because Pollio had a son, appears so wild a fiction, that I am ready to suspect the poet of having written, for some other purpose, what he took this opportunity of producing to the publick.'[30]

II.   An expected child of Mark Antony and Octavia. Antony's children by Cleopatra would clearly have been ineligible to Romans. Antony claimed descent from Hercules and Clausen supports this identification by pointing to several reference to Hercules in the poem. In fact Antony and Octavia did in time have two daughters but no son.

III.   A child of Octavian and Scribonia. She did bear a daughter to him, the elder Julia, whereupon Octavian divorced her. But Octavian was very much the junior partner at this time and Pollio was a partisan of Antony not Octavian so this seems unlikely.

IV.   The son of Octavia and Marcellus, Marcus Claudius Marcellus, who had been born in 42 B.C. and was later adopted by Octavian, then Augustus, as his heir. He died young as is mentioned in a famous passage in *Aeneid* VI (860-92). But a reference to him in the terms of the poem in the year 40 B. C. would have been wildly inappropriate.

It seems impertinent to suggest this, but what the commentators seem curiously reluctant to consider[31] was that Virgil was deliberately hedging his bets. He thought some child would be born who would come to dominate the Roman world though he couldn't at this stage be sure who it would be. If you had come to him with any of these specific candidates he would surely have smiled and murmured: *Bene est si tu ita putas* (Well might you think so) and kept his counsel. But later, long after Actium, when the outcome had been decided, he knew who was the right person to celebrate:

hic uir, hic est, tibi quem promitti saepius audis,
Augustus Caesar, diui genus, aurea condet
saecula qui rursus Latio regnata per arua
Saturno quondam ... (*Aeneid* VI.792-4)

Here is the man—this is he—whom you so often hear promised, Augustus Caesar, son of a god, who will again establish a golden age in Latium among fields once ruled by Saturn ...

In effect he pretends that Augustus, the renamed Octavian, was the marvellous child all along. The *Eclogues* had already been published so it was too late to change the wording there. However, again we have a human being who is treated as not, or not only, the son of his birth father but also of a god; Augustus' adoptive father Iulius had been deified in 42 B.C., whereupon he adopted the title *Diui filius*.[32]

So much for the poem's original context and the intentions of the author. But origins are not meaning and there is a long tradition of understanding that the original author may not fully understand his own meaning and may not be its best interpreter. The locus classicus of this in the ancient world is the speech of Socrates to the rhapsode Ion. It is too long to quote in full, but here are some key passages:

> The Muse ... first makes men inspired, and then through these inspired ones others share in their enthusiasm, and a chain is formed, for the epic poets, all the good ones, have their excellence not from art, but are inspired, possessed, and thus they utter all these admirable poems ... A poet is a light and winged thing, and holy, and never able to compose until he has become inspired, and is beside himself and reason is no longer in him ... Herein lies the reason why the deity has bereft them of their senses and uses them as ministers, along with soothsayers and godly seers; it is in order that we listeners may know that it is not they who utter these precious revelations while their mind is not within them, but that it is the god himself who speaks, and through them becomes articulate to us... . The poets are nothing but interpreters of the gods, each one possessed by the divinity to whom he is in bondage. (Ion 533e-534e)[33]

Socrates and Ion were both speaking particularly of Homer, and an allegorical tradition of interpreting Homer developed and held sway for centuries.[34]

A similar allegorical tradition also developed in respect both of the Jewish and also of the Christian Bible, with Origen and Augustine being prominent in the latter. A common feature of these allegorical interpretations is that the historical or literal meaning becomes secondary to the allegorical one. In Christianity this led to typology, a particular kind of allegory whereby events (not predictions) in the Old

Testament were considered to prefigure events, characteristically in Jesus' life, in the New. Eventually this led to the fourfold interpretation of scripture, of which a convenient example is provided by Dante in discussing his *Commedia*:

> To elucidate, then, what we have to say, be it known that the sense of this work is not simple. But on the contrary it may be called polysemous, that is to say 'of more senses than one'; for it is one sense which we get through the thing the letter signifies; and the first is called literal, but the second allegorical or mystic. And this mode of treatment, for its better manifestation, may be considered in this verse: 'When Israel came out of Egypt, and the house of Jacob from a people of strange speech, Judaea became his sanctification, Israel his power.' For if we inspect the letter alone the departure of the children of Israel from Egypt in the time of Moses is presented to us; if the allegory, our redemption wrought by Christ; if the moral sense, the conversion of the soul from the grief and misery of sin to the state of grace is presented to us; if the anagogical, the departure of the holy soul from the slavery of this corruption to the liberty of eternal glory is presented to us. And although these mystic senses have each their special denominations, they may all in general be called allegorical, since they differ from the literal and historical.[35]

Dante's application of a technique for reading the Bible to his own secular writing is worth noting. With this in mind and considering first the prophecy in Isaiah, we can see that, whatever child the writer might have had in mind, the passage in its Septuagint version works typologically as a foretelling of the birth of Jesus from a virgin.

Allegorizing declined after the Reformation, since the Protestant reformers put the emphasis in Biblical interpretation on the literal sense. Similarly commentators on literary texts look nowadays for the sense they would have had for their author and first audience, as indeed I have been doing for most of this paper. But in fact there is a modern way to open the door to the allegorical approach, one which has developed in connection with the interpretation of ordinary secular writings rather than sacred ones. This is the notion of the intentional fallacy, propounded by W. K. Wimsatt in an influential article with this title. Wimsatt suggested that 'the design or intention of the author is neither available nor desirable as a standard for judging the success of a work of literary art.'[36] This is not quite the same thing as saying that the intention of the author is not available for judging the *meaning* of the work but it is very close, and Wimsatt goes on to discuss some doubtful cases and also to quote part of the same passage of the *Ion* which I quoted earlier. Or to put the same point more crisply in the celebrated words of D. H. Lawrence: 'The artist usually sets out—or used to—to point a moral or adorn a tale. The tale, however, points the other way, as a rule. Two blankly opposing morals, the artist's and the tale's. Never trust the artist. Trust the tale. The proper function of a critic is to save the tale from the artist who created it.'[37]

With this in mind let us try the experiment of reading the fourth eclogue with the Christian interpretation. Forget the contextual interpretation which I have been at some pains to expound. Forget Pollio, the goddess Astraea, the Pact of Brundisium, the dynastic marriages of warlords, speculation about their children and the Roman civil war. These are, after all, all things we bring *to* the poem: of them only Pollio and an unidentified Virgin are truly there *in* the poem. In fact the poem can easily sustain the Christian interpretation: of the key characteristics, the prophecy of the sibyl, the Virgin and the death of the serpent work perfectly well. Of the other two, the wonderful child and the new golden age, I would contend that the Christian interpretation actually makes better sense and a better poem than the contextual one. Jesus fits the description of the wonderful child a good deal better than any of the other candidates proposed. And then, Virgil's gradually developing golden age, so different from that of Hesiod before him, Horace at about the same time or Ovid after him, is an excellent analogue for Jesus' teaching about the kingdom of God. This is both 'already' (e.g. Matt. 12.28; Luke 17.20-1) and also 'not yet' (e.g. Luke 19.11), if we accept the interpretation known in theology as inaugurated eschatology. This then allows for the fact that, despite the new age having started, wars and rumours of wars can still happen, as Virgil rightly says. I acknowledge that this last suggestion is not part of the traditional Christian interpretation, as far as I know, but it fits with it.

Abstracting still further we can see that Virgil's poem, Isaiah's prophecy and the accounts of the Nativity in the gospels of Matthew and Luke are all examples of the common motif in mythology and folklore known as the miraculous birth of the culture hero.[38] The analysis by Lord Raglan has not been superseded: he distinguishes 22 characteristics of the life of the mythological hero, not all of which are of course present in every case. The first five and tenth are relevant to our birth stories:

1. The hero's mother is a royal virgin;
2. His father is a king, and
3. Often a near relative of his mother, but
4. The circumstances of his conception are unusual, and
5. He is also reputed to be the son of a god.
10. On reaching manhood he returns or goes to his future kingdom.[39]

Virgil's child satisfies points 4, 5 and 10 and, on the Christian interpretation, 1 as well partly. Isaiah's child satisfies points 1, 2, 4, 5 and 10. Jesus satisfies points 1, 2 by descent, 4, 5 and 10. (Raglan's type example who satisfies all the points is Oedipus.) And the eclogue takes its place in the genre of panegyrical odes to a human representative of deity, of which the *Carmen Saeculare* of Horace is another example.[40]

Northrop Frye provides an apposite summary:

> The interpretation of Virgil's Fourth Eclogue as Messianic ... assumed that Virgil was "unconsciously" prophesying the Messiah. But the poet unconsciously meant the whole corpus of his possible commentary, and it is simpler merely to say that Virgil and Isaiah use the same type of imagery dealing with the myth of the hero's birth, and that because of this similarity the Nativity Ode, for instance, is able to use both.[41]

We can now answer the question I put at the beginning. If Christians are prepared to look beyond the typology which sees only events in the Old Testament as foreshadowing those in the New to a common set of archetypal or mythological motifs which are exemplified not only in the Bible but also in non-Biblical mythology, then Virgil's poem can take its place as part of the *praeparatio evangelica*. And this is enough to rehabilitate the Christian interpretation of the poem.

---

1. Constantine, *Oration to the Assembly of the Saints*. In *Nicene and Post-Nicene Fathers*, Second Series, Vol. 1. Edited by Philip Schaff and Henry Wace, Buffalo, NY: Christian Literature Publishing Co., 1890.

2. There is a useful summary of this process in Sabine MacCormack, *The Shadows of Poetry: Vergil in the Mind of Augustine*, Berkeley and Los Angeles, 1998, 22-34.

3. This is explicit in *Monarchia* I. xi.1: *'Virgo' nanque vocabatur iustitia, quam etiam 'Astream' vocabant ;* For 'the virgin' was their name for justice, whom they also called 'Astraea', *Monarchia* ed. and trans. Prue Shaw, Cambridge, 1995, 22-3.

4. Domenico Comparetti, *Vergil in the middle ages*, trans. E. F. M. Benecke, London 1966 (1908²), 310-11.

5. See Bruno Santi, *The Marble Pavement of the Cathedral of Siena*, Florence, 1982.

6. Jerome, Letter 53.7, *Letters* trans. W. H. Fremantle, G. Lewis and W. G. Martley, Buffalo, 1893.

7. See Joseph B. Mayor *et al.*, *Virgil's Messianic Eclogue: its meaning, occasion and sources*, London, 1907 and T. F. Royds, *Virgil and Isaiah: A Study of the Pollio*, Oxford, 1918.

8. Most of my discussion of this is based on the current standard commentaries of Coleman and Clausen, to which I do not give detailed references. Nisbet, 'Virgil's Fourth Eclogue: Easterners and Westerners' in Katharina Volk (ed.), *Virgil's Eclogues*, Oxford, 2008, is a fascinating study in sources and parallels; a possible weakness in his approach is that he is very reluctant to consider that Virgil could have branched out on his own and not followed an earlier model.

9. For this I have relied on Ronald Syme, *The Roman Revolution*, Oxford, 1967 (1939), 217-20.

10. J. J. Collins: 'Sibylline Oracles', 355, dates this book to 163-45 B.C.. See next note.

11. *Sibylline Oracles* ed. J. J. Collins in James Charlesworth (ed.), *The Old Testament Pseudepigrapha*, New York, 1981, I.317-472.

12. Josephus, *Antiquities*, XV.10 (343).

13. Martin Goodman, *Rome and Jerusalem: the Clash of Ancient Civilizations*, London, 2007, 57, 92-103, 385ff..

14. Further examples in Émile Mâle, *The Gothic Image*, London, 1961 (1913), 336-340 and Diane Apostolos-Cappadona, *Dictionary of Christian art*, Cambridge, 1994, s.v. sibyl.

15. The idea of the Great Year goes back to Heraclitus and Plato; in this form it is Stoic, see S. Sambursky: *Physics of the Stoics*, London, 1987 (1959) 106, with references and citations.

16. Nisbet, 'Virgil's Fourth *Eclogue*', 159-60, points out various inconsistencies.

17. Gordon Williams, 'A version of Pastoral', in Tony Woodman and David West (eds.), *Quality and Pleasure in Roman Poetry*, Cambridge, 1974, 36.

18. Michael Putnam, *Virgil's Pastoral Art: Studies in the Eclogues*, Princeton, 1970, 140.

19. Geri Parlby: 'The origins of Marian Art', in Sarah Jane Boss (ed.) *Mary: the complete resource*, Oxford, 2007, see particularly 111.

20. *A New English Translation of the Septuagint* ed. Albert Pietersma and Benjamin G. Wright, New York, 2007.

21. This account is necessarily very compressed. For a full discussion see Raymond E. Brown, *The Birth of the Messiah*, New York, 1993, 145ff.. Brown also offers a study of the fourth eclogue from the point of view of a Biblical scholar in Appendix IX of his book.

22. I owe this point to M. L. West's edition of *Works and Days*, Oxford, 1978, 172-7.

23. Nisbet: 'Virgil's Fourth *Eclogue*', 161.

24. Accepting, with Goold, Klouček's transposition of 23 and Campbell's *fundet* in 20.

25. Hesiod, *Theogony, Works and Days, Testimonia*, ed. and trans. Glenn W. Most, Harvard(LCL), 2006.

26. Putnam, *Virgil's Pastoral art*, 152.

27. This is an old theory, expounded and defended by Marjorie Crump, *The epyllion from Theocritus to Ovid*, London, 1997 (1931), 154-6. R. O. A. M. Lyne argues for a late date in his edition of the *Ciris*, Cambridge, 1978, 54, but Goold in his revision of the Loeb Virgil, Harvard, 1999, II, 377, considers this impossible because of its echoes of Catullus 64 which dropped out of common knowledge.

28. These examples from A. D. Nock, *Conversion: the Old and the New in Religion from Alexander the Great to Augustine of Hippo*, Oxford, 1965 (1933), 232-3.

29. The original wording of the Nicene Creed, J. N. D. Kelly, *Early Christian Doctrines*, London, 1977[5], 232.

30. Samuel Johnson, *The Adventurer* No. 92.

31. Gordon Williams is an exception: *Tradition and Originality in Roman Poetry*, Oxford, 1968, 283 and 'A version of Pastoral', 45, where he suggests that Virgil is thinking of both II and III.

32. Syme, *The Roman Revolution*, 202.

33. Plato, *The Collected Dialogues*, ed. Edith Hamilton and Huntington Cairns, New York, 1963. *Ion* trans. Lane Cooper.

34. Robert Lamberton, *Homer the theologian*, London, 1986, is a good exposition of this.

35. Dante, *Epistola* X, §7 in *Latin Works* trans. Philip Wicksteed, London, 1904, 347-8. The psalm quoted is 113 in the Vulgate, 114 in English versions. For the Latin see *Dantis Alagherii Epistolae* ed. Paget Toynbee, Oxford 1966 (1920), 173-4.

36. W. K. Wimsatt, *The Verbal Icon*, Kentucky, 1954, 3.

37. *Studies in Classic American Literature*, London 1937 (1923), 2.

38. Stith Thompson, *Motif-Index of Folk-Literature*, Bloomington, 1997, Vol I, 116-7, topic A511.

39. Lord Raglan, *The hero*, London, 1949 (1936), 178ff..

40. I take this point from Northrop Frye, *Anatomy of Criticism*, Princeton, 1957, 295.

41. Frye, *Anatomy of criticism*, 342. The Nativity Ode is that of Milton.

7

FEAR AND TEMPTATION IN
THE ATTIS POEM OF CATULLUS

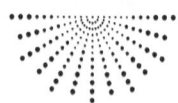

I remember hearing Sophocles the poet greeted by a fellow who asked,
'How about your service of Aphrodite, Sophocles—is your natural force
still unabated?' And he replied, 'Hush, man, most gladly have I escaped
this thing you talk of, as if I had run away from a raging and savage
beast of a master.' (Plato, Republic 329b. Trans. Paul Shorey)

"Né creator né creatura mai,"
  cominciò el, "figliuol, fu sanza amore,
  o naturale o d'animo; e tu 'l sai." (Dante, Purgatorio XVII.91-3)

He began: "Neither Creator nor creature, my son, was ever without
love, either natural or of the mind, and this you know." (Trans.
Singleton)

This strange poem tempts the reader to explore many
fascinating by-ways: the cult of Anatolian Cybele and her
eunuch priests, the *galli*, the rare galliambic metre of the poem named
after them,[1] the use of archaic words and special coinages, the problems

of the text[2] and, finally, the question of to what extent this poem might reflect a personal issue for Catullus, who is celebrated for bringing his personal life so vividly into his work. But to succumb too soon to these lures risks turning the poem into a document of social anthropology or a riddle. Catullus does, I think, play straight with his reader and he provides most of the information we need to understand his poem—though it is part of the Alexandrian technique to avoid over-explicitness and we need to be alert to matters presented unobtrusively. I shall therefore neglect his vivid descriptions of the exotic paraphernalia of the cult to concentrate on the central character and his motivation.

Who is the Attis of the poem? Clearly he is not the Attis of the various myths, the lover of Cybele who then destroys him; an essential feature of this was his self-castration.[3] In the poem Attis is a human being who travels to Phrygia, the home of the cult, who there emasculates himself and becomes a devotee. Where does he come from? Attis was a common personal name in Phrygia,[4] but the figure in this poem is not Phrygian since he travels there. The poem seems to imply, though it does not state, that he was Greek. This comes out most clearly from line 60:

abero foro, palaestra, stadio et gyminasiis?

I shall be lost to market place, wrestling ground, racetrack and playground.

Three of these four places are actually Greek words, and the fourth, the *forum*, represents the Greek ἀγορά. Furthermore the journey from Greece to Phrygia[5] is much shorter and simpler than that from Rome or anywhere in Italy. The loss of his native country, mentioned four times (*patria*, 50 twice, 55 and 59) is something he felt keenly so it is interesting that Catullus does not actually specify the country in question. Commentators are sure that he was straightforwardly Greek, thus Harrison: 'a young man of traditionally Greek culture.'[6] I think this makes definite what Catullus deliberately left undefined and that he is leaving open the possibility that the Attis of the poem might conceivably be a Roman and so someone like the reader he envisaged. Romans felt strongly about *patria*. And indeed I would go further: I think the ostensibly Greek and Phrygian settings of the poem are a cover, a distancing device, for Roman concerns and specifically for issues which were live ones for Catullus.

I take some support for this from a story recounted by Julius Obsequens, a much later writer, but referring to the year 101 B.C.:

> seruus Q. Servilii Caeponis Matri Ideese se praecidit, et trans mare exportatus, ne unquam Romae reverteretur (Julius Obsequens 44a)

> *A slave of Q. Servilius Caepio mutilated himself in honour of the Idaean Mother and was deported across the sea, lest he ever return to Rome.*

This is the comparison Attis explicitly draws, though, as we shall see, he cannot be a slave:

> 'patria o mei creatrix, patria o mea genetrix,
> ego quam miser relinquens, dominos ut erifugae
> famuli solent, ad Idae tetuli nemora pedem ...
> ubinam aut quibus locis te positam, patria, reor?' (50-2, 55)

> *Oh my country which gave me life, my country which gave me birth, which I, wretched man abandoning as runaway slaves desert their masters and brought my steps to Ida's woods ... where and in what places do I think I shall find you, my country?*

But for this consideration a Roman Attis could have followed the cult in Italy, since it was tolerated though not encouraged, as the passage from Julius Obsequens shows. Roman citizens were not permitted to join the cult and make themselves eunuch priests of Cybele,[7] which suggests that many wanted to and some did; the cult was widespread across the Roman world.[8] We need to appreciate that the temptation to join was a real one. Yet, with the flight to Phrygia, Attis has lost, as well his country, also his possessions, friends and parents (*bonis, amicis, genitoribus*, 59). But an even greater loss, implied but not stated, is that of his original name: it could not have been Attis. I find it rather strange that none of the commentators remark on this. The leader of a troop of *galli*, the eunuch priests of Cybele, was often called Attis,[9] and it is from this that Attis is now re-named. His rather shadowy companions (*comitibus*, 11, 15 and 27) represent such a troop. We call him Attis because we are not told his original, his real name, and so have nothing else to call him. (The spelling varied; in this form it can also be a female name, and in the form Atthis can mean 'woman of Attica', reinforcing his quasi-female identity and supporting the suggestion of Greek origin.)[10] His original identity is completely suppressed in his new role.

There are some other circumstances of his flight which seem strange. According to our sources[11] men made themselves *galli* characteristically during the excitement of the festival of Cybele, on the Day of Blood (*dies sanguinis*). His personal motivation would then have been reinforced by the passion and ecstasy which groups and crowds can generate, which Durkheim termed 'collective effervescence.'[12] But Attis apparently does not perform his act of self-mutilation in the context of a festival but after travelling to Phrygia. He has abandoned his *patria* already. This can only suggest unusual determination on his part since the support and excitement of the festival are absent. There must have been something else to strengthen his motivation.

He is indeed a very young man. We hear of his snowy or delicate hands (*niueis ... manibus*, 8) and soft fingers (*teneris ... digitis*, 10) and later that he has rosy lips (*roseis ... labellis*, 74). There is no mention of a beard: we may presume he was too young to have one. I have seen a suggestion that he acquired these characteristics miraculously after his self-emasculation;[13] this seems to me far-fetched, unnecessary and contrary to his character as Catullus presents it. A revealing passage rehearses his earlier life:

> ego iuuenis,[14] ego adolescens, ego ephebus, ego puer,
> ego eram gyminasii flos,[15] ego eram decus olei:
> mihi ianuae frequentes, mihi limina tepida,
> mihi floridis corollis redimita domus erat,
> linquendum ubi esset orto mihi Sole cubiculum. (63-7)

I have been a man, an adolescent, youth and boy: I was the flower of the
playground, I was the idol of the arena: mine were the crowded doors,
mine the worn thresholds, mine the house decorated with flowery garlands
when at sunrise it was time to leave my bedroom.

This is a key passage in the poem, and line 63 is the longest single
line with nearly every opportunity for resolution taken so the repeated
ego twice elided seems almost swallowed:

ĕgŏ iŭuĕnĭs, ĕgo‿ădŏlēscēns, ‖ ĕgo‿ĕphēbŭs, ĕgŏ pŭĕr

The weight falls on *adolescens* and the naturalized Greek word
ephebus. And after one line summarizing athletic exploits—which helpfully informs us that he is indeed freeborn, since these are not the activities of a slave—we have three whose burden is his attractiveness. This is
his most important memory. The whole setting is that of courtship of
an adolescent boy by older male admirers, of a kind well attested at
Athens and also known at Rome. Attis had in fact been a pretty boy
with suitors, a *puer delicatus*, a fact he was proud of. And he had had the
looks which went with this. To understand this is to begin to make sense
of the poem.

Why then did he rush to Phrygia, making haste both by sea (*celeri*
rate, in a swift boat, 1) and by land (*citato ...pede*, with restless foot, 2)?
The simple explanation is that he was overcome by madness:

stimulatus ibi furenti rabie, uagus animis (4)

urged on there by raging madness and wandering in his mind

And this is the mental state Cybele herself requires in a devotee
when at the end of the poem she instructs one of her lions to pursue
Attis to return him to the manic phase:

fac uti furoris ictu reditum in nemora ferat (79)

Make him by a stroke of madness make a return to the woods.

And in the last line the poet prays to be spared this state of mind:

alios age incitatos, alios age rabidos (93)

Drive others to frenzy, drive others mad.

This is not, of course the language of modern mental health services —the modern might murmur bi-polar disorder linked to gender dysphoria—but we can see what Catullus is getting at: to a normal Roman man the prospect of emasculating oneself and joining the cult was abhorrent and anyone who did it was crazy.

But this explains nothing: there has to be more to Attis' motivation than this. Catullus gives us the information we need but he does it very economically and if we are not attending we can easily overlook it. The crucial line is this: Attis is addressing his companions, but he clearly includes himself with them:

et corpus euirastis Veneris nimio odio (17)

You have unmanned your bodies from utter revulsion from Venus.

A great deal of weight rests on *nimio*, and my translation here as *utter* is only a stopgap. *Nimis* can mean either *excessively*, or *exceedingly* (OLD s.v. 1 and 3); although in casual speech these are often used interchangeably, the meanings are distinct. The Latin word is ambiguous; what does Catullus mean by it here? To understand his usage I used a concordance to identify all his uses of *nimis* and its cognates. The results are in Appendix 4. To summarize: on four occasions he means *excessively*, on three *exceedingly* and three, not counting the present line, are ambiguous.[16] Of the two other uses in this poem, one (36) means *exceedingly* and one (80) *excessively*.

Attis himself has to mean *exceedingly*: at this point he is in the manic phase. But I think the poet, *while using exactly the same word*, means *excessively*: the poet conveys his character's enthusiasm but stands at a distance from it as is clear from the sequel and the prayer at the end. For the poet, his character's madness consists precisely in this excessive hatred. And *Veneris*, often translated as *love*, can also mean quite simply *sex*, which is what it surely means here.[17] Would this be the sex he might have had with his older male admirers, or the sex—specifically penetrative sex—he would have gone on to have with women—or boys—as an adult man—had he not taken his fateful decision? Is he looking backwards or forwards? At one point I wondered whether he had been sexually abused[18] and whether his hatred of Venus might have stemmed from this. This might have been the case with other *galli* but for Attis the memory seems a good one so it does not seem that his revulsion can be from what happened in the past. It therefore has to refer to the future: with his companions he rejects adult male sexual life. In its stead he is choosing devotion to the goddess, which presumably is a form of love or takes its place in his life. (I think on this point Catullus is with Dante in the passage I used as epigraph.) Arguably, the comparison of him to a heifer—the only simile in the poem—expresses his feeling of rejection of sexual life as well as his female identification:

> ueluti iuuenca uitans onus indomita iugi (33)

like an untamed heifer shaking off the burden of the yoke.[19]

And we do need to raise the issue of exactly what he did do to himself. The Latin is:

> deuulsit ili acuto sibi pondera silice[20] (5)

He sliced off with a sharp flint the weights of his groin.

Pondera, weights, is of course plural: does the poet mean the testicles specifically? That would be castration, which is the term every commentator I have looked at uses. But from *sine uiro*, without manhood (6), *corpus euirastis*, you have unmanned your bodies (17) and *notha mulier*, a counterfeit woman (27) it appears that he and, presumably the other devotees, were left without any external genitals. This is technically more than castration: it is emasculation. So *pondera* refers to all the male genitalia, though euphemistically, since, in a serious poem like this, Catullus does not permit himself the explicit sexual language he uses elsewhere.[21] Attis wished to remove every trace of his masculinity.[22]

Catullus emphasizes the precipitous haste of Attis' action: *celeri*, fast (1), *citato*, speedy (2). This contrasts markedly with the way gender reassignment is handled by doctors nowadays. A trans-gender person is required to live for at least a year in the preferred gender before surgery is offered, to test the strength and stability of the motivation. In the case of Attis the strength is not in doubt: *stimulatus ibi furenti rabie, uagus animis* (goaded by raging madness and wandering in his mind, 4), and it was strong enough to take him from his home to Phrygia and to draw companions (*comites*, 15) with him. But the stability is not there: it was all part of a distracted state of mind, the acting out of a fantasy which collapses when the collective effervescence subsides and he regrets it as soon as the following day.

At this point we come to a powerful rhetorical device. After his emasculation Attis is referred to in the feminine gender. In the first long sentence of the poem we have Attis as the subject in the first line followed by a whole succession of verbs in the third person singular perfect: *tetigit* (reached, 2), *adiitque* (entered, 3), *deuolsit* (sliced off, 5), *sensit* (felt, 6), *cepit* (seized), where the gender of the subject is not confirmed. Even *citata* (swift) in the eighth line could be another neuter plural but is only clarified as feminine when we reach *adortast* (she began) in line 11. Catullus continues to use the feminine gender for Attis after this point right up to *famula*, handmaid, in line 90 but reverts to the masculine when reflecting on his earlier life. Or that at any rate seems to be his intention: it requires some regularizing of forms in the transmitted text by editors.[23] The rest of his first speech is full of the excitement of the cult.

Aristotle had argued that 'All animals when castrated change to the female character.'[24] However, despite his use of feminine word forms, Catullus does not accept this. His attitude seems closer to that in a court case reported by Valerius Maximus: in 77 B.C. a *gallus* named Genucius was denied an inheritance on the basis that he was neither man nor woman. He was not even allowed to put his case to court.[25] In the first sentence after the first speech of Attis the narrator immediately undermines any idea of his femininity by two words:

simul haec comitibus Attis cecinit notha mulier ... (27)

As soon as Attis sang in this way to the companions, a woman but a counterfeit one ...

The excitement continues for another sixteen lines but here Catullus has planted the seed of the coming depressive passage, in which Attis contemplates his past and from which I have already quoted. The *galli* may have used feminine terms of and to one another; Catullus himself does so in the person of Attis at 12, *Gallae*, and as narrator at 34. This convention—if it was one—does not reduce the rhetorical force of his usage of feminine terms in this poem. A later example is in Apuleius where a group of *galli* are addressed as *puellae*: girls.[26] In our own time camp gay men also used to do so, at least until recently. But Catullus regards this as only a pretence. For Catullus, emasculation and the use of feminine pronouns do not in themselves turn a male into a female. *Notha mulier*, a counterfeit woman. That, in his view, is the brutal truth.

In the depressive phase he is now in, Attis contemplates his future as a devotee:

ego Maenas, ego mei pars, ego uir sterilis ero?
ego uiridis algida Idae niue amicta loca colam?
ego uitam agam sub altis Phrygiae columinibus,
ubi cerua siluicultrix, ubi aper nemoriuagus?
iam iam dolet quod egi, iam iamque paenitet. (69-73)

Am I to be a Maenad, I part of myself, a sterile man? Am I to inhabit the icy places covered with snow of leafy Ida? Am I to pass my life beneath the loft peaks of Phyrgia, where the forest-haunting hind is, where the boar ranging the woodland is? Now now I rue what I have done, now now I repent.

Maenas is normally a follower of Bacchus rather than Cybele but it seems that some aspects of the cults were interchangeable.[27] The coming to a realization of what he has done is also specifically reminiscent of Agave in the *Bacchae* of Euripides, who realises that she has murdered her son and is holding his head in her hands. Attis, like Agave, finds the realization horrific. This is his lowest point; not only is he here in the depressive phase but it seems that, underneath all the frenzy, this is his real considered reflection. Notice that there is no further mention of the companions: he separated himself from them to rush to the shore and the possibility that they could give him comfort does not even occur to him. Sociability and collective effervescence belong only to the manic phase; the depressive one he must face alone. The hurtling rush of the verse is slowed in the culminating line which is the shortest, the heaviest and the saddest in the poem:

iām iām dŏlĕt quŏd ēgī, ‖ iām iāmquĕ paēnĭtĕt. (73)

Now, now, I regret what I have done, now, now, I repent.

Other *galli* may have been content in their new identity; we know this is possible from considering their modern equivalent: the hijras of modern India who are eunuch priests of the mother goddess they know as Bahuchara Mata.[28] The Attis of our poem is clearly not. Nor does this seem simply the reaction in the depressive phase to the frenzy of the manic phase. His action is madness because hatred of adult sexuality— or fear of it—has led to horror, misery and regret. And he now has no future except to return to the manic phase. Catullus symbolizes this by adopting and adapting the *topos* of an encounter between a *gallus* and a lion. This had been a popular subject in the Hellenistic period and several examples survive in the Greek Anthology.[29] They have in common the theme of a *gallus* coming across a lion in a waste place and frightening it off with his tambourine. In these poems the lion has no connection with Cybele. Catullus makes three changes: he makes the lion one of Cybele's own, he has her set it on Attis in punishment for his expression of regret, and he has it win the encounter:

facit impetum. illa demens fugit in nemora fera;
ibi semper omne uitae spatium famula fuit. (89-90, accepting
Lachmann's *illa* for the transmitted *ille*)

*It made a charge. Out of her mind she fled into the wild groves. There for
the whole course of her life she was a handmaid (of the goddess).*

One imagines that this Attis could not have stood many recurrences
of the depressive phase and might well have committed suicide fairly
soon. *Omne uitae spatium*, the whole course of her life, might have been
short, an ironic reference by Catullus to the fact that in the myths Attis
is killed or dies from his wound.

I have said nothing about the other details of the cult because they
speak for themselves. It was widespread across the Roman world. We
probably know it best from literary accounts such as those in Lucretius
(2.602-643) and Ovid (*Fasti* 4.179-246). The first of these was probably
available to Catullus if he needed it, but he presumably witnessed the
cult often enough himself at first hand. There is nothing to suggest that
he personally talked to *galli* and heard their stories or researched the
cult's history. The poem does not present any view of the life of a *gallus*
outside the observance of the cult or revulsion from the self-
mutilation.[30]

What then is the significance of the poem? One possible answer is
that it is a poem about someone who has rejected the possibility of
marriage and offspring, to contrast with neighbouring poems in the
collection which do variously treat of marriage: poems 61 and 62 are
both marriage hymns; poem 64 celebrates two marriages, each involving
a divine being and a mortal;[31] poem 66 the marriage of Berenice; poem
67 presents an unsatisfactory marriage; and poem 68 handles the fact
that Lesbia is married to someone else. Poem 63 is then a poem which
deals with someone who has made marriage impossible for himself. And
one could argue that its structure, with its movement from frenzy to
regret and back again, is there simply to create a narrative so that
Catullus could concentrate on the scenes of ecstatic excitement which
form the bulk of the poem. There is also a strong contrast between civi-

lized Greek—or Roman—culture and the frenzy of an Asiatic cult: a form of Orientalism, in the negative sense of that term. The poem is then primarily a technical exercise, to contrast with the neighbouring poems and to show off the poet's knowledge and his skill in writing in this difficult metre.

Some poets enjoy technical challenges of this kind; that Catullus was one of them is shown by the variety of metres in his collection. The poem could have started as a technical exercise, perhaps in friendly rivalry with Caecilius, who was also working on a poem to Cybele (see poem 35). The galliambic metre was traditional for hymns to Cybele, though apparently these were always in Greek.[32] In any case this is the only surviving complete poem in this metre from the ancient world. It poses particular challenges in Latin because of the need for many short syllables. One can imagine Catullus relishing the challenge. In doing so he departs both from the conversational tone which he normally deploys in tandem with a strict metre in his short poems and which to an English reader seems to anticipate Donne's combination of passion and elegance, and also from the epigrammatic style which suggests Pope. He meets it in a number of ways, usefully listed by Fordyce;[33] I shall give examples from passages I have already cited: archaic forms such as *gyminasiis*, playground 60, and *columinibus*, summits 71; poetic plurals such as *maria*, seas, for sea, 1, and arguably *pondera*, weights, 5; compounds after the Greek manner such as *siluicultrix*, woodland haunting and *nemoriuagus*, forest ranging 72; repetition of certain words such as *ferus*, wild, and *uagus*, wandering, or the fourfold *iam*, now, in line 73. And the poem is certainly a technical tour de force. Yet, despite its excitement, intensity and pathos there is a certain coldness about it, particularly when compared to the Lesbia poems: it is a piece in which one admires the virtuosity of the poet's skill but remains unmoved.

However, the technical challenge could have led to a very different kind of poem. This is clear from the only other complete poem in galliambics known to me. This is the *Hymn to Bacchus* by the Renaissance poet Michael Marullus, one of a collection of neo-pagan hymns, published in 1497.[34] The cult of Bacchus was of course long dead when he wrote, but he writes as if it were active and he has certainly done his research. As we have seen, it was a similar cult to that of Cybele and used some of the same paraphernalia. Michael's poem is of sixty lines, so two thirds the length of the *Attis* but longer than many others in his collection. He clearly has the *Attis* in mind but takes his subject in a quite different direction. The speaker is a devotee, as is Attis, and he begins with an elaborate invocation and encouragement to himself to engage in worship:

> Agedum, canite patrem, Thespiades, mihi Bromium,
> Sobolem igneam Iovis, quem peperit bona Semele
> Puerum coma praesignem et radiantibus oculis.
> Euoe! sonant furenti mihi pectora rabie
> Nimioque deo plenus concutitur gravis animus. (1-5)

> *Come now Muses, sing to me of father Bromius, fiery offspring of Jupiter, whom the good Semele brought forth, the boy distinguished by his locks and radiant eyes. Euoe! My breast sends forth a sound emanating from a frenzied rage and my soul, overflowing with the god, is shaken.* (Trans. Charles Fantazzi)

Michael has picked up the theme of frenzy (*rabie*) from Catullus and he clearly takes *nimioque* as *excessive*. But the excitement is not painful and leads to praise which takes up all the rest of the poem, which is well over half, beginning with a roll call of the god's titles:

> Euoe! impotenti thyrso gravis, alme Dionyse,
> Martie, bicornis, rex, omnipotens, femorigena,
> Mystice, Thioneu, ultor, solivage, Euie, sature,
> Genitor deorum idem atque idem germen amabile etc (24-8)

> *Weighed down by the wild thyrsus, O life-giving Dionysus, martial, two-horned king, almighty one, born from the thigh, initiate in the sacred mysteries, son of Thyone, avenger wandering alone, Euius, Satyr, at once father of the gods and loveable infant ...*

Catullus could perfectly well have met the technical challenge and constructed his Attis poem on similar lines. He would then have given us a genuine hymn to Cybele, a far from impossible thought. After all he gives us a genuine hymn to Diana in poem 34. But this is precisely what he does not offer us.[35] Instead we have this poem about a *gallus* who regrets becoming a *gallus*, who misses his homeland and original identity and whose enthusiasm for worship of the goddess is soon exhausted. We come back to *Veneris nimio odio*, exceeding or excessive hatred of sex, and his past as a pretty boy with admirers. To make sense of his story we have to reconstruct his motivation from the hints Catullus gives us. This I think we can do. The problem for Attis was that he had enjoyed being a pretty boy, but in the nature of things this is only a short phase in the development towards adulthood. He wanted somehow to perpetuate it or go back to it. He did not want to grow up.[36] Whether the drive was primarily to retain the effeminate looks which had brought him attention which he had welcomed, or whether it was rather to avoid adult sexuality and responsibilities is left uncertain. But one element was that he was afraid of adult sexuality and so tempted to a course of action which would excuse him from it. We have to understand that this was a real temptation, one to which he succumbed, as did others, including so many Romans that the practice had to be forbidden. He carried it through: he emasculated himself and then found that instead of staying a pretty boy he had become an object of horror to ordinary people and even to himself. He had cut himself off from everything that had made or could make life worth living. He fancied that he had made himself a woman, but Catullus will have none of that: he calls Attis a *notha mulier*, a counterfeit woman. Not that he comes across as someone who really wanted to be a woman or at least a transgender woman anyway, as one imagines some of the *galli* were. What he wanted was to avoid being an adult man; he could not really be a woman; what he was now was a eunuch. To be a eunuch was social death, as we learned from Valerius Maximus.[37] Eunuchs were used as slaves or tolerated as devotees of Cybele but any chance of the normal life he would have had as a man was gone. His story is a personal tragedy.

With this in mind we can consider what significance this poem might have had for Catullus and what light this might throw on the poem. He is celebrated particularly for making poems out of the events of his life, and above all for the disastrous relationship with Lesbia. And we can see this affecting his other poems. In poem 64, the *Peleus and Thetis*, the immediate next poem of the collection, everyone remembers Ariadne abandoned on the beach by Theseus:

nulla fugae ratio, nulla spes: omnia muta,
omnia sunt deserta, ostentant omnia letum (64: 186-7)

No means of escape, no hope: everything is silent, everything is aban-doned, everything points to death.

We can imagine Catullus abandoned by Lesbia identifying with this; and apart from *omnia muta*, everything silent, it could be the feeling of Attis also, in the depressive phase, and also looking out from the shore to the waste sea (*maria uasta*, 48) and reflecting on the waste of his life.[38] But are there any direct parallels between Catullus and Attis? Well it is worth remembering that as well as the Lesbia poems which everyone remembers, Catullus also wrote about his attachment to a boy or young man whom he calls Juventius. (This name, which means something like *youthful*, is presumably a surrogate for the boy's real name, as Lesbia was for, probably, Clodia Metelli.) There are some half dozen of these, of which poems 48 and 99, at least, seem as genuine in their feeling as the poems about Lesbia.[39] We can't imagine this attachment as being simul-taneous with that to Lesbia, or later, so presumably it was earlier. Juven-tius would have been a free Roman, not a slave, and he was clearly a *puer delicatus* who had other admirers of whom Catullus was jealous—see poems 15, 21 and 24. Wiseman called him 'the spoilt young aristocrat who made his admirers beg for kisses and played the field with casual heartlessness.'[40] In other words he would not have been so very different from Attis before his flight. In his relationship to Catullus he would have been the *eromenos*, the younger love object, and Catullus the *erastes*, the older lover, to use the Greek terms for these relationships.

Now Juventius would have been expected to mature through this phase and after ceasing to be an *eromenos* possibly become an *erastes* himself before putting such things behind him as an adult man who would in due course take a wife. (Whether he did or not, of course we do not know.) At least that seems to be the theory—unofficial adult liaisons with women, such as that of Catullus with Lesbia, are outside this scheme. There were therefore two possible transitions as part of normal male development: from *eromenos* to *erastes* and from *erastes* to married man or at least heterosexual man.[41] That these transitions were seen as normal and expected is shown by a passage in the wedding hymn poem 61. This is perhaps a literary imitation of a choral ode rather than the thing itself, but that it was written for a real wedding is shown by the fact that the names of the bride and groom are known: L. Manlius Torquatus and Iunia or Arunculeia. The context of the passage I discuss is the scattering of walnuts in the wedding procession, symbolizing putting away childish things.

> ne diu taceat procax
> Fescennina iocatio,
> nec nuces pueris neget
> desertum domini audiens
>   concubinus amorem.

> da nuces pueris, iners
> concubine! satis diu
> lusisti: nucibus iubet
> iam seruire Talassio.
>   concubine, nuces da.

> sordebant tibi uilicae,
> concubine, hodie atque heri:
> nunc tuum cinerarius
> tondet os. miser a miser
>   concubine, nuces da.

> diceris male te a tuis
> unguentate glabris marite

abstinere, sed abstine.
io Hymen Hymenaee io,
   io Hymen Hymenaee.

scimus haec tibi quae licent
soli cognita, sed marito
ista non eadem licent.
io Hymen Hymenaee io,
   io Hymen Hymenaee. (61.119-143)

May naughty Fescennine [obscene] *teasing not be silent for long nor let the favourite fail to scatter nuts to the boys on hearing that his master's devotion has been abandoned.*

Give nuts to the boys, lazy favourite: you have played long enough: now you must enjoy serving nuts to Talasius [the equivalent of Hymenaeus]. *Favourite, scatter the nuts.*

Today and yesterday, favourite, you scorned stewards' wives: now the hairdresser shaves your cheeks. Wretched, ah wretched favourite, scatter the nuts.

They say that you, perfumed bridegroom, are reluctant to give up beardless boys, but give them up. O Hymen Hymenaeus O, O Hymen Hymenaeus.

We know that the pleasures allowed a bachelor are known to you, but they are not permitted a husband. O Hymen Hymenaeus O, O Hymen Hymenaeus.

The tone is light and the suggestions may not be seriously meant, but they have to be plausible and the transitions referred to are real. The word I have translated *favourite* is *concubinus*: a slave boy who has been the bedfellow or catamite of his master. Catullus deliberately uses the relatively neutral term *concubinus*, rather than the strongly derogatory *cinaedus* or *pathicus*, which he uses in poem 16. These refer to receiving anal and oral penetration, either of which might have been required of the *concubinus*. But he is losing his position, not only because his master is marrying, but also because he himself is growing too old for the role since he is developing facial hair. The master is also moving on from a role in which such liaisons were permitted to one where they are not—at least officially. The catamite is obviously in a weaker position than Juventius, since he is a slave whereas Juventius was a free Roman, but they each have to make this transition. And the master has to make the next one: from a same-sex relationship with a boy to an opposite sex one with a wife.

Freud's classic discussion of male same-sex relationships seems particularly appropriate here—we should remember that Freud had a classical education:

> What excited a man's love was not the masculine character of a boy, but his physical resemblance to a woman as well as his feminine mental qualities—his shyness, his modesty and his need for instruction and assistance. A soon as the boy became a man he ceased to be a sexual object for men and himself, perhaps, became a lover of boys ... The sexual object is not someone of the same sex but someone who combines the characters of both sexes; there is, as it were, a compromise between an impulse that seeks for a man and one that seeks for a woman, while it remains a paramount condition that the object's body (i.e. genitals) shall be masculine. *Thus the sexual object is a kind of reflection of the subject's own bisexual nature* (my emphasis).[42]

This helps understand the motivation of people like Catullus and Manlius: part of the attraction of the *eromenos* for the *erastes* is that he reflects aspects of the *erastes* back to him. Catullus created his Attis to be a similar figure to Juventius and the *concubinus*. And a long footnote Freud later added to the passage just quoted contains a passage which is particularly helpful in clarifying the corresponding motivation of the *eromenos*:

> Future inverts, in the earliest years of their childhood, pass through a phase of very intense but short-lived fixation to a woman (usually their

mother), and ... after leaving this behind, they identify themselves with a woman and take *themselves* as their sexual object.

This is exactly the stage of development Attis had reached. As a *puer delicatus* he has been a sexual object of this kind and he tries to make himself or at least see himself as a woman but this only works for him in the manic phase. Whereas Catullus and Manlius moved on to relationships with women, Attis was fixated at an earlier stage; he was on the way to becoming what Freud calls an invert.

Catullus moved on from relationships with the likes of Juventius. Nevertheless, Lesbia was not and would not have been a wife to him—that is part of the point of poem 68. In contemplating the torment of his relationship with her he must have wondered, like Sophocles in the remark attributed to him by Plato, whether the pain of an adult sexual relationship was worth it. Some commentators have drawn a parallel, summarized conveniently by Nauta:

> It has often been felt that Attis is in a sense an allegory for Catullus, and Cybele for Lesbia: like Attis, Catullus was brought out of his mind by a dominant female, like him he tried to free himself from her sway, and like him without success.[43]

In this vein Wiseman suggests that madness and slavery were characteristic both of Attis' marriage (*sic*) to Cybele and of the language Catullus used for his own love, and that Lesbia was a *domina*.[44] This seems to me to involve some forcing of the text. For example I do not think *domina* at 68B.68 and 156 refer to Lesbia but to Allius' accommodating housekeeper.

But the claim of madness seems tempting so I looked through the poems and Wiseman's citations to see if the evidence supported such a view. The pickings are slim:

tam te basia multa basiare
uesano satis et super Catullo est, (7.9-10)

So many kisses for kissing you would be enough and more than enough for crazy Catullus.

sed toto, indomitus furore, lecto
uersarer cupiens uidere lucem,
ut tecum loquerer, simulque ut essem. (50.11-13)

I tossed all over the bed with unmanageable madness, longing to see dawn so that I could talk with you and also that I might be with you.

non est dea nescia nostri,
quae dulcem curis miscet amaritiem (68.16-17)

Not unknown to me is the goddess who mingles a sweet bitterness with her burdens.

nam, mihi quam dederit duplex Amathusia curam
scitis, et in quo me torruerit genere. (68.52-3)

For you know how the treacherous Amathusia (Venus) has given me suffering, in what way she scorched me.

me miserum aspicite et, si uitam puriter egi,
eripite hanc pestem perniciemque mihi,
quae mihi surrepens imos ut torpor in artus
expulit ex omni pectore laetitias. (76.19-20)

Look on me in in my wretchedness and, if I have led a pure life, cast out this plague and pestilence from me, which, creeping like paralysis into the depths of my being, has expelled joy from all my heart.

cum uesana meas torreret flamma medullas (100.7)

When a crazy passion scorched my innermost being.

non potui, si possem, tam perdite amarem (104:3)

I could not, nor, if I could, love so hopelessly.

I may have missed some references but these are sufficient to give the picture: Catullus suffers indeed, but *uesanus*, crazy (7.10 and 100.7) and *furore*, madness (50.11) are the only words to suggest anything approaching madness, and even they are not literally meant. And they are weaker than the *furenti rabie* at the beginning of our poem (raging madness, line 4), *furor* (madness) at the end (91) and similar uses throughout our poem. No, if we want the authentic tone of a lover who thinks he is really being driven mad we have to look to another poet:

Febris amor meus est, adeo desiderat ille
    Cuncta quibus possit perpetuare malum;
Semper uterque etenim vel nutrimenta doloris
    Appetit, incertae si placuere gulae.
Nam ratio, tantis in amoribus una medela,
    Consilia indignans me data nulla sequi,
Cessit, et agnosco letale cupidinis omen
    Esse, medelarum reicientis opem.
Sic ratio victa est, nec restat cura salutis
    Vlla, sed huc illuc irrequietus agor;
Ac velut insani mea sensa ac verba vagantur
    Longius a veris, ut sine mente sonus;
Nam mihi nonnunquam tu visa es dictaque, virgo,
    Candida, quae tanquam Nox Erebusque nigras.

I must admit to cheating: this is a translation by Alfred Thomas Barton of Shakespeare's sonnet 147.[45] Here is the original:

My love is as a fever, longing still
For that which longer nurseth the disease,
Feeding on that which doth preserve the ill,
The uncertain sickly appetite to please.
My reason, the physician to my love,
Angry that his prescriptions are not kept,
Hath left me, and I desperate now approve

Desire is death, which physic did except.
Past cure I am, now reason is past care,
And frantic mad with evermore unrest;
My thoughts and my discourse as madmen's are,
At random from the truth vainly express'd;
> For I have sworn thee fair, and thought thee bright,
> Who art as black as hell, as dark as night.

The point is clear: there is nothing like this in Catullus. I see no parallel between the suffering in his devotion to Lesbia and that of Attis in his devotion to Cybele because there is no similarity in their motivation.[46] Catullus suffered from sexual jealousy, Attis from a revulsion from sex. We should resist the temptation to see Attis as a mere mask for Catullus[47] rather than a fictional character with his own integrity. If we want to make a personal comparison we must look elsewhere.

My suggestion is that the issue for Catullus is not madness but temptation. He could have looked back not only to his role as *erastes* to Juventius but possibly also to an earlier time when he himself had been an *eromenos*. That he had been at least thought so seems one possible reading of poem 16, to which his response is not denial but sexual threats attacking his accusers' masculinity and a claim that as a dedicated poet he has to live a decent life (*nam castum esse decet pium poetam*, 16.5). He was not always a dedicated poet; what kind of life did he live as a boy? How are we to take *parum pudicum* (not exactly chaste) at 16.4? Had he in fact been another Juventius? And, as a poet, he might have wondered what it would have been like to refuse to make the transition we have been discussing. This would have been to refuse to become an adult man, in short to make the decision that Attis did. The *Attis* is then an imaginative exploration of the possible consequences. Catullus might have started by asking himself: 'What kind of person chooses to become a *gallus* and a devotee of Cybele. Would it be someone who had been an *eromenos* and wanted to remain so?' And he could have reflected on the *concubinus* of poem 61—who was or could have been a real person as the hymn was written for a real marriage—and on Juventius. The *concubinus* has to forego his privileged status and Juventius will have to outgrow his; what would they have been like had they wished or tried to retain it? I repeat: the temptation must have been real. The poetically interesting situation is then not that of a slave, whose choices are limited —and who could have been forcibly castrated at the whim of his master —but that of a free-born youth, who is not compelled and freely makes that choice or gives in to that temptation. And then to give the poem shape and point he could have asked himself: 'The act is irreversible: what if my character regrets it afterwards, when it is too late?' He therefore imagines a motivation for Attis which he can identify with, one which represents a real temptation, and which he suggests in the poem but does not emphasize. It is this which takes it some way beyond a technical exercise or a straightforward hymn and gives it its pathos.

My final argument for a personal reference of this kind comes from the concluding prayer by the poet. He wishes to avoid a fate like that of his Attis:

dea magna, dea Cybebe, dea domina Dindymi,[48]
procul a mea tuus sit furor omnis, era, domo.
alios age incitatos, alios age rabidos (91-3)

Great goddess, goddess Cybele, goddess lady of Dindymum, may all your madness be far from my house, mistress. Drive others to frenzy, drive others mad.

Some commentators take this prayer as not serious and the poet's apparent attitude of great reverence as tongue in cheek.[49] They also find the episode with Cybele's lion funny. On both points this view seem to me grotesque: it devalues the central character and with it the poem. I take a different view. Although the setting of the poem is ostensibly Greek, Catullus sees the fate of Attis as a possible one for him. He, a Roman, might share that fate if the prayer is not answered. He might make the choice that Attis did. You do not pray to be delivered from that which you do not fear or which does not present a temptation.

---

1. Having not found any of the standard expositions of this very helpful, I have drawn from them to make my own, in Appendix 3.

2. I am taking Harrison as my basic text for this poem and discuss controversial readings as they arise, with line mumbers; Harrison's text is in Ruurd Nauta and Annette Harder (eds.), *Catullus' poem on Attis: Texts and Contexts*, Leiden, 2005. For other poems I mainly follow G. P. Goold (ed.), *Catullus: the Poems*, London, 2001 (1983).

3. The best general survey of these I have found is in Lynn E. Roller, *In search of God the Mother: the cult of Anatolian Cybele*, Berkeley, 1999, 238-243, with a convenient summary at 259. A study of them with particular reference to this poem is Jan N. Bremmer, 'Attis: a Greek God in Anatolian Pessinous and Catullan Rome' in Nauta and Harder.

4. Roller, 245.

5. Phrygia around Pessinous was the original home of the cult, but the later mentions in the poem of Mount Ida and Mount Dindymon suggest that Catullus meant Phrygia in the Troad—unless he conflated the two. places. This is of course where the Trojans, the ancestors of the Romans, came from, and some commentators have seen in this a veiled allusion to the issue of effeminacy at Rome. See T. P. Wiseman, *Catullus and his world: A Reappraisal*, Cambridge, 1985, 119-120; Roller, 302-3.

6. Stephen J. Harrison, 'Altering Attis: Ethnicity, Gender and Genre in Catullus 63', in Nauta and Harder, 13.

7. Dionysius of Halicarnassus, *Roman Antiquities*, 2.19.

8. Martern J. Vermaseren, *Cybele and Attis: the myth and the cult*, London, 1977, and, more recently Roller, *In search of God the Mother*, give comprehensive accounts. Vermaseren is particularly well illustrated.

9. Vermaseren, 98 with references.

10. Harrison: *Altering Attis*, 13.

11. Summarized in Vermaseren, 96-7.

12. Durkheim, The *Elementary Forms of the Religious Life*, trans Cosman, Oxford, 2001 (1912),164.

13. Nauta, 'Catullus 63 in a Roman context', in Nauta and Harder, 92.

14. I have adopted Schwabe's *iuuenis* for the *mulier* of the MS tradition. *Mulier* is printed by Mynors and Quinn and defended by Fordyce though it forces *fui* in the next line to mean *sum* here. Furthermore, it has already been contradicted by *notha mulier*, 'a woman though a counterfeit one', in 25, so to use it here would be bathetic; it would also inappropriately anticipate *ego Maenas* at 67 where Attis starts exploring his new quasi-female identity. As Thomson says: 'The line begins with the present and goes back by stages to Attis' childhood.' We therefore need a word for *man* or *adult*. There have been many suggestions: see the website *Catullus online*. Goold and Thomson favour Scaliger's *puber*, but Harrison and Heyworth point out that this nominative is not attested in classical Latin and prefer Schwabe's *iuuenis*, which I have accepted.

15. Thus Heyworth for the standard *ego gymnasi fui flos*: Nisbet argued that the perfect *fui* and imperfect *eram* cannot stand together. See S. J. Harrison and S. J. Heyworth, 'Notes on the text and interpretation of Catullus,'
    https://users.ox.ac.uk › ~sjh › documents › catconj accessed 2.4.2025.

16. I have considered the possibility that for Romans there was no clear distinction between *exceedingly* and *excessively* and that we have desynonymized what for them was a word with a wide extension. And no doubt there are many examples which are ambiguous. But the concepts are distinct and I would point to this passage as

showing that at any rate this writer was well aware of the distinction; it makes it a better poem to accept this.

17. James Michie's generally admirable verse translation offers *limitless loathing of love* for this phrase; *limitless* is an ingenious way of rendering *nimio*, effectively straddling the ambiguity, but *love* is surely wrong: *lust* would have been more appropriate and preserved the alliteration of the rendering.

18. I am aware that customs and values in the ancient world were different from those of now. The issues are the reality of consent and the mutuality of pleasure. Then, as now, these could be present or absent. If absent then the relationship would be abusive and exploitative. The absence of an age of consent and the freedom of adult male citizens to indulge in sex with slaves of either gender meant that slaves and children had to put up with it or might think cooperation the best or only strategy. See the discussion of poem 61 later. However, it is clear, for example from the Juventius poems which I shall come to, that free-born boys had to be courted.

19. K. M. W. Shipton, 'The Iuvenca image in Catullus 63', *Classical Quarterly* N. S. Vol. 36, No. 1, 1986, points out that violent head-tossing is characteristic of the cult and that the *iugum* is willingly accepted here though of course it is later (83) associated with Attis' slavery to Cybele. Horace has a whole poem, *Odes* 2.5, applying this comparison to a young girl who has just been married but is not yet ready for sex.

20. The line as quoted relies on emendations but these are universally accepted.

21. J. N. Adams, *The Latin sexual vocabulary*, London, 1982, discusses the available words; see 51-69. Catullus is often very explicit, notoriously so in poem 16, which I touch on later. David Wray, 'Attis' Groin Weights', *Classical Philology*, Vol. 96, No. 2 (Apr. 2001), 120-6, points out that *pondera* was also used of the weights of a loom which were sliced off when the fabric was finished. (He cites Seneca, *Epistles* 90.20 which describes the process.)

22. Ovid makes this explicit in his echoing of this: *Fasti*, 4.241-2: *onus inguinis aufert/ nullaque sunt subito signa relicta uiri*, he cut off his groin's weight, and suddenly there were no signs left of his manhood.

23. Kenneth Quinn (ed.), *Catullus: The Poems*, London, 1970, 286-7, discusses this in detail. I use the masculine form throughout my discussion.

24. See David Wray, 'Attis' Groin Weights.' *Classical Philology*, Vol. 96, No. 2 (Apr., 2001), pp. 120-126, citing Aristotle, *On the generation of animals* 787b-788a.

25. Valerius Maximus 7.7.6. See Roller, 292.

26. *Metamorphoses* 8.25.

27. Compare the description of the Cybelian procession at 63.19-26 with that of the Bacchic one at 64.255-263. Harrison 'Altering Attis' finds several parallels between our poem and the *Bacchae* of Euripides. G. O. Hutchinson, notes: 'The sequence of madness, irreversible act, and realization and lament occurs in several tragedies', instancing *Bacchae* among others, *Hellenistic Poetry*, Oxford, 1988, 312.

28. See Roller, *op. cit.*, 320-5, and Serena Nanda, *Neither man nor woman: the hijras of India*, Belmont 1999.

29. These are discussed by Roller, 229, and Harder, 'Catullus 63: a 'Hellenistic poem?', 69-70. The poems in question are A.P. 6.217 (Simonides), 218 (Alcaeus), 219 (Antipater), 220 (Dioscorides) and 237 (Antistius), *Greek Anthology* trans. W. R. Paton, London (Loeb Classical Library), Vol. I, 1916, 410ff.. A. P. 234 (Erycinus) ,which is sometimes grouped with these, concerns a *gallus* but not meeting a lion.

30. To be fair, hardly anyone else in the ancient world does either. The passage in Apuleius referred to above is the only one I know. The distinction of Nanda's book, *op. cit.*, is precisely that she does this for the hijras.

31. Peleus and Thetis, whose marriage in this version is happy (*non despexit hymenaeos*, 20; *concordia*, 336) and Bacchus and Ariadne.

32. Servius on Virgil, *Georgics* 2.394: *hymni Libero apud Graecos Graeca, apud Latinos Latina uoce dicuntur; hymni uero Matris Deum ubique propriam, id est Graecam, linguam requirunt,* (Hymns to Bacchus are recited in Greek among Greeks and in Latin among Latins; however, hymns to the Mother of the gods everywhere need her own language, which is Greek.)

33. C. J. Fordyce, *Catullus: A Commentary*, Oxford, 1961, 262.

34. Text in Michael Marullus, *Poems* trans. Fantazzi, Harvard (I Tatti), 2012.

35. Wiseman's suggestion, *Catullus and his world* 205-6, that the poem is a Romanized version of the cult suitable for the Megalesia seems implausible and has been rejected by Bremmer, 'Attis: a Greek god', 59, and by Nauta, 'Catullus 63 in a Roman context', 100.

36. At his point I find my argument coincides with that of Kenneth Quinn, *Catullus: An Interpretation*, London, 1972, though he puts the emphasis entirely on Attis' refusal of adulthood and does not explore his motivation; I think Attis also hankers back to his past. Marilyn B. Skinner, 'Ego mulier: the construction of male sexuality in Catullus,' in Judith P. Hallett and Marilyn B. Skinner (eds.), *Roman sexualities*, Princeton, 1997, presents an argument closer to mine but moves into gender politics which I cannot follow.

37. See above and note 25.

38. Harrison, 'Altering Attis' 18, also draws parallels with the laments of Euripides' Medea and suggests: 'Attis is a strange example of the species "lamenting abandoned literary heroine," though he is not strictly female and has not strictly been abandoned.'

39. The celebrated poem 5, *uiuamus, mea Lesbia, atque amemus*, let us live, my Lesbia, and let us love, seems to me a reworking of poem 48.

40. Wiseman, *Catullus and his world* 122.

41. I do not want to appear excessively schematic about this. In Tibullus 1.4 and 9 the poet is the *erastes* and a boy named Marathus is the *eromenos*, but in 1.8 Marathus has a girlfriend, Pholoe, so is in the process of making the transition even while still being an *eromenos* to the poet. Catullus' poem 56 presents a comparable situation. I am aware that the use of the term heterosexual for relationships in the ancient world can be thought anachronistic: I do not think it is so for Catullus.

42. Freud: *Three Essays on the Theory of Sexuality*, trans. Strachey ed. Richard, London 1977 (1905 with later revisions), 56. For a Jungian account, offering a mythological rather than a psychological interpretation, on similar lines but with a greater emphasis on the destructive power of the Great Mother, see Erich Neumann, *The Origins and History of Consciousness*, New York, 1964, 49-52.

43. Nauta, 'Catullus 63 in a Roman context', 89. However, Nauta does not himself support this view.

44. *Catullus and his world*, 181.

45. Alfred Thomas Barton, *Latin elegies after William Shakespeare's Sonnets*, Thurgau, 2006 (1923), 160.

46. A stronger version of this thesis is that by Roller, who sees the poem as 'a pointed allusion to his powerful mistress who draws innocent young men into her circle, then gelds and enslaves them', *op. cit.*, 306. But in what sense does Lesbia geld Catullus?
47. As does Daniel A. Miller, *Devotion and disillusionment: the Catullus persona in Carmen 63*, *Vexillum* No. 1, 2011, who sees Attis as a surrogate (mask is his term) for Catullus. He draws attention to his frequent feminine identification, but none of the commentators discuss Attis' motivation as a character.
48. The punctuation of this line is as recommended by Harrison and Bremmer.
49. So Hutchinson, *Hellenistic Poetry*, 314 and Bremmer, 'Attis', 60.

8

FATALE MONSTRUM:
THE FIGURE OF CLEOPATRA
IN HORACE ODE I.37

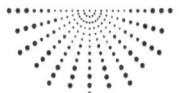

NUNC EST BIBENDUM, NUNC PEDE LIBERO

*O*n first reading this poem might seem rather crude: a celebration of a Roman victory in a jingoistic tone understandable in the circumstances, particularly if it were written only shortly after Actium, but rather lacking the balance we expect from Horace. However, I shall argue it deliberately moves from the theme of Roman success to a genuine admiration for the defeated Cleopatra and that it is her courage we are left with as the dominant idea. Horace did indeed write a rather crude and jingoistic poem about Actium, but that is Epode 9, not our poem.

In handling the theme of Roman success, Horace distorts history considerably. In discussing this I shall draw on the work of modern scholars who have assembled the numerous ancient sources and reconstructed what seems to have happened.[1]

The first stanza is straightforward. Horace takes off from a poem of Alcaeus, which began 'Now must men get drunk and drink with all their strength, since Myrsilus has died,'[2] Myrsilus being a tyrant. Horace's opening *nunc est bibendum*, now is the time for drinking, directly alludes to this and by implication prepares the reader who recognizes this for the death of a tyrant, meaning here Cleopatra. (Whether her rule of Egypt was actually harsh and arbitrary—tyrannical in the modern sense—is a possible inference he is happy to leave hanging in the air.) The association of feasting with political success was traditional. He also writes this poem, appropriately enough, in Alcaics. Lest this seem too Greek, we then immediately have some distinctively Roman references:

> Nunc est bibendum, nunc pede libero
> pulsanda tellus, nunc Saliaribus
>   ornare puluinar deorum
>   tempus erat dapibus, sodales.

> *Now is the time for dancing, now the ground should be trodden with unfettered feet, now would be the time, my friends, to decorate the couches of the gods with a feast worthy of the Salii.*

The *Salii* were a Roman priesthood of Mars, known for their leaping dances, and the reference to the *puluinar* is to the festal ceremony known as the *lectisternium*, in which images of the gods were placed on couches in the streets and offered food. In shifting from *nunc est* to *tempus erat* rather than *tempus est*, Horace is suggesting that this would be an appropriate celebration rather than actually advocating its performance, as the real celebration will be the triumph of Octavian, hinted at also in the central simile of the poem and directly referred to at the end. *Sodales*, which can mean both priests, i.e. here the Salii, and also friends, is a neat way of combining the ceremonial with the simply social aspects of this notional celebration. So the rest of this first stanza brings us firmly back to Rome and its customs.

The second stanza gives the reason for the celebration, namely Cleopatra's defeat, but the characterisation of her is unstoppable and runs over to the third:

> antehac nefas depromere Caecubum
> cellis auitis, dum Capitolio
>   regina dementis ruinas
>   funus et imperio parabat

contaminato cum grege turpium
morbo uirorum, quidlibet impotens
      sperare fortunaque dulci
         ebria.

Before this it would have been wrong to bring out the Caecuban wine from our fathers' cellars while the queen was planning mad ruin for the Capitol and death for the empire, with her diseased and disgusting degraded men, unable to hope for anything at all, drunk as she was with sweet fortune.

Here the historical distortions begin. One can appreciate that it might not have been appropriate to drink the vintage wine in a time of civil war, but Horace does not refer to that. Instead, he suggests that Cleopatra had aggressive designs on Rome. This is nonsense: Egypt had not been an expansionist power for centuries; it was Rome which was increasing its empire in the Eastern Mediterranean. And the main agent in that was Antonius, Mark Antony in English, who is significantly not named at all in this poem. This is in marked contrast to Epode 9, where his defeat is the main subject. When Octavian declared war on Cleopatra, he was really attacking Antony, by then allied to her: he passed off a new phase in the civil war as if it were a war against a foreign power. This was good politics but bad history and Horace must have known it. The strange thing is that the details he offers to characterise Cleopatra have the effect of minimizing rather than enhancing the threat she supposedly presented. If she was surrounded with ineffectual eunuchs and was wildly overoptimistic about her chances of success, presuming on her previous relationship with Julius Caesar and current one with Antony, then she was not really that formidable an opponent. (The eunuchs also turn up in Epode 9; Horace's fascinated disgust leads him to overrate their importance.) It is in refusing to name her that he really suggests her power—everyone knows who he means. And everyone also knew that she was allied to Antony, Octavian's real enemy.

We come then to his version of Actium:

>   sed minuit furorem
> uix una sospes nauis ab ignibus,
> mentemque lymphatam Mareotico
>   redegit in ueros timores
>   Caesar ab Italia uolantem
>
> remis adsurgens, ...

But the fact that scarcely one ship escaped unharmed from the flames reduced her mania and what brought her mind, maddened by Mareotic wine, back to real fear was Caesar, pressing on with his oars as she flew away from Italy ...

What actually happened was that Cleopatra, rather than fleeing, broke out from Octavians's blockade, retained her fleet of sixty ships and, most importantly, her treasure, and got safely back to Egypt. Antony's task was to hold Octavian at bay to cover her. This he achieved. What was disastrous to their cause was Antony's abandonment of his land army and many of his ships when he followed her. This destroyed his standing as a war leader. As for Octavian, he did not set off for Egypt until the following year, so to suggest that he was pressing on after Cleopatra is fanciful. To be fair to Horace, he would have had to rely on accounts of Actium by Octavian and his key supporters; he was not writing history where he would have expected to talk to eyewitnesses on both sides, so he might have been misled about the conduct of the battle. But that does not apply to the year's delay before Octavian went to Egypt to mop up. He even went back to Italy for part of the interim so Horace would have known this. This telescoping of history is both to project Octavian as an effective war leader following up his success and to prepare us for the following simile.

This simile, which Horace then introduces to characterise him, is placed at the centre of the poem and is its turning point:

> accipiter uelut
> mollis columbas aut leporem citus
>   uenator in campis niualis

Haemoniae, daret ut catenis

fatale monstrum;

like a hawk after a gentle dove or a swift huntsman after a hare on the snowy fields of Thessaly, to give the death-dealing apparition to chains;

We need to examine this closely. Clearly Octavian is the hawk and the huntsman—both objects of admiration—and the image of the hawk also takes up the previous one of him flying over the waves to pursue Cleopatra. Though he did no such thing, that is doubtless how he wished to be thought of. Both the dove and the hare are defenceless against their predators but the corollary of this is that they then represent Cleopatra and so are quite unsuitable images for someone who supposedly is the aggressor. Their vulnerability might arouse our sympathy for them,[3] but carefully Horace does not dwell on this but proceeds immediately to the key image of Cleopatra as a *fatale monstrum*. Unfortunately, the phrase is almost untranslatable: *fatal monster* does not catch it at all. *Fatale* means something like 'doom-laden' and a *monstrum* is normally a portent or a prodigy outside the norm of nature.[4] Of course, this is a ridiculous exaggeration of the threat she presented—or even of that which the unmentioned Antony presented by then. He had already been outnumbered at Actium and by the time the conflict had moved to Egypt he had lost most of his army. However, it may well accurately represent the way Octavian wanted the threat to be represented, and this whole simile is a vignette of how he wished to be seen. Perhaps he would want us to consider Cleopatra a *monstrum* because she was very probably the product of brother-sister incest, of Ptolemy XI and Cleopatra V. As for the chains, they are the second oblique reference to the triumph he planned, at which he would have liked to be able to parade Cleopatra in fetters.

But it was not to be. The final three stanzas all present Cleopatra positively:

quae generosius
perire quaerens nec muliebriter

> expauit ensem nec latentis
> > classe cita reparauit oras;

But she, wanting to die in a nobler way did not fear the sword in a
womanish way nor with her swift fleet did she reach for a secret shore;

From this point on, the characterisation of her from earlier in the poem is reversed: instead of being despised for being surrounded by degraded men, i.e. eunuchs, womanish men, she is praised for not being womanish; instead of being left with scarcely one ship she now has a fleet; and the possible escape to a safe haven is presented as a realistic option and not a contemptible flight. She is no longer represented as either drunk or mad. Furthermore, she is daring and brave in her famous suicide:

> ausa et iacentem uisere regiam
> uultu sereno, fortis et asperas
> > tractare serpentis, ut atrum
> > > corpore combiberet uenenum,

but dared to contemplate the royal city lying defeated with a calm expres-
sion and she was brave enough to handle the sharp-toothed serpents so that
she absorbed their black venom in her body,

The final reflection on her is wholly admiring:

> deliberata morte ferocior,
> saeuis Liburnis scilicet inuidens
> > privata deduci superbo
> > > non humilis mulier triumpho.

more fiercely resolved on death, no doubt determined to cheat the cruel
Liburnians in their wish for her, no humble woman, to be led out,
deprived of her royal status, in a proud triumph.

It is impossible really to convey the effect of the Latin word order in

English. The Liburnians were fast manoeuvrable galleys, possibly originally developed by the tribe of that name. Here they are a proxy for Octavian, whom Horace does not wish to present as vindictive. Still, he is implicitly there in the final word of the poem, where at last his twice anticipated triumph is finally heralded. The effect of *superbo*, proud, in this context is unsettling: of course, for Octavian the triumph would be proud, but surrounded by words emphasizing Cleopatra's defiance the meaning is almost *insulting*, as of course it would have been for her. Furthermore, the direct rhyme between *superbo* and *triumpho*, something Roman writers normally avoided, emphasizes for Octavian and an unreflective audience the completeness of his victory but to more sensi٠tive readers also its crudity.

The Ode as a whole has been called 'unpleasantly vindictive.'[5] I hope I have demonstrated that it is more complex than that, moving as it does from a total identification with Octavian's cause to a genuine admiration for Cleopatra. Horace gives two stanzas to denigrate her but three to admire her. Clearly his attitude to her across the poem as a whole is complicated. And something similar has to be true of his attitude towards Octavian. He had reason to be grateful to Octavian, as well as of course to Maecenas, but this was not just for patronage and personal kindness: even more important was that the victory at Actium and its follow-up in Egypt put an end to the civil war. If the price of that was accepting what one might call the official propaganda about Actium, it was a price well worth paying. But treating Cleopatra rather than Antony as the enemy also made for a more balanced, a more interesting poem than writing about Antony directly, as we can see from comparing our poem with Epode 9. This is Antony in Epode 9:

Romanus, eheu,—posteri negabitis—
    emancipatus feminae
fer uallum et arma miles et spadonibus
    seruire rugosis potest,
interque signa turpe militaria
    sol aspicit conopium.

A Roman, alas—our successors will deny it—subservient to a woman, carries a stake and weapons as a soldier and can endure serving wrinkled eunuchs, while the sun shines down on the disgraceful mosquito net among the military standards.

Antony is absent from our Ode and Cleopatra from Octavian's triumph; Horace exploits these absences in constructing this much more subtle poem.

Horace's treatment of the defeated Cleopatra is worth comparing with Virgil's. This is Virgil's representation of the aftermath of Actium on the shield of Aeneas:

ipsa uidebatur uentis regina uocatis
uela dare et laxos iam iamque immittere funis.
illam inter caedes pallentem morte futura
fecerat ignipotens undis et Iapyge ferri,
contra autem magno maerentem corpore Nilum
pandentemque sinus et tota ueste uocantem
caeruleum in gremium latebrosaque flumina uictos.

(Aeneid VIII.707-13)

The queen herself, after she had invoked the winds and was seen to spread the sails and now, even now, to loosen the slackened ropes. Among the slaughter the god of fire had fashioned her, pale at approaching death, being carried by the waves and by Iapyx [the wind blowing South from the Adriatic], *while opposite her was the mourning Nile with his great body, opening out his folds and with all his clothing calling the defeated into his sea-blue lap and sheltering streams.*

Virgil dwells on her defeat and can afford to be compassionate about it. Furthermore, the phrase *pallentem morte futura*, is almost exactly what he had said about Dido, who was *pallida morte futura* (*Aeneid* IV.644), pale at approaching death.[6] Both Dido and Cleopatra were foreign queens who nearly seduced Roman leaders from their destiny. They had to be rejected but our sympathies are with Dido—and can be with Cleopatra.

Horace's note of proud defiance provides a different resolution for the fate of the queen. But the motivation is similar. Admiration for a defeated enemy is the lesson of the *Iliad* and it was not lost on either Horace or Virgil.

---

1. The ancient sources include Dio, Plutarch, Suetonius and others. I have relied on Ronald Syme, *The Roman Revolution*, Oxford, 1952, Si Sheppard, *Actium 31 B.C.: Downfall of Antony and Cleopatra*, Oxford, 2009 and the introduction to this poem in Nisbet and Hubbard's Commentary. I shall not cite individual sources as the points I shall rely on are uncontroversial.

2. Alcaeus fragment 332 Lobel-Page; *Greek Lyric: Sappho and Alcaeus*, trans. David A. Campbell, Harvard, 1990 (1982), 372.

3. To the suggestion that people in the ancient world were not as sympathetic to animal suffering as moderns often are I would point to the image of the hare in the first chorus of the *Agammemnon*, 119-137, and that of the nightingale in *Georgics* IV.511-5.

4. Eduard Fraenkel, *Horace*, Oxford, 1957, 160.

5. W. H. Alexander quoted in Fraenkel, *Horace*, 160.

6. I owe this point to Michael Putnam, *Virgil's Epic Designs: Ekphrasis in the Aeneid*, New Haven, 1998, 148.

9

TIME AND TRANSITION
IN HORACE ODE 2.5

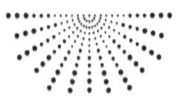

NONDUM SUBACTA FERRE IUGUM UALET

*a*t first reading this is a rather unpleasant poem and also badly balanced: the picture of the girl being like a heifer not yet able to bear the weight of the bull rushing to mate (*nec tauri ruentis |in uenerem tolerare pondus*) seems crude, the man seems to be a philanderer who wants to win over an underage girl and why does Horace give a whole stanza to celebrating the androgynous charm of the man's previous fancy boy? However, this is both a better and a subtler poem than first appears.

We need to start with some background. Roman girls were commonly betrothed shortly after they became sexually mature, the age of consent being twelve, while marriage followed when they were able to bear children. Their husbands were usually older, sometimes substantially so. These unions were not necessarily unhappy: Pompey the Great was famously devoted to his much younger wife Iulia, daughter of Julius Caesar. Augustus notoriously strengthened marriage laws in 18 B.C. with a view to increasing the number of legitimate children born. However, this ode was published along with the rest of the first three books in 23 B.C. so the new marriage legislation was not yet on the horizon. Even so, the issue which gave rise to it—the reluctance of men to marry—would have been apparent. A poem which examines how to make marriage work would have been seen as supportive of the regime, even though it does not deal with the bearing of children.

It is indeed marriage which is the setting of our ode: the word *maritum* in line 16 among animals means a mate, as in the metaphor of the heifer which makes its last appearance in the poem in this line, but among human beings it means a husband or a bridegroom, not a lover, who is *amans* or *amator*.[1] So this is a poem whose setting is a typical marriage of an as yet immature girl with a rather older man and whose immediate counsel is of restraint. This at once puts the poem in a better light, so with this in mind we can examine it in detail.

Nondum subacta ferre iugum ualet
ceruice, nondum munia comparis
    aequare nec tauri ruentis
      in uenerem tolerare pondus.

She is not yet strong enough to bear the yoke with a meek neck, nor is she ready to take equal responsibility nor to endure the weight of a bull rushing to mate.

The comparison of a girl or woman with a heifer or cow who is wild and needs breaking in by marriage was a familiar trope. But when the metaphor is extended like this, the Roman reader would immediately think of two figures from mythology. The first is Io, seduced by Zeus and punished, in one version by Hera, by being turned into a cow; Zeus turned himself into a bull to continue to mate with her. Io went on to be tormented by a gadfly.[2] The second is even more sinister and is evoked specifically by the fourth line: Pasiphaë, made to lust after a bull, for whom Daedalus made a wooden cow in which the bull impregnated her; their offspring was the Minotaur.[3] This had been evoked by Virgil a few years earlier in a passage Horace and his readers would have known:

fortunatam, si numquam armenta fuissent,
Pasiphaën niuei solatur amore iuuenci.
a, uirgo infelix, quae te dementia cepit! (*Eclogues* 6.45-7)

He [Silenus] *consoles Pasiphaë, who would have been happy if herds of cattle had never existed, with her desire for the snow-white bull—ah, unhappy girl, what madness has overcome you!*

Horace's line manages to evoke both the eager desire of the bridegroom and the tragic destiny of the girl if it is satisfied. Horace does not parade his mythological references, and the poem makes sense without them, but it is richer if we can recognize them. The line, though strong, is not crude.

I need to stress this as the English reader of Horace's line will immediately think of Cleopatra's 'O happy horse, to bear the weight of Antony!'[4] Shakespeare's line is quite opposite in its implications to Horace's: his Cleopatra is an experienced woman who relishes the prospect of a sexual encounter with Antony; Horace's girl is inexperienced and not ready for sexual activity.

After an initial stanza which looks forward, the second stanza looks back to the life the girl prefers, presented with such enthusiasm that it runs over into an extra line:

circa uirentis est animus tuae
campos iuuencae, nunc fluviis grauem
   solantis aestum, nunc in udo
     ludere cum uitulis salicto

praegestientis.

The thoughts of your heifer are on green fields, sometimes relieving great heat in the river, sometimes having an overpowering desire to play with the younger ones in a thicket of willows.

However it may be with heifers, the girl is still at the age when she prefers the company of those of her own sex and age or younger—the *uitulae*, calves, are younger than the *iuuenca*, heifer—and is not ready for married life. But, now sensitized to mythological references, we can think of another girl who was playing with her friends when she was snatched away: Persephone, or Proserpina as she is in Latin.[5] As with the previous mythological references this is just sufficiently hinted at to put a cloud over too early a consummation of the marriage.

This is reinforced by Horace's use of the extraordinary word *praegestientis*. This is obviously intended to draw attention, reinforced not only by its rarity but also by its position after an enjambment. The fact that he fits it into half an Alcaic line may have been one of his reasons for choosing this metre: it scans *praēgēstiēntīs*. OLD notes only three occurrences of this verb; this is the third, and the two earlier ones would both have been familiar to Horace:

> nunc iam nulla uiro iuranti femina credat,
> nulla uiri speret sermones esses fideles;
> quis dum aliquid cupiens animus praegestit apisci
> nil metuunt iurare, nihil promittere parcunt.
>
> (Catullus 64: 143-6)

> *From now on let no woman believe a man who swears oaths, nor look for truthful speeches from a man; while his desirous nature is very eager to gain something, they will not fear to make oaths, nor be sparing of promises.*

> Praegestit animus iam uidere, primum lautos iuuenes mulieris
> beatae ac nobilis familiaris, deinde fortis uiros ab imperatrice in
> insidiis atque in praesidio balnearum conlocatos.
>
> (Cicero, *pro Caelio* 67)

> *I am really enthusiastic to see, firstly, those smart young men, the friends of a happy and noble lady, then on the brave men placed by their mistress in a fortified ambush at the baths.*

The Catullus is part of Ariadne's lament, the Cicero part of his ironical attack on Clodia; what they have in common is the atmosphere of seduction and betrayal. Horace turns the word to a quite different use: his girl's enthusiasm is to continue playing girlish games and precisely not to engage in the kinds of adult activities which the earlier authors present. Rhetorically, it is an implied antithesis.

After these complexities the remainder of the third stanza is straight-forward:

> tolle cupidinem
> immitis uuae: iam tibi liuidos
>   distinguet autumnus racemos
>   purpureo uarius colore.

Remove your wish for an unripe grape: soon Autumn with its many colours will mark out for you the ripening bunches.

Horace has changed the metaphor from a heifer to a grape as he wants to bring out that the girl is maturing and that this will happen soon (*iam*). Ripeness is presumably easier to see in a grape than maturity in a heifer. (For the colour words *liuidos* and *purpureo* the version I have given is obviously a stopgap, but precise renderings of these, as of other Roman colour words is a difficult issue, and not central to the meaning here.)

We are now at the centre of the poem and at its central idea:

> iam te sequetur; currit enim ferox
> aetas et illi quos tibi dempserit
>   adponet annos;

Soon she will follow you: for her wild time runs out and will give the years to her which it takes from you.

The crucial sentence *iam te sequetur*, soon she will follow you, would be the more powerful for the Roman reader who recognised it as deriving from Sappho: 'If she runs away, soon she shall pursue.'[6] It is not just that the girl will grow up, stop playing games with her girl-friends and be ready for sexual activity: she will actually be enthusiastic about it. He need only wait for that. However, while she makes the transition to adult woman, he will be getting older. The time for love is a relatively restricted period; she is entering it but the time will come for him to leave it. We would say that he is not getting any younger. So the underlying idea, the framework on which the poem is constructed, is that of the passage of time and what it does to human beings.

In the second half of the poem the attention shifts from the girl to her husband and we move from mythological allusions to references to real or at least possible people. This turn is neatly done:

> iam proterua
> fronte petet Lalage maritum,
> dilecta, quantum ...[7]

Soon Lalage will encounter her husband head on, loved more than ...

This is the only time that the girl is actually named. Lalage, like the other names in the poem is a Greek name, but this does not mean either that the poem has a Greek setting or that the people named in it are slaves or recently freed; rather it has a generalising effect, that Horace has no particular girl in mind but is writing about a typical situation.[8] He also uses these names again in other poems,[9] but there is no reason to suppose that the same individuals, real or imagined, are intended. It is interesting then that the nominal addressee of the poem, the husband, is not named. He is clearly a Roman husband, so a Greek name would be inappropriate but a Roman one too specific and could be taken as referring to a particular individual. Some critics, such as Nisbet and Hubbard, consider that Horace could be addressing himself; however, not only would this contradict my reading of *maritum*, given that Horace never married, but it would turn the poem back to the rather sleazy interpretation which the purpose of this paper is to argue against. Taking the addressee as someone else, real or imagined, makes it a better poem.

As an older man, he can be expected to have had previous relationships. However, we should be wary: the situation may be no different from that of best man speeches in weddings nowadays: it is customary to present the bridegroom as a bit of a lad, but the sexual adventures alluded to may be more aspirational than achieved.[10] With this in mind we can consider the first two credited to him:

dilecta, quantum non Pholoe fugax,
non Chloris albo sic umero nitens
   ut pura nocturno renidet
      luna mari

*loved more than the flighty Pholoe, more than Chloris with her white
shoulders shining like the cloudless moon as it reflects in the night sea*

The force of *fugax* in connection with Pholoe is a little difficult to
establish: 'elusive' (Quinn), 'shy' (Rudd), 'unapproachable' (Michie) are
some suggestions. I prefer 'flighty' as I imagine this was the husband's
first attempt at a relationship, and that it was really more of a crush;
Pholoe was inaccessible to him, for whatever reason. This is in any case
the only thing we are told about her.

We learn a little more about Chloris, but only about her looks, not
her personality. Her name means pale (Greek χλωρός); this was the name
of the surviving daughter of Niobe, originally named Meliboia and
renamed after surviving the tragedy. She later married Neleus and was
mother of Nestor.[11] However, this does not add anything to Horace's
poem, so I do not think there is an implied reference to it here. We also
wonder whether she too was admired from a distance, as the addressee
does not seem to know anything about her.

Now we come to the third of the bridegroom's previous loves, who
is given more space than the two predecessors:

   Cnidiusue Gyges,

quem si puellarum insereres choro,
mire sagacis falleret hospites
   discrimen obscurum solutis
      crinibus ambiguoque uultu.

*and more than Cnidian Gyges, whom if you put him in a troop of
dancing girls, it would trick even perceptive visitors to their surprise, for
the difference* [between the sexes] *would be concealed by his flowing hair
and androgynous face.*

Pholoe gets one line, Chloris three and Gyges nearly five. It becomes clearer that it is indeed a bridegroom rather than simply a husband to whom the poem is addressed. The need to put aside a sexual interest in pretty boys, whether real or imagined, was perhaps a traditional theme at weddings; the *Fescennina iocatio* (Fescennine teasing) of Catullus 61 suggests exactly this. In fact, the man, as well as the girl, needs to grow up; she has to give up playing with her girlfriends, he has to give up love affairs, both hopeless crushes on unattainable girls and also affairs with pretty boys.

As for Gyges himself, his name has a history of its own and with him we return to mythological allusions. He is from Cnidus, now Knidos in Turkey, famous for its statue of Aphrodite by Praxiteles, so a suitable origin for a boy who is a love object. Gyges was the name of a bodyguard of king Kandaules, who induced him to let him see his queen naked, following which Gyges conspired with the queen to kill the king and take the throne and the queen.[12] The relevance of that story to this Gyges is that of contrast, indeed another implied antithesis: we cannot imagine this Gyges getting caught up in such a plot. There was another Gyges: the hundred-handed Titan Gyas or Gyges probably referred to at Odes 2.17 and 3.4.[13] This ferocious character is even more different from this Gyges, though I think it is rather the Gyges of Herodotus whom Horace has in mind here. The point is surely that effeminate good looks such as this Gyges has are very fleeting, far more so than those of pretty girls; the time for him to be a love object is briefer than for Lalage and her husband.

And with this we can see why Horace gave this issue a whole stanza. The first stanza dealt with Lalage's sexual immaturity but went on to envisage her maturing and in due course her readiness for sexual life as a married woman. The last stanza balances this by considering Gyges, who has no future as a pretty boy: his maturing will mean he loses his effeminate appearance. Furthermore, it will no longer—according to Roman norms—be appropriate for him to have a sexual relationship with a man, or, if he does, he becomes an object of scorn. Compared to that grim fate, Lalage's future of normal married life is something not to be feared.

Underlying the whole poem is therefore not only the passage of time but the necessity and inevitability of transition. This is what gives it its unity and makes it a better poem than may first appear.

---

1. Lewis and Short and OLD, supported by Quinn. Nisbet and Hubbard, however, explicitly prefer 'mate' rather than 'husband.' I thought I should test this by examining a couple of love poets. Catullus uses *maritus* several times, for example in his marriage hymn, poem 61, but always to mean husband, bridgegroom or spouse. In Propertius 2.7 the *maritus* is explicitly contrasted with *amantes*.

2. The source of this version is Aeschylus, *Suppliants* 291-307; Io appears and tells her own story in *Prometheus Bound*, 640-86. The earliest version was in the Hesiodic *Catalogue of women*, fr. 72 Most.

3. The story was very well known through vase paintings though the earliest literary sources are now fragmentary: *Catalogue of women* fr. 93 Most and Euripides, *Cretans*, of which, however, enough remains of a big speech by Pasiphaë to give the story, fr. 472e Kannicht. She blames Minos for her predicament.

4. *Antony and Cleopatra*, I.5.21.

5. The primary literary source is the *Homeric Hymn to Demeter*.

6. Sappho 1.21,.

7. I have followed Klingner, Quinn and Shackleton Bailey in preferring *petet* to *petit* in line 16, from a different branch of the manuscript tradition.

8. I have followed Quinn's discussion of Horace's use of Greek names here, his edition 131.

9. There is a Pholoe in Odes 1.33, described as *asperam ... Pholoen* and both names occur in Odes 3.15. The Gyges of Odes 3.7 is clearly older than the one here. I consider Gyges the hundred-handed Titan below.

10. I agree here with Nisbet and Hubbard: 'Horace seems to suggest the indecisive yearnings of the unfulfilled lover.'

11. The only unambiguous source for this now is Pausanias, 2.21.9, which of course is later than Horace. However, there are earlier scatted allusions, assembled by Timothy Gantz, *Early Greek Myth: A Guide to Literary and Artistic Sources*, Baltimore, 1993, 538-9, notably in the fragmentary *Niobe* of Sophocles, particularly fr. 444 Radt.

12. Herodotus I.8-13. There is a different version of this story in Plato, *Republic*, 359d-360b, but the Herodotian version makes the better contrast here.

13. The text is uncertain and depends on emendation in each place.

10

JUNO'S CHANGE OF MIND IN HORACE ODE 3.3

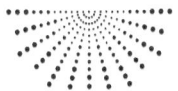

HORACE'S DIALOGUE WITH VIRGIL

*J*uno's speech traverses, though of course much more briefly, some of the same themes as the *Aeneid*, though in a different setting and to a different end. The similarities are so close that they are worth examining. Obviously, Horace and Virgil were contemporaries, colleagues and friends and they also worked under the same constraints, such as the need to acknowledge the principate of Augustus. I am not here concerned whether there was a direct influence of one on the other, though this is likely; Horace's ode had been written before 23 B.C. when it was published; the *Aeneid* did not become generally available until after Virgil's death in 19 B.C. though it is possible, and indeed probable, that the two poets showed each other their work and may have discussed their handling of themes they were both interested in.

The occasion for Juno's speech is the death and apotheosis of Romulus, so well after both the Trojan war and the adventures of Aeneas and also well before the time Horace is writing. He begins by praising the virtue of tenacity in the upright man who sticks to his purpose (*iustum et tenacem propositi uirum*), as exemplified immediately by Augustus but also in the past by Romulus, who was deified because of it, setting a happy precedent. Romulus became identified with Quirinus, who may originally have been a Sabine god; the name means spear-wielder. Horace imagines a council of the gods, such as took place in the Homeric epics and also in the *Aeneid* Book X, and at his council Juno praises this virtue of tenacity:

> hac Quirinus
> Martis equis Acheronta fugit (15-6)

Through this (virtue) Quirinus avoided Acheron by the horses of Mars.

It seems that the idea for this apotheosis came, as a literary device, from Ennius[1] and it certainly later became a topos, though used only here by Horace. However, he does not include a demand for the exaltation of Romulus in the actual speech he gives Juno. Virgil, however, does hint at this:

> uiden, ut geminae stant uertice cristae
> et pater ipse suo superum iam signat honore?
> > (*Aeneid* VI.779-80)[2]

Do you see how twin plumes stand on his head and how the father of the gods now marks him with his own honours?

This topos was then taken up by Ovid, who used it twice. It also appears in Livy and Plutarch.[3]

The theme of the speech itself is Juno's hatred for Troy and the Trojans, and hence of Aeneas and, by implication, the Romans. However, half way through her speech she renounces this hatred provided certain conditions are met. What are her reasons for her hatred? She gives two:

> Ilion, Ilion
> fatalis incestusque iudex
> > et mulier peregrina uertit

in puluerem, ex quo destituit deos
mercede pacta Laomedon, mihi
   castaeque damnatum Mineruae
      cum populo et duce fraudulento. (18-24)

A disastrous and adulterous judge and a foreign woman reduced Troy to dust, Troy given to me and chaste Minerva for punishment, because Laomedon cheated the gods despite having agreed the payment and it was condemned, together with its people and treacherous leader, to the judgement of myself and chaste Minerva.

Unfortunately, a reasonably fluent English version cannot convey the force of the opening apostrophe to 'Ilion, Ilion,' nor the sequence of thought in the Latin order. In mythological terms Juno's argument is coherent enough. But without turning the poem into a political allegory we can see that it also alludes to contemporary events. The foreign woman, *mulier peregrina*, Helen, would immediately also suggest Cleopatra, the Egyptian queen who supposedly had designs on Rome, from which it is a short stretch to see in the reference to Paris a reference to Antony. The fact that Juno names neither Helen nor Paris also strengthens these oblique hints; psychologically it is an expression of her contempt, rhetorically an ingenious use of metonymy. Similarly, the mention a few lines later to the supposed extension of the Trojan war by the conflict of the gods, a detail not in Homer or the epic cycle, seems a glancing reference to the civil war:

nostris ductum seditionibus
bellum resedit. (29-30)

The war which was prolonged by our treacherous quarrels has finished.

The reference to Laomedon may seem cryptic—he had promised to pay Apollo and Neptune for building the walls of Troy but reneged on the agreement—but it is explained by looking at Virgil's use of this myth:

di patrii Indigetes et Romule Vestaque mater,
quae Tuscum Tiberim et Romana Palatia seruas,
hunc saltem euerso iuuenem succurrere saeclo
ne prohibete. satis iam pridem sanguine nostro
Laomedonteae luimus periuria Troiae;
iam pridem nobis caeli te regia, Caesar,
inuidet atque hominum queritur curare triumphos.
                                    (Georgics I.498-505)

*Gods of my fatherland, heroes of the land, both you, Romulus, and you,
mother Vesta, who protect the Tuscan Tiber and the Roman Palatine, do
not prevent this man from rescuing a fallen world! We have paid with
our blood for Laomedon's treachery at Troy for long enough; heaven's
kingdom has grudged you, Caesar for long enough, and complained that
you care for earthly triumphs.*

Virgil had completed the *Georgics* by 29 B.C., when he and
Maecenas read it to Augustus, so this passage would have been familiar
to Horace while composing the Odes. Horace might well have expected
Augustus and Maecenas, his patrons, to recognize in his passage an allusion to Virgil's and hence another reference to Augustus, whom he has
already suggested deserves divine honours for his possession of the
virtue of tenacity:

hac arte Pollux et uagus Hercules
enisus arcis attigit igneas,
    quos inter Augustus recumbens
        purpureo bibet ore nectar; (9-12)

*With this quality Pollux and wandering Hercules reached the fiery
citadels by their own efforts; among them Augustus reclining will drink
nectar with bright red lips.*

Juno's hostility to Troy and hence to Aeneas and his companions is
a major theme in the *Aeneid*. Right at the beginning Virgil presents this,
referring to Juno as *regina deum*, queen of heaven, and asking:

tantaene animis caelestibus irae? *(Aeneid* I.11.)

Are there really such great resentments in heavenly beings?

In recounting the fall of Troy he presents Juno as leading the attack:

> hic Iuno Scaeas saeuissima portas
> prima tenet sociumque furens a nauibus agmen
> ferro accincta uocat (*Aeneid* II.612-4)

Here, Juno, the fiercest one, is in the front to hold the Scaean gates and, girded with iron, wildly calls on her allied company from the ship.

The sibyl says to Aeneas in passing:

> nec Teucris addita Iuno
> usquam aberit (*Aeneid* VI.90-1)

Nor will Juno ever desist from dogging the Trojans.

Juno only finally ceases her hostility at the direct command of Iuppiter:

> uentum ad supremum est. terris agitare uel undis
> Troianos potuisti, infandum accendere bellum,
> deformare domum et luctu miscere hymenaeos:
> ulterius temptare ueto. (*Aeneid* XII.803-6)

The end has come. You have been able to pursue the Trojans by land and sea, to inflame dreadful war, to spoil homes and mix weddings with misery. I forbid you to go further.

She yields, but with certain conditions, which I shall return to:

et nunc cedo equidem pugnasque exosa relinquo...
occideritque sinas cum nomine Troia.
(*Aeneid* XII 818, 828)

And now I give way and abandon the conflict in disgust... Let Troy be
fallen together with her name.

Cyril Bailey suggested that Juno is 'Aeneas' evil; genius, the fate
which drives him into misfortune, *Teucris addita Iuno*.' Contrasting her
with Venus, Aeneas' mother, he says: 'It would perhaps be truest to say
that Venus represents that which, in the divine will, made for the success
or happiness of the Aeneadae, Iuno that which made for their misery
and thwartings; they are the good and evil sides of the divine will
expressed in their μοῖρα.'[4] It takes the whole of the *Aeneid* for Juno's
resistance to Aeneas and the Trojans to be overcome.

In Horace, however, her change of mind comes by her own will and
is summed up in one word:

protinus et grauis
iras et inuisum nepotem,
Troica quem peperit sacerdos,

Marti redonabo. (30-33)

From now on, my deep anger and hatred for the grandson which the
Trojan priestess bore, for the sake of Mars I shall renounce.[5]

There is enormous emphasis on the crucial word *redonabo*, which is
the turning point of her speech. Firstly, it is a rare verb, attested only
here and at 2.7.3 before Apuleius.[6] It is further emphasized by enjambment, the sentence being run on from the preceding quatrain. Finally, it
is emphasized metrically by being placed where it overrides the normal
caesura after the fifth syllable with an elision:

Mārtī rĕdōnābō; (i)ll(um) ĕgŏ lūcĭdās

It would not be too much to say that in this one word Juno makes the transition which in Virgil takes her the whole of the *Aeneid*.

She proceeds to describe what the apotheosis of Romulus involves:

> illum ego lucidas
> inire sedes, ducere nectaris
>   sucos et adscribi quietis
>   ordinibus patiar deorum. (33-6)

I shall allow him to enter the regions of light, to drink the juice of nectar and to be enrolled in the rank of the gods.

Horace has already made it clear, as noted above, that Augustus is in line for similar honours.

As in Virgil, Juno imposes conditions on her renunciation. In Virgil there are four of these:

> ne uetus indigenas nomen mutare Latinos
> neu Troas fieri iubeas Teucrosque uocari
> aut uocem mutare uiros aut uertere uestem.
> sit Latium, sint Albani per saecula reges,
> sit Romana potens Itala uirtute propago:
> occidit, occideritque sinas cum nomine Troia.
>   (*Aeneid* XII.823-8)

Do not order the native Latins to change their ancient name or to become Trojans and be called Teucrians or to change their language or alter their manner of dress. Let Latium be, let Albans be kings for ages, let there be a Roman race, strong in Italian courage: let Troy be fallen together with her name.

Horace uses only the last of these conditions and adds two of his own. In each case, providing the condition is observed, there will be a glorious future for the future Romans. This is the first:

> dum Priami Paridisque busto

insultet armentum et catulos ferae
celent inultae (40-2)

*while a herd of cattle tramples on the funeral pyre of Priam and Paris
and wild beasts hide their young unpunished.*

Abandoned cities becoming waste places seems to have been not
only a reality in the ancient world but also a literary topos; it turns up
also in various places in the Old Testament, such as Isaiah 13:21-2.

Then gold, representing wealth, is not to be pursued:

aurum inrepertum et sic melius situm,
cum terra celat, spernere fortior
   quam cogere humanos in usus
      omne sacrum rapiente dextra. (49-52)

[Rome will be] *stronger in rejecting gold, better placed when the earth
hides it than when forcing it into human uses with a thieving hand
snatching at everything sacred.*

The suggestion that Troy was wealthy and decadent can also be read
as another glance at the conditions in pre-Augustan Rome when wealth
bought private armies and could lead to the desecration of sanctuaries.

The final condition is really the same as the first, and is where
Horace coincides with Virgil:

sed bellicosis fata Quiritibus
hac lege dico, ne nimium pii
   rebusque fidentes auitae
      tecta uelint reparare Troiae.

Troiae renascens alite lugubri
fortuna tristi clade iterabitur,
   ducente uictrices cateruas

coniuge me Iouis et sorore.

ter si resurgat murus aeneus
auctore Phoebo, ter pereat meis
   excisus Argiuis, ter uxor
      capta uirum puerosque ploret. (57-68)

But I reveal the future to the warlike Quirites [citizens] with this condition, that they should not, from excessive piety or overconfidence try to rebuild their homes at ancestral Troy. The destiny of a reborn Troy by an evil omen would be repeated in a dreadful slaughter, and leading the conquering troops would be myself, Jove's wife and sister. If the wall of bronze were to rise up a third time with the help of Apollo, it would fall demolished three times through my Argives, and three times would the captive wife weep for her husband and sons.

The prohibition on rebuilding Troy can be understood in several different ways. In Virgil it is part of the general theme that Aeneas should look forward rather than back. For the first half of the *Aeneid* he does indeed look back and indeed recounts much of his story himself. After the visit to the underworld in Book VI and the colloquy with the spirit of his father he looks forward. Virgil shows what can happen if one looks back in Book III, in which Aeneas visits Buthrotum and finds Andromache and Helenus wholly absorbed by the lost Troy which they have tried to recreate in miniature in a hopeless and futile gesture:

procedo et paruam Troiam simulatque magnis
Pergama et arentem Xanthi cognomine riuum
agnosco, Scaeaeque amplector limina portae.
              (*Aeneid* III 349-52)

I go forward and recognize a little Troy and a copy of great Pergamus and a dry stream named after Xanthus and embrace the threshold of a Scaean gate.

That there is no hope in going back is the inference Virgil wants us to draw. However, this idea does not seem relevant to Horace in the same way: I shall come to Horace's treatment shortly.

Another more topical reference was that the idea had been around that the capital might be moved from Rome further East. Julius Caesar had considered both Alexandria and Troy as alternatives and Antony had considered Alexandria.[7] Agrippa was based in Lesbos so a secondary centre of power in the East was already in place. However, Augustus must have decided to retain Rome as his capital and emphasized this by his rebuilding programme. The whole of the *Aeneid* is based on Aeneas reaching Italy and looking forward to Rome as having a glorious future as predicted by the spirit of Anchises. Similarly, Horace links the abandonment of Troy with the future of Rome. The passage about cattle treading on the pyres of Priam and Paris continues:

> stet Capitolium
> fulgens triumphatisque possit
> Roma ferox dare iura Medis.
>
> horrenda late nomen in ultimas
> extendat oras, qua medius liquor
> secernit Europen ab Afro,
> qua tumidus rigat arua Nilus; (42-8)

may the gleaming Capitol stand and may fierce Rome give laws to the conquered Medes. Feared from afar, may she make her name known in the most distant shores, where the middle sea [the Mediterranean] *separates Europe from Africa, where the swollen Nile irrigates the fields;*

Horace, unlike Virgil, deals with the consequences of rebuilding Troy. These would be disastrous, as Juno pointed out. Going back for Horace would not mean a hopeless attempt to recreate the past but the repetition of a disastrous war. It is impossible not to read this, in the light of the earlier similar references, as a warning about the risk of a return to civil war.

In his final stanza Horace abruptly dismisses his subject with no conclusion drawn; rhetorically this is the trope known as aposiopesis.

Why does he do so at this point? It is a final parallel with Virgil. Virgil is fond of making his points by implication rather than by statement. Horace does the same here. In Virgil, Aeneas has to let go of the memory of lost Troy, learn how to be an effective leader in Italy and look forward to future Rome. He has to learn to be precisely the kind of man of tenacity whom Horace celebrates in our poem. It take the whole of the *Aeneid* for him to achieve this. Horace, however, deliberately refrains from explicitly drawing the implied conclusion of his poem and leaves it to the reader: it is Augustus who through his tenacity saves Rome from a return to civil war.

---

1. *Remains of Early Latin I: Ennius, Caecilius* trans. E. H. Warmington, Harvard (LCL) 1935, fragments 62-4.
2. I am taking *pater ipse superum* with Austin as referring to Iuppiter.
3. *Metamorphoses* XIV, 812ff.; *Fasti* II, 485 ff; Livy I.16; Plutarch, *Romulus* 27-8.
4. Cyril Bailey, *Religion in Virgil*, Oxford 1935, 224.
5. Literally: 'I shall return to Mars', i.e. forgive him for his father's sake (Quinn).
6. OLD and Nisbet and Rudd *ad loc.*
7. Suetonius, *Julius Caesar* 79.3, Dio Cassio 50.4.1 and discussion by Nisbet and Rudd, 37-8.

11

OVID'S HAPPY AFTERNOON: A READING OF AMORES I.5

In this charming poem Ovid attempts something surprisingly difficult: a poem about making love which is not also about other things. Love poems are rarely about happy and successful love-making. Longing, courtship, frustration, disappointments, rivalries, separations and the like usually make up much more of the content. So this poem of Ovid is unusual in being a straightforward account of a happy afternoon in which lovers make love. However, it has several features which make it interesting, which I want to bring out by comparing it with passages from two earlier poems with which Ovid would have been familiar: one by Catullus and one by Propertius. I start with these.

The Catullus poem is LXVIII, like Ovid's in elegiacs, which deals with the kindness of his friend Allius (possibly a disguise for Manlius, who features in the immediately previous poem) in making a house available in which the poet could achieve a successful sexual encounter with his beloved, presumably Lesbia, though unnamed in this poem. This is a long poem of nearly 150 lines, though some argue that the first forty and the last twelve lines, dealing with his brother's death, may be separate pieces. In the first passage I want to cite, his beloved enters the house:

is clausum lato patefecit limite campum,
     isque domum nobis isque dedit dominam,
ad quam communes exerceremus amores.
     quo mea se molli candida diua pede
intulit et trito fulgentem in limine plantam
     innixa arguta constitutit solea. (LXVIII.67-71)

He [Allius] *opened up a broad path across a fenced field, and he gave me a house and he gave me its mistress, under whose roof we we might enjoy our shared love. To there my shining goddess came with dainty steps and checked her bright foot on the glittering threshold, as she stepped on it with a tap of her sandal.*

We notice here that the beloved is a mistress in the sense of being the person in charge, compared to whom the poet is then as a slave, that she is explicitly said to be a goddess, which is the theme of divinization of the beloved, a common topos in love poetry, and that, unlike the bride in a Roman marriage, she steps on the threshold rather than stepping carefully over it.[1] We should bear these points in mind when we come to Ovid.

The second passage is near the end of the poem, after several mythological passages and one autobiographical one, when the lovers finally achieve what they have been preparing for:

nec tamen illa mihi dextra deducta paterna
     fragrantem Assyrio uenit odore domum,
sed furtiua dedit muta munuscula nocte,
     ipsius ex ipso dempta uiri gremio.
quare illud satis est, si nobis is datur unis,
     quem lapide illa diem candidiore notat.
                         (LXVIII 143-8)[2]

Nor indeed did she come led by her father's hand to a house fragrant with Oriental perfume, but gave me her little stolen presents in the silence of the night, taken from the very embrace of her husband. Therefore it is

enough, if to me alone is given the day which she marks with a whiter
stone than any other.

Notice that the love-making is referred to but not described, with
the emphasis being that this is not a bride being received into a suitably
decorated home and that their time together is stolen from her life with
her husband. (The white stone is the mark of a lucky day, a reference
taken up by Propertius in the passage I am about to quote.)

I turn now to Propertius, where the poem I want to consider is
II.15, which, like Ovid's poem, deals with a successful erotic encounter.
This is a shorter poem than the Catullus but over twice the length of the
Ovid. It falls into several different sections:

I. direct reminiscence: lines 1-10;
II. direct address to Cynthia: lines 11-36;
III. reflection: lines 37-48;
IV. direct address: lines 49-54.

It is the first section which provides the most direct parallel to Ovid.
Here it is:

O me felicem! nox o mihi candida! et o tu
      lectule deliciis facte beate meis!
quam multa apposita narramus uerba lucerna,
      quantaque sublato lumine rixa fuit!
nam modo nudatis mecumst luctata papillis,
      interdum tunica duxit operta moram.
illa meos somno lapsos patefecit ocellos
      ore suo et dixit 'sicine, lente, iaces?'
quam uario amplexu mutamus bracchia! quantum
      oscula sunt labris nostra morata tuis!
                         (II.15.1-10)[3]

O happy me! O lucky night for me! And O you little bed made happy by
my darling. How many words we exchanged while the light was next to us
and what a fight there was when the light was put out! For at one time she

fought with me with her breasts bared and at times she brought about delay with her tunic covered. She opened my eyes which had drooped in sleep with her kiss and said: 'Are you really lying there like that, slow-coach?' How we shifted our arms in a variety of embraces! How long did my kisses linger on your lips!

Note that the time of day for Propertius is night, which is hardly surprising as a good time to make love. Now let us look at Ovid, and the time of day is the first matter on which he differs:

Aestus erat, mediamque dies exegerat horam;
    adposui medio membra leuanda toro.
pars adaperta fuit, pars altera clausa fenestrae;
    quale fere siluae lumen habere solent,
qualia sublucent fugiente crepuscula Phoebo,
    aut ubi nox abiit, nec tamen orta dies. (V.1-6)

It was hot and the day had gone past noon; I had put my limbs ready to rest in the middle of a divan. Part of the window [i.e. the shutter] was open, the other part closed; the light was the kind which woods almost always have, the kind of twilight which glimmers when the sun is departing or when night has gone but day has not yet dawned.

The time of day, which Catullus and Propertius had each disposed of with one word for night, is now instead early afternoon and Ovid gives six lines to developing this. The mood is determined by the use of the word *crepuscula*: this is a liminal time. The half-light in the wood suggests the world of Virgil's *Eclogues*, with the possibility of an erotic encounter always present. However, Wilkinson considers that Ovid then over-extended his scene setting. He suggests:

The comparison in lines 3-4 between the chiaroscuro in a room at noon with one shutter open and the half-light in a wood is excellent; the further comparison with the twilight after sunset or before sunrise adds nothing, and in fact slightly changes and spoils the picture.[4]

In fact, the wording Ovid has chosen has some close parallels with that in Virgil in the *Aeneid* for the appearances of gods, except that where Virgil characteristically has *nox erat*,[5] Ovid has *aestus erat* but then there was also a belief that 'supernatural beings were to be encountered at noon-day.'[6] Ovid is preparing us for someone who would be his equivalent of Catullus's *candida diva* (shining goddess).

However, he conspicuously refrains from using that language about Corinna, and in fact there is a good deal of irony about her arrival, though we notice that he does drop in the word *candida*:

> illa uerecundis lux est praebenda puellis,
>   qua timidus latebras speret habere pudor.ˋ
> ecce, Corinna uenit tunica uelata recincta,
>   candida diuidua colla tegente coma,
> qualiter in thalamos famosa Semiramis isse
>   dicitur et multis Lais amata uiris. (V.7-12)

That (kind of) light should be given to scrupulous girls, where their timid modesty may hope to have hiding places. See, Corinna comes, dressed in an unbelted tunic, her parted hair covering her white neck, just as lovely Semiramis is said to have gone to her chamber and Lais, loved by many men.

Corinna turns out to be far from timid, and the implication is reinforced by the comparisons with two historical figures: Semiramis and Lais may both have been famously beautiful but both were also said to have been promiscuous. The theme of the divinization of the beloved, present in the Catullus—and one which Propertius will take up later in his poem—is conspicuous by its absence in Ovid; indeed, the references to Semiramis and Lais implicitly contradict it: this is a normal, beautiful though possibly promiscuous, human girl.

We also notice that Catullus writes a whole poem about setting up an opportunity for him to meet up with his beloved, but that Propertius does not tell us how he and Cynthia managed to get together. Ovid's presentation, in contrast to both of these, immediately begs a number of questions. We seem to be in his house, but how did Corinna come to be there? In the immediately preceding poem Ovid is separated from his girl (not there said to be Corinna and possibly a different girl entirely) by *saeuas fores* (cruel doors, IV.62), a stock situation in Roman love poetry. But here she is there in the house already. How does she come to be there? What is her social status? She certainly does not come in either as a bride or in contrast to a bride. Ovid leaves us wondering.

At this point commentators like to speculate as to whether Corinna was a real person, as Catullus' Lesbia and Propertius' Cynthia certainly were, whether she was a composite of several women, or entirely imaginary,[7] or even, in one pleasant fancy, Ovid's first wife.[8] This cannot now be determined and anyway is irrelevant to the appreciation of this or any of the *Amores* as poems. Nor is she—or the girl in the poems where she is not named—necessarily the same girl each time. I think it is enough to consider that, whether real or fictional, at least in this poem she must have been a freedwoman, as a married Roman woman would have been officially out of bounds and a slave would not have had to be courted. More relevant is the issue of her name. The historical Corinna was a Boeotian poet of the fifth century and an occasionally successful rival to Pindar. Some fragments of her work survive.[9] Propertius refers to her once (II.3.21) and this might have suggested the use of her name by Ovid, as suggesting a girl who is a *docta puella*, a clever girl, in the sense proposed by Sharon L. James,[10] a girl who is an independent and resourceful agent and who deliberately exploits her sexual attractiveness to win money and gifts in order to earn a living. The traditional English term for this role is a courtesan. There is certainly no suggestion in Ovid that Corinna is in any way like a goddess, nor Ovid like a slave to her.

However, despite laying the grounds for Corinna to be a *docta puella*, Ovid promptly confounds our expectations and also does the opposite of Propertius. Propertius had exclaimed *quam multa apposita narramus verba lucerna* (How many words we exchanged while the light was next to us). Ovid makes no mention of any words being exchanged at all. By this account, his Corinna could be a complete ignoramus, or at least a woman who knows that some men do not like their women to appear intelligent. In fact, his account suggests to a modern reader the ideal sexual fantasy of a certain kind of young man: the girl comes in of her own accord; no words are needed; the man dispenses with all preliminaries to move as soon as possible to bed.

However, after having just departed from Propertius, Ovid now coincides with him on the issue of play fighting and byplay with Corinna's clothes. Propertius says:

> nam modo nudatis mecumst luctata papillis,
> > interdum tunica duxit operta moram. (II.15.5-6)

> *For at one time she fought with me with her breasts bared and at times she prolonged delay covered with her tunic.*

Ovid's equivalent is this:

> deripui tunicam; nec multum rara nocebat,
> > pugnabat tunica sed tamen illa tegi,
> cumque ita pugnaret, tamquam quae uincere nollet,
> > uicta est non aegre proditione sua. (V.13-6)

> *I pulled off her tunic; being loosely woven it didn't hurt much, but she struggled to be covered by it, and since she struggled like one who did not want to win, she was conquered without difficulty.*

I am clearer with Propertius than with Ovid that the girl genuinely enjoyed the play fighting. For *deripui* McKeown argues *ad loc.* that 'the sense required is "pull down" rather than the more violent "pull apart."' We must hope he is right and that the Ovid of the poem correctly judged that Corinna's resistance was just token and that he did not actually tear her tunic.

He goes on with a passage for which there is no equivalent in Propertius: a catalogue of Corinna's charms.

> ut stetit ante oculos posito uelamine nostros,
> > in toto nusquam corpore menda fuit:
> quos umeros, quales uidi tetigique lacertos!
> > forma papillarum quam fuit apta premi!

quam castigato planus sub pectore uenter!
  quantum et quale latus! quam iuuenale femur! (V.17-22)

As she stood before my eyes with her clothing put aside, nowhere on the
whole of her body was there a blemish; what shoulders, what arms I saw
and touched! The contour of her breasts was so suitable for caresses! How
flat her belly below her trim breast! How long and lovely her flank! How
youthful her thigh!

I find this both pedestrian and voyeuristic. Ovid seems to be indirectly praising himself for having won a girl with such a good figure.
Although he does refer to caressing her (*tetigique ... premi*), his appreciation seems to be primarily visual. There is a poem by Donne which has
been considered a free imitation of this one,[11] but in the equivalent
place Donne presents himself as very much actively exploring his girl's
body rather than just gazing at it:

Licence my roaving hands, and let them go,
Before, behind, between, above, below.
O my America! my new-found-land,
My Kingdome, safeliest when with one man man'd.
My Myne of precious stones: My Emperie,
How blest I am in this discovering thee!
To enter in these bonds, is to be free;
Then where my hand is set, my seal shall be.
(*Elegie XIX To his Mistress Going to Bed*, 25-32)

The way Donne involves himself with his girl here seems to me at
once both more erotic and more respectful than Ovid. In fact, Ovid
seems himself to realize something of this in his next couplet:

singula quid referam? nil non laudabile uidi,
  et nudam pressi corpus ad usque meum. (V.23-4)

Why should I recount her individual charms? I saw nothing not praise-
worthy, and I pressed her naked body against mine.

Line 24 is straightforward and admirable. Yet just before, he still seems to be awarding her marks and implicitly complimenting himself on having secured her. Donne gets rid of that idea and has a better one, using a witty double-entendre:

> To teach thee, I am naked first; why then
> What needs thou have more covering than a man.
> (*Elegie XIX* 47-8)

Before we get to Ovid's last couplet, it is worth turning back to Catullus and Propertius. Catullus's poem covers many topics, including his brother's death and various mythological figures, in the general context of Allius creating an opportunity for the lovers to meet. Their actual sexual encounter is referred to only in the words *furtiua munuscula* (stolen presents). So it is the opportunity rather than the encounter which is the theme of his poem.

Propertius, having dealt with his sexual encounter with Cynthia in the opening of his poem, goes on to a range of reflections, in particular emphasizing his devotion to her:

> atque utinam haerentis sic nos uincire catena
>   uelles, ut numquam solueret ulla dies!
> exemplo iunctae tibi sint in amore columbae,
>   masculus et totum femina coniugium.
> errat, qui finem uesani quaerit amoris:
>   uerus amor nullum nouit habere modum.
> terra prius falso partu deludet arantis,
>   et citius nigros Sol agitabit equos,
> fluminaque ad caput incipient reuocare liquores,
>   aridus et sicco gurgite piscis erit,
> quam possim nostros alio transferre dolores:
>   huius ero uiuus, mortuus huius ero.
> quod mihi si interdum talis concedere noctes
>   illa uelit, uitae longus et annus erit.
> si dabit et multas, fiam immortalis in illis:

nocte una quiuis uel deus esse potest. (II.15.25-40)[12]

And would that you wanted to bind us together with a chain, so that no day would ever separate us as we cling together. Let doves yoked together in love be your model, male and female a complete union. He errs who tries to put an end to mad love: true love does not know how to have any limit. The earth shall sooner mock ploughmen with wrong crops, the sun will sooner drive black horses and rivers begin to call their waters back to their source and fish be left thirsty from the drying up of the deep than I could transfer the sufferings of my love to another: I shall be hers while I am alive, in death I shall be hers. But if she were willing to grant me such nights from time to time, even a year of life would be long. If she will give me many, I shall become immortal in them: with one night any man could become a god.

Ezra Pound's free interpretation of part of this (he uses an older text and cuts and transposes lines) catches the tone well:

Nor can I shift my pains to other,
    Hers will I be dead,
If she confers such night upon me,
              long is my life, long in years,
If she give me many,
    God am I for the time.
       (*Homage to Sextus Propertius*, VII.35-40)[13]

This kind of sentiment is far from unusual in lovers: the divinization of the beloved leads to at least momentary divinization of the lover. However, there is nothing corresponding to this in Ovid: there is nothing in the experience beyond itself. This we can see from his ending:

cetera quis nescit? lassi requieuimus ambo.
    proueniant medii sic mihi saepe dies! V.25-6

Who does not know the rest? Tired, we both rested. May my mid-days often so come about.

It is hard to catch the right tone for this in English. Here, for contrast, is Christopher Marlowe, translating when a student in 1582:

Judge you the rest; being tir'd she bade me kiss;
Jove send me more such afternoons as this.

Here the tone is right, but the translation is very free: neither judging, kissing, nor Jove appear in the original.

It seems, at first, as if Ovid has flinched from the final challenge: describing his lovers making love. Yet, I would suggest that his account, what has been called the erotic aposiopesis,[14] is actually more erotic and powerful than any alternative which could be offered. After all, what is the alternative? Actual descriptions of sexual activity are notoriously difficult to carry off, as D. H. Lawrence unwittingly demonstrated, despite his best intentions, in *Lady Chatterley's Lover*, and many lesser writers have confirmed since. They tend to be either ridiculous or pornographic, or both, being in neither case satisfying from a literary point of view.

Actually, in this case we have the opportunity to see what it would have been like had Ovid decided to continue with a direct description. This is exactly what he does towards the end of the *Ars Amatoria*:

ulteriora pudet docuisse: sed alma Dione
    'praecipue nostrum est, quod pudet,' inquit 'opus.'
nota sibi sit quaeque; modos a corpore certos
    sumite: non omnes una figura decet.
quae facie praesignis erit, resupina iaceto;
    spectentur tergo, quis sua terga placent.
Milanion umeris Atalantes crura ferebat;
    si bona sunt, hoc sunt aspicienda modo.
                    (*Ars Amatoria* III.769-776)

The rest I blush to explain, but kindly Dione [mother of Venus, or alternatively the goddess herself] *says, 'The task which leads to blushing is my task above all.' Let each woman be familiar with herself: one method does not suit everyone. Let she who is fair in her face lie on her back; those whose backs are pleasing should be seen from behind. Milanion carried Atalanta's legs on his shoulders; if they are attractive, let them be seen like this.*

This account of various sexual positions goes on for nearly forty lines. Of course, the *Ars* purports to be not a love poem but a didactic poem about finding, if not love, at least sex, though it is no more a real handbook than are the *Georgics* a real handbook on farming. In any case, I defy anyone to argue that this is either more powerful or more erotic than the artful evasion at the end of the poem at hand.

In conclusion we can note that Ovid seems to have made a point of rejecting a number of possible ways of handling the challenge he set himself. There are no obstacles to be overcome, no implicit comparison to a bride, no rival lover or husband to be cheated, not even any conversation. Above all, there is no divinization and no abject self-abasement: Corinna is a pretty and willing girl, that is all. Given these restrictions, it is impressive that he manages to make a poem of twenty-six lines out of it. Although his poem is a good deal shorter than the one of Catullus and about half the length of that of Propertius, he concentrates entirely on their encounter. Admittedly he uses six lines to set the scene, in a passage I have defended, and eight to describe her charms, in one I have criticized, but overall his achievement is impressive. In particular, in avoiding a direct description of their making love he achieves by suggestion what he could not have done by direct statement and thereby makes his poem a success.

---

1. The exact interpretation of line 71 is disputed: see Fordyce and Quinn *ad loc.*
2. In line 145 *muta* (Heyse) is an emendation for the transmitted *mira*. In line 148 *diem* (1473 Parma edition) is an emendation for transmitted *dies.*
3. The text of Propertius is notoriously uncertain, particularly in Book II. I have consulted four respected texts and basically rely on Goold, with notes where variants are relevant. In this passage Camps and Fedeli give the same text as Goold (though without the prodelision of *mecumst*), but Heyworth's 2007 Oxford text gives the first line as *io me felicem! io nox mihi candida! io tu* (Housman) and transposes lines 7-10 between 2 and 3 (Carutti); see S. J. Heyworth, *Cynthia: A Companion to the*

Text of Propertius, Oxford, 2007, 173-5. These emendations do not affect my argument.

4. L. P. Wilkinson, *Ovid recalled*, Cambridge, 1955, 73.

5. Aeneas' vision of the Penates at *Aeneid* III.147ff.; the vision of Tiberinus at *Aeneid* VIII.26ff.. I take these references from W. S. M. Nicoll, 'Ovid, *Amores* 1.5,' *Mnemosyne* Vol. XXX Fasc.1 (1977), 42-3.

6. T. D. Papanghelis: 'About the hour of noon: Ovid, *Amores* 1.5,' *Mnemosyne*, Vol. XLII, Fasc. 1-2 (1989), 54-5.

7. There is a comprehensive summary by McKeown, *Ovid: Amores*, I.19-24.

8. Diane Middlebrook, *Young Ovid*, Berkeley, 2014, 69.

9. I do find it odd that none of the standard commentators on Ovid make the link with the historical Corinna, but Diane Middlebrook mentions it, *op. cit.* 60.

10. I have not been able to see the original work by Sharon L. James, *Learned Girls and Male Persuasion: Gender and Reading in Roman Love Elegy*, Berkeley, 2003. I am relying on a review by Alison Sharrock, *Bryn Mawr Classical Review*, 2003.09.29.

11. J. B. Leishman, *The Monarch of Wit: an analytical and comparative study of the poetry of John Donne*, London, 1962[6], 76.

12. The transmitted *tecum* at 37 is rejected by all editors. The main alternatives are *secum* (an early conjecture), *interdum* (Housman) and *tantum* (Camps). Goold, Fedeli and Heyworth prefer *interdum*. *et* in 39 is an emendation by Shackleton Bailey for the transmitted *haec*. It is accepted by Camps, Goold and Fedeli but Heyworth deletes the couplet. See Heyworth, *Cynthia*, 176.

13. Pound's text, though not as uncertain as that of Propertius, has its own problems. I cite this passage from J. P. Sullivan's study, *Ezra Pound and Sextus Propertius*, London, 1965, which contains the only critical text. That in *Ezra Pound: Poems and Translations*, ed. Richard Sieburth, New York, 2003, reprints the text of the first edition. There are several variants in the passage quoted.

14. McKeown *ad loc*. Aposiopesis is the figure of speech in which a phrase is deliberately broken off and left unfinished.

12

THE PRESENTATION AND INFLUENCE OF OVID'S CIRCE

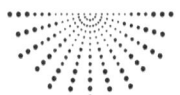

*I*n deciding to bring forward Circe as a major character in Book XIV of the *Metamorphoses* Ovid took a risk and faced a challenge: many of his first audience would remember her from her appearance in the *Odyssey* read in their school days and many would also know the references to her in that recent work already accepted as a classic, Virgil's *Aeneid*. He had to tell a story which would both be convincing in its own terms but also interesting to those who knew either or both of the previous versions. A modern parallel might be for a contemporary writer to decide to treat the subject of Salome for an audience who might or might not remember the death of John the Baptist from the Gospels or Oscar Wilde's play or the opera Richard Strauss based on it.

I shall consider Ovid's presentation of her, with some comparison with Homer and Virgil; then the interpretation and significance of metamorphosis in the episodes concerning her; and finally touch on the influence of the Ovidian Circe in some later literature.

Ovid chose to present Circe in three episodes: Scylla, Ulysses and Picus. These are strongly contrasted: the Scylla episode is, in the mythological chronology, pre-Homeric, and is recounted by the poem's narrator; the Ulysses episode is a retelling of the episode in the *Odyssey*, but by Macareus, a participant who had suffered metamorphosis, whereas in Homer it is part of the long account of his adventures by Odysseus who had not at first been present or involved; and the Picus episode is an embedded narrative within that of Macareus and so also earlier in the imagined chronology. Furthermore, the pre-history of Scylla, although the subject of a lost Alexandrian poem and a mention in the *Ciris*,[1] would have been relatively unfamiliar to the first audience compared to *Odyssey*, and the story of Picus and Canens has no known predecessors.

The Picus episode is also the first explicitly Italian one in the poem, and this introduces the poem's turn towards Italian and Roman subjects. This is supported by the post-Homeric location of Circe's island offshore from Italy, and Ovid's suppression in this Book of its Homeric name Aeaea.[2] Perhaps this turn was also one reason Ovid did not introduce another episode involving Circe, that of Medea's request for ritual purification after her flight from Colchis with Jason, which Apollonius of Rhodes had treated in his *Argonautica*. Not only had Ovid already given Medea a full treatment in his Book VII but this would have represented a reversion to Greek subjects inappropriate at this stage of his poem.

I consider now some of her characteristics. It is part of the tradition that Circe is a goddess, daughter of Helios, the sun. This makes her a Titan, but only Ovid insists on this: Glaucus addresses her as *Titani* (14); she is twice referred to as *Titania* (382, 438) and she refers to herself as *Titanida* (376); I shall return to the significance of this. On the other hand, he does not mention her mother Perse, daughter of Oceanus (*Odyssey* X.139),[3] nor use her Homeric epithet αὐδήεσσα, *using human speech*. Possibly more significant is that he departs from both Homer and Virgil in not having her carry out weaving, mentioned by both Homer (*Odyssey* X.222 ff.) and Virgil (*Aeneid* VII.14). In fact, he explicitly denies this:

> pulchro sedet illa recessu
> sublimi solio pallamque induta nitentem
> insuper aurato circumuelatur amictu.
> Nereides nymphaeque simul, quae uellera motis
> nulla trahunt digitis nec fila sequentia ducunt; (261-5)[4]

She sat in a lovely inner chamber on a lofty throne, clothed in a shining mantle covered with a golden veil. With her were Nereids and nymphs, who card no fleece nor spin threads with nimble fingers.

Instead, Ovid presents her as a witch who is specifically a herbalist. The passage above continues:

gramina disponunt sparsosque sine ordine flores
secernunt calathis uariasque coloribus herbas.
ipsa quod hae faciunt opus exigit, ipsa, quis usus
quoque sit in folio, quae sit concordia mixtis,
nouit et aduertens pensas examinat herbas. (266-70)

they arrange herbs and flowers scattered at random and place herbs arranged by colour into baskets; she herself examines what they do; she herself knows what value there may be in each leaf and what makes a good combination and she attentively checks the weight of the herbs.

This is a more extended treatment of her herbal skills than in Homer or Virgil. And she personally adds her poisonous juices (*sucos*, 275) to the posset she gives Ulysses' followers and which transforms them into pigs though still with human minds.

Ovid also insists on her herbalism in the Scylla episode. Glaucus suggests that herbs may be more potent than spells (*siue expugnacior herba est*, 21), and when he rejects her, Circe resorts to them first:

Venerisque offensa repulsa,
protinus horrendis infamia pabula sucis
conterit et tritis Hecateia carmina miscet (42-4)

furious at the rejection of her love she immediately pounded plants notorious for their noxious juices and mixed magical spells in with the good herbs.

And she poisons Scylla's bathing pool in a process with two stages:

hunc dea praeuitiat portentificisque uenenis
inquinat; hic pressos latices radice nocenti
spargit et obscurum uerborum ambage nouorum
ter nouiens carmen magico demurmurat ore (55-8)

This the goddess contaminates in advance and pollutes with supernatural powers; she sprinkles liquids squeezed out from poisonous roots and mutters three times nine times with magical speech a spell riddling in the obscurity of its strange words.

However, in the Picus episode we are specifically told that the sight of him is so overpowering to her that she drops her herbs (*cecidere manu, quas legerat, herbae*, the herbs which she had gathered fell from her hand, 350) and turns instead to other kinds of magic.

As a witch she is part of a family which includes Hecate and Medea among her relatives—there are various versions of their relationships. There is perhaps an implication that as a Titan rather than an Olympian she cannot perform magic through command alone, but does actually need to possess technical skills.

These she uses in the service of her lust. This is the motive in two of the episodes, and an emphasis specific to Ovid. So she offers herself to Glaucus in words featuring word play of the type associated with spells:

en ego, cum dea sim, nitidi cum filia Solis,
carmine cum tantum, tantum quoque gramine possim,
ut tua sim uoueo. spernentem sperne, sequenti
redde uices, unoque duas ulciscere facto. (33-6)

See, I, although I am a goddess, although I am daughter of the shining Sun, and although I can do a great deal with spells and also with herbs, I beg that I might be yours. Reject the one who rejects you and turn to the one who follows you, and with one act requite both.

This is elaborately constructed: note the tricolon with *cum*, the rhyme of *carmine* with *gramine*, the chiasmus and antimetabole with *tantum*, and the alliteration on 'm' in that line and on 's' in the next, the polyptoton of *spernentem sperne* and the apparent paradox of *unoque duas*.

Her attempted seduction of Picus is verbally less intricate but develops an apostrophe to his eyes and figure:

> 'per o tua lumina' dixit
> 'quae me ceperunt, perque hanc, pulcherrime, formam,
> quae facit ut supplex tibi sim dea, consule nostris
> ignibus et socerum qui peruidet omnia Solem
> accipe, nec durus Titanida despice Circen.' (372-6)

> *Oh, by those eyes which have captivated me, by that figure most lovely one,*
> *which has made me a goddess a suppliant to you, indulge my passion and*
> *accept the Sun which sees everything as your father-in-law, and do not,*
> *cruel one, spurn Circe the daughter of a Titan.*

This is the language of love poetry, given some grandeur at the end by the use of Greek accusative forms (*Titanida, Circen*).

However, in the Ulysses episode the emphasis is not on lust; Ovid treats briefly and cryptically the issue of his acceptance of her:

> inde fides dextraeque datae, thalamoque receptus
> coniugii dotem sociorum corpora poscit. (297-8)

> *Then faith was pledged and right hands given and once received into the*
> *wedding chamber he demanded the bodies of his companions as dowry.*

The implied context is a Roman marriage ceremony, but Ovid's use of *fides* surely would evoke the ambiguous union of Aeneas with Dido in Virgil, which Venus and Dido regarded as a *coniugium*, a marriage (*Aeneid* IV.126, 172, 316) but which Aeneas denied (IV.338). And indeed, Ulysses was already married. In the *Remedium Amoris* 263-88 Ovid had presented Circe as at first hoping then despairing that Ulysses would marry her; in this passage this is compressed into the one word *fides*. And Ovid withholds an account of the advice which Mercury (Cyllenius, 291) gave him but which Homer provides: he needs to insist on a second oath from Circe not to hurt him as otherwise he might be deprived of his courage and unmanned (ἀνήνορα, *Odyssey* X.301).

Although Ovid withholds this detail I would argue that it is in fact essential to an understanding of his Circe: she is in fact a lustful and destructive castrating female, and the fate that Aeneas avoids through being forewarned would have been waiting possibly for Glaucus (though as a god he might have been immune) and certainly for Picus had they succumbed to her blandishments. And possibly it is because of this that Ovid insists on her identity as a Titan: she is a being of an earlier divine dynasty, one in which the castration of Uranus by Saturn was a central episode, an earlier and cruder time which he finds repellent and avoids spelling out in detail: neither here, nor in Book I, nor in Book III of the *Fasti* does he explain Saturn's mutilation.

Support for this view comes as I move to my second topic: the treatment and significance of metamorphosis in these episodes. Scylla's transformation, although presented in the third person, is seen from Scylla's point of view:

> Scylla uenit mediaque tenus descenderat aluo,
> cum sua foedari latrantibus inguina monstris
> aspicit; ac primo, credens non corporis illas
> esse sui partes, refugitque abigitque timetque
> ora proterua canum. sed quos fugit, attrahit una
> et corpus quaerens femorum crurumque pedumque
> Cerbereos rictus pro partibus inuenit illis;
> statque canum rabie subiectaque terga ferarum
> inguinibus truncis uteroque exstante coercet. (59-67)

Scylla came and has gone down as far as her belly when she saw her loins disfigured with barking monsters; but at first, not believing that these were parts of her own body, she runs away and thrusts off and is frightened of the savage jaws of the dogs. But the things she flees she draws along with her, and when looking for the solidity of her thighs and legs and feet she finds instead of those parts gaping Cerberean mouths; she stands on raging dogs and the attached hinder part of wild beasts is constrained by her mutilated body and protruding belly.

I cannot agree with Otis when he says 'our sympathy with Scylla is minimal';[5] granted, the story is realistically impossible, but this is a characteristic example of Ovid's technique, which is to imagine what it would have been like had it been possible. (Shakespeare's technique in his romantic comedies of imagining real psychology in fairy tale situations owes a good deal to Ovid.) And Ovid retains our sympathy for Scylla by transforming only the lower part of her body, the part which came into contact with the poisoned water. Her upper half is still that of the girl she was. In doing so Ovid departs from Homer, in whom she is a monster with six heads and necks and twelve legs (*Odyssey*, XII.89-92). Such a monster could indeed snatch six sailors from a boat, as she does; the transformed Scylla of Ovid could not in fact achieve this and he touches only briefly on her doing so (71).

I should point out that in this treatment of her transformation Ovid is not original but following Virgil who describes her much as in Ovid, with the addition of dolphins' tails (*delphinum caudas*, Aeneid III.428). In this they both seem to be following an earlier post-Homeric tradition:[6] she is so presented in a Greek red figure vase.[7]

Ovid presents this transformation as Circe's revenge on Scylla as the successful rival for the love of Glaucus. But in fact, Glaucus was not successful in his love for Scylla, and surely Ovid also implies that Scylla's transformation is also her punishment for rejecting Glaucus' love. So this is then another version of the rejected female becoming a destructive monster. This point is clearly brought out in a recent treatment of the story:

Because he wouldn't enter me
I made her unenterable—Scylla,
the nymph who fled from the god
whose spawn and thrashing fish tail
I wanted. I spilled my powders
into the pool where she waded
to cool herself in the gauzy
noon heat—stayed to see her crotch
grow teeth, to watch her run
from her own legs. (Vicki Feaver: 'Circe')[8]

However, I must concede that the Renaissance view of Scylla, as embodied in the celebrated commentary of George Sandys of 1632, was quite different. Perhaps surprisingly she is considered not primarily as a female but as embodying the higher and lower parts of human nature:

That the vpper part of her body, is feigned to retaine a humane figure, and the lower to be bestiall; intimates how man, a diuine creature, endued with wisdome and intelligence, in whose superiour parts, as in a high tower, that immortall spirit resideth, who only of all that hath life erects his lookes vnto heauen, can neuer so degenerate into a beast, as when he giueth himselfe ouer to the lowe delights of those baser parts of the body, Dogs and Wolues, the blind & saluage fury of concu-piscence.[9]

Unusually, Ovid gives her a second transformation, into a rock (73-4), conveniently in time for Aeneas and the Trojans to escape her. This may well be, as Myers suggests (note *ad loc.*), a rationalizing interpreta-tion for the promontory known as the Rocca di Scilla, but it is surely also a way of releasing the girl from her misfortune. For Sandys, however, this was 'in regard of the impudency of lasciuious women, hardned by custome.'

There is a double transformation also of Macareus, this time retold in the first person: together with his other companions he is given the body of a pig. This transformation and its undoing is a story which positively invites allegorizing or psychologizing interpretations, which indeed it has received from early days. For example, Socrates is reported as refusing a feast:

he believed it was with such meats as those that Circe changed men into swine, and that Ulysses avoided that transformation by the counsel of Mercury, and because he had temperance enough to abstain from tasting them.[10]

Admittedly this concerns the Homeric rather than the Ovidian Circe. And in general, the Greek Neoplatonic philosophical tradition of interpreting Circe, based on the *Odyssey*, seems to have been more benign than the Latin literary and artistic one, based on Virgil and Ovid.[11] Dante, who did not know Homer but who certainly knew Ovid, compares the degenerate Florentines to the pigs transformed by Circe:

> ond'hanno sì mutata lor natura
>   li abitator de la misera valle
>   che par che Circe li avesse in pastura. (*Purgatorio*, XIV.40-2)

wherefore the dwellers in that wretched valley have so changed their nature that it seems that Circe had them at pasture (trans. Singleton).

Dante's use of Ovid is in fact a creative misinterpretation which points to the meaning of the original: the point here, as in Homer (*Odyssey* X.240), is that Macareus and the others had their minds unchanged and this of course is the source of the suffering: a real pig does not object to being a pig. By the time of the fourteenth century *Ovide moralisé* Circe was being interpreted as the Whore of Babylon in the Book of Revelation,[12] tempting men to lust and bestial behaviour. In the Renaissance the direct Christian reference was dropped but Circe was still seen as seducing men and turning them into beasts. This is Sandys' interpretation:

So the fortitude and wisedome of *Vlisses*, preserues him in the midst of vices against their strongest inuasions, when some of his Companions are deuoured by the *Cyclops*, some destroyed by the *Laestrigonians*, and others converted into beasts by *Circe*: their head strong appetites, which reuolt from the soueraignty of reason (by which wee are onely like vnto God, and armed against our depraued affections) nor euer returne into their Country (from whence the soule deriueth her caeles- tiall originall) vnlesse disinchanted, and cleansed from their former impurity. For as *Circes* rod, waued ouer their heads from the right side to the left: presents those false and sinister perswasions of pleasure, which so much deformes them: so the reuersion thereof, by discipline, and a view of their owne deformity, restores them to their former beauties.[13]

But this is just to touch on the fringe of a vast subject.[14]

I should mention that in none of the classical sources is anything further said about the rest of Circe's entourage, the people who have been turned into animals other than pigs. It would be pleasant to imagine that they were also restored to their original bodies but we are not told so.

The Picus episode is in contrast to the Ulysses one, in that what is significant is not the transformation itself but the reason Picus gives for refusing Circe:

> 'quaecumque es,' ait 'non sum tuus; altera captum
> me tenet et teneat per longum, comprecor, aeuum,
> nec Venere externa socialia foedera laedam,
> dum mihi Ianigenam seruabunt fata Canentem.' (378-81)

> *'Whoever you are', he said, 'I am not for you; 'another woman holds me captive and, I pray, will do so for a long time. Nor shall I break my oath for an adulterous love while the fates preserve for me Canens daughter of Janus.*

He refuses Circe not for any qualities she may or may not have but because he chooses to be faithful to his wife. Although these lines are not without word play it is their simple dignity which predominates. It is interesting then that Circe here revenges herself not on her successful rival, as she imagined Scylla to be, but on the rejecting male; perhaps the fact that Canens was daughter of a goddess gave her pause—the nonce word *Ianigenam*, daughter of Janus, otherwise unattested, supports this. The eventual transformation of Canens was a consequence of Circe's action but not directly instigated by her. Indeed, I wonder whether Canens was Ovid's invention, so that he could make a point of Picus' fidelity.

These two outer episodes therefore demonstrate in various ways the destructiveness of thwarted sexuality, specifically female sexuality. And if we doubted whether Ovid was really conscious of what he was doing we can consider two passages later in this book in which Ovid is more explicit. Diomedes tells Venulus:

antiquo memores de ulnere poenas
exigit alma Venus (477-8)

nurturing Venus exacted the penalty she had in mind for her old injury.

Admittedly the injury here is not thwarted love but a physical injury. But we should read this along with the words of Vertumnus to Pomona a little further on:

ultoresque deos et pectora dura perosam
Idalien memoremque time Rhamnusidis iram. (693-4)

Fear the avenging gods and the Idalian goddess [Venus] *detesting hard hearts and the wrath of remembering Nemesis.*

The Greek names and forms and the Homeric diction add to the solemnity of this warning. Ovid was therefore quite clear about the significance of these stories, which despite their fantastic setting have a serious point as well.

As for the Ulysses story, this was the one which is closest to the Homeric source. Perhaps Ovid is inviting us to consider the differences among the three males: Glaucus and Picus both reject Circe and both end up losing their loves; Ulysses accepts her under advice and unfaithfully—though we should imagine the double standard operating—and eventually gets back to his Penelope. She represents—mythologically she is—a power not to be trifled with.

Finally, I want to glance briefly at the influence of the Ovidian Circe. Shakespeare, like Dante, knew Circe from Ovid not Homer,[15] so it is disappointing that his only two direct references[16] are both early:

See how the ugly witch doth bend her brows
As if, with Circe, she would change my shape
(*I Henry VI*. V.3.34-5)

I think you all have drunk of Circe's cup
(*Comedy of Errors*, V.1.271)

However, at the other end of his career, in *The Tempest*, we have a magical island which had been ruled over by a witch who knew the properties of plants (or Sycorax's son Caliban could not have learned them) and who imprisoned her unwilling servant Ariel in a pine tree. This is very close to Ovid's Circe. Even the name Sycorax, possibly derived from the Greek for sow (σῦς) and raven (κόραξ) is similar to Circe (from κίκρος, a hawk).[17]

Milton was a classicist of professional standing and had easy access to Homer as well as to Virgil and Ovid. Comus is the son of Circe, with the same powers. The Attendant Spirit warns the Brothers against him:

> Boldly assault the necromancer's hall;
> Where if he be, with dauntless hardihood,
> And brandished blade rush on him, break his glass,
> And shed the luscious liquor on the ground,
> But seize his wand ... (*Comus*, 648-52)

Milton has here taken the brief version of the warning to Ulysses about Circe as given in Homer (*Odyssey* X.293-5) and expanded it with material from the episode as given by Ovid:[18]

> tutus eo monitusque simul caelestibus intrat
> ille domum Circes et ad insidiosa uocatus
> pocula conantem uirga mulcere capillos
> reppulit and stricto pauidam deterruit ense. (293-6)

> *Safe with this* [the mysterious *moly*] *and also having been warned by heavenly powers he entered the realm of Circe and when invited to the deceitful cup he pushed aside the wand trying to stroke his hair and threatened the frightened goddess with his drawn sword.*

The fullest treatment of Circe in modern times is that of Joyce, in *Ulysses*. The incidents of one day in Dublin in 1904 are based on the episodes of the *Odyssey*. The fifteenth and longest chapter, the climax of the book, is Circe,[19] and is located in the nighttown or red light area of Dublin. The equivalent of Circe is Bella Cohen, the brothel madam, who subjects Leopold Bloom to a series of hallucinatory fantasies of sexual guilt and humiliation. The principal classical source is obviously Homer but the occupation of Bella Cohen in presiding over lust and her degrading treatment of Bloom derive from the Ovidian tradition, with which Joyce was, of course, familiar.[20]

The continuing vitality of the Ovidian Circe has been shown recently in the collection *After Ovid: New Metamorphoses*, which has two treatments of Circe, to one of which I have already referred. For a more positive treatment see Madeline Miller, *Circe*. It is likely that she with her lustfulness, her magic cup and malevolent intent will continue to fascinate writers for a long time to come. And there is not much that men can do to oppose her.

---

1. The body of the *Ciris* deals with the other Scylla, the daughter of Nisus, treated by Ovid in Book VIII. If one accepts the early date for this poem it would have been available to Ovid.
2. He uses it earlier in the poem, IV 205, as does Virgil at *Aeneid* III 386.
3. At VII.74 Hecate is referred to as daughter of Perse, which would make Circe's invoking of her at XIV.44 rather odd. See below.
4. Accepting *sublimi* in 262 with Kenney, Myers and Hardie. Quotations are from Book XIV unless otherwise noted.
5. Brooks Otis, *Ovid as an epic poet*, Cambridge, 1966 289.
6. Timothy Gantz, *Early Greek Myth: A Guide to Literary and Artistic Sources*, Baltimore and London, 1993, 731-2, assembles the evidence.
7. CA 1341 in the Louvre.
8. From Michael Hofmann and James Lasdun (eds.): *After Ovid: New Metamorphoses*, London, 1994.
9. George Sandys, *Ovid's Metamorphosis Englished, Mythologiz'd and Respresented in Figures*, Oxford, 1932. Accessed on line.
10. Xenophon, *Memorabilia* I.3.
11. See references to Circe in Robert Lamberton, *Homer the theologian: Neoplatonist Allegorical Reading and the Growth of the Epic Tradition*, Berkeley and Los Angeles, 1986.
12. I take this from the article by Gareth Roberts, 'Circe', in A. C. Hamilton (ed.), *The Spenser Encyclopedia*, Toronto 1990.
13. Sandys, *Ovid's Metamorphosis Englished*.
14. On Renaissance interpretations of Ovid see Jonathan Bate, *Shakespeare and Ovid* Oxford, 1993 and Malcolm Bull, *The Mirror of the Gods: How Renaissance Artists rediscovered the Pagan Gods*, Oxford, 2005.
15. The researches of modern scholars such as T. W. Baldwin, *Shakespere's Small Latine and Lesse Greeke*, Urbana, 1944, A. D. Nuttall: 'Action at a distance: Shakespeare and the Greeks', in Charles Martindale and A. B. Taylor (eds.): *Shakespeare and the Clas-*

sics, Cambridge 2004 and Jonathan Bate, *Shakespeare and Ovid*, have demonstrated that Ben Jonson's comment that he had 'small Latine and lesse Greeke' should be revised into 'Shakespeare's considerable Latin and Non-existent Greek.' He certainly could and did read Ovid in the original as well as in Golding's version of 1567. Chapman's translation of the *Odyssey* did not appear until 1615, after Shakespeare had retired.

16. To these could be added the name Titania from *A Midsummer Night's Dream*, but there is no implied reference to Circe there.

17. Frank Kermode (ed.): Shakespeare, *The Tempest*, London, 1958, 26.

18. I owe this example to Leishman: *Milton's minor poems*, London, 1969, 233.

19. The Homeric chapter titles are not given in the book but are universally used by readers and commentators.

20. He had modelled Stephen Dedalus in *A Portrait of the Artist as a Young Man* on Ovid's Icarus, and references to his unsuccessful flight continue to accompany his appearances in *Ulysses*.

13

WHAT CAN DR JOHNSON'S 'THE VANITY OF HUMAN WISHES' TEACH US ABOUT JUVENAL'S TENTH SATIRE?

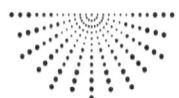

*D*r Johnson was a great admirer of Juvenal and claimed to have all his poems by heart. That this was no idle boast is shown by a couple of occasions recorded by Boswell, in which a quotation from, or allusion to, a passage of Juvenal came up, and Johnson was each time able to quote the original.[1] He made English versions of Juvenal's third and tenth satires, with the titles 'London' and 'The Vanity of Human Wishes.' These, however, were not translations, such as Dryden and others had made before him, but what he called imitations. He explained this once in a letter: 'part of the beauty of the performance (if any beauty be allowed it) consisting in adapting Juvenal's sentiments to modern facts and persons.'[2] Here I want to use 'The Vanity of Human Wishes' to help understand the original, reading it, as it were, over Johnson's shoulder. There are three aspects of this I want to concentrate on: prayer, the use of historical references, and the use of the grand manner.

We immediately learn something from Johnson's title; Juvenal, of course, gave his satires no individual titles as this was not practice in the ancient world. In using 'vanity' in his title Johnson was not referring to fashion or narcissism but empty and futile effort, as in the 'Vanity of vanities, all is vanity' of Ecclesiastes, or Vanity Fair in *Pilgrim's Progress*.[3] This is fair enough as applied to Juvenal's poem, but in fact Juvenal does not deal simply with wishes, but quite specifically with prayers as well. Courtney[4] suggested that his poem could be summarised as 'The Right and Wrong Objects of Prayer.' Now Johnson has no problem with wishes but avoids or minimizes any link with prayers. Juvenal says:

> quid enim ratione timemus
> aut cupimus? quid tam dextro pede concipis ut te
> conatus non paeniteat uotique peracti? (3-5)[5]

For what reason do we fear or desire? What is there that you plan so auspiciously for which you do not regret the effort or the wish once completed?

Johnson's equivalent for this is:

> How rarely reason guides the stubborn choice
> Rules the bold hand, or prompts the suppliant voice. (11-12)[6]

This is fair enough, as it deals simply with wishes. However, just a few lines further down we read:

> euertere domos totas optantibus ipsis
> di faciles. (7-8)

The compliant gods have completely ruined whole families by fulfilling their actual wishes.

For this, Johnson gives:

> How nations sink, by darling schemes oppress'd,
> When vengeance listens to the fool's request. (13-14)

Here, an abstract 'vengeance' has replaced the compliant gods. We should also note that *optantibus* can mean prayers as well as wishes and that the Romans did not clearly distinguish the two. Then Juvenal observes:

prima fere uota et cunctis notissima templis
diuitiae, crescant ut opes, ut maxima toto
nostra sit arca foro. (23-5)

Almost the first prayers very often noticed in all temples are for wealth,
that resources may grow, that my treasure chest may be the biggest in the
forum.

Johnson has no equivalent of these prayers.
In contemplating the fate of the powerful, Juvenal asks:

ergo superuacua aut quae perniciosa petuntur?
propter quae fas est genua incerare deorum? (54-5)

So what pointless or pernicious things do people seek? For what things is it
right to grease the knees of the gods with wax?

Johnson has no equivalent of this either.
Juvenal's aspiring young orator invokes the appropriate goddess to
help him:

eloquium ac famam Demosthenis aut Ciceronis
incipit optare et totis quinquatribus optat
quisquis adhuc una parcam colit asse Mineruam (114-6)

Whoever begins to wish for the eloquence and reputation of Demos-
thenes or Cicero and continues so to wish (or pray) throughout the
festival of the Quinquatrus worships thrifty Minerva with a single
coin.

The Quinquatrus was not only a spring festival in honour of
Minerva, goddess of learning, but also a school holiday, so the boy's
continued devotion during the holiday was evidence of his enthusiasm
to learn oratory with the help of the goddess. Johnson's student, on the
other hand, who is actually not a schoolboy but a student at university
in Oxford, has ambitions but no prayers:

When first the college rolls receive his name,
The young enthusiast quits his ease for fame;
Through all his veins the fever of renown
Burns from the strong contagion of the gown. (133-6)

However, Johnson does occasionally allow a note of prayer. Juvenal's old man prays:

da spatium uitae, multos da, Iuppiter, annos. (188)

Give me a long life, Jupiter, give me many years.

Johnson's old man does pray:

Enlarge my life with multitude of days
In health, in sickness, thus the suppliant prays. (253-4)

And the mother in Juvenal prays:

formam optat modico pueris, maiore puellis
murmure, cum Veneris fanum uidet, anxia mater
usque ad delicias uotorum. (289-291)

The anxious mother wishes (or prays) for good looks, in a quiet voice for her sons, in a louder one for her daughter, when she sees the shrine of Venus, going into details in her prayers.[7]

The mother in Johnson also prays, but less clearly and specifically:

The teeming mother, anxious for her race,
Begs for each birth the fortune of a face. (317-8)

At the conclusion, when Juvenal finally gets round to saying what he thinks people should pray for, he is quite specific about the role of the gods:

nil ergo optabunt homines? si consilium uis,
permittes ipsis expendere numinibus quid
conueniat nobis rebusque sit utile nostris;
nam pro iucundis aptissima quaeque dabunt di.
carior est illis homo quam sibi. (346-50)

*So will people hope (or pray) for nothing? If you want my advice, allow the
powers that be themselves to assess what suits us and will be useful in our
affairs; for the gods will always give whatever things are most suitable
rather than what are most pleasant. Mankind is dearer to them than to
itself.*

Johnson's version is much more muted:

> Must no dislike alarm, no wishes rise,
> No cries attempt the mercies of the skies?
> Enquirer, cease, petitions yet remain,
> Which heav'n may hear, nor deem religion vain.
> Still raise for good the supplicating voice,
> But leave to heav'n the measure and the choice.
> Safe in his pow'r, whose eyes discern afar
> The secret ambush of a specious pray'r. (345-352)

In this Johnson moves from 'Heaven' to 'his'[8] and the passage
continues with more specifically Christian references to love, patience
and faith. I take these up later.

It is not surprising that Johnson removed references to the pagan gods
in what is supposed to be a poem dealing with his world, not that of Juvenal. (I should note that earlier English versions of this poem, by Vaughan
and Dryden,[9] retain the references to the pagan gods but these are specifically offered as translations and not as imitations.) Furthermore, he also
knew that Christians should not be praying for worldly success and for this
reason also toned down the references to prayer. For Johnson, as a devout
Christian, knew that one's own will may not be God's will and that one
should pray for the latter, not the former.[10] What this tells us about Juvenal

is how easily the people of his time could move from wishes to prayers. OLD makes it clear that *optare* could be used for either wishing or praying, thereby implying that the difference between them was either not sharp or was actually nonexistent to Romans. People therefore felt much closer to their gods than we might have expected and for them the move from wish to prayer did not have the clear boundary that it did for Johnson.

I need also to note that Juvenal appears to shift his position on the willingness of the gods to grant prayers or wishes by the end of his poem. He writes:

nam pro iucundis aptissima quaeque dabunt di.
carior est illis homo quam sibi. (349-50)

For the gods will always give whatever things are most suitable rather than what are the most pleasant. Mankind is dearer to them than to itself.

This contradicts what he said in lines 7-8, quoted above. I have not found the commentators pointing this out, but Courtney is surely right when he says 'Juvenal does not spell out (indeed probably had not thought out) the implications of what he saying;' Johnson, on the other hand, had a coherent creed, Anglican Christianity, which he could have defended.

With the historical references, the first thing to note is that Juvenal's are nearly all to much earlier figures, ranging backwards from figures in the previous century all the way back to Xerxes and the Persian invasion of Greece in the fifth century B.C., and even beyond that to the heroes of the Trojan war several centuries earlier still. His contemporary references, on the other hand, are to people either unnamed, such as his schoolboy, old man and mother, or unidentifiable. Of course, it was much safer for him to mock figures who were long dead, such as Marius, or disgraced, such as Seianus, or foreign, such as Hannibal, than to attack contemporaries. (Johnson's targets are also all safely dead, though often quite recently.) Here for example, is a passage about the ills of old age full of apparently contemporary references, which is also interesting for another reason:

praeterea minimus gelido iam in corpore sanguis
febre calet sola, circumsilit agmine facto
morborum omne genus, quorum si nomina quaeras,
promptius expediam quot amauerit Oppia moechos,
quot Themison aegros autumno occiderit uno,
quot Basilus socios, quot circumscripserit Hirrus
pupillos, quot longa uiros exorbeat uno
Maura die, quot discipulos inclinet Hamillus (217-224)

Moreover the tiny amount of blood in his old body warms only in a fever,
and every kind of illness jumps round him in an orderly line, whose
names, if you were to ask, I would sooner relate how many lovers Oppia
had, how many patients Themison killed in one autumn, how many
business partners Basilus has rung rings round, how many wards Hirrus
has deceived, how many men tall Maura may suck off in one single long
day, how many pupils Hamillus buggers.[11]

There was apparently a historical Themiston, a doctor in the days of
Augustus, but the other names cannot be related to known individuals,
and might well have been invented. Even so they were probably recog-
nizable types in Juvenal's day: promiscuous women, unsuccessful
doctors, swindlers and corrupt teachers were stock characters. Johnson's
version of this is instructive; he simply gives:

Unnumber'd maladies his joints invade,
Lay siege to life and press the dire blockade. (281-2)

He completely omits the comparisons, and that in Juvenal they
become explicitly sexual was surely part of the reason for this. Despite
Johnson's admiration for Juvenal, he did say that some of the satires
'were too gross for imitation.'[12] His attitude here is markedly different
from that of Dryden a century earlier, admittedly offering a translation,
not an imitation, who renders this passage quite closely. Nevertheless,
even he flinches from the implications of *exorbeat*, though he finds a fair
equivalent to *inclinet*:

> Ask me their names, I could sooner relate
> How many drudges on salt Hippia wait;
> What crowds of patients the town-doctor kills,
> Or how, last fall, he raised the weekly bills:
> What provision by Basilus were spoil'd,
> What herds of heirs by guardians are beguiled:
> How many bouts a day that bitch has tried;
> How many boys that pedagogue can ride!
> (Dryden, *The tenth satire of Juvenal* 348-355)

In contrast Johnson omits all the sexual references, and this sense of decorum persisted for some centuries, in fact until the 1960s. During this period we find that texts of the Latin classics, especially those intended for schoolboys, were routinely expurgated, without the fact being signalled, and that translations were omitted, curtailed, sanitized or provided only into another foreign language.[13] Duff's generally good 1898 edition of Juvenal omits the two lines with sexual references here, with only the jump in the line numbering to betray the cut. (Of course, these measures were wholly futile: they simply showed the schoolboys which passages to look up in a complete edition.) But my main point is that Juvenal wrote for a culture in which such passages were completely acceptable, in fact one more like that of the present day than like that of Johnson.

Even so, Johnson may be right not to offer an equivalent for these lines, and for another reason than decorum. The appropriateness of such a list here may well be questioned: the comparisons are arguably not apposite or relevant and have nothing to do with the ills of old age; it looks as if Juvenal has got carried away, moving from illness through fraud to his favourite sexual obsessions.

Returning to historical comparisons, one of the most impressive passages in the original is that on Hannibal, exemplifying the alleged futility of seeking military glory. Johnson's equivalent is Charles XII of Sweden (1682-1718), who successfully defeated neighbouring armies, but spent some time in exile and was eventually killed, probably by a sniper's bullet. It is an irony of fate that, except possibly in Sweden, he is less well remembered than Hannibal. I want to consider two passages in both versions. Here is Hannibal on his wish to conquer Rome:

> 'acti' inquit 'nihil est, nisi Poeno milite portas
> frangimus et media uexillum pono Subura.'
> o qualis facies et quali digna tabella,
> cum Gaetula ducem portaret belua luscum! (155-9)

> *'There is nothing achieved,' he said, 'unless we break down the gates with*
> *a Carthaginian army and plant our standard in the middle of the Subu-*
> *ra.' What a sight and how worth caricature,*[14] *when the Gaetulian beast*
> [an elephant] *carries the one-eyed commander!*

Johnson's equivalent is:

> 'Think nothing gain'd,' he cries, 'till nought remain,
> On Moscow's walls, till Gothic standards fly,
> And all be mine beneath the polar sky.'
> The march begins in military state,
> And nations on his eye suspended wait. (200-205)

Johnson's general imagines planting his flags in a place which clearly signals victory and his military progress impresses other nations. Juvenal adopts a tone of mockery, even in Rome's most dangerous moment. He imagines Hannibal in the Subura, the valley between the Viminal and Esquiline hills, which was the 'red-light area' and 'notorious for noise, filth and crime.'[15] The effect is one of bathos; Courtney suggests 'a humourless writer would have made Hannibal name the Capitol.' And what would have been Hannibal's greatest moment of triumph is treated scornfully: Juvenal is not impressed by the *Gaetula belua*, and thinks that Hannibal's loss of sight in an eye a matter for contempt. This is in marked contrast to his source:

> ipse Hannibal aeger oculis ex uerna primum intemperie uariante
> calores frigoraque, elephanto, qui unus superfuerat, quo altius
> ab aqua exstaret, uectus, uigiliis tamen et nocturno umore

palustrique caelo grauante caput et quia medendi nec locus nec
tempus erat altero oculo capitur. (Livy 22.2.10)

*Hannibal himself, suffering from an eye infection since the spring with
its unhealthy varying hot and cold weather, was carried by the one
surviving elephant to lift him higher from the water, but the sleepless
nights, their dampness and the marshy climate seriously affected his head
and, because there was neither place nor time for treatment, he went
blind in one eye.*

Livy, though writing about an enemy general, is neutral in his
account; Juvenal belittles him. He writes as if he does not realize that it
does his country no service to treat an enemy as contemptible. This has
been a truism ever since the *Iliad*, with Caesar's treatment of Vercinge-
torix along with Livy's of Hannibal familiar Roman examples. Johnson
has deliberately rejected this effect. We need hold no particular admiration for Hannibal to realize that he was a formidable opponent and it is
absurd for Juvenal to treat him otherwise.

The way the two generals are dismissed is also worth comparing.
Here is Juvenal:

> I, demens, et saeuas curre per Alpes
> ut pueris placeas et declamatio fias. (166-7)

*Go, madman, run through the savage Alps to please boys and be the
subject of their speeches.*

Juvenal here mocks Hannibal's most celebrated exploit, the crossing
of the Alps, and wittily and correctly identifies that he will become the
subject of school exercises,[16] such as he mocks in more detail in an
earlier satire:

> culpa docentis
> scilicet arguitur, quod laeuae parte mamillae
> nil salit Arcadico iuueni, cuius mihi sexta
> quaque die miserum dirus caput Hannibal inplet,

quidquid id est de quo deliberat, an petat Urbem
a Cannis, an post nimbos et fulmina cautus
circumagat madidas a tempestate cohortes. (VII.158-64)

Clearly it is the fault of the person teaching, that nothing pounds on the
left side of the breast of an Arcadian youth when he fills my wretched
head with dread Hannibal whatever the debate is about, whether he
should make for Rome from Cannae or whether after the rains and light-
ning he should be prudent and turn his sodden troops round away from
the storm.

In comparison, Johnson is weighty rather than witty:

He left the name, at which the world grew pale,
To point a moral, or adorn a tale. (219-20)

School exercises in rhetoric have been abandoned: Johnson is
thinking of the moral to be drawn from Charles's career. Juvenal has
consistently belittled his general while Johnson for his has both respect
and pity, emotions foreign to Juvenal.

Turning to the use of the grand manner, Johnson's general characterization of Juvenal is this: 'The peculiarity of Juvenal is a mixture of
gaiety and stateliness, of pointed sentences, and declamatory
grandeur.'[17] Let us then consider part of the concluding paragraph of
Juvenal's satire, continuing from where my earlier quotation left off:

nos animorum
inpulsu caeco magnaque cupidine ducti
coniugium petimus partumque uxoris, at illis
notum qui pueri qualisque futura sit uxor.
ut tamen et poscas aliquid uoueasque sacellis
exta et candiduli diuina tomacula porci,
orandum est ut sit mens sana in corpore sano.
fortem posce animum mortis terrore carentem,
qui spatium uitae extremum inter munera ponat
naturae, qui ferre queat quoscumque labores,

nesciat irasci, cupiat nihil et potiores
Herculis aerumnas credat saeuosque labores
et uenere et cenis et pluma Sardanapalli. (350-62)

We are led by the force of our instincts, by blind and empty desire, and seek marriage and offspring from a wife, but it is known only to them what kind of sons and what kind of wife she will be. But so that you may ask for something with the entrails and the little sacred sausages and of a gleaming white piglet offered at the shrine, what should be prayed for is a sound mind in a sound body. Ask for a strong mind lacking fear of death, which puts a long life among the least of nature's gifts, which can bear any kind of trouble, which does not know how to get angry, desires nothing and thinks the hardships and cruel labours of Hercules preferable to the sex and dinners and downy cushions of Assurbanipal.

What we notice about this is the continuing variation of tone, Johnson's 'mixture of gaiety and stateliness,' because of the variation of content, within the grand manner. What we are driven to ask for in the form of a wife and children are reasonable desires for a man and not normally to be deprecated. But immediately we get a sardonic comment about what the wife and children might be like. Animal sacrifice is difficult for modern readers to get their heads round, but there is surely a slightly mocking tone about the diminutive in *exta et candiduli diuina tomacula porci*, the entrails and the little sacred sausages and of a gleaming white piglet. And then immediately the tone changes back to serious with one of Juvenal's most famous epigrams. He goes on with a series of perfectly serious wishes; these may be Stoic commonplaces but their handling here is straight, unlike with the instincts a few lines earlier. The labours of Hercules had become a stock example of virtuous behaviour, but are immediately followed by the contrast with the notorious Assyrian king. We also notice the curious fact that three lines rhyme, with the same word used twice: *labores,*[18] *potiores, labores.* This gives emphasis. And the fact that the Assyrian king can be fitted into the last two feet of a hexameter was too good a gift not to take: *Sārdănă I pálli.* But this is not just about metrical convenience: *Sardanapalli* at the end of the phrase about him contrasts with *Herculis* at the beginning of the previous one, both lines following from *potiores* at the end of the prevous line and the central rhyming word and making a neat antithesis.

When we look at what Johnson himself has at the equivalent place we find this:

Implore his aid, in his decisions rest,
Secure whate'er he gives, he gives the best.
Yet when the sense of sacred presence fires,
And strong devotion to the skies aspires,
Pour forth thy fervours for a healthful mind,
Obedient passions, and a will resign'd;
For love, which scarce collective man can fill;
For patience, sov'reign o'er transmuted ill;
For faith, that, panting for a happier seat,
Counts death kind Nature's signal of retreat. (353-62)

Gone are the paraphernalia of worship, the Stoic commonplaces, the references to exempla, Hercules and Assurbanipal, and the variations in tone. Instead, we have a consistently weighty manner, varied by moving the pause from line to line. Christian virtues have replaced the Stoic ones, though there is some overlap, as in the acceptance of death. Johnson has deliberately sacrificed 'the mixture of gaiety and stateliness' and gone for the 'declamatory grandeur.' And indeed, in his own terms, he has succeeded.

What then has Dr Johnson taught us about this poem of Juvenal? That the Romans had a different kind of relationship with their gods from that of Christians; that our society is more like the Romans than that of Johnson in openness about sexual matters; that worldly success, even though ultimately nugatory, can, despite Juvenal's contempt, nevertheless inspire some positive feelings; that it was not safe in either society to attack identifiable contemporaries; that there are both continuities and differences between Stoic and Christian virtues; and that Juvenal's frequent changes of tone bespeak a nervous energy admired by Johnson but eschewed by him in favour of the sententiousness he can so well provide, and which derives from a more coherent ethical outlook.

T. S. Eliot once said, writing of both 'London' and 'The Vanity of Human Wishes,' 'both of them seem to me among the greatest verse Satires of the English or any other language; and, so far as comparison is justifiable, I do not think that Juvenal, his model, is any better.'[19] Fortunately we have both and do not have to choose between them.

---

1. James Boswell, *The Life of Dr. Johnson*, London, 1992, 462, 808.
2. Undated letter of 1738, Boswell, *Life*, 72.
3. Johnson greatly admired *Pilgrim's Progress*, Boswell, *Life*, 469.
4. E. Courtney, *A Commentary on the Satires of Juvenal*, London, 1980, 446.
5. All Juvenal quotations are from satire X unless otherwise stated.
6. Quotations from *The Vanity of Human Wishes* are from the modern spelling text in Donald Davie, ed., *The Late Augustans*, London, 1958, with historical annotations on which I have drawn.
7. The best explanation of this phrase I have seen is that by Duff, who suggests that the mothers 'are not content to ask simply for beauty; they want something more out of the common, specifying e.g. the colour of hair or eyes they wish their children to have.'
8. I have been quoting Johnson in Davie's modernized text, but I should note here that in the original spelling 'his' is not capitalized, though the reference is clearly to the Christian God.
9. Vaughan's translation, greatly expanded from the original, appeared in his first volume, published in 1646, included in Henry Vaughan, *The Complete Poems* ed. Alan Rudrum, New Haven, 1981 (1976). Dryden translated five of the satires for a complete translation by various hands in 1693, popular in their own day but now rarely reprinted, and I have had recourse to a Victorian edition: *The Poetical Works of John Dryden* ed. Joseph and John Warton, London, 1851.
10. The *locus classicus* for this is Christ's prayer in the garden of Gethsemane: 'Abba, Father, all things are possible unto thee, take away this cup from me: nevertheless not that I will, but what thou wilt.' Mark 14: 36 KJV, with parallels in Matthew and Luke.
11. *Exorbeat*, literally 'may swallow' and *inclinet*, literally 'may bend over,' but these sexual meanings, not in OLD but accepted by the commentators, are confirmed by J. N. Adams, *The Latin sexual vocabulary*, London 1982, 139 and 192, discussing these lines. Although the meanings are unequivocal, Juvenal's words are slightly less explicit than my translations. The explicit verbs would be *fello* and *pedico*.
12. Boswell, *Life*, 116.
13. This has become an aspect of classical reception which has started to attract its own literature. See Stephen Harrison and Christopher Stray (eds.), *Expurgating the Classics: Editing Out in Greek and Latin*, London, 2014.
14. *Tabella* is literally a little tablet or picture, but commentators are unanimous about the diminutive implying contempt: Duff and Courtney have 'caricature,' Ferguson and Braund 'cartoon.'
15. Ferguson *ad. loc.* and on III.5.

16. The function of such exercises in Roman education, with a reference to the passage from Juvenal's seventh satire, is discussed by H.I. Marrou, *A History of Education in antiquity*, Madison, 1982, 286.
17. *John Dryden*, in *Lives of the English Poets*, ed. G. B. Hill, 3 vols., Oxford, 1905, I.447 §300.
18. So OCT, Ferguson and Hanson. But Courtney prefers *dolores*, attested in some manuscripts, to avoid the identical rhyme.
19. T. S. Eliot, *London: A Poem and The Vanity of Human Wishes by Samuel Johnson, LL. D. with an Introductory Essay by T. S. Eliot*, London, 1930; *The Complete Prose of T. S. Eliot: The Critical Edition*, ed. Ronald Schuchard and others, Baltimore, 8 vols., 2014-9, IV.172.

14

IN THE SATYRICON
OF PETRONIUS IS THE
RELATIONSHIP BETWEEN
ENCOLPIUS AND GITON
REALLY ONE OF LOVE?

The relationship between Encolpius and Giton is the only one which continues throughout the *Satyricon*,[1] as we have it, and yet it has received curiously little attention from the commentators.[2] Nevertheless it raises many questions. Is it really a love relationship? Is it relevant that it involves two people of the same sex? Are the vicissitudes in this relationship just things which happen, or is there something more to them? What literary significance, if any, does this relationship have?

Let me start with a few general points. The fragmentary nature of the work imposes its own limitations. The text we have has been assembled from four separate, partly overlapping traditions. There are lacunae throughout the text, which in places seems more a florilegium of interesting passages than a proper transcript. It is frequently obscure and sometimes unintelligible. Even the *Cena Trimalchionis*, which is the best preserved section, has lacunae in it. Therefore, I have to range across the whole work as we have it, picking up clues to my topic from wherever I can find them.[3]

Then there is the issue of genre. The work looks like a modern novel, and it is sometimes loosely called one. However, it seems best considered as a Menippean satire, a form which may have developed out of verse satire by adding prose interludes, but which we know as a prose form with the use of incidental verse.[4] Northrop Frye, whose discussion I am drawing on here, distinguishes four main forms of prose fiction: novel, romance, confession and anatomy, which last is his preferred replacement term for Menippean satire. He characterizes it as follows:

> The Menippean satire deals less with people as such than with mental attitudes. Pedants, bigots, cranks, parvenus, virtuosi, enthusiasts, rapacious and incompetent professional men of all kinds, are handled in terms of their occupational approach to life as distinct from their social behaviour. The Menippean satire thus resembles the confession in its ability to handle abstract ideas and theories, and differs from the novel in its characterization, which is stylized rather than naturalistic, and presents people as the mouthpieces of the ideas they represent.[5]

He offers as examples, as well as the *Satyricon*, also Apuleius' *Metamorphoses* from the ancient world, Boethius' *Consolatio Philosophiae* from the medieval world, and Swift's *Gulliver's Travels*, Voltaire's *Candide* and Huxley's *Brave New World*, from the modern one.[6] He also allows for mixed and combined forms. In the case of Petronius, the *Satyricon* seems very loosely structured on the *Odyssey*, in that Encolpius, the central character, moves through a series of adventures, beginning, most commentators agree, in Massilia, and ending possibly in Egypt or in Lampsacus, the birth place of Priapus.[7] The *gravis ira Priapi* (the great anger of Priapus, 139.4), which Encolpius has aroused is a parody of that of Poseidon for Odysseus and is probably the mainspring of the plot.[8] In contrast to the *Odyssey*, in which the hero Odysseus is superior to other men and the environment, and moves in a world in which the ordinary laws of nature are slightly suspended, Encolpius is himself a man *declassé* (*infamus*) and he moves through a world of parvenus, vagabonds and outcasts, to whom the reader is assumed to be superior. To use more of Frye's terminology, the *Odyssey* is written in the mode of romance, the *Satyricon* in that of irony.[9] It can also be seen as a kind of parody of the Greek novels of romance and adventure, with the fickle same-sex pair of Encolpius and Giton replacing the devoted opposite-sex pairs of lovers of the Greek novels;

although the extant ones we have are all later than Petronius, there are earlier fragments, suggesting that this was a familiar form when he was writing; the fact that most of the characters in the *Satyricon* are Greek, and have names derived from Greek, supports this. Indeed, Jensson considers that the work 'is a Greek story, notwithstanding the language and the audience.'[10] And the fact that the text is presented as the recollections of Encolpius raises questions about the relation between Encolpius as narrator, Encolpius as protagonist and Petronius the actual author.[11] The book also contains self-contained short tales, including folk tales such as Niceros' one of the werewolf and Trimalchio's of the changeling, and so-called Milesian tales—short narratives with an erotic content—such as Eumolpus' stories of the widow of Ephesus and the Pergamum boy. There is also a good deal of other literary influences, often by way of parody, such as that of Plato's *Symposium* on the *Cena Trimalchionis*. The commentaries by Courtney and Schmeling are thick with allusions—not just parallels—to other literary works, almost to the point of implying that the *Satyricon* is a collection of situations which parody those in serious literature with no real coherence of its own at all.

The issue is complicated by the fact that Encolpius is both the mouthpiece for satire on the other characters and the object of satire himself. As Sullivan explains:

> It is more important to see Encolpius as the narrator rather than as a realistic hero. Even though he himself is often the subject of the plot and the humour, our interest is not focused on him as a person, but as the occasion for sexual adventures, parody and burlesque. Petronius' interests, it must not be forgotten, are literary rather than psychological.[12]

However, I suggest that Sullivan rather overstates his case. Although none of the characters is obviously and immediately sympathetic, the effect of reading the work is that one gradually develops a rather grudging respect for them. In the case of Trimalchio, who, apart from Encolpius himself, is the most fully developed character in the text we have, we move from amusement at his pretensions, ignorance and exhibitionism to some affection for a man who is generous and hospitable, who in practice though not in theory is kind to his slaves,[13] having not forgotten his slave past, and whose follies harm nobody and whose boasting stems from insecurity. I am going to argue that something similar happens with Encolpius and Giton; at any rate I am going to treat their characterisation as being sufficiently consistent and realistic to make the questions I asked at the opening real ones, even though in places this assumption is tested.

I then need to say something about the theme of same-sex love between males—I am avoiding the word homosexuality, which belongs to our culture and not that of the ancient world. This was, of course, not new, either in literature or in life, and a few references are enough. In Greek literature Achilles and Patroclus are famous examples; their relationship is not represented as sexual in Homer but is in Aeschylus and Plato.[14] Plato's *Symposium* is of course the *locus classicus* for same-sex love, but one must remember that, for Plato, forswearing a physical relationship was an essential early step. Nevertheless, he includes among the characters in the work Agathon and Pausanias, who were lovers. The Greek Anthology has a whole section devoted to epigrams on pretty boys, with the themes of adoration and courtship occuring over and over again. Among Greek novels, the story of Hippothous and Hyperanthes from the *Ephesian Tale* of Xenophon of Ephesus features two same-sex lovers in a brief account with similarities to the relationship between Encolpius and Giton; this probably dates from the second century A. D., later than Petronius.[15] In Roman literature there is Virgil's second eclogue, in which the uncouth Corydon sighs hopelessly for the unattainable Alexis, so in fact there is a crush but no actual relationship, while in the *Aeneid* we have Nisus and Euryalus, who are lovers who live together, fight together and die together. Catullus, as well as his disastrous relationship with Lesbia, also has, perhaps earlier, one with a fancy boy, Juventius. He is careful not to claim on the physical side any more than kisses (*basia*) as Juventius would appear to be freeborn,[16] though this language may disguise a fuller physical relationship,[17] but there seems to be, as well as sexual desire, affection and jealousy and so at least some mutuality. The same is true of Tibullus, whose fancy boy Marathus is actually old enough to have his own girlfriend.[18] In a different context, it was common to abuse political or personal enemies by suggesting they got up to sexual practices such as fellatio or anal intercourse which were considered degrading for free adult males unless they exercised the penetrative role exclusively. Martial's preferred sexual activity is anal penetration of slave boys; he rejects the idea of giving the boy pleasure so there is no mutuality.[19] In fact, in modern terms we would consider him a paedophile, and indulging his proclivities would land him in prison. Even worse was the behaviour of Petronius' patron, Nero: after he had killed his wife Poppaea, he took the freed slave boy Sporus, who looked like her, had him castrated and made him take her place, known as Sabina, Poppaea's second name. He formally married 'Sabina' in 66 A.D. After Nero's suicide Sporus was passed around among other imperial aspirants and eventually committed suicide.[20] So in the ancient world, as in the modern, same-sex relationships, like opposite-sex ones, could range from unrealistic crushes through faithful and devoted or briefer but still mutual relationships through to exploitation, abuse, degradation and mutilation. Common features were that the lover, the *erastes*, to use the Greek terms, was an adult man, while the love object, the *eromenos*, was usually a boy, a *puer delicatus* in Latin, rather than an adult, and that freeborn boys, such as Juventius, had to be courted, whereas slaves were considered fair game. (In today's world the boys might well be under age and such relationships illegal.) Adult men might be sexually interested in women, boys or both, as is Encolpius and possibly also Giton; the moral distinction was not between same or opposite sex activity but between penetrative or receptive roles. (The fact that both Encolpius and Giton may well take both roles is an important feature of the *Satyricon*.) Relationships of adult men with boys were normally transient and were expected to end when the boy started developing facial hair, which was an important rite of passage,[21] while the man might move on to other boys, or to women, or get married, when he was at least supposed to leave such things behind.[22] However, Trimalchio, himself a former *puer delicatus* (75.10-11, quoted below), though married, maintains not only an official favourite, Croesus (28.4 and 64.5-13), but also provokes a row with his wife through prolonged kissing of another boy to whom he seems to have given rewards for services received (74.8-75.5).

The theme of mentoring by the *erastes* of the *eromenos*, which hovers in the background of ancient male same-sex relationships, appears in the *Satyricon* in reverse: you might expect Encolpius to be some sort of mentor to Giton, but in fact Giton shows himself to be much more practical, marking the way home (79.4) when Encolpius had previously got lost and ended up in a brothel (6.2-4), distracting the guard dog at Trimalchio's house with scraps of food (72.9) and being the only one of the trio with Ascyltos not to fall into the fishpond (72.7-8). Another kind of reversal of mentoring appears in the story of the Pergamum boy, with Eumolpus as the duplicitous mentor who seduces the boy (85-7).

With this range of possibilities in mind, let us turn to Encolpius and Giton. I begin with Encolpius. His name means 'in the bosom,' so 'bosom companion,' or, more indecently, 'in the crotch' from Greek κόλπος.[23] Commentators agree that he is the person referred to in the first of the Petronius fragments:

> sacra id est execrabilis. tractus est autem sermo ex more Gallorum. nam Massilienses quotiens pestilentia laborabant, unus se ex pauperibus offerebat alendus anno integro publicis sumptibus et purioribus cibis. hic postea ornatus verbenis et vestibus sacris circumducebatur per totam civitatem cum execrationibus, ut in ipsum reciderent mala totius civitatis, et sic proiciebatur. (Frag. 1)

> *sacra means accursed. The term is from a custom among the Gauls. Whenever the residents of Massilia [now Marseilles] suffer from plague, one of their poor residents offered to be fed for a whole year at public expense and fed with very specially ceremonially refined food. Afterwards he was decorated with sacred foliage and with ceremonial vestments and led round the whole city with curses, so that the ills of the whole city fell on him, and so he was cast out.*

The person who took on this role of professional scapegoat, so to speak, could obviously not afterwards return to the city. The identification with Encolpius is supported by two passages in the main text: he describes himself as an *exul* (exile, 81.3) and Eumolpus jeers at him as *pharmake* (107.15). This is the the only attested use of this word in

Latin; Sullivan takes it as representing Greek φάρμακος (note the accent), *poisonous fellow*, but more recent commentators take it as representing Greek φαρμακός, *scapegoat*.[24]

As a native of Massilia he would be Greek, and he has certainly had a degree of education, as is shown by his discussion about rhetoric with Agamemnon at the beginning of our extant text, where he cites several authors, all of whom are Greek.

His original social status is unclear.[25] Eumolpus tells Lichas that both Encolpius and Giton are free citizens:

flectite ergo mentes satisfactione lenitas, et patimini liberos homines ire sine iniuria quo destinant. (107.3)

Let gentleness soften your hearts now that satisfaction has been given, and allow the free men to go where they wish.

Admittedly, Eumolpus is here engaged in special pleading, and *patimini liberos homines* might simply mean *let them go free*. However, Encolpius, after losing Giton to Ascyltos, says to himself, threatening revenge: *nam aut vir ego liberque non sum, aut noxio sanguine parentabo iniuriae meae* (for either I am not a free man or I shall make an offering to my wrong with their guilty blood, 81.6). This suggests that he is free, though he may previously have been a slave. Although older than Giton he is still young (he describes himself as a *iuuenis*, 130.1) and effeminate, as appears when Circe's maid Chrysis at Croton speaks to him:

quia nosti venerem tuam, superbiam captas vendisque amplexus, non commodas. quo enim spectant flexae pectine comae, quo facies medicamine attrita et oculorum quoque mollis petulantia, quo incessus arte compositus et ne vestigia quidem pedum extra mensuram aberrantia, nisi quod formam prostituis ut vendas? (126.1-2)

Because you know you are sexually attractive, you put on haughty airs and sell your embraces instead of giving them away freely. For what other reason does your hair look waved with a comb, why is your face rubbed with rouge and your eyes also have a gentle lasciviousness, your carefully

controlled way of walking and even your footsteps are carefully measured,
unless you are selling your good looks for money?

She does not add, because at that stage she does not know, that
Encolpius' attractions include the fact that he is well endowed.[26] A
particularly hilarious moment comes when, in a parody of the recogni-
tion by Eurycleia of Odysseus by his scar, Lichas recognises him, not by
his face but by his genitals:

Lichas, qui me optime noverat, tamquam et ipse vocem audisset,
accurrit et nec manus nec faciem meam consideravit, sed continuo ad
inguina mea luminibus deflexis movit officiosam manum et 'salve'
inquit 'Encolpi.' (105.9)

Lichas, who knew me extremely well, as if he himself had heard my voice,
ran in and examined neither my hands nor my face but with his eyes cast
down immediately moved his investigating hand to my private parts and
said 'Hallo, Encolpius.'

In recounting this, Encolpius accepts that he is a runaway (*fugitivi*,
105.10), and it is clear he had a previous sexual relationship with Lichas.
He may look like a prostitute but the only point in the story where he
actually seems to present as one is after the row on board ship, when
Eumolpus brokers a peace, whose terms are these:

ex tui animi sententia, ut tu, Tryphaena, neque iniuriam tibi factam a
Gitone quereris, neque si quid ante hunc diem factum est obicies vindi-
cabisve aut ullo alio genere persequendum curabis; ut tu nihil imper-
abis puero repugnanti, non amplexum, non osculum, non coitum
venere contrictum, nisi pro qua re praesentes numeraveris denarios
centum. item, Licha, ex tui animi sententia, ut tu Encolpion nec verbo
contumelioso insequeris nec vultu, neque quaeres ubi nocte dormiat,
aut pro singulis iniuriis numerabis praesentes denarios ducenos. (109.2-
3)

> *In all honesty, that you Tryphaena, neither complain of past injury done to you by Giton, nor will you allege, avenge or in any other way attempt to pursue anything done before this day; that you will impose nothing objectionable on the boy, neither embrace, nor kiss, nor enforced sexual intercourse, unless for each occasion you indulge you pay one hundred denarii. Secondly, Lichas, in all honesty, that you pursue Encolpius neither with insulting language nor with looks, nor investigate where he sleeps at night, or for every individual offence you commit you pay two hundred denarii.*

Stripped of its mock legal language, this means that the going rate for sex with Giton is one hundred denarii, and with Encolpius it is twice that. These terms are not invoked in the book as we have it, and Encolpius seems to live mostly by theft and sponging off others. He has also had an ambiguous sexual history, which could have included being a prostitute, or a *puer delicatus*, or both.

Otherwise the most important characteristic of Encolpius is the theme of the *gravis ira Priapi* which runs throughout the book and which has rendered him unable to perform sexually. In fact, he has, or had, or attempts to have, sexual contact with several other people in the course of the book apart from Giton. They include Psyche (20.2), an unnamed *cinaedus* (23.5), Quartilla (26.5), Lichas (implicit from 105.9, quoted above), his wife Hedyle (if this conjecture is correct, 113.3), Tryphaena (113.8), the mysterious Doris (126.18),[27] Circe (127) and Philomela's son (140.11). What is noteworthy is that none of these attempts in the extant book succeed, and at times it resembles one of those farces in which couplings are always about to occur or have occurred but somehow never do occur on stage. Furthermore, in the extant book the initiative is always taken by the other party, except in his relationship with Giton. Because of his repeated sexual failures he abuses his penis (132.8-11) and shortly afterwards is found offering a prayer to Priapus for forgiveness and so restoration of his sexual powers (133.3). His inability to perform sexually may account for his voyeurism, a consistent theme in the book.[28]

Turning then to Giton, whose name means 'neighbour,' Greek γείτων, we know something of his appearance and his history. When

Eumolpus first sees him, he refers to him as a Ganymede, ravished by Zeus to be his cupbearer and catamite (92.3). When Ascyltos is searching for him after he returned to Encolpius, he got a town crier to proclaim, with the offer of a reward:

> puer in balneo paulo ante aberravit, annorum circa XVI, crispus, mollis, formosus, nomine Giton. (97.2)

> *A little while ago in the baths a boy wandered off, aged about sixteen, curly-haired, with soft skin* [i.e. without facial hair], *handsome, named Giton.*

A little earlier, while Giton still appears lost to him, Encolpius mentally upbraids first Ascyltos then moves on to Giton:

> quid ille alter? qui tamquam[29] die togae virilis stolam sumpsit, qui ne vir esset a matre persuasus est, qui opus muliebre in ergastulo fecit, qui postquam conturbavit et libidinis sua solum vertit, reliquit veteris amicitiae nomen et, pro pudor, tamquam mulier secutuleia unius noctis tactu omnia vendidit. (81.5)

> *What about the other one? Who on the day he would have been eligible for the* toga virilis *took a woman's robe, who was persuaded by his mother not to be a man, who took the role of a woman in the slave-barracks, who after he confused and switched the direction of his sexual favours, abandoned the claim of a long-standing friendship and—in the name of decency!—sold everything like a nymphomaniac for a one night stand.*[30]

To put it briefly and brutally, Giton is a pretty boy who was pimped by his mother; *opus muliebre* is to be receptive in anal intercourse. Throughout the book he shows the characteristics of someone who has been sexualised young: it is the main way he knows how to relate to others and he manipulates and provokes them to try to ensure their continuing interest in him. With Encolpius he is successful. However, there is more to their relationship than this, as we shall see.

The use of the word *ergastulum* is significant. This was 'a kind of prison on a large estate to which refractory or unreliable slaves were sent for work in chain-gangs' (OLD). Giton therefore was or had been a slave, and this is consistent with his ability to cook (9.1, 16.1), to act as an attendant at dinner (26.10), at the baths (73.2; 91.1) and to lay the table (92.3). He also has some literary education as is shown by his references to Lucretia and Tarquin (9.5), the Theban brothers Eteocles and Polyneices (80.3), and his sarcastic thanks to Encolpius for loving him *Socratica fide* (with Socratic integrity, i.e. without sexual activity, 128.7, a reference to the celebrated instance of Socrates and Alcibiades, *Symposium* 207, 219b-d). However, there is no mention of a master for him—in the story he assumes slavery only as a role (103.4)—so he is presumably also a runaway freedman. Given how such a boy would have found life in a chain-gang and in the *ergastulum*, this is hardly surprising: life with the adoring Encolpius would have seemed a much better bet.

As well as his personality, we also have to consider his physical development. Puberty came later in the ancient world than it does now. In boys it nowadays usually begins at around age twelve. The penis and testicles grow and boys may have involuntary ejaculations (wet dreams). The break in the voice and the development of facial hair come later. This process is usually complete by age sixteen, though the full adult body type is not achieved until eighteen.[31] In the ancient world these processes started later, at around age fourteen.[32] At the age of sixteen, Giton was therefore nearer the beginning of physical maturation than would be a boy nowadays. Crucially for his role in the book, his genitals have matured though are still not fully grown: Quartilla, *pertractato vasculo tam rudi* (having fondled[33] his little tool, so immature), looks forward to enjoying it *promulside* (as an hors d'oeuvre, 24.7). However, he still has the smooth face of a child (*mollis*, 97.2 quoted above). (Petronius does not tell us whether his voice has broken, so this is presumably not an issue either way.) It is a moot point to what extent he experiences sexual desire—he accepts kissing by Psyche and Tryphaena but Petronius does not say whether he actively reciprocates. Psyche kisses him *non repugnanti puero* (while the boy did not resist, 20.8) while Tryphaena *implebat osculis pectus* (filled his chest with kisses, 113.5). Both of these could be the passively compliant behaviour of a boy accustomed to being treated as a sexual plaything. Meanwhile, the absence of facial hair allows him to retain his role as a *puer delicatus*, for example attracting both Ascyltos and Eumolpus and scorning Encolpius' impotence (128.7, already quoted above) and eliciting an apology (129.1), which suggests that he enjoys being penetrated, at least by Encolpius. In this he resembles the Pergamum boy of Eumolpus' story, who, he tells us, was an *ephebus plenae maturitatis et annis patiendum gestientibus* (a youth who was fully ripe and of an age that was eager to be submissive, 87.7).[34] However, while Giton is clearly anally receptive to his lover, it is not clear whether he can himself achieve penetration and orgasm: in the episode in which he is encouraged to deflower Pannychis—to a modern sensibility far and away the most objectionable thing in the book as *non plus quam septem annos habere videbatur* (she seemed to be no more than seven years old, 25.2)—Quartilla and Encolpius watch their *lusumque*[35] *puerilem* (their childish sexual play, 26.4), and Petronius' wording leaves it ambiguous as to whether Giton's attempt succeeded, *lusum* being qualified by *puerilem*. Note, incidentally, that Encolpius shows no jealousy of Giton attempting sexual intercourse with a girl but enjoys being a voyeur, whereas thoughts of Giton with Ascyltos torment him.

He is also potentially in the position that Trimalchio himself was, as he tells his dinner guests, although Giton, unlike the young Trimalchio, is in no hurry to develop the facial hair of adulthood:

> tam magnus ex Asia veni quam hic candelabrus est. ad summam, quotidie me solebam ad illum metiri, et ut celerius rostrum barbatum haberem, labra de lucerna ungebam. tamen ad delicias domini annos quattuordecim[36] fui. nec turpe est quod dominus iubet. ego tamen et ipsimae satis faciebam. scitis quid dicam: taceo, quia non sum de gloriosis. (75.10-11)

> *I came from Asia as big as this candlestick. In short, every day I used to measure myself against it, and to get a whiskery beak sooner, I oiled my lips from the lamp. But I was my master's fancy boy at the age of fourteen. What the master commands is not wrong. But I also did the job well enough for herself. You know what I mean: I don't say anything because I am not the kind who boasts.*

Giton, like the young Trimalchio and also Tibullus' Marathus, is able to function both as a *puer delicatus* and, at least aspirationally, as a penetrative male, and much of the action of the book exploits this dual role.

In considering the relationship between Encolpius and Giton, we notice that it continues throughout the book, that Encolpius refers early on to his wish *ut veterem cum Gitone meo rationem reducerem* (to return to my old understanding with Giton, 10.7), and to their *vetustissimam consuetidinem* (their very long intimacy, 80.6), and Giton to their *amicitiae sacramentum* (sworn friendship, 80.4), even though this is immediately before Giton leaves him for Ascyltos. It seems sensible to assume that Giton also came from Massilia and that his relationship with Encolpius began there. Encolpius frequently refers to him as his *frater*, normally brother or at least a close male relative, but here equivalent more to partner in the modern sense of sexual partner; Sullivan usually translates it as *boyfriend*.

The vicissitudes in their relationship are an important feature of the plot, with actual or attempted sexual relationships by each with others, a breakup and tearful reunion, and a complicating third party, mostly Ascyltos but later Eumolpus. They both at various times threaten suicide and self-castration. I shall concentrate on some representative moments.

At the beginning, Encolpius, Giton and Ascyltos form a trio, but Encolpius falls out with Ascyltos when the latter assaults Giton, who reports it in these words:

Tuus ... iste frater seu comes paulo ante in conductum accucurrit coepitque mihi velle pudorem extorquere. cum ego proclarem, gladium strinxit et "si Lucretia es," inquit "Tarquinium invenisti." (9.4-5)

That mate of yours ran into my lodging and began wanting to have his wicked way with me. When I called out, he pulled out a knife and said "If you are Lucretia, you have found your Tarquin."

In the ensuing confrontation Ascyltos taunts Encolpius in these words:

non taces, nocturne percussor, qui ne tum quidem, cum fortiter faceres, cum pura muliere pugnasti, cuius eadem ratione in viridario frater fui qua nunc in deversorio puer est? (9.9-10)

You don't keep quiet, you stabber in the dark, who, even at your strongest struggled to go with a decent woman, and I was your partner in the garden in the same way that the boy is now here in the guesthouse.

Encolpius, that is, had a previous sexual relationship with Ascyltos (note that Giton refers to him as his *frater*) in which he took the active role, presumably before he offended Priapus, but could not satisfy a woman; Ascyltos now wants to take the active role with Giton and at this point Giton rebuffs him. However, his later behaviour with Ascyltos is much more ambiguous, as we shall see.

Encolpius later attempts an affair with Circe, and this piece of dialogue with her is revealing:

'si non fastidis' inquit 'feminam ornatam et hoc primum anno virum expertam,[37] concilio tibi, o iuvenis, sororem.[38] habes tu quidem fratrem, neque enim me piguit inquirere, sed quid prohibet et sororem adoptare? eodem gradu venio. tu tantum dignare et meum osculum, cum libuerit, agnoscere.' 'immo' inquam ego 'per formam tuam te rogo ne fastidias hominem peregrinum inter cultores admittere. invenies reli-giosum, si te adorari permiseris. ac ne me iudices ad hoc templum gratis accedere, dono tibi fratrem meum.' (127.1-3)

'If you don't look down on a stylish woman,' she says, 'and in her first year of experience with a man, I'll be a girlfriend to you, young man. You already have a boyfriend, because I wasn't ashamed to find out, but what stops you choosing to have a girlfriend? I come on the same basis (as he does). You need only think me worth it and receive my kiss whenever it might please you.' 'Indeed,' I say, 'I ask you that because of your beauty you don't scorn to admit a wandering stranger among your devotees. You will find him devout, if you permit him to worship you. Nor need you think I am entering the temple without an offering, as I give up my boyfriend to you.'

Circe is amazed at Encolpius' proposed renunciation of Giton, and indeed it seems inconsistent with the whole of the rest of the work. It is the strongest argument against my case that the *Satyricon* can be read in terms of consistent characterization. Petronius offers no clarification or explanation of this in the extant work; we could think of several, such as that Encolpius is getting his own back for Giton having gone off with Ascyltos. I shall return to this later. However, the main point here is that, despite willingness on both sides, Encolpius is unable to perform sexually with her. She asks *numquid Gitona times?* (Surely you aren't afraid of Giton? 128.1) but his reaction is:

perfusus ego rubore manifesto etiam si quid habueram virium[39] perdidi, totque corpore velut laxato 'quaeso' inquam 'regina, noli suggillare miserias. veneficio contactus sum.' (128.2-3)

I blushed with obvious embarrassment and lost whatever remained of my potency, with the whole of my body limp. 'I beg you, my queen,' I say, 'don't add insults to my misery. I have been polluted by witchcraft.'

And shortly afterwards Giton makes his sarcastic remark, already referred to, that Encolpius has been unable to perform with him either.

Next, I shall consider Encolpius' temporary breakup with Giton. After they have all returned from dinner with Trimalchio and Encolpius is happily in bed with Giton—I shall return to this—Ascyltos spirits him away to his own bed while Giton either is, or, like the Pergamum boy, pretends to be, asleep. Encolpius confronts him and he and Ascyltos agree to go their separate ways. What is to happen to Giton? Ascyltos proposes:

'ego ... finem discordiae imponam. puer ipse quem vult sequatur. ut sit illi saltem in eligendo fratre libertas.' ego qui vetustissimum consue- tudinem putabam in sanguinis pignus transisse, nihil timui, immo condicionem praecipiti festinatione rapui commisique iudici litem. qui ne deliberavit quidem, ut videretur cunctatus, verum statim ab extrema parte verbi consurrexit et fratrem Ascylton elegit. (80.5-6)

'I shall put an end to this argument. Let the boy himself follow whom he wishes. So that he at least may have freedom in choosing his lover.' I, who thought that our long intimacy had become a guarantee equivalent to blood ties, feared nothing, and indeed jumped rapidly at the proposal and gave the dispute to the judge. He did not hesitate a moment, lest there be any appearance of delay, and immediately got the word out of his mouth and chose Ascyltos as his lover.

I am surprised that two commentators view Encolpius' action negatively here: Schmeling says 'Encolpius again takes a passive approach ... and gets what he deserves,' and Richlin suggests that he 'loses Giton because he is too weak to fight for him.'[40] However, Giton is not a slave, at least not Encolpius' slave, and Encolpius has to court him, like Catullus with Juventius, and risk losing. Encolpius thinks he has rights —he frequently refers to Giton's betrayal as *iniuria*, a legal term (81.6, 83.4, 91.6, 94.2), but this can only be metaphorical— he has only a relationship based on love and commitment with no other power to compel. What would they have him do? Physically coerce him, aggravated by rape?

Why did Giton make this choice? His own explanation, offered at their tearful reunion, was:

quaeso ... Encolpi, fidem memoriae tuae appello: ego te reliqui an tu me prodidisti? equidem fateor et prae me fero: cum duos armatos viderem, ad fortiorem confugi. (91.8)

Please, Encolpius, I ask you to be true to your memory: did I leave you or did you abandon me? I admit and make no secret of it: when I saw two men with weapons, I turned to the stronger.

This is already a tendentious interpretation by Giton of the scene I have quoted, but Encolpius is so besotted that he accepts it. And we remember that Giton, in an earlier passage I have also quoted, had said Ascyltos had tried to rape him. However, Encolpius later questions Giton about their separation:

'narra mihi' inquam 'frater, sed tua fide: ea nocte, qua te mihi Acyltos subduxit, usque in iniuriam vigilavit an contentus fuit vidua pudicaque nocte?' tetigit puer oculos suos conceptissimisque iuravit verbis sibi ab Ascylto nullam vim factam. (133.1-2)

'Tell me, my darling,' I said, 'but on your honour: in that night when Ascyltos took you away from me, did he stay awake to the point of injustice or was he content with an empty and chaste night?' The boy touched his eyes and swore solemnly that Ascyltos had used no violence on him.

Giton does not want to lie directly to Encolpius but what he implies is that sex between Ascyltos and himself that night was consensual, not that it didn't take place. Of course, this could mean anything from passive compliance by Giton—he was, after all, supposed to be asleep— to active participation. At least Ascyltos had not used violence, as he had previously threatened to. Encolpius, while asking, is also evading the fact that Giton remained with Ascyltos not just for a one night stand (*unius noctis tactu*, 81.5, quoted above) but for at least several days. He does not want to know about any further betrayal by Giton beyond compliance in his abduction that first night. Once again, he shows that he will accept any explanation from him.

Yet Giton's real motivation remains obscure. Did he consider Ascyltos simply a bully who has the better of him, or more positively that he is stronger and might be a better protector (he is violent and has already beaten up Encolpius once, 11.4), the more resourceful companion (he wangled the dinner invitation with Trimalchio, 10.6), or simply the better lover (he is very well endowed, 92.9, while Encolpius is the victim of the *gravis ira Priapi*)? Or did he think one or more of these might be true, went with Ascyltos to find out and decided he was better off with his old lover? Or had he learned from experience to be sexually compliant as the best way of surviving? Or was he deliberately provoking jealousy in Encolpius, with no real intention of staying with Ascyltos for long? Or was Petronius simply exploiting the known fickle-ness of boy lovers, a standard topos,[41] without any psychological inten-tion? If this last, then the book dissolves into a series of episodes with no coherence at all and there is nothing to discuss. It is more interesting to take one of the earlier alternatives, and the one which helps makes sense of the motivation is the last of these: that Giton was provoking jealousy with the aim of binding Encolpius even more firmly to him. Why he should behave in this way is an issue I shall come to. Of course he need not have been conscious of his manipulative behaviour: he was sexualised young, as I have noted, and one way he functions is to encourage and exploit scenes with a third person, Ascyltos or Eumolpus in the text we have; I would be surprised if the complete version did not have a succession of such third parties.

Encolpius' distress at their separation is real enough:

> collegi sarcinulas locumque secretum et proximum litori maestus conduxi. ibi triduo inclusus redeunte in animum solitudine atque contemptu verberabam aegrum planctibus pectus et inter tot altissimos gemitus frequenter etiam proclamabam: 'ergo me non ruina terra potuit haurire?' (81.1-3)

> *I collected up my little bags of belongings and took myself off sadly to a quiet place near the beach. There for three days I shut myself up, brooding on my loneliness and humiliation and I beat my breast, sore with weeping, and through all my great groaning would keep calling out, 'Why could that earthquake not have swallowed me up?'*

I have quoted only the opening: Encolpius goes on the rehearse the history of both Ascyltos and Giton, and I have quoted the latter section already. Encolpius has tied his happiness to a boy with a history of being sexually exploited by others and the behaviour that goes with this. Jensson, 208, suggests that 'the driving force of the plot is not so much the "wrath of Priapus" as the jealousy of Encolpius.' I do not think this is quite right: Encolpius becomes understandably jealous of the sexual interest of others in Giton, who acts a kind of male *femme fatale* in the book, and his behaviour, here and throughout, though emotional, seems natural given his devotion to him; yet his many weaknesses do not include attempting to control and restrict Giton in the way characteristic of jealous partners. But Giton is compulsively driven to act seductively with others, to test Encolpius' devotion to him, to try to provoke the rejection that at some level he feels he deserves. This is typical behaviour for a deprived and sexually exploited child. And the fact that Encolpius loves him, always accepts him back and indeed accepts his flimsy explanations for his conduct is the reason that Giton returns to him. Psychologically, Encolpius is as much a father figure to Giton as a lover. It is unlikely that Giton had much of a father and part of his attachment to Encolpius would be due to unconscious yearning for a father-substitute. Of course, Encolpius is not very effective in this role, but that is secondary.

Of course, I do not suggest that Petronius would have expressed the motivation of his characters in these terms. He would not have needed to: all he had to do was to observe the behaviour of slaves, freedmen and *pueri delicati* in particular, which he would have had ample opportunity to do.

The real test of Giton's feelings for Encolpius comes in the ship-wreck, when they both think they are going to drown. The fact that this is a stock situation from the Greek novels and that Petronius is here more than usually rhetorical do not detract from the truth and vividness of the characterisation here:

> applicatus cum clamore flevi et 'hoc' inquam 'a diis meruimus, ut nos sola morte coniungerent. sed non crudelis fortuna concedit. ecce iam ratem fluctus evertet, ecce iam amplexus amantium iratum dividet mare. igitur, si vere Encolpion dilexisti, da oscula, dum licet, ultimum hoc gaudium fatis properantibus rape.' haec ut ego dixi, Giton vestem deposuit, meaque tunica contectus exeruit ad osculum caput. et ne sic cohaerentes malignior fluctus distraheret, utrumque zona circumveni-enti praecinxit et 'si nihil aliud, certe diutius' inquit 'iuncta mors feret, vel si voluerit mare misericors ad idem litus expellere, aut praeteriens aliquis tralaticia humanitate lapidabit,[42] aut quod ultimum est iratis etiam fluctibus, imprudens harena componet.' (114.8-11)

> *Hugging him with a cry, I wept and said, 'We deserved this from the gods, that only death would unite us. But cruel fate does not permit it. Look, the waves are now capsizing the ship and the angry sea breaks the embraces of lovers. So, if you ever loved Encolpius, kiss me while you can*

and take this last pleasure from the fate which is rushing upon us.' As I said this, Giton slipped off his clothes and, covered with my tunic, lifted up his head for a kiss. And lest the envious flood should drag us apart, he tied us each together with his encircling belt and said, 'If nothing else, death will carry us off more slowly joined, or if the pitying sea casts us up on the same shore, either someone passing by will cover us with stones out of common humanity or, as a last action by the angry waves, the sands, unconscious of their pious act, will cover us.'

Despite the artificiality of the situation, we can take their emotions as genuine: the best side of Encolpius is his enduring love for Giton—if one can excuse the lapse with Circe—and the best side of Giton is his willingness, as far as he is capable, to accept and return it.

The shipwreck is their lowest point in the book and it brings out the best in them. Finally, I want to consider their highest point, the start of the night after the dinner party with Trimalchio. Encolpius is stirred to verse:

qualis nox fuit illa, di deaeque,
quam mollis torus. haesimus calentes
et transfudimus hinc et hinc labellis
errantes animas. valete, curae
mortales. ego sic perire coepi. (79.8)

What a night that was, gods and goddesses. How soft the bed was. We embraced so warmly and poured our wandering souls in our lips from one to another. Farewell, earthly troubles. I was ready to die like this.

This is not as straightforward as it seems. We note that Encolpius has expressed himself in hendecasyllables, one of the favourite metres of that notable erotic poet Catullus. Then we note the theme of the exchange of souls through kisses. This was a celebrated topos in ancient love poetry, deriving from an epigram which was for long attributed to Plato:

Τὴν ψυχὴν, Ἀγάθωνα φιλῶν, ἐπὶ χείλεσι ἔσχον ·

ἦλθε γὰρ ἡ τλήμων ὡς διαβησομένη.
(*Greek Anthology*, V.78)[43]

My soul was on my lips when I was kissing Agathon. Poor thing! she came hoping to cross over to him.

However, despite these marks of joy, Petronius does all he can to undermine Encolpius' happiness. Notice the odd construction of the last line: Schmeling says that *perire+coepi* 'seems to be unique in Latin to this poem: Encolpius could be signalling that he was involved with foreplay when he fell asleep, *solutus mero remississem ebrias manus*' (I relaxed my drunken hands, loosened with wine, 79.9). In fact, he was under the *gravis ira Priapi*, so probably did not achieve penetration or orgasm, and we have already registered doubts about Giton's ability to do so. Then this passage is immediately followed by Ascyltos' abduction of the unresisting Giton, which I have already discussed. And the whole scene is called into question by the use of the same image when Encolpius unsuccessfully attempts to make love to Circe:

> iam pluribus osculis collisa labra crepitabant, iam implicitae manus omne genus amoris invenerant, iam alligata mutuo ambitu corpora animarum quoque mixturam fecerant. (132.1)

> *Now our joined lips sounded in many kisses, now our entwined hands found every way of making love, now our bodies tied in our joint embrace also made a union of our souls.*

If he was unsuccessful with Circe, then he probably was with Giton also. But even more important is that he uses the same language and image in both situations. If Circe means as much to Encolpius as does Giton, then the central relationship of the plot collapses, as his relationship with Giton continues for the whole of the work as we have it and seems to have begun in Massilia, possibly even before the *gravis ira Priapi*. The effect of this is, as when we considered the motivation for Giton's betrayal, and that of Encolpius' proposed renunciation of him, again to risk dissolving the work into a series of episodes. There are three possible resolutions of this issue. One is that parts of the work now missing might have resolved it, with Encolpius excusing himself to Giton about Circe as did Giton to him about Ascyltos. Their other sexual escapades would count as minor in comparison. Supporting this is the fact that in the passage I have just quoted Müller indicates lacunae immediately before and after it and in numerous other places during the Circe episode. Secondly, I cannot wholly dismiss the thought that Petronius may be simply putting together a series of scenes without caring too much about consistency, which, if true, destroys my thesis. Finally, his actual achievement may be somewhat different from his conscious intention—and he would not have been the first writer for whom this is true. He might have intended his book as a comic parody of a Greek romance, but, in the course of developing his characters, made them more sympathetic than he expected. (Something similar seems to have happened with Dickens and Mr Pickwick.) I mentioned at the outset that, for all the ridicule which is directed at Trimalchio, we end up feeling rather fond of the old fellow. I find something similar is true of Encolpius and Giton, even though they are not, in any ordinary sense, admirable characters. However, I would be willing to make considerable allowances for them as Giton was certainly, and Encolpius very possibly, a survivor of what we would consider sexual abuse. Their love comes over as more than sexual attraction; indeed, sexual activity between them as distinct from embraces is somewhat lacking in the extant work.

The answers to the questions I posed at the beginning are therefore as follows: yes, their relationship is one of love. The significance of their being of the same sex is that it carries with it the probability that their relationship may not be permanent. It is really tested, by Encolpius' timidity and impulsiveness, by Giton's tendency to manipulate, and by the tendency of both to accept other partners when offered, but nevertheless they always return to each other. Its literary significance was probably, in Petronius' intention, simply to parody the devoted couples of Greek romances but in fact it comes over as more than that.

It is hard to imagine how the book would have ended. Even if Encolpius manages to appease Priapus and be wholly reconciled to Giton, could their relationship last? What possible future could the two of them have, whether separately or together? However, even if they were to separate, it does not mean that there was not something true and good about their relationship. At their high point Encolpius draws on an epigram attributed to Plato. I shall end with a thought about lovers which comes undoubtedly from Plato himself:

> *It is ordained that all such as have taken the first steps on the celestial highway shall no more return to the dark pathways beneath the earth, but shall walk together in a life of shining bliss, and be furnished in due time with like plumage the one to the other, because of their love.* (*Phaedrus* 256d-e trans. R. Hackforth)

Encolpius and Giton have at least taken those first steps.

---

1. I follow the usual custom in the form of the title, i.e. taking *Satyricon* as a Greek genitive plural, short for *libri Satyricon*, as opposed to the Greek nominative singular *Satyrica*, a Satyr-like, i.e. erotic tale, which some scholars prefer.

2. There are brief discussions in Edward Courtney, *A Companion to Petronius*, Oxford, 2001, 49-53, and Amy Richlin, 'Sex in the *Satyrica*: Outlaws in Literatureland', in Jonathan Prag and Ian Repath (eds.), *Petronius: a Handbook*, Chichester, 2009. to which I make reference later.

3. I worked mainly from the 2003 edition of Müller's Teubner text.

4. *Prosimetrum* is a medieval term for the mixed form of verse with prose; discussion and further examples in Peter Dronke, *Verse with Prose from Petronius to Dante: The Art and Scope of the Mixed Form*, Harvard, 1994. Some scholars also find an affinity between the *Satyricon* and ancient mimes.

5. Northrop Frye, *Anatomy of Criticism*, Princeton, 1957, 309.

6. These more recent works are entirely in prose. For modern examples of the mixed form consider the Lewis Carroll Alice books, W. H. Auden, *The Orators* and *The Sea and the Mirror*, and David Jones, *In Parenthesis*.

7. Discussions in J. P. Sullivan, *The Satyricon of Petronius: A Literary Study*, London, 1968, 39 and 77; Gareth Schmeling with Aldo Setaioli, *A Commentary on the Satyrica of Petronius*, Oxford, 2011, xxii-xxv; Courtney, *A Companion*, 44-9; Gottskálk Jensson's thesis, *The Recollections of Encolpius: A reading of the Satyrica as Greco-Roman erotic fiction*, University of Toronto Ph. D. thesis, 1987, is a detailed and convincing reconstruction of the original plot of the *Satyricon*, from hints and references in the extant text. (Jensson later published *The Recollections of Encolpius: the* Satyrica *of Petronius as Milesian fiction*, Groningen, 2004, presumably based on his thesis, but I have not seen this.)

8. Sullivan, *The Satyricon of Petronius*, 92-3. Opinions differ as to whether the anger of Priapus lasted throughout the whole of the original work or is an episode. Courtney, 153-5, surveys the issue and thinks it probably was 'an objective motivating force in the wanderings and tribulations of Encolpius.'

9. Frye, *Anatomy*, 33-4.

10. Jensson, *The Recollections of Encolpius*, 109. He thinks it was adapted from a Greek model, 289.

11. Jensson, for example, who explores this in detail, sees Encolpius the narrator as considerably older than Encolpius the protagonist of the story, and the whole work as an imagined oral performance.

12. Sullivan, *The Satyricon of Petronius*, 117.

13. The reported crucifixion of the slave Mithridates at 53.3 is an apparent exception, but this, like many others of the reported *acta diurna*, daily records, is likely to be an exaggeration or an invention.

14. Aeschylus, *Myrmidons* fragments 135-7; Plato, *Symposium* 179e-180b.

15. Xenophon of Ephesus, *An Ephesian Tale* 3.1-2, in B. P. Reardon (ed.), *Collected Ancient Greek Novels*, Oakland, 1989, 146-8.

16. Catullus 48 and 99. The other poems which name Juventius are 24 and 81, though he may be intended in some others.

17. Petronius also follows this convention, see *osculum meum*, my kiss, 127.2, quoted below. Poets still do this. In William Empson's 'Aubade,' in which the lovers in bed are woken by an earthquake, he writes 'After two aliens had one kiss;' *Complete Poems* ed. Haffenden, London, 2000, 70.

18. Tibullus 1.8. Marathus is also the subject of poems 1.4 and 1.9.

19. Martial 11.22; see J. P. Sullivan, *Martial: the unexpected classic*, Cambridge, 1991, 207-9.

20. The story is assembled from various sources by T. P. Wiseman, *The Myths of Rome*, Exeter, 2004, 273.

21. Craig A. Williams, *Roman Homosexuality*, Oxford, 1999,72-7. In the *Satyricon* see 29.8 and, especially, 75.10-11. I quote the latter below.

22. Catullus 61.119-138.

23. There is a Encolpos who is the slave boy lover of his master Aulus Pudens in an epigram by Martial, I.31; *Epigrams* ed. and trans. Walter C. A. Ker, London, 1919, I.48-9.

24. Jensson 126, Schmeling *ad loc*. LSJ gives examples of the two differently accented forms.

25. Richlin, "Sex in the *Satyrica*," 86-8, has an extended discussion of this in relation to Encolpius, Giton and also Ascyltos, and concludes that 'Both the sexual and social status of all three characters seems mischievously indeterminate in the novel; they are living outside the law.'

26. This seems the obvious meaning of the passage I am about to quote. However, it may mean that there was something else unusual about Encolpius' genitals as Eumolpus is amazed when Encolpius shows them to him (140.13.)

27. Jensson, 192, thinks Doris is not a real woman but a *nom de guerre* which Giton assumed at some time in the past.

28. Sullivan, 238-245, offers a discussion of this.

29. Müller deleted *tamquam* from the text, but Courtney, 41, argues that it should be retained somewhere, so that 'the reference becomes merely a comparison to a similar stage in the growing up of a citizen boy.'

30. I have adopted various suggestions reported by Schmeling in this rendering.

31. *NHS Choices: Stages of puberty: what happens to boys and girls*, accessed on line 23.1.2023.

32. T. K. Hubbard, 'Puberty', *The Encyclopedia of Ancient History*, Chichester 2012, 1–2.

33. '*Tracto* itself was commonly used of masturbation,' and its compounds were used for a range of sexual activities, J. N. Adams, *The Latin Sexual Vocabulary*, London, 1982, 186-7.

34. Williams's rendering, *Roman Homosexuality*, 185.

35. '*Ludo* and *lusus* take their implication from the context ... Both the noun and the verb are often used of the amatory indulgence granted to youth,' Adams, *op. cit.*, 162. He does not cite this passage of Petronius.

36. Assuming, with Reeve, an ellipsis of *natus*, so that he only assumed the role at the age of fourteen rather than that he performed it for fourteen years. See discussion by Schmeling *ad loc.* and LCL.

37. The claim that she had been a virgin until recently cannot be true in view of what Chrysis has already told Encolpius, that Circe looks for lovers *in extrema plebe* (from the lowest of the low, 126.7).

38. Circe is playing with words. If Giton is Encolpius' *frater*, she can be his *soror*, and pretend that the kiss she offers is the chaste *ius osculi* of family affection.

39. i.e. his erection. Here, as with Circe's kiss and the use of *frater* and *soror*, Petronius, unlike, say, Catullus, uses decorous language even though it is perfectly clear what he means.

40. Schmeling *ad loc.*; Richlin, "Sex in the Satyrica," 94.

41. E.g. Catullus 24, 81, 82; Tibullus 1.9.

42. Covering their imagined bodies with stones would constitute a technical burial and so allow their spirits to cross Acheron. The allusion is to Palinurus, *Aeneid* VI.365-6.

43. Greek text from Walther Ludwig, 'Plato's Love Epigrams', *Greek, Roman and Byzantine Studies*, 1963, 4, 59–82; translation from *Greek Anthology*, ed. and trans. W. R. Paton, London, 1918, I, 166-7. Ludwig points out that this Agathon cannot be the tragic poet. For other examples of this topos see Appendix 5.

15

REALISTIC PSYCHOLOGY IN
THE TALE OF CUPID AND PSYCHE

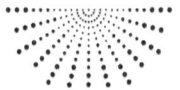

THE RELATIONSHIP OF VENUS AND CUPID

Neither must we admit at all, said I, that gods war with gods and plot against one another and contend ... Hera's fetterings by her son and the hurling out of heaven of Hephaestus by his father when he was trying to save his mother from a beating, and the battles of the gods in Homer's verse are things we must not admit into our city either wrought in allegory or without allegory. (Plato, *Republic* 378b-d trans. Paul Shorey)

Tantaene animis caelestibus irae? (Virgil, *Aeneid* I.11)

Are resentments so great in divine spirits?

The tale of Cupid and Psyche has been admired for many reasons, one of the chief being its significance as a Platonic allegory. However, in this paper I wish to consider another aspect, the realistic psychology Apuleius gives in particular to the divine characters Venus and Cupid.

In using this, he develops three narrative techniques, one of which reaches back to Homer, one of which anticipates Shakespeare, and one is particularly characteristic of himself. The Homeric technique is to treat the gods as if they had the same kinds of passions and behaviour as do ordinary human beings. As a good Platonist, Apuleius was naturally familiar with the passage of Plato I have quoted above. However, as an original writer of fiction, instead of accepting the advice Socrates gives in this passage and elsewhere, he does the opposite: he deliberately gives his divine characters human passions and, if anything, exaggerates these in his characterisation, as we shall see.

The second technique is to present the characters of what, after all, is a fairy or folk tale, as if their situations were entirely normal and for them to respond to them as would ordinary people if placed in those situations. This is more remarkable than it may seem, because English readers have got used to Shakespeare doing exactly the same thing in his romantic comedies. The clearest example is *The Merchant of Venice*, which employs two folk tale plots, the pound of flesh and the three caskets. Shakespeare may well have been influenced in this directly by reading Apuleius, either in William Adlington's translation of 1566, or indeed in the Latin original. The transformation of Bottom in *A Midsummer Night's Dream* shows the direct influence of the framing story of Lucius. Apuleius uses this technique with both his divine and his human characters, though arguably more with the former than the latter, hence the focus of this paper.

The third technique is the elaborate and flowery language in which he writes the tale, which is at odds, both to the character of the old woman who is supposedly retelling it, and to the normal way in which folk tales are retold. This creates a dissonance between the content of the story and the clever rhetoric of the narration, which serves to emphasizes the artificiality of the whole work. This points towards the allegorical meaning of both the framing story and the inset tales—not only this one—but I shall not be exploring this here.

We start with Venus. We realize straightway that there is going to be trouble when we learn that Psyche was being worshipped as an incarnation of Venus:

> Multi denique civium et advenae copiosi ... inaccessae formonsitatis admiratione stupidi et admoventes oribus suis dexteram, priore digito

in erectum pollicem residente, ut upsam prorsus deam Venerem uener-
abantur religiosis adorationibus. (IV.28.3)[1]

Many citizens and numerous visitors ... were amazed at her unparalleled
beauty, moving their right hand to their lips, with their index fingers
resting on their upright thumbs, as they worshipped her with religious
devotions in every respect as the goddess Venus.

As a result:

Paphon nemo, Cnidon nemo, ac ne ipsa quidem Cythera ad
conspectum deae Veneris navigabant. Sacra differuntur, templa defor-
mantur, pulvinaria proteruntur, caerimoniae negleguntur; incoronata
simulacra et arae viduae frigido cinere foedatae. (IV.29.3)

No one sailed to Paphos, no one to Cnidos, nor even to Cythera to see the
goddess Venus. Her rituals were abandoned, her temples were continu-
ously neglected, her ceremonial cushions trampled on, her ceremonies
ignored; her statues were left ungarlanded and her widowed altars,
deprived of offerings, were polluted with cold ashes.

Although this is not a situation Psyche had willingly or deliberately
brought about, Venus reacts as if it were. She is filled with resentment
and promises revenge on the entirely innocent girl:

En rerum naturae prisca parens, en elementorum origo initialis, en
orbis totius alma Venus, quae cum mortali puella partiario maiestatis
honore tractor! ... Sed non adeo gaudens ista, quaecumque est, meos
honores usurpabit: iam faxo eam fastus huius etiam ipsius inlicitae
formonsitatis paeniteat. (IV.30.1, 3)

See the original parent of all nature, the first source of the elements, see
Venus, nurturer of the whole world, who am being driven to share the
honour of my majesty with a mortal girl! ... But she will not be rejoicing
much, whoever she is, who will usurp my honours: I shall soon make sure
that she regrets the arrogance of that illegitimate beauty of hers.

She then commissions Cupid to punish Psyche by making her fall in love with the basest possible human being, reinforcing her wishes with *osculis hiantibus filium diu ac pressule saviata* (having kissed her son long and hard with parted lips (IV.31.4), which suggests an almost incestuously close relationship, immediately contrasted with her ceremonial return to Ocean.

We can reconstruct what happens next: Cupid goes to take a look at Psyche and falls in love with her himself. He then gets Apollo to issue the oracle with its apparently dire prophecy, which, however, is a grandiose example of irony and is fulfilled in every particular except one, in the opposite sense. The exception is the adjective *vipereum*, snake-like, for the *gener*, son-in-law (IV.33.1). This is not true of Cupid but is taken up by Psyche's sisters as part of their deceitful warning, that Psyche's husband is really an *immanen colubrum multinodis voluminibus serpentem* (a monstrous snake creeping with many-knotted coils, V.17.3).

At this point I digress briefly to point out that Cupid in this version is not the naughty child of traditional mythology, as for example in Apollonius of Rhodes, in which Aphrodite asks Eros to make Jason fall in love with Medea, which was Apuleius' model for this scene.[2] In Apuleius he is old enough to be physically mature and able to father a child, but also young enough to be somewhat under his mother's sway, and to be beardless, and with rosy cheeks (*genasque purpureas*, V.22.5), in fact what we would call an adolescent. Indeed, it is interesting how easily Apuleius's characterization transfers into modern terms.

Anyway, he does nothing to fulfil his mother's command, and instead spirits Psyche away to his palace where he visits her only at night and forbids her to see his face. Why does he do this? Clearly, he does not want his mother to find out that he has disobeyed her instructions and done the opposite; furthermore, he is in the position of a teenage boy whose mother thinks he is too young to be sleeping with his girlfriend. Of course she finds out, as mothers always do, because a little bird tells her (V.28.2, 8). Her first thought is that a scheming girl has seduced him:

Ergo iam ille bonus filius meus habet amicam aliquam? Prome agedum, quae sola mihi servis amanter, nomen eius, quae puerum ingenuum et investem sollicitavit (V.28.7)

So now that fine son of mine has some girlfriend? Come on then, you who are the only one to attend me willingly, tell me the name of the female who seduced that simple and immature boy.

When she finds out that the girlfriend is not a nymph or similar but in fact Psyche, and that Cupid has made her his wife (*nuptias*, V.30.3) she launches into a long tirade against him, whose underlying feeling is that his starting a new family has made her feel old and infertile, a sentiment more probable in a human mother than a goddess:

Honesta ... haec et natalibus nostris bonaeque tuae frugi congruentia, ut primum quidem tuae parentis—immo dominae—praecepta calcares, nec sordidis amoribus inimicam meam cruciares, verum etiam hoc aetatis puer tuis licentiosis et immaturis iungeres amplexibus, ut ego nurum scilicet tolerarem inimicam. Sed utique praesumis, nugo et corruptor et inamabilis, te solum generosum, nec me iam per aetatem posse concipere. (V.29.2-4)

What a good show, and really suitable for our family origins and your reputation for decency, that first you trample underfoot the command of your mother—in fact your sovereign—and do not torture my enemy with a demeaning passion, and, in fact, you, still a child in age, copulate with your uncontrolled adolescent lovemaking, so that obviously I should accept an enemy as a daughter-in-law. No doubt you take it for granted, you worthless and unlovable seducer, that only you are fertile and that I am now unable to conceive because of my age.

She goes on, in a finely comic passage, to propose replacing him:

Velim ergo scias multo te meliorem filium alium genituram, immo ut contumeliam magis sentias, aliquem de meis adoptaturam vernulis eique donaturam istas pinnas et flammas et arcum et ipsas sagittas et omnem meam supellectilem, quam tibi non ad hos usus dederam. nec enim de patris tui bonis ad instructionem istam quicquam concessum est. (V.29.5-6)

So I want you to know that I shall produce another son much better than you; in fact so that you should feel the disgrace all the more, I shall adopt one of my young household slaves and give him those wings and torches and bow and those arrows and all my equipment, which I did not give you for this purpose. For there was not anything handed over from your father's property for your outfit.

What makes this especially witty is that her tone of an outraged and unsupported single mother is completely belied by the mythological facts which would have been well known to Apuleius's readers, namely Venus's adultery with Mars and the complete uncertainty as to who Cupid's father actually was.[3]

She goes on to complain that he abuses her, as a consequence of having been badly brought up:

Sed male prima tu a pueritia inductus es et acutas manus habes et maiores tuos irreverenter pulsasti totiens, et ipsam matrem tuam, me inquam ipsam, parricida denudas cotidie et percussisti saepius et quasi viduam utique contemnis, nec vitricum tuum fortissimum illum maxi-mumque bellatorem metuis ... (V.30.1)

But right from the beginning you were badly brought up in your child-hood and you are quarrelsome and have disrespectfully hit your elders so many times, and even your own mother, myself I say, you expose every day, you batterer, and you have very often hit me and jeered at me as if I were a widow, nor do you have any respect for your stepfather, the bravest and greatest warrior ...

This falls apart as soon as you examine it. If Cupid was badly brought up, it is her responsibility. The physical abuse she complains of is of course the use of his bow and arrows, which, as she has just said, she gave him. And he uses them to provoke love, something which, as

Venus, she is generally enthusiastic about. As for respect for his stepfather, this is Mars, with whom she has had an adulterous affair and for whom there is no reason for Cupid to feel any respect at all.

Towards the end of this she asks herself:

Quibus modis stelionem istum cohibeam? (V.30.3)

By what means may I stop that reptile?

This is an interesting return of the snake imagery for Cupid, which lurks in the background for the first half of the story.

In fact, though she shuts Cupid up in her own house after he has been injured by the drop of boiling oil—though his adverse reaction to this seems extreme—she carries out none of her threats against him and instead transfers her anger to Psyche, who has innocently provoked her. She gets Jupiter's permission to use Mercury as her messenger for the asking, and flatters and commissions him to find Psyche in these words:

Frater Arcadi, scis nempe sororem tuam Venerem sine Mercuri praesentia nil umquam fecisse, nec te praeterit utique quanto iam tempore delitescentem ancillam nequiverim repperire. Nil ergo superest quam tuo praeconio praemium investigationis publicitus edicere. (VI.7.3)

Arcadian brother, you surely know that your sister Venus has never achieved anything without the presence of Mercury, nor can it have passed you by for how long I have already been unable to find my disappearing slavegirl. So nothing remains but for a reward for finding her to be publicly announced through your office.

The crucial word here is *ancilla*, which Venus repeatedly uses for Psyche. However, you translate it: slave, handmaid, maidservant, it implies that Psyche is in a publicly recognized position of servitude to Venus, and that in not being present and available to her she is a runaway. Neither of these is true: Psyche is a king's daughter, and also, as Venus has angrily conceded, her daughter-in-law. But Venus has persuaded herself that Psyche owes her duties which she has not discharged and pursues her with a fury that is reminiscent of that of Juno in the *Aeneid*—hence my second epigraph above.

In the setting of impossible tasks—a traditional folklore motif—the issue is not that Psyche manages to accomplish them, because in this kind of story that always happens, but how she manages to do so. (It is perhaps a slight blemish that there are four tasks instead of the traditional three.) What Apuleius tells us is that a little ant (*formicula*, VI.10.5) pities her and gets his colony to sort out the heap of seeds, a frank and kind reed (*harundo simplex et humana* (VI.13.1) advises her on handling the wild sheep, an eagle, Jupiter's own bird (*supremi Iovis regalis ... aquila*), acting on behalf of good Providence (*Providentiae bonae* , VI.15.1) obtains the waters of the Styx for her and a far-seeing tower with a duty of prophecy (*turris illa prospicua vaticinationis munus*, VI.20.1) advises her on how to go safely to the underworld and return with Proserpina's ointment. Juno, however, is convinced that Psyche has only managed to achieve the tasks with the covert help of Cupid, despite his being on his sickbed and locked in a room. For example, she says after the first task has been completed:

> Non tuum ... nequissima, nec tuarum manuum istud opus, sed illius, cui tuo, immo et ipsius, malo placuist. (VI.11.2)

> *That work, you dreadful creature, is not yours nor from your hands, but from him to whom you were attractive, to your misfortune and his too.*

However, what Apuleius actually tells us is that good Providence has been looking after Psyche. This happened first when she arrived at Cupid's palace (*sensit Psyche divinae Providentiae beatitudinem*, Psyche felt the blessing of divine Providence, V.3.1). Providence is an important power for Apuleius and she turns up repeatedly as an attribute of Isis in the Isis book (e.g. XI.5.4, XI.15.4 accepting Beroaldus' emendation, XI.18.1). I am therefore not sure that Kenney is right when he says flatly that 'this power is Cupid.'[4] He—and Venus—may be right, but the issue is unsettled. We may suspect the hand of Isis behind all of this.

Whatever the truth of this, Cupid definitely does himself come to rescue Psyche when her fatal curiosity leads her to open Proserpina's box. He breaks out from his mother's house without difficulty, the decision never to see Psyche again is quietly abandoned, and he goes to her. To resolve the matter finally, he goes to appeal to Jupiter. Apuleius characterizes this by saying *ad armillam redit*, literally he returned to the wine-jug (VI.22.1). This is an idiomatic phrase which Kenney translates 'he returned to type,' and Hanson 'turned back to his old tricks.' The implication is clearly that he is doing something mischievous or deceitful, but within the conventions of the story there is nothing better or more appropriate he could do than to appeal to the supreme god. Kenney suggests, rightly in my view, that this is to draw attention to a change in the allegory; however, it breaks the consistency at the literal level. Venus had also appealed to Jupiter, and without censure, even though she did not give her reasons.

In all this, we see Cupid growing up and taking responsibility. He has broken out from his mother's possessive and somewhat suffocating love (we remember that kiss), which turned out not to be difficult after all, rescued Psyche, and gone over the head of his mother to get the matter resolved by the one authority who is in a position to do it. He is no longer behaving like an adolescent with a secret girlfriend whom he hides away but as an adult, young indeed but an adult, who wants to have his position regularized according to the conventions of the time and the story and who publicly acknowledges his wife. After some prevarication, Jupiter accedes to his request and goes on to mollify Venus by addressing her real concerns:

> Nec tu ... filia, quicquam contristere, nec prosapiae tantae tuae statuque de matrimonio mortali metuas. Iam faxo nuptias non impares, sed legitimas et iure civili congruas.[5] (VI.23.4)

> *Nor should you, my daughter, be distressed about anything, nor should your fear for your distinguished dynasty nor your status because of marriage to a mortal. I shall make the wedding no longer unequal but legitimate and in agreement with civil law.*

As a result he makes Psyche immortal, there is a wedding feast, and—

Sic rite Psyche convenit in manum Cupidinis. (VI.24.4)

In this way Psyche came properly to the hand of Cupid.

Was then Psyche's first, funereal wedding (*funerei thalami*, IV.33.1, also IV.34.1) then not valid? Venus certainly seemed to think it was valid, because her indignation, as we have seen, is that she has acquired a mortal daughter-in-law who will have her grandson or granddaughter. She would probably not have felt the same if Cupid had merely entered into a brief liaison with a mortal woman, as the male gods did that all the time. Perhaps there is a parallel with Catullus, where the marriage of Peleus and Thetis is celebrated separately by the mortals and the immortals, though admittedly on the same occasion. Maybe we need not be too concerned about the correct etiquette when an immortal marries a mortal, particularly if the latter is going to be deified. Now that Venus's dynastic fears have been assuaged—and, though she does not say so, the issue of paying the mortal Psyche divine honours has been removed— she indicates her willingness to accept the situation by dancing at the wedding (*saltavit*, VI.24.3); however, apologizing to Psyche for her cruel and unfair treatment of her is beyond her.

For an allegory to succeed, it must maintain consistency at the literal level. Examples include *Pilgrim's Progress* and *Animal Farm*. Apuleius does this brilliantly, finessing potentially awkward points, such as the validity of Psyche's wedding to Eros, and how she manages to achieve her tasks. I have noticed only two places where there is a slight awkwardness: the use of *vipereum* in Apollo's prophecy and that of *ad armillam redit* in Cupid's appeal to Jupiter, both of which I have discussed. And even these may be deliberately planted clues pointing to the allegorical meaning. He tells the story so well that the reader can relax and enjoy it in its own terms without worrying about the allegory, but that is precisely what his use of realistic characterization of his divine characters is intended to achieve and does achieve.

---

1. All quotations have been taken from Maaike Zimmerman's 2012 OCT.
2. Kenney *ad loc.*; Apollonius Rhodius, *Argonautica*, III.111-153.

3. Cicero rehearses the various theories, *De natura deorum* III.58-60; see also Pierre Grimal, *Dictionary of Classical Mythology*, Oxford, 1986, s.v. Eros, 152-3, 483, with copious references.
4. Kenney, 142.
5. Taking *iure* as dative; see Kenney *ad. loc.*, also Gildersleeve and Lodge, *Gildersleeve's Latin Grammar*, Wauconda 2000 (1895), 257. Jahn emends to *iuri*.

APPENDICES

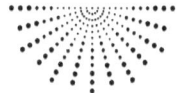

1

A NOTE ON THE HELEN EPISODE

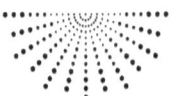

his passage (lines 567-88) is not in the early manuscripts of the *Aeneid* and is supplied from Servius *auctus*, who comments on 566: *post hunc uersum hiuversum fuereunt, qui a Tucca et Vario obliti sunt* (after this line came these lines, which were removed by Tucca and Varius); they were the editors of the text appointed by Augustus, though it seems that the work was probably done just by Varius. Modern texts, such as the Oxford, include the lines in continuous numbering with the rest of the book, but with brackets or italics or other indications to show their separate line of transmission and doubtful status.

Servius *auctus* gives the reason for deletion as follows:

> ut enim dictum est, uersus illos qui superius notati sunt, hinc constat esse sublatos, nec immerito. nam et turpe est uiro forti contra feminam irasci, et contrarium est Helenam in domo Priami fuisse illi rei, quae in sexto dicitur, quia in domo est inuenta Deiphobi, postquam ex summa arce uocauerat Graecos. hinc autem uersus esse sublatos Veneris uerba declarant dicentis 'non tibi Tyndaridis facies inuisa Lacaenae.'[1]

As was said before, it is agreed that those lines which were recorded above were removed from here, and rightly so. For it would both be wrong for a strong man to get angry with a woman and it would be contradictory for Helen to have been in the house of King Priam, because it is said in the sixth book that she was found in the house of Deiphobus, after she had summoned the Greeks from the rooftop. Moreover Venus' words confirm that lines were removed from here when she says [in 601] *'It is not the face of the Laconian woman, the daughter of Tyndarus* [Helen], *that should be hateful to you.'*

Scholars have disagreed about the authenticity and appropriateness of these lines, and one could provide a roll call of those on either side of this debate. The three fullest relatively recent discussions I am aware of are by Austin, Goold and Horsfall.[2] Horsfall helpfully quotes Murgia's summary: 'In general, textual critics, on grounds of the suspect quality of the tradition and of the language and style, deny authenticity, while literary critics maintain it.'[3] Horsfall himself is primarily a linguistic commentator and denies authenticity, as does Goold, who suggested Lucan as the putative author of the episode. I am not competent to enter into the linguistic arguments, but from the literary point of view I would expect a forger to make sure his addition was consistent with the Deiphobus passage in book VI and would not have had Aeneas even contemplate killing a woman. For these reasons I tend to support authenticity and prefer Austin's view, which he summarizes in his commentary as follows:

My view ... is that the passage is by Virgil: and that it is a collection of drafts forming a series of approaches to ideas that were never worked up into a finished unitary whole. My main arguments are these: (*a*) Servius' reasons for the deletion are worthless; (*b*) the criticisms made against style, language, and metrical technique are unsound; (*c*) the passage is too brilliantly imaginative to have been composed by a poet-aster and too full of obvious difficulties to be the work of a forger who hoped to deceive scholars; (*d*) in its unpolished, inchoate form it was removed by Virgil's executors as being just the kind of thing that ought not to be 'authorized' for posterity.[4]

Certainty in this is not obtainable, but one could add that something must have stood, or been intended to stand, in this place, and some version of the Helen episode meets the need

---

1. Comment on 592. To add to the complications, the text of Servius *auctus* is far from certain and neither the Thilo-Hagen nor the Harvard edition is regarded as reliable by specialists. I have cited the passage as quoted from the Harvard edition by Austin, 'Virgil, *Aeneid* 2.567-88,' *The Classical Quarterly*, Nov. 1961, Vol. 11, No. 2 (Nov. 1961). The text of Servius is also discussed at length in Goold's article 'Servius and the Helen episode,' *Harvard Studies in Classical Philology*, 1970, Vol. 74.
2. Austin's article, noted above, is briefly summarized in his commentary; Horsfall's is an appendix to his commentary.
3. Horsfall 566.
4. Austin's commentary, 218.

2

CHART OF NAMES
IN THE ECLOGUES

Eclogue	1	2	3	4	5	6	7	8	9	10
Tityrus	✓		✓		✓	✓		✓	✓	
Meliboeus	✓		✓		✓		✓			
Amaryllis	✓	✓	✓					✓	✓	
Galatea	✓		✓				✓		✓	
Corydon		✓			✓		✓			
Alexis		✓			✓		✓			
Pan		✓		✓	✓			✓		✓
Menalcas		✓	✓		✓				✓	✓
Damoetas		✓	✓		✓					
Daphnis		✓	✓		✓		✓	✓	✓	
Amyntas		✓	✓		✓					✓
Aegon		✓			✓					
Micon		✓					✓			
Damon		✓						✓		
Phyllis		✓			✓		✓			✓
Pollio		✓	✓							
Linus			✓			✓				
Codrus					✓		✓			
Alphesiboeus					✓			✓		
Mopsus						✓		✓		
Gallus						✓				✓
Varus						✓			✓	
Lycidas							✓		✓	
Moeris								✓	✓	

3

THE GALLIAMBIC METRE

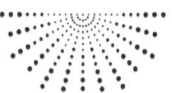

he Attis poem is the only surviving complete poem in this metre from the ancient world. It was surprisingly difficult to reach an understanding of this metre as no single work seemed to give all we need in one place. So I am setting out my understanding of how it works.

The galliambic is a type of Ionic metre. The basic *metron*, or metrical unit, is one of two kinds: either ‾ ‾ ˘˘ which is the Ionic *a maiore* or ˘˘ ‾ ‾ which is the Ionic *a minore*. This is not a common metre in Latin and there is only one standard example, which uses the *a minore* version:

> miserarum est neque amori dare ludum neque dulci
> mala uino lauere, aut exanimari metuentis
> > patruae uerbera linguae. (Horace: *Odes* 3.12)

Poor girls, not able to give free play to their love or wash their troubles away with sweet wine or, if they do, fearing the lash of an uncle's tongue.

The galliambic is based on the Ionic in the *a minore* version. The basic galliambic line starts as a sequence of four Ionics *a minore*:

⏑⏑ – – | ⏑⏑ – – | ⏑⏑ – – | ⏑⏑ – –

However, the last one has its last syllable removed; this is termed *catalectic*. There is also a always a word end after the second *metron*. Such coincidence of word and *metron* end is termed *diaeresis*.[1] The line is therefore always broken in two. This is termed *asynarteton*. This gives us:

⏑⏑ – – | ⏑⏑ – – ‖ ⏑⏑ – – | ⏑⏑ –

However, Catullus commonly modifies this line with three devices. First is *anaclasis*, where a short element (a *breve*) changes its place with an adjacent long element (a *longum*). This is common in the first half of the line and occasional in the second. Here is the line with both changes:

⏑⏑ – ⏑ | – ⏑ – – ‖ ⏑⏑ – ⏑ | – ⏑ –

ălĭēnă | quaē pĕtēntēs ‖ uĕlŭt ēxŭl- | ēs lŏcă (14)

In this form the line now consists of two anacreontics, the second of which lacks its final syllable and is therefore *catalectic*.

Second is *resolution*, which is the substitution of two short syllables for one, particularly used late in the line. In the words of the ancient metrist Caesius Bassus, this is done *quo magis hic uersus, quod matri sacer est Idaeae, uibrare uideatur*, 'in order that this verse, since it is sacred to the Idaean mother, should seem all the more frantic.'[2] This then gives us:

⏑⏑ – ⏑ | – ⏑ – – ‖ ⏑⏑ – ⏑ | ⏑⏑ ⏑ –

This pattern forms the standard line, which is used in by far the greatest number of verses, and can be seen in the first line; the last syllable can be long, or, as here, short:

sŭpĕr āltă | uēctŭs Āttīs ‖ cĕlĕrī ră- | tĕ mărĭă (1)

The two longs in the first half and that on the third syllable of the second half are never resolved, and these give some stability as the rest rushes along.

The use of resolution is taken to an extreme in the longest line in the poem:

ĕgŏ iŭuĕnĭs, | ĕgo‿adŏlēscēns, ‖ ĕgŏ‿ephēbŭs, | ĕgŏ pŭĕr (63)

The third device is *contraction*, which is the replacement of two short syllables by one long one, as in the shortest line in the poem:

iām. iām dŏ- | lēt quŏd ēgī. ‖ iām iāmquĕ | paēnĭtĕt. (73)

Word accent is a controversial issue with this metre. The consensus seems to be that long syllables should be stresses, or the first of the two shorts substituted for a long. The final syllable *anceps* is stressed.

The use of this metre by Michael Marullus in his Hymn to Bacchus is clearly modelled on the example of Catullus.

Tennyson attempted an English equivalent to the galliambic metre in his *Boadicea*. Here is the opening:

> While about the shore of Mona those Neronian legionaries
> Burnt and broke the grove and altar of the Druid and Druidess,
> Far in the East Boädicéa, standing loftily charioted,
> Mad and maddening all that her heard her
>   in her fierce volubility,
> Girt by half the tribes of Britain, near the colony Cámulodúne,
> Yell'd and skrie'd between her daughters o'er a wild confederacy.

---

1. In line 37 he permits himself an elision over the break: *pĭgĕr hīs lăbāntĕ lānguōre͜ ŏcŭlōs sŏpŏr ŏpĕrĭt*. This is the only place he does this.
2. Quoted with translation from Llewelyn Morgan, *Musa pedestris: metre and meaning in Roman verse*, Oxford, 2010, 82.

4
NIMIS AND ITS COGNATES IN CATULLUS

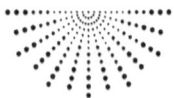

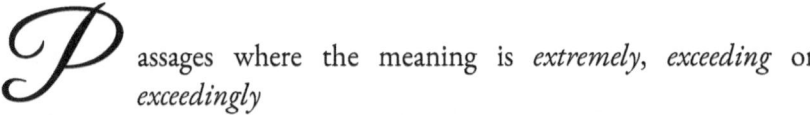Passages where the meaning is *extremely, exceeding* or *exceedingly*

63.36   nimio e labore somnum capiunt sine Cerere
after extremely great effort they fall asleep without eating.

43.4   nec sane nimis elegante lingua
without an exceedingly refined tongue

56.4   res est ridicula et nimis iocosa
it is an absurd and extremely funny story

Passages where the meaning is *excessive or excessively*

51.14   otio exsultas nimiumque gestis
you run riot in your idleness and get about too much

60.5   ah nimis fero corde
ah with an excessively cruel heart

63.8   omea libere nimis quae fugere imperia cupit
she wants to be excessively free and escape my rule

64.169   sic, nimis insultans extreme tempore saeua
so, excessively cruel, mocking me in my hour of need

Passages where the meaning is ambiguous, translated as *very* or *utter*:

63.17   et corpus euirastis Veneris nimio odio
You have unmanned your bodies from utter revulsion from love.
[see discussion in text]

64.22o   nimis optato saeclorum tempore nati
Oh born in that very happy period of time

68.137   ne nimium simus stultorum more molesti
lest I be tiresome in the manner of very stupid men

93.1   nil nimium studeo, Caesar, tibi uelle placere
I am not very keen, Caesar, to be pleasing to you

Notice that apart from line 17 under consideration there are two other uses in this poem, one at at 36 where the meaning is *exceedingly* and the other at 80 where it is *excessively*.

5

THE SOUL IN THE KISS

The epigram which Encolpius quotes has a considerable history, both because of the idea itself, and also because of its attribution to Plato, which was for long accepted. Gaselee, whose 1924 article remains fundamental,[1] was inclined to think that it might be genuine, reflecting the views of scholars of the day. More recently, Walther Ludwig considered that this and other erotic epigrams attributed to Plato came probably from the third century B. C., and were inserted by Diogenes Laertius into his biography of him from a collection assembled by an unidentifiable Aristippos.[2] Gaselee gives examples from Greek, Roman and some later writers. Schmeling gives Latin ones, though some of these are more to do with catching the breath of the expiring soul (see the Bion and Virgil passages below) than the exchange of kisses, and others are later than Petronius. I give below a selection from these, together with some English examples I have found.[3]

From the Alexandrian poet Bion, probably late second century B. C.:

Rouse yourself a little, Adonis, and kiss me for a final time; kiss me as your kiss has life, until you breathe your last into my mouth, and your spirit flows into my heart, and I drain your sweet love. *(Lament for Adonis, 45-8)*[4]

This Bion passage also draws on the idea of catching the last breath of a loved one. Anna tries to do this with Dido:

> date uulnera lympha
> abluam et, extremus si quis super halitus errat,
> ore legam. (*Aeneid* IV.684-5)

Give me water to wash her wounds and catch with my lips whatever last breath may be wandering.

The idea that the soul of the dying person could be caught by the living relative was a popular belief,[5] though one I would distinguish from the idea of exchanging souls in kisses. Petronius also draws on this idea (74.17), but separately from the theme of the exchanges of kisses.

Returning to Greek, there are two passages from Meleager, first century B.C.:

> The wine cup feels sweet joy and tells me how it touches the prattling mouth of Zenophila the friend of love. Happy cup! Would she would set her lips to mine and drink up my soul at one draught. (*Greek Anthology* V.171)[6]

> For now that I have kissed Antiochus, fairest of our youth, I have drunk the sweet honey of the soul. (*Greek Anthology* XII.133)[7]

The two passages from Petronius come next chronologically. Gaselee's other Greek examples are later than Petronius, but it is worth noting one from the third century A. D. Achilles Tatius, since this kind of book seems to have been Petronius' model:

> The union and commingling of two mouths radiates pleasures down into the bodies and draws up the souls towards the kissing lips. (*Leucippe and Clitophon*, II.8)[8]

Of Gaselee's examples from late antiquity I note only that Aulus Gellius quotes and discusses the original pseudo-Platonic epigram[9] and then come to the Renaissance. Castiglione introduces the poet and churchman Pietro Bembo as a character at the end of his *Il Cortegiano* (*The Courtier*). Bembo makes a speech about love which includes the following:

> A kisse may be saide to be rather a coupling together of the soule, than of the body ...For this doe all chaste lovers covet a kisse, as a coupling of souls together. And therefore Plato the devine lover saith, that in kissing, the soule came as farre as his lippes to depart out of the bodie. (*The Courtier*, 315)

I have cited Thomas Hoby's 1561 translation, as English writers who did not read Italian would probably have read this.[10] So in Sidney we find:

> O kisse, which soules, even soules together ties
> By linkes of *Love*, and only Nature's art
> > (*Astrophil and Stella* 81.5-6)[11]

And in Donne:

> So, so, break off this last lamenting kiss,
> Which sucks two souls, and vapours both away
> > (*The Expiration)*[12]

Also from Donne:

> Sir, more than kisses, letters mingle souls
> > (*To Mr Henry Wotton)*[13]

This epigram is from Herrick:

> I prest my *Julia's* lips, and in the kisse

Her Soule and Love were palpable in this.
(Love palpable)[14]

Probably the most famous use of the image in English is this, from Marlowe:

Was this the face that launched a thousand ships,
And burnt the topless towers of Ilium,
Sweet Helen, make me immortal with a kiss,
Her lips suck forth my soul: see where it flies.
Come, Helen, come, give me my soul again.
Here will I dwell for heaven is in those lips,
And all is dross that is not Helena. (*Dr Faustus* 5.1.97-103)[15]

Gaselee offers later examples from Shelley and Tennyson. I dare say a systematic search would produce several more.

---

1. Stephen Gaselee, 'The Soul in the Kiss,' *The Criterion*, 2, April 1924, 349-59.
2. Ludwig, Walther, *ibid*. The relevant passage is Diogenes Laertius, *Lives of Eminent Philosophers*, III.1.32.
3. I have not used Gaselee's texts or his versions, which cannot be relied on: for example in the Agathon epigram he renders his name by Kate! Schmeling gives only references.
4. *Theocritus, Moschus, Bion* ed. and trans. Neil Hopkinson, Harvard, 2015, 510-1.
5. The commentary on the Virgil passage by A. S. Pease gives many parallels from classical literature and folklore.
6. *Greek Anthology, op. cit.*, I.210-1.
7. *Op. cit.* V, 350-1
8. *Achilles Tatius*, trans. Gaselee rev. Warmington, Harvard, 1969, 170-1; translation from *Ancient Greek Novels*, 192.
9. Aulus Gellius, *Attic Nights* ed. J. C. Rolfe, IX, 11, London, 1927, III. 392. He gives the text of the epigram in Greek without a Latin translation.
10. It was conveniently reprinted in the Everyman series, London n.d. [1928].
11. *The Poems of Sir Philip Sidney* ed. William A. Ringler, Jr., Oxford, 1962, 207. *Astrophil and Stella* was probably written in 1582 and circulated originally in manuscript. Ringler gives Hoby's Castiglione as Sidney's source.
12. *The Songs and Sonets of John Donne* ed. Theodore Redpath, London, 1983, 201. These poems date mainly from the 1590s. Redpath notes that Donne quotes the original pseudo-Plato from Aulus Gellius in a (much later) sermon.
13. *The Complete Poems of John Donne*, ed. Robin Robbins, London, 2010 (2008), 83.
14. *The Poems of Robert Herrick* ed. L. C. Martin, Oxford, 1965, 240.

15. Marlowe, *Plays and Poems* ed. M. R. Ridley, London, 1955, 154. *Dr Faustus* probably dates from 1588 or 1589.

LIST OF ABBREVIATIONS

CGLC / Cambridge Greek and Latin Classics

LCL / Loeb Classical Library

OCT / Oxford Classical Texts

Teubner / Bibliotheca Scriptorum Graecorum et Romanorum Teubneriana

Apuleius

Kenney / Apuleius, *Cupid and Psyche* ed. E. J. Kenney, Cambridge (CGLC), 1990

Hanson / Apuleius, *Metamorphoses* ed. and trans. J. Arthur Hanson, Harvard (LCL), 1989, 2 vols.

OCT / *Apulei Metamorphoseon libri XI* ed. M Zimmerman, Oxford (OCT), 2012

Zimmerman / Maaike Zimmerman: *Metamorphoses books IV 28-35, V and VI 1-24: the tale of Cupid and Psyche*. Groningen commentaries on Apuleius. Groningen: Egbert Forsten, 2004.

Catullus

Mynors / *C. Valerii Catulli Carmina* ed. R. A. B. Mynors, Oxford (OCT), 1967 (1958)

Fordyce / *Catullus: A Commentary* by C. J. Fordyce, Oxford, 1961

Michie / *The Poems of Catullus*, translated by James Michie, London, 1969

Quinn / Catullus: *The Poems*, ed. Kenneth Quinn, London, 1970

Goold / *Catullus* ed. G. P. Goold, London, 2001 (1983)

Thomson / *Catullus* ed. D. F. S. Thomson, Toronto, 2003 (1997)

Harrison / in Nauta and Harder: see below, 2005 (poem 63 only)

Nauta and Harder / Ruurd R. Nauta, and Annette Harder: *Catullus' poem on Attis: Text and Contexts*, Leiden, 2005

Catullus online: an online repertory of conjectures on Catullus: http://www.catullusonline.org/CatullusOnline/?dir=edited_pages&pageID=5

Catullus Concordance: available at http://www.obscure.org/obscene-latin/carmina-catulli/

Dante

Singleton / *The Divine Comedy*, translated with a commentary by Charles S. Singleton, Princeton University Press, 1970-5, 6 vols.

Horace

Klingner / *Horatius Opera* ed. F. Klingner, Leipzig (Teubner) 1957[3]

Michie / Horace: *The Odes*, trans. James Michie, London 1963

Nisbet-Hubbard / Nisbet, R. G. M. and Margaret Hubbard: *A Commentary on Horace* Odes, *Book I*, Oxford 1970, *Book II*, Oxford 1978

Nisbet-Rudd / Nisbet, R. G. M. and Niall Rudd: *A Commentary on Horace: Odes Book III*, Oxford 2004

Quinn / Horace: *The Odes* ed. Kenneth Quinn, London 1980

Shackleton-Bailey / *Horatius Opera* ed. D. R. Shackleton Bailey, Stuttgart 1970,(Teubner) 1985

LCL / Horace: *Odes and Epodes* ed. and trans. Niall Rudd, Harvard (LCL). 2004

Juvenal

Braund / *Juvenal and Persius* ed. Susanna Morton Braund, Harvard (LCL), 2004

Clausen / *A. Persi Flacci et D. Iuni Iuuenalis Saturae* ed. W. V. Clausen, Oxford (OCT), 1959

Courtney / E. Courtney, *A Commentary on the Satires of Juvenal*, London, Athlone Press, 1980

Duff / *D.Iuni Iuuenalis Saturae XIV* ed. J. D. Duff, Cambridge, 1966 (1898)

Ferguson / Juvenal: *The Satires* ed. John Ferguson, London, Bristol Classical Press, 1999 (1979)

Ovid

Mozley-Goold / Ovid: *The Art of Love and other Poems* ed. J. H. Mozley rev. G. P. Goold, Harvard (LCL), 1979 (1929)

Miller-Goold / Ovid: *Metamorphoses* ed. F. J. Miller rev. G. P. Goold, Harvard (LCL), 2 vols., 1977 and 1984

Barsby / John Barsby (ed.), *Ovid: Amores I*, London, Bristol Classical Press, 1991 (1973)

McKeown / *Ovid: Amores, Text, Prolegomena and Commentary*, ed. J. C. Mckeown, 4 vv., Liverpool: Francis Cairns, 1987-1998

Kenney / *P. Ovidi Nasonis Amores* (etc.) ed. E. J. Kenney, Oxford (OCT), 1994^2

Tarrant / *P. Ovidi Nasonis Metamorphoses* ed. R. J. Tarrant, Oxford (OCT), 2004.

Myers / Ovid: *Metamorphoses XIV* ed. K. Sara Myers, Cambridge (CGLC), 2009

Hardie / Alessandro Barchiesi and others, *A Commentary on Ovid's Metamorphoses*, Cambridge, 2024, 3 Vols. Commentary on Book XIV by Philip Hardie in Vol 3.

Petronius

Smith / Petronius, *Cena Trimalchionis* ed. Martin S. Smith,
Oxford, 1975

Müller / Petronius, *Satyricon Reliquiae* ed. Konrad Müller,
Munich and Leipzig (Teubner), 2003 (1995⁴).

Sullivan / Petronius, *The Satyricon* and Seneca, *The Apocolocyntosis* trans. J. P. Sullivan, revised edition, London, Penguin
Books, 1986 (1965)

Schmeling / Gareth Schmeling with Aldo Setaioli, *A Commentary on the* Satyrica *of Petronius*, Oxford, 2011

LCL / Petronius, *Satyricon* with Seneca, *Apocolocyntosis* ed. and
trans. Gareth Schmeling, Harvard (LCL), 2020

Plato

The Collected Dialogues ed. Edith Hamilton and Huntington
Cairns, New York, Bollingen Foundation,1961. Translations
credited individually.

Propertius

Camps / *Propertius Elegies Book II* ed. W. A. Camps,
Cambridge, 1967

Goold / *Propertius Elegies* ed. and trans. G. P. Goold, Harvard
(LCL), 1990

Fedeli / *Sexti Properti Elegiarum Libri IV* ed. P. Fedeli, Stuttgart
and Leipzig (Teubner), 1994

Heyworth / *Sexti Properti Elegos* ed. S. J. Heyworth, Oxford (OCT), 2007

Virgil

Alpers / Alpers, Paul: *The Singer of the Eclogues: A Study of Virgilian Pastoral*, Berkeley, 1979

Clausen / Virgil: *Eclogues with an Introduction and Commentary by Wendell Clausen*, Oxford, 1994

Coleman / Vergil: *Eclogues* ed. Robert Coleman, Cambridge (CGLC), 1977

LCL / Virgil: *Eclogues, Georgics, Aeneid, Appendix Vergiliana*, trans. Fairclough rev. Goold, Harvard (LCL), 1999, 2 vols.

Mynors / *P. Vergili Maronis Opera*, ed. R. A. B. Mynors, Oxford (OCT), 1969

Putnam / Michael Putnam, *Virgil's Pastoral Art: Studies in the Eclogues*, Princeton, 1970

Austin / *P. Vergili Maronis Aenidos Liber Secundus, Quartus, Sextus with a Commentary by R. G. Austin*, Oxford 1964, 1955, 1977

Horsfall / Horsfall, Nicholas, *Virgil, Aeneid 2: A Commentary*, Leiden, Brill, 2008

Horsfall / Horsfall, Nicholas, *Virgil, Aeneid 6: A Commentary*, Berlin, De Gruyter, 2013, 2 vols.

www.ingramcontent.com/pod-product-compliance
Lightning Source LLC
Chambersburg PA
CBHW030631030726
47497CB00006B/1727